FAR FAR BEYOND BERLIN

C000216564

FAR FAR BEYOND BERLIN

To Kim,

Hope you enjoy this signed copy from Scotland's *biggest author (*in terms of weight)

X

CRAIG MEIGHAN

Elsewhen Press

Far Far Beyond Berlin

First published in Great Britain by Elsewhen Press, 2021
An imprint of Alnpete Limited

Copyright © Craig Meighan, 2021. All rights reserved
The right of Craig Meighan to be identified as the author of this work has been asserted in accordance with sections 77 and 78 of the Copyright, Designs and Patents Act 1988. No part of this publication may be reproduced, stored in a retrieval system or transmitted in any form, or by any means (electronic, mechanical, telepathic, supernatural, or otherwise) without the prior written permission of the copyright owner.

Elsewhen Press, PO Box 757, Dartford, Kent DA2 7TQ
www.elsewhen.press

British Library Cataloguing in Publication Data.
A catalogue record for this book is available from the British Library.

ISBN 978-1-911409-82-3 Print edition
ISBN 978-1-911409-92-2 eBook edition

Condition of Sale
This book is sold subject to the condition that it shall not, by way of trade or otherwise, be lent, re-sold, hired out or otherwise circulated in any form of binding or cover other than that in which it is published and without a similar condition including this condition being imposed on the subsequent purchaser.

This book is copyright under the Berne Convention.
Elsewhen Press & Planet-Clock Design are trademarks of Alnpete Limited

Printed and bound by CPI Group (UK) Ltd, Croydon, CR0 4YY

This book is a work of fiction. All names, characters, places, observation satellites, planets, universes, eternal realms and events are either a product of the author's fertile imagination or are used fictitiously. Any resemblance to actual events, paradises (or the other place), worlds, moons, places or people (living, dead, or immortal) is purely coincidental.

Audi A5 is a trademark of Audi AG; BBC is a trademark of The British Broadcasting Corporation; Carling is a trademark of Molson Coors Brewing Company (UK) Limited; Casio is a trademark of Casio Computer Co., Ltd; Citroën is a trademark of Automobiles Citroën; Dulux is a trademark of Akzo Nobel Coatings International BV; Hungry, Hungry Hippos is a trademark of Hasbro U.K. Limited; Ikea is a trademark of Inter IKEA Systems BV; Incredible Hulk, Iron Man, Thor are trademarks of Marvel Characters, Inc.; James Bond is a trademark of Danjaq, LLC; Jean-Luc Picard is a trademark of CBS Studios Inc.; Lord Voldemort is a trademark of Warner Bros. Entertainment Inc.; Mary Poppins is a trademark of Disney Enterprises, Inc; NASA is a trademark of National Aeronautics and Space program ; National Trust is a trademark of The National Trust (Enterprises) Limited; Netflix is a trademark of Netflix, Inc.; Photoshop is a trademark of Adobe, Inc.; Pink Floyd is a trademark of Pink Floyd (1987) Limited; Post-it is a trademark of 3M Company; Scooby Doo is a trademark of Hanna-Barbera Productions, Inc.; Space Invaders is a trademark of Kabushiki Kaisha Taito; Stella Artois is a trademark of Anheuser-Busch InBev S.A.; Swingball is a trademark of Swingball Limited; TED talks is a trademark of Ted Conferences, LLC; Telegraph is a trademark of Telegraph Media Group Limited; Tomb Raider is a trademark of Square Enix Limited; Travelodge is a trademark of Travelodge Hotels Limited; Twix is a trademark of Mars Wrigley Confectionery UK Limited; Whatsapp is a trademark of WhatsApp Inc.; Wikipedia is a trademark of Wikimedia Foundation, Inc.; Windows is a trademark of Microsoft corporation; YouTube is a trademark of Google LLC. Use of trademarks has not been authorised, sponsored, or otherwise approved by the trademark owners.

Contents

For Jen, who is clearly the best human. The only reason I have ever done anything good and without whom this book would still be a post-it note stuck to the corner of my monitor.

Chapter 1
Genesis

IN the beginning, there was darkness. God said "Let there be light" and there was light.

And it helped Him find that thing He'd been feeling about for in the darkness.

Now He could see what He was doing, God set about creating the small blue planet, He moulded the core, shaped the crust, laid down the rocks and the soil. He created the grass and the hills; He made the lakes, the plants, the trees, the oceans and the seas.

Standing back and looking upon His creation, He frowned with His massive face. He saw that it was good, but 'good' is not 'perfect'. He made the oceans and lakes a more brilliant blue. He made the grass greener, then, wanting to increase the greenness even further, He realised that as God he could just make 'Green' more green. After all, it was He who defined what 'green' was in the first place, having invented it earlier that morning.

He positioned two suns in such a way that the warm light would hit the surface evenly at all times.

Like all creative projects, there was a period of pointless tweaking. Leaves were reshaped, the grass blades thickened then thinned again, the consistency of sand went through about nineteen iterations and because He couldn't decide which was best, He deployed all of them to different parts of the planet. Eventually, He felt comfortable to declare it finished.

When all was right with the new world He carefully, lovingly fashioned the tiny creatures and granted them life.

It was to be a faultless world without sadness, violence or disease. It was perfection. Eternal sunshine would light his idyll forever.

He called it Joy World.

Needless to say, it was a fucking disaster.

****

A long way away and 5 billion years later, on my thirty-second birthday I was killed. I understand that, as a piece of story-telling, that is like saying "I went to the shops yesterday and then in 1958 a dog fell over in Berlin", but I do hope to explain how those two events are related items.

We will start on Earth one week before my birthday. I was still breathing and about to have an odd morning…

Glasgow – 7:30 a.m.

It was a Monday morning, and I was alive.

Checking if I was dead was not part of my morning routine at that stage, so I didn't note that fact at the time, but it's probably an important distinction to make now. Unknowingly, I ventured outside to what was going to be my last ever day at the office.

It was 8 a.m., frost was clinging to every surface, the park was extremely cold; I buttoned up my overcoat and tried to find the motivation for my walk to work. Unfortunately, I work in a local council office as an administrator, so occasionally my motivation buggers off without warning. Thankfully the job I do is utterly pointless and circular to the extent that if anyone thought about it for five seconds, I could be replaced by a filing cabinet and an answering machine, so I don't have to expend too much effort on it.

My walk to work is a time for contemplation. I wasted it entirely by fantasising about winning the lottery and what I would do with the money. As my head cycled through all the possibilities, my feet pounded the ground in front of me. I was absolutely immersed in the fantasy to the extent that I actually reached out to rev a jet ski that wasn't there and in doing so cracked my hand off a lamppost. All this excitement sadly meant that by the time I reached the office I was spent; slightly physically, partly mentally and completely imaginarily financially.

The office was a large open plan affair with many desks separated with wobbly baffle board dividers that had pictures of football teams, children and George Clooneys for decoration. On the wall, some motivational artwork was framed. There was something or other about teamwork with a black border around a picture of some synchronised swimmers. As I arrived, I said hello to a few people and switched on my computer. Whilst it was starting up, I had the usual small talk with the people sitting nearby. John said "Cold outside isn't it?" as he does every morning, regardless of the temperature. As usual, I replied, "Yes, I'm glad I didn't put my shorts on today!" and we both laughed. This is office banter. As anyone who works in an office will know, it's like regular banter, but at roughly 0.1% of the quality.

Little tiny, old Margaret said "I think you're getting taller every day! Have you grown?" I haven't. I wanted to say that I've been exactly the same height since 2002, which is one of the very few things I have in common with the Town Hall. Instead, I trotted out an old standard, "Yes, I've been standing in the miracle grow again!"

People often say when working in an office "Oh I could write a sitcom about the stuff that goes on in here!" and they probably could, but it would be the same tame episode week after week.

Not that being in a tame sitcom is anything to complain about. I know that many people have it a lot worse, but I was stuck in a rut big time. Every day was of the same average quality, but it was the repetition that got me down. It was akin to being told a decent joke, it's nice, but imagine then being told it a further 15,000 times. Life had somewhat lost its punch.

The computer finally logged itself in, so I sat down at my desk and started going through my inbox.

After an hour or so, I gathered up some random documents and walked across to the tiny photocopier room. (By that, of course, I mean a tiny room in which a normal size photocopier sits rather than a normal size room where we kept a load of tiny photocopiers).

I closed the door behind me and started feeding paper into the tray. I set the machine to make fifty copies. I had always found it relaxing to get some quiet solitude, feel the warmth of the hot confined space, listen to the sound of the machine and risk closing my eyes for a few brief seconds.

Sometimes I'd come in and make unnecessary copies just to get away from it all.

Sometimes I'd come in and make unnecessary copies just to get away from it all.

Sometimes I'd come in and make unnecessary copies just to get away from it all.

Sometimes I'd come in and make unnecessary copies just to get away from it all.

Sometimes I'd come in and make unnecessary copies just to get away from it all.

Sometimes I'd come in and make unnecessary copies just to get away from it all.

Sometimes I'd come in and make unnecessary copies just to get away from it all.

On that day, whilst I was standing there, a familiar thought entered my head and waved its arms about trying to get my attention.

Although never having tried it, making a copy of my face had been something of a lifetime ambition. Now I'm aware that in terms of ambition, making a photocopy of your own face is up there with doing 31mph on a 30 road or sending a piece of second-class post, but when your life is as dull as mine, you have to lower the bar for excitement somewhat.

I stared at the copier. I wanted to do it, but I could also faintly remember someone telling me that looking into the light from a photocopier can blind you. As a result, I had always managed to talk myself out of it, but on this day, I was feeling a little devil-may-care.

Thirty seconds later with my nose pressed up against the glass and my finger on the button, an odd thought came to me; not 'This could blind me' or 'What if someone comes through the door right now?' No, the thought was 'Wouldn't it be great just to be somewhere else right now?'

I was feeling extremely indifferent about life. My job could be done by office furniture; I had no love-life, no family, and no real friends. In short, I had nothing. And so, I surmised, nothing to lose.

I pressed 'Copy'.

I opened my eyes.

Chapter 2
Somewhere Else

Everything was white, my knees buckled and then everything was dark, with purple bits.

It had been foolish and extremely painful to copy my face, but I was still hopeful that it would at least provide me with a funny picture of my squashed features. After a few seconds, my eyes started to feel a bit better again, but I still couldn't make anything out. I groped in the darkness trying to feel my way around; the world was extremely sluggish about coming back into focus.

I couldn't even feel where the copier was anymore. I reasoned that I must have blindly stumbled backwards. I felt in front of me with my hands, like a mummy, as I continued to wait for my vision to return. What I didn't know was, that it already had.

It was when I actually looked down at where my hands were, I realised that I could see them faintly. My vision had returned almost immediately, but the lights in the photocopier room were out. I fumbled around looking for a switch and silently prayed that I hadn't shorted out the whole floor by copying my face. I was now extremely glad that it wasn't my arse I'd been copying.

About thirty or forty seconds of groping the air passed, and a slow realisation dawned. I'd been walking continuously in the same direction for half a minute without collision in a room I knew to only be 8x8 feet in size. I sighed, now aware that I must have wandered out into the office and that I had indeed shorted the fuse everywhere. Shite.

I crept about like a bloody idiot for a minute before realising that the reason I was creeping about was that there was absolute silence in the office, no talking, no whirring, no breathing, nothing and this was very odd for a power out. Normally there would be commotion and jokes and footsteps and breathing and rummaging, but there wasn't. There was nothing.

"Hello?" I called out, like a twat in a horror film.

I waited.

"Hello?" I said again, just in case it wasn't stupid enough the first time.

I waited, and I listened, trying to ascertain a clue to what could have happened. It was then I remembered with a chill that it was 9:30 a.m. and the office had floor-to-ceiling windows. Regardless of a power-out, I should have been able to see everything.

At this point I started to get properly worried. I didn't know where I was or what was going on, so I thought the best response was simply to wait. I'm sure I had read a quote about that somewhere.

I think it was Kevin Costner who said – "Just hang about and wait – someone else will hopefully appear and fix the problem without you having to actually do anything" – I may have misremembered that though.

I eased myself down onto the floor which felt unusually cold and smooth – for carpet. I commenced Operation: Hope For the Best.

Ten minutes passed, and as they did so, I became increasingly nervous. I got up and started pacing gently back and forth. It was then that I heard a low whooshing sound, like an aeroplane idling on the runway. This did not help with my feeling of nervousness. Worryingly it then became louder and louder, thundering, roaring, shaking, vibrating and growing until eventually it could be felt as much as heard. As it reached a crescendo, it cut out, and the lights clicked on.

When I looked around, I gaped, I stared and I stumbled back in horror. I didn't even have time to shit myself, as I was far too busy having a heart attack. I was not in the office any longer. Shiny white hard floor stretched out in front of me for miles.

Humans often have trouble with scale, especially when it dwarfs them. I fear the open sea for this very reason.

The white floor hit the horizon and curved upwards; I followed it and immediately fell to the floor trying to grip on to the smooth surface in vain as vertigo paralysed me. It was so high. I mean really high, sickeningly, painfully high. Think of the highest thing you can think of, then add the second highest thing you can think of to that and whatever you're imagining is still not quite as high as this wall. It continued all the way up for miles on miles until I could see that it formed the side of an enormous sphere in which I was a tiny, insignificant speck of absolutely nothing.

The view I currently had inside this massive globe was akin to the view given to a solitary brain cell at the bottom of a vacant moron's hollowed-out head. I was minute, miniscule, minor, miniature, immaterial, irrelevant, tiny, trivial, small, wee, and scared shitless.

I lay on the ground, curled up and prayed I was insane.

****

Meanwhile there was chaos in a control room. Almost exactly 3,743 Kilometres above the white floor, a red indicator light began to flash on a wall mounted control panel.

The light was really pleased about this, as it had never had the opportunity to light up before. In fact, it had been poised and ready to glow for a few million years.

The creature looking at the flashing light was *not* pleased and mashed the keypad with its face in distress.

The Intruder Light had never flashed before and nor was it supposed to. Some of his colleagues firmly believed it was installed as a joke by security, but the creature, whose name is unpronounceable in our language, knew that the scaly race of beings that were hired as security had no capacity for humour.

He had hoped never to have to push the big red button that summoned them.

They were not friendly or forgiving.

He pushed the big red button and prayed that it didn't cost him his job. Or his life.

Or some money; generally, he was just hoping it had no negative consequences whatsoever.

****

I had gathered my stomach together enough to try and find a way out. I tried to make my way towards a wall as my human brain told me that's where the exit would be housed. However, looking ahead at the terrifying incline on the wall was giving me major heebie-jeebies. Instead, I stared at the floor and this made me notice a hatch and a button set into the white floor that I might have walked past otherwise.

I crouched, pressed the button, and the hatch slid back to reveal a ladder leading down to a small, dark room. I climbed down and noticed that the tiny space had seats carved into the wall. It looked like an escape pod in every sci-fi film I'd ever seen. Suddenly above me, the hatch closed and there was a heavy clunk suggesting a lock had been engaged. I panicked and scrambled at the hatch lid, but it was sealed, with no opening from my side.

A dark, deep, pulsing sound began to reverberate through everything in the tiny pod. My eyes were painfully vibrating in their sockets. I could hear my bones. It made the walls ripple and the floor look like a shimmering liquid; I felt it in my soul. The air was like soup and it felt like being deep underwater during a tsunami. Grabbed by this pulsing, crushing force, I was lifted off my feet six inches into the air where I was suspended by the pounding sonic waves. My head was spinning, my chest was compressing and I felt like I was being crushed in the hand of an invisible giant.

In my state of extreme distress, I was surprised to notice a ghostly apparition developing in front of me. This further cemented my instinct that I was about to die. I was confused about what I was seeing though. I had heard of people's life flashing before their eyes before they died; however, this phenomenon was not one I had previously heard of. What I was experiencing was a goose flashing before my eyes, not my life – a photorealistic goose. He was floating in the air in front of me. I supposed that this was my brain trying to show me something calming before death, so I just looked at it, focussed on his soft eyes and waited to die.

He seemed to regard me with a benign smile and then began to speak.

"Good day! I am Graham the Gravity-Goose. If you have never experienced a sudden transition between two very strong gravitational areas before you may be experiencing some discomfort."

My eyes began to bulge, and I was struggling to breathe. The Goose continued:

"I am here to talk you through the process and ensure that

you have a good transition. You are being transported from the natural gravity of the Infinite Hollow to the artificial gravity of the command and engineering decks. At present you are halfway between these two zones and the two gravitational forces are pulling you in opposite directions. Unfortunately, this can cause severe physical trauma, cellular damage, brain tissue degradation, and these elements can occasionally make the journey less enjoyable. Also, there is a chance that depending on what kind of life-form you are that the blood no longer knows which direction to flow around your body and this may feel unpleasant."

My legs and arms felt like they were being crushed in a vice. With all of the effort I could muster I managed to suck some paltry morsels of air into my burning lungs. I could not talk. I was now suspended in the flickering, wavering, breathless, vortex being condescended by a goose.

Graham went on, "The process will be complete in a few moments and at that time you should feel as good as new. However, if you feel that any of your limbs have significantly changed in size then please inform a member of our staff who will put you in touch with our tailor. Thank you for your patience."

He waved a wing and then faded from view. The noise began to shudder to a halt, and I felt the death grip on my limbs loosening. I was lowered slowly back to the floor and collapsed into a heap. Breathing greedily and rubbing my aching limbs, I began to laugh uncontrollably. The sheer euphoria of being alive and feeling the blood rush back to my oxygen starved cells was giving me a crazy, euphoric high and I laughed and laughed and laughed until I cried from the exhaustion of laughing. Eventually wiping the tears from my eyes, I climbed to my feet, reinvigorated and ready for whatever else this crazy day could throw at me.

Above me, I noticed that the hatch was now open again and I climbed the ladder to get back out.

However, far from being in the infinite whiteness, I was now in a dark, hot, extremely claustrophobic corridor filled with steam and pipes, like the inside of a submarine. A sign in front of me said 'Engineering Deck 12'.

Looking down the corridor, I began to get the unsettling feeling of being watched. I slowly turned, and in the mess of steam, pipes, wires, and grating, there were six of the ugliest creatures I had ever seen. They had short legs, stocky, scaly, grey, glistening bodies and chubby arms. But it was their faces that were the real worry; faces that looked as though they had been sculpted by a psychopath who was attempting to use tar and walruses to recreate a Picasso.

All I managed to whisper in my shock was, “Hello”.

“Mrdermurmur”, they said and hit me with a very, very hard blue shiny thing.

Chapter 3
Man in the Moon

When I woke up, my head was pulsating, my eyes were sore, and I couldn't think. The room was bright, white and there were lots of shapes. Beyond that, my eyes were either unwilling or unable to give me any further details.

I was bound to a chair, and I could hear murmuring and shuffling all about me. My head hung heavily as I tried to lift my eyes for a look around. This was far too painful, so I continued to look down at the floor. The background noise stopped abruptly when a door whirred open. Someone important had arrived. I saw large sandalled feet approaching, human-looking feet, with normal skin and toes, but of an inhuman size, they were enormous, far too big for a person to have. The owner of the feet parked them in front of me and spoke.

"Welcome to the Master Observatory and Orbit Navigator, or as you may know it, the Moon." The soft, but authoritative baritone was a pleasant sound; however, I hadn't really understood the sentence.

"Who are you?" I tried to look up, but my head was heavy and my eyes still reluctant to fully open.

"I am the controller of the universe as you understand it."

"What's your name?" I asked, struggling to regain some normality.

"I'm afraid my real name is not within your pronunciation capability."

"Ha!" I said. "Why? Because my tiny human brain can't cope with your complex alien language?"

"No. Because you are British and therefore even if I had a Belgian name it would probably be outside of your pronunciation capability. You're just rubbish at it."

"Oh."

"If you wish to assign me a human name, you may call me 'Terry – Master of the Universe'".

"Terry?"

"Master of the Universe", he reminded me.

"Terry – Master of the Universe?"

"Yes"

I blinked slowly and tried to ward off a smile. The room was slowly coming into focus. The cloaked man in front of me was about seven feet tall; he had extra-large facial features, big bright eyes, and long grey hair. Enormous hands and feet were accompanied by an endearingly wide smile. On first glance, you might have said he looked like a part-time wizard or like a bank manager on a hippy team-building retreat. The ugly violent creatures from the hallway continued to mill around in the background, but there was a definite lack of menace about the situation.

"Ok. So let me get this straight – I'm on the Moon?"

"No, you're inside the MOON." He smiled.

"Be honest. Are you just saying the first thing that comes into your head?"

"It's a hollow structure, an enormous cavity, surrounded by a layer of corridors, control rooms, and offices. Above that is the dusty surface of the station which we use to disguise it as a satellite of your planet. The whole world, as you know it, is carefully monitored by us."

"That's ridiculous," I said smiling. "We can't get a phone signal near tall buildings, and you're saying you're monitoring everything from the Moon? Is this a cult? It's a cult, right? You've kidnapped me for a cult, yes? I don't want to do a suicide pact to get to level five or something. Just let me go. I promise I'll read your leaflet carefully."

"Ah. I understand the reference; you think I am a madman. I assure you I am not deluded." He did his widest smile. It did not help his case.

I looked around at the clean white room, there were several pieces of technology which I did not recognise. It did reek of the future somewhat, but I'm a sceptical man and wasn't up for being taken in by some hippy cult-leader and his Moon story without a little bit more pressing. "Ok for the sake of argument let's say this is the Moon. How did I get here?"

"I do not know, that is what we wish to ask you. What were you doing precisely before you left the Earth?"

"Making photocopies."

There was a murmur of appreciative noise around the room. Terry smiled, and everyone seemed more at ease.

"Well that explains a lot." He said brightly.

"How does that explain a lot?" I said, looking around – everyone just ignored me.

However, a few seconds later I was released from my bindings and took a deep breath for the first time in a while.

As I massaged my wrists, a disgusting cup of thick brown liquid marked 'coffee' was brought to me and Terry – Master of the Universe – began to explain.

"You see," he said, "we have been observing Earth for a very long time. And while we've been doing that, we've tried many different techniques of gathering data on humans. One such technique was called 'Photocopying'". He made air quotes.

"Yes, I know what photocopying is," I said irritably.

"No. You only know what we told you it was. You think photocopying is making identical sheets of paper. We planted the technology on your planet and told you that's what it did. Photocopiers actually use a special concentrated light to copy what is on the glass and send it back here for storage and analysis. We've built a pretty good knowledge of your business world, literature and arses through this method alone."

"So how does that explain how I got here? Am I a copy?"

"No. We did test this as a method of transport, but never really got it to a level where it was reliable. You see the soul cannot be copied; it's far too vast an amount of data, so the light transports the original back here for analysis. Like a teleport system, as you would understand from your science fiction. However, most of our test subjects were dead on arrival or mangled beyond recognition – I tell you if I never see another inside-out intern I'll be a happy man. You're very fortunate to be alive. Why did you look into the light?"

I was confused. "How do you know I looked into the light?"

"Because that is how the system identified your soul so clearly. The eyes truly are windows to the soul, because they directly connected to the brain and our light had direct access when you looked into it. So, again, why did you look into the light?"

I tried to answer as honestly as possible whilst retaining my dignity. "I was trying to make a funny picture."

"Weren't you worried about it blinding you? I'm pretty

sure we got that rumour round as fact a long time ago." He looked around at his team who nodded in confirmation.

"I was past caring really."

"Well, that's quite sad, if uninteresting. Would you like a tour of the place?"

I set my cup down and stood up, nodding. "I would like that very much."

"You don't like your coffee?" Terry asked pointing at the cup.

"This isn't coffee", I said.

"Oh."

"It's just mush."

"Oh."

****

Like everything inside it, the universe is controlled by a group of old, out of touch men.

God has assembled a group of specialists, and high above the universe, they decide how to mess with your life. The line-up is impressive, God is there obviously. Every boardroom has a chairman.

Fate, the fuck face, is also there, a walking talking philosophical concept – sometimes with his wife Destiny. She's not a concept though, she's just a stripper.

Irony is there with his fashionable clothes and sushi. He's wearing a t-shirt that says 'The Universe is Infinite' because he's cleverer than you. However, he is outdone completely by the Devil who strolls in smoking a cigarette wearing a 'What would Jesus do?' t-shirt that is at least ten-times as ironic as Irony's shirt. This also pisses God off, because He has to be polite when He really wants to say:

"What would Jesus do? I'll tell you what…He'd smack *you* upside ya head!"

But that would be childish, and He is not a child. He is God; maker of children.

And anyway, Jesus isn't here to defend himself; he's not allowed to sit on the committee until he has tidied his room.

Chapter 4
Revelations

I was still getting used to the idea of being inside the Moon whilst getting a tour from Terry. Life had just become interesting for the first time in twenty years.

Despite my initial cynicism, I was shown clear proof that the entire Moon was an enormous space station dedicated to the observation and protection of Earth. A mile-thick crust all the way round was, in fact, the twenty huge decks of the space station. The hollow sphere in the centre was used for storage, but also necessary for a piece of technology they possessed. Frustratingly, Terry was very cagey about this. Anything that needed a planet size space to operate in was obviously very, very powerful.

We walked around the station, and I got the full breakdown. He showed me the security and monitoring departments. They had created an efficient IT system whereby the computers were powered by the frustration of the beings attempting to use them. They had so much extra power left over from this that it ran their gravitational field as well as an absolutely cracking hot chocolate machine.

The station was partially staffed by a mute race called the Sentos. They were friendly slug-like creatures with three-fingered hands on the end of short arms. They were able to plant images in your mind to communicate, but could not read your thoughts. They had a wonderful way with visual metaphors, which instantly made them seem like a noble race of liberal poets until you remembered that they were staffing a covert space station, which controlled the universe in its entirety.

The security creatures were called the Haag. They did not have a wonderful way with visual metaphors. They had a wonderful way with blunt instruments. Their culture had no humour and was entirely literal, so they hated the Sentos with a passion. Terry said they ended up working here together as they were the last surviving members of their respective races and the station had taken them in.

He showed me the command centre which genuinely

looked space age, the first such example I'd seen. It was all white; clean with big screens, swivel chairs, touch screen controls and people talking to 'computer'. No frustration in here, no-one trying to run Windows Universe Edition on an out of date set-up, no wires, no smoke, no alarms, no banging, just a sense of control that was actually calming. Terry explained to me that here the technology was powered in a different way. It was charged by the smug satisfaction of the beings using them. This powered their IT, life support, propulsion, a gym and an absolutely irritating organic coffee machine. It was staffed by beings who looked just like Terry, but slightly younger and slightly smaller.

He saw me looking at them and must have sensed the question coming. "Yes. We too are the last of our people."

"I'm sorry Terry. What happened?"

"A great disaster befell us, but that is another story for another time." He looked wistfully away.

"Right of course. I didn't mean to be insensitive. It's just, can you give me a heads up when it ***is*** time for that story because it really sounds interesting?"

He ignored me and we continued walking into the centre of the room. From here we could see a spectacular image of the Earth on a giant viewing screen; the entire planet blown up on a huge screen at incredible resolution. It was one of the coolest things I had ever seen. I stood with my jaw open staring at it until he spoke.

"This is our bridge," he remarked unnecessarily, but proudly.

"It's pretty nice," I said.

He looked at me in absolute horror; like I'd just described his four-year-old son as 'sexy'.

"What?" I said. Because I hadn't.

"*Pretty* nice? *Pretty* nice?" His eyes were dangerously large. "Have you ever been anywhere nicer?"

"Probably not, no."

"Okay then. So, it's got to be better than pretty nice." He held out his hand towards the room, as if encouraging me to make it feel better.

I now understood. Terry was dredging for compliments.

"It's quite certainly the most attractive place I've ever been, and it also has a lovely atmosphere." I offered.

"Thank you."

"You're welcome," I said carefully, hoping that this odd piece of theatre was over. Thankfully Terry seemed pretty chuffed by the exchange. He turned to me and smiled.

"Now would you like to see the sum of all human knowledge?"

"Yeah, why not?"

****

The board had run the Universe for as long as it had existed.

Time wasn't a factor they measured, but it was something they noticed. The board members all had different jobs, some were vital, some were ceremonial and some were just distractions to keep everybody entertained:

Irony was in charge of arranging Coincidences and Ironic Events and was also Head of Sarcasm. His day to day included happenstance, comeuppances, comebacks, poetic justice of any kind and precisely none of the things in that Alanis Morissette song.

The Buddha was in charge of calm and kindness. His job was to defuse any potentially threatening incidents and make everyone relax. It used to be that he would do this by planting wise and soothing words in people's minds. They would be compelled to speak the words and people would stop in their tracks and think. And when people think they tend to realise they need to calm down, and thus the system worked.

However modern culture and advertising slogans desensitised the world to his influence so he had been forced to invent marijuana. Now all he has to do is identify dangerous individuals early on and guide their minds and bodies towards some weed, rendering them completely useless.

The Devil was created by God to provide some balance to the Universe, also partially to give God a worthy nemesis. It would make things interesting. He was in charge of Evil which has many subdivisions including paedophilia, ISIS and politicians. It was the biggest job outside of God's. He was extremely creative and was passionate about his work. From wars to depression he touched billions, but not in a nice way, more like if say, your weird Uncle touches you. However, The Devil was a benign old man compared to the prick of providence that is Fate. Someone, (possibly Kevin Costner) once wrote 'Fate is a hunter'. They were right.

Fate was the board's assassin; a born killer who relished his work. His role was in deciding people's ultimate fate; he chose whether people were allowed a painful or peaceful demise. In popular culture he was known by many names; The Angel of Death, Death, The Grim Reaper – well not that many names actually, but they were all a bit deathy, so he preferred to be called Fate because he thought that was much cooler.

He was also God's henchman, sworn to deal with threats to the stability of the universe. However, as you'll no doubt be relieved to hear, threats to the stability of the Universe are few and far between so, in times of peace, he indulged in a little unilateral population control. He picked favourites, he developed grudges, he watched the theatre of the world play out then intervened when he saw fit. He roamed the earth taking human form. He has killed men to get to women he wanted to sleep with, from time to time he killed people for their political beliefs, but it can be far pettier than that.

He has killed people for choosing the wrong snack from a vending machine. Basically, he is a big evil bastard.

When people meet after ten years of being apart and lonely, they say "Fate brought us together" "It was destiny". Well they're wrong; it's just life. Humans are predictable; they go to the same places and do the same things. Events will coincide from time to time; it would be strange if they didn't. Fate has nothing to do with it. He doesn't bring people together; he's a cold-blooded killer.

And if you're wondering, it was a Twix.

****

I was returned to the vertigo-inducing white space again, although, this time, in much more comfortable circumstances. It turned out that the hatch I had been through was for use in emergencies only – Terry had a little revolving door in his office which led to the hollow. You could step into it and be shielded from the transition as you rotated. It was much more civilised.

Terry wanted to show me the sum of human knowledge they had gathered; I was expecting something substantial, something spectacular. Maybe an empire state building size pile of boxes full of paper, maybe a large mainframe computer room with hundreds of busy archivists filing and cataloguing; anything really, except what I actually had to look at.

A cube.

One cube.

One solitary cube, silver and metallic; about the size of a microwave oven.

"What's this?" I asked, pointing at it.

"This is the sum of all human knowledge," said Terry, confused.

"But…"

"But what?"

"But…it's so small. I mean, it's too small. That can't be everything we know. *I* know more than that on my own."

"No, I'm afraid not." He patted the plastic cube. "These storage cubes are fairly spacious."

"Is it something fancy? Like a really futuristic hard disk drive?" I asked hopefully.

"No. It's like a hard disk drive." He looked away awkwardly.

"But what about the internet? That's huge! And books! What about all the books? They must have taken up some space." I was on to something here.

"And films! Yes, what about all those BBC four programmes?" I demanded, never having watched one. "They must count as knowledge; some of the programmes had French words in the title!"

"Um. Well this box has on it all the useful data from the internet. We originally tried having one of our technicians' download the entire internet, but there were so many malicious files and junk and pornographic images we decided to just take what we needed. All our technician got first time around was three viruses and an erection."

"But…." I trailed off, unable to argue.

"Once you took away the porn, You-Tube and social networking sites there was a lot less than we expected."

"But…what about…uh…. what about Wikipedia!"

Aha comeback to that!

"A significant amount of the information on Wikipedia was found to be erroneous." Terry laughed a little laugh.

"Come on, most of it was right." I said huffily, having used it for all of my research for my degree.

"Yes, but all of the true parts were available from other more reliable sources so we deleted it."

He paused, observing my dismay. Then continued, ignoring it.

"We also deleted a fair portion of your scientific research because much of it was planted by us, for example anything about photocopiers or George Foreman Grills. You do indeed have many books, but all works of fiction were excluded and much of the non-fiction contained repetition or restatement of facts from other sources so they were also disregarded."

"But these things are important."

"Yes of course. So we store them in your culture cubes."

My face lifted. 'Cubes' is a plural word.

Chapter 5
Nice Guys Finish Last

Alan Barnet was in IT. He was forty-seven, mildly overweight, single and balding.

Alan Barnet had it going on.

He lived in a flat above a Turkish restaurant and met his friend Dave for drinks three or four times a week. He collected movies and read comics. He was harmless and all who knew him would have used words like kind, easy-going, friendly and funny to describe him.

Alan Barnet was a nice guy.

On a rainy Tuesday he toddled on downstairs to the Turkish restaurant where, because he knew the owners, he was occasionally given free food in exchange for mending their old puffer of a computer. They liked him because he was a good neighbour and a regular customer. However, on this night Fate was dining at the restaurant. He was on a date with Destiny. Literally. Upon seeing Alan receive his free meal and chat jovially to the owners, Fate's date remarked jokingly, "Maybe I should have gone out with that guy – he gets free food!"

Fate's eyes turned to black. Jokes weren't really his thing.

Alan Barnet died that night after choking on his spicy, spicy falafel. Living alone at forty-seven there was no-one to help him or give him that manoeuvre.

Flailing around his living room floor, struggling for breath, he looked around for something or someone that could save him. His wax, life-size model of Jean-Luc Picard did nothing.

Alan Barnet is dead.

Chapter 6

Release Forms

I sat on the polished white floor browsing through the entire spectrum of human culture. I realised how little I knew outside of my British and American comfort zones. It was shameful and fascinating and humbling and awe-inspiring, but after a while, like anything, it got a bit boring. I pulled a device from my pocket that Terry had given me to communicate with him; it appeared to be a pre-touchscreen mobile phone from about 2007.

I pressed '1' as instructed and was connected directly to Terry.

"Hello, Terry MOTU speaking."

"What's MOTU?"

"Master of the Universe"

"Right."

"How can I help you?"

"I'm bored now, can I come back to the bridge?"

"Yes, just press the hash key."

I pressed the hash key. A bright flash fired out of the device and smashed into my face. It was a horrific sensation which combined pain, discomfort and motion sickness; like being hit with a hammer whilst being stuffed into a suitcase which was being thrown off a cliff. I vomited all over Terry's face on arrival and then collapsed on the floor.

"Convenient isn't it?" he said with a smile, reaching for a towel.

"I thought it was going to connect me to a taxi number or something," I groaned, unable to focus my eyes, talk or stand up for the third time that day.

"No, it uses standard cell phone bandwidth and literally squeezes you along the connection and out of the handset on the other side. It's effective, but quite primitive which is why there is occasional fluid discharge or expulsion, head pain and joint damage."

In my opinion this was one of those times when the word 'occasional' was inappropriate. Like when it precedes the word 'Holocaust' or 'Armageddon'.

> Exemplum –
> *"Hi I'd like to go skydiving please."*
> *"Certainly sir."*
> *"Just one thing though, it is completely safe isn't it?"*
> *"Oh yes sir, apart from the occasional plane crash and chute malfunction, no worries at all."*
> *"I'll just watch."*

I rolled over on the floor to face Terry. "Terry" I said, pointing like a drunk, "I never ever want to do that again"

"That's wise, I hate it. So, once you are together again, we need to see the boss about how to get you back to Earth."

"The Boss?"

"Yes."

"I have to say Terry, that the fact you even have a boss seriously undermines your title of Master of the Universe."

****

God's living space was the staging area from which all things were monitored and where all things were created. It was a series of cloud platforms which looked down on all of creation. It was outside of the Universe, but from it you could go anywhere you needed to go.

He sat down on his main cloud after the board had finished their meeting. He dangled His big legs off the side and stared down at the magnificent sight below. Gleaming shining orbs representing all of creation lay far, far below Him. He couldn't take any joy from it in that specific moment as a niggling concern was constantly bothering Him, like toothache. He was displeased with the way things had slipped. They were getting lax about discipline. He was thinking about Fate and his all too frequent trips to Earth. He was worried that the deaths He'd discovered were mounting up and that Fate was out of control. Just then He noticed Satan lingering at the doorway on the far side of the cloud, pensively chewing on his red tail.

"You ok?" asked God, although He knew already.

"No. I'm concerned about Fate," said Satan.

"Me too." God said, looking up at Satan. "Come and sit

down if you like."

Satan came and sat down.

"Beer?" asked God.

"Yeah, thanks. Actually, have you got any light beer?"

"Um hold on." God rummaged in His big cooler.

"I'm just kidding," said Satan.

"Oh."

God handed him a Bud.

Satan cracked it open with the pointed end of his tail and took a sip before he spoke, "Have you noticed there's been a significant deviation from the planned mortality rate?"

"Yes, I have."

"Good", the Devil nodded awkwardly. "Good."

"I mean, I'm God, of course I've noticed."

"Right yeah sorry. It's just it could destabilise the universe which would end existence for all of us as we know it."

"Yeah I know. As I said I am *God*. I know these things."

"So it seems like the sort of thing you-know-who might do."

"You-know-who? He's Fate, not Voldemort and yes it does seem like the sort of thing he might do, but I don't have any proof so I don't want to get into it with him until I do."

"We'll need to do something eventually."

"I'll pull him in for a chat, see if I can catch him out in a lie. It could just be co-incidence; there are aberrations in the stats all the time, for all sorts of reasons."

"Yes, but I think we'd better be sure. And you know I normally love the murders and all that. I think he's a creative genius, but if he kills us all and takes the universe with it, I'll be bloody-well hopping mad!" said Satan.

"Well we won't let it get to that stage."

"If it goes south, we may have to destroy him," said Satan.

"Yes. I've been thinking that."

"So, it begs the question; does he know his own Fate?"

"Yes, it does," agreed God, sipping His beer.

Satan looked down at the universe, then sharply back up at God.

"Wait what? You don't know? How can you not know? You created him!"

"Yeah. But I was tired. I couldn't be bothered hearing all your thoughts so I made board members exempt so we could have a normal friendship."

"You were TIRED?!" The Devil's eye's bulged.

"Well, I'd just created heaven, the universe, billions of people, designed all the animals and made the angels. Then for balance I made you and as a result I had to build hell and demons and then purgatory as an overspill area."

"Yeah I suppose."

"So, it was late on Monday night and I *was* concentrating, but I wasn't *really* concentrating. You know?"

"Mmm."

"I do a lot of my designs by gut feeling alone. If anything, I try not to think about them too much."

"Yeah?" Satan arched an eyebrow.

"Yeah," nodded God.

Satan got out his notepad and started writing. "Do you find that works though? I'm quite obsessive; I make notes, draw diagrams, put flowcharts up on the wall and do mind maps and stuff."

"Yeah, I mean whatever works for you, I just get ready and do it, I just do it. It's instinct, I just see it, then I do it." God sipped His beer, finishing it.

"Could I sit in on one of your sessions and learn that method?"

"You can if you like, but I'm warning you, it's pure instinct, you can't teach it, it's there or it isn't, there's no course for instinct."

"Ok cool." Satan nodded.

"Anyway, listen to me, gabbing away like a schoolgirl! Do you want something to eat?" said God.

****

Terry sat me down at a table. He looked at me seriously. I looked back attempting to be equally as serious.

He slid a piece of paper across the table to me.

"What's this?" I said.

"It's a release form."

"What for?"

"It's just to say that you swear upon pain of a very, very real and tangible death not to tell anyone, anything of what you saw and learned here." Terry inclined his head solemnly.

"Sure." I signed the form. "You have my word."

"Excellent." He beamed and slid another piece of paper across to me.

"What's this?"

"It's a release form."

"I've just signed a release form, what's this one for?"

"It's just to say that if you die on the way back to Earth or from a heart attack or other symptom upon arrival then it was at your own risk entirely."

"Why, what could go wrong?"

"Oh nothing, it's perfectly safe, although at one point we did have the occasional disembowelling."

"Hmmm." I said unhappily. "When do I meet this boss of yours?"

"I've decided just to send you back without bothering him with this. He's very busy and important you know." Terry looked at me witheringly.

"Really? The guy who is the boss of the Master of the Universe is busy and important? That shocks me."

"Well it shouldn't, it's obviously a big job; I have to say that even for a human you are hopelessly naïve," Terry scoffed. I laughed, but Terry hadn't engaged with my sarcasm.

He led me along a white corridor that I may or may not have been in before. It all looked the same. I had no idea how people found their way around this place. We came to a white metal sliding door and it opened up revealing a room, which looked like it contained four shower cubicles on each of its four walls. Each cubicle had a glass door and a large dark opening in the ceiling above it.

"These are the teleportation booths. This is how we will return you to Earth. We will programme the destination and you should arrive instantly."

"Should? You don't know?" I yelped.

"Well it *is* quite a new system."

He quickly eased me into one of the booths and slid the glass door closed.

"Wait, how many of these have you done?" I demanded.

He hesitated. "About five."

"What's 'about' five? Not five then?"

"Well ok, four. We've done four."

"Four? FOUR? You've only done four? What does occasional disembowelment mean then? How many did that happen to?"

"Just one. But that was the only issue," he said earnestly.

He pushed the ignition. It counted down.

3

2

1

"Oh, and we had one death."

0

"AAAAAAAAAAAAAAAAAAAAAAAAAAAAAAAAAA
AAAAAAAAAAAAAAAAAAAAAAAAAAAAAAAAAAAA
AAAAAAAAAAAAAAAAAAAAAAAAAAAAAAAAAAAA
AAAAAAAAAAAAAAAAAAAAAAAAAAAAAAA!"

"Seen you soon!" shouted Terry, waving cheerfully as I bellowed at him. He pressed the button that split me into 5 million bits.

Chapter 7
The Nightly Update

It was late and there were beer cans all over the place as Terry arrived for his nightly update with God. You used to have to climb a stairway to this vantage point, but God had put in a lift recently, which had sped things up no end.

It only had three buttons, one had the word 'Bells' on it, one had 'Boardroom' and the third had 'Above' written on it. God made that little joke to Terry the first time He showed him it.

"You press the middle one, Terry, always the middle one. The bottom button goes to hell and the one at the top goes to Heaven. Another way to put that is:

"HELL'S BELLS AND HEAVEN'S ABOVE!!!!!"

God had laughed for about fourteen days straight. He likes jokes, especially wordplay. After all, He invented puns. Terry had just stood there for the entire fortnight in terror. Not wanting to turn his back on God or interrupt Him he had just stood there and waited for the laughter to stop. By the time he returned to the MOON he collapsed, starved, exhausted and delirious.

This time God just waved him in. Terry stepped around the beer cans and stood in front of God.

"Hello God," said Terry, cheerfully.

"Terryyyyyyyyyyy!" said God and then gave him a hug.

"You are my main man, Terry, I knew you'd come, you're always on time. Have I ever told you how much that punctuality means to me? I love you man. That's how much it means to me. That's how much. I mean, it says in the Bible 'For God so loved the world... yada yada', it should have just said 'For God so loved Terry and his AMAZING punctuality'. It should have just said that."

They sat down and God put His arm around Terry's shoulder.

"Give me some knuckles," said God, holding out His giant fist.

God was drunk and Terry had absolutely no idea what to do. He heard a clatter of cans moving and a groan and turning his big long face he saw the Devil struggling to sit up holding his head and grimacing.

"Saaatttaaaaaan! Hey, I thought you went home hours ago!" said God, laughing.

"What?"

Satan looked pretty dazed.

"I said, I thought you went back to Hell already." God tapped His wrist, but He wasn't wearing a watch.

"Oh. No man. I was over here and then I fell down."

"You are mental."

"Me? I can't believe you're still standing after that. I mean I can't even sit up properly and I only had 18,000 beers. You were doing them three at a time."

The devil stood up a little too quickly. Then he vomited violently, which caused every child in Taiwan to cry.

"I'm going home." And with that he left in a puff of red smoke.

Terry fidgeted nervously with his report. He was worried that God was going to forget about it and he was anxious to tell God about the interesting day he'd had. So, he just passed the report across and began talking as God leafed through it laughing at words like 'moon' and 'crevice'; but as Terry described the events that had taken place that day God sobered up pretty quickly.

"A human," He said, seriously.

"Yes. A nice one."

"And you told him what you do."

"Well yes. Of course."

"Ok."

God stood up and began pacing; without thinking He crushed the beer cans into a large cube, which disappeared.

The cube reappeared in Hell that instant and The Devil read the note God had attached, which said 'F.A.O. Hitler's ass.' The Devil laughed for ages, which also caused every child in Taiwan to cry. God was always doing stuff like that.

"Did he ask a lot of questions?" God said.

Terry frowned, "He asked – I would say – a normal amount of questions for someone who just discovered that aliens and teleportation were both real before lunchtime."

There was an awkward silence.

God looked at Terry. "Terry do you trust me?"

"Yes of course."

"I need you to do something for me."

"Anything."

"Terry what I need you to do is awful. It will seem quite immoral and extremely unfair."

"What is it?"

"I need you to kill the human. I'm sorry Terry, it's not what I want, but I need you to kill him. Can you do that for me?"

"Oh. I'm afraid not sir. I didn't want you to have any hassle on my account so I sent him back to Earth already."

"Ah."

"I'm sorry sir, have I done something wrong?"

"No, you're a good man Terry, devoid of murderous thoughts. It has just made things slightly more complicated."

God dismissed Terry and summoned Fate. The human was now in so much more trouble than he could ever have known.

Chapter 8
A Calculated Risk

The wind blew across an empty street in Tokyo. Mr. Namosaki stepped out from his calligraphy workshop and locked the door behind him. It had been a good day; he had made many fine signs, displays and even designed a tattoo.

His daughter was making him dinner that evening, which was good because he was hungry and she was an excellent cook. His work and his family were more important to him than anything – to have an enjoyable day and then spend time with his wife and daughter was his idea of a perfect day.

He thought back to the tattoo he had designed that day. He was asked to do them occasionally because of his great and famous artistic skill. However, in Tokyo it was mainly western tourists who had them done. The couple that day had been odd; she was tall, friendly, peroxide blonde and spoke in loud slow-motion English. He was *really* tall, with scary dark eyes and spoke quietly, but authoritatively. He was also very rude. He asked her to 'hurry the hell up' when she was choosing and told Mr Namosaki that he 'better do it right or there will be consequences'.

She asked for her name in Japanese on her forearm.

Her name was 'Destiny'.

Mr Namosaki was a serious professional, but he did not tolerate rudeness. So, gambling that they could not understand Japanese, he wrote 'My boyfriend is an ass' in beautiful script on the special paper.

He had directed them to the nearest tattoo parlour and then when they had left, he had a very long laugh at them.

He looked out across the empty street and paused for a moment to appreciate the fresh air.

Two hundred feet above him, the piano was moving at quite a speed. As it fell, the air rushed through its insides and the strings began to vibrate. The men operating the now broken crane could only stare in slow-motion horror.

The last thing Mr Namosaki heard was a perfectly tuned F sharp.

Fate had struck again. Mr Namosaki is dead.

Chapter 9

The REALLY Green Grass of Home

I opened my eyes. This teleportation device was obviously better designed than Terry's hash key vomit phone or his photocopier transport system which could have turned me inside out. This jump had simply left me a little dazed, but otherwise unharmed.

I was slightly confused though. I could not place my location. The green grass I was standing on was really, really green. I mean superbly, extraordinarily green, like think of the greenest thing you've ever seen and then double the amount of green – you're still not even getting close to the greenness. If Dulux had to name it on their colour chart, they'd have to call it something like Super-Mega-Ultra-Lime-Wallop.

The sky was blue, perfect blue and there was not a cloud to be seen. The rolling grassy hills stretched out in front of me to the horizon. The air was warm, fragrant, but not stifling, it was faultless, I had never been anywhere quite like it. It looked like a computer-generated image. It was like being in a photoshopped screensaver landscape from Windows 98, it didn't seem real. It was an extremely nice place to be, although I was struggling to enjoy it because I appeared to be in the middle of nowhere; possibly in a foreign country, with no money, no passport and no idea of the language or customs.

I began to walk and to my right I saw movement. From behind a hill an adorable little grey rabbit emerged, hopping along the ground with carefree abandon. When it saw me it stopped dead, frozen in fear and tensed as if ready to run. Its white fluffy tail suddenly rigid.

"Don't worry" I said softly, "I won't hurt you," and moved slowly down to a crouch to look at his cute wee face.

The rabbit straightened up on to his hind legs. "Why the fuck should I believe you?" he said, very unexpectedly.

"Ummmmmmm," I hesitated, unsure how to cope with the extremely sudden onset of mental illness I now found myself burdened with.

"Well?" said the insistent bunny; now with his little paws on his hips.

I didn't handle it entirely well. "I'm going mad – I'm actually going mad", I started to rub my face vigorously and walk in little circles.

"And that's supposed to get me to trust you is it?" the rabbit continued.

"There's a talking rabbit. There's a talking rabbit." I repeated and repeated; slowly coming to the realisation that teleportation had mangled my mind rather than my body this time. I looked through my fingers at him. I muffled a scream of frustration by placing a hand over my mouth.

"Are you alright? You don't look right," he said gently. Well this was just great. A tiny rabbit was pitying me now. Looking at *me* how *I* look at junkies.

"I'm fine, just insane unfortunately. Do you know where we are?"

"We're on Joy-World!"

"What?"

"We're on Joy-World!"

Of course we were. When you have mentally deteriorated to the level where you are having imaginary conversations with talking bunnies, you shouldn't be surprised when they answer your questions with nonsense. "Do you know where the nearest train station is?" I said, changing tack.

"No sorry – I don't know what a train station is," the little bunny replied.

"Of course, sorry, my apologies, I keep forgetting you're a rabbit I'm imagining."

"You're not imagining me. At least, I don't feel like you are imagining me," he said patting his little white chest.

"That's not psychologically helpful to either of us."

"Very true," agreed the talking rabbit.

"Ok, can you take me to where the other people are?"

I was hoping this would lead to a conversation with a human and a ticket home. He looked me up and down suspiciously. Unsure of something.

"I don't know mate; you seem dodgy as fuck."

"Me? At least I'm not a talking rabbit. I am doing everything within normal parameters," although the timbre of my voice as I said this went out of normal parameters.

"What's a talking rabbit?" he shot back, "And who told you that you look normal? You're a terrifying, giant, pink creature with no hair on your face or paws. I nearly shat all over this lovely field when I saw you. You're looking at normal from a distance, mate."

I didn't know what to do with that statement as it flew in the face of all the information I had available to me. I dropped to my knees and looked him in the eye "Look, I just want to get home. Is there anyone who can help me?"

"I'll take you to see the Chief," he said reluctantly. He began to walk away and beckoned me to follow him. I got up and trudged off behind him.

****

Fate in his chosen form was tall, pale, smartly dressed, with slicked hair and would have been handsome if not for his dead black eyes. He basically looked like if Dracula was an estate agent from the 1980s. Terry bumped into him lurking by the door on his way out and gave him a friendly hello. The look that Fate gave Terry caused him to have nightmares about crows for five weeks. Terry wondered why Fate had been eavesdropping on their chat, but not enough to stay and ask.

Fate waited for Terry to get out of sight, took a breath and then swept into God's chamber confidently.

"Good Morning. You wished to speak to me?"

"Yes Fate," said God. "I have a question to ask you."

"Ask it." His voice imperceptibly cracked with nerves.

"Are you aware of a series of deaths that have occurred on Earth which are not in accordance with our submitted plans?"

"Yes. It was this matter I was attending to when you summoned me."

"In what way were you attending to it?"

Fate eyed God aggressively. "What do you mean by that?"

"In what way were you attending to it?"

"Are you suggesting that I would carry out these killings?"

God smiled – "I made you. I know you. I can't read your mind as I can the humans. After all who could maintain a friendship with someone who could see their every idle thought?"

"Quite."

"However, I made you to be a killer. Someone who would be able to cope with, even enjoy the task."

"I take great pride in my work."

"As well you should, it's an important task that I have burdened you with. That being said, we have had to speak about your temper before."

"I have apologised for those lapses in judgement," Fate reminded God.

"There were several."

"And I have apologised," Fate snapped back.

"And my son, you are forgiven. But I need to know now, this minute – have you 'lapsed' again?"

"I have not," said Fate, unable to meet God's gaze.

"I do not wish to offend you, but Satan and I are not entirely convinced about that."

"Well I'm glad you've found yourself such a trustworthy confidant," Fate sneered.

"I know it is counter-intuitive, but sadly he is the most honest of us all."

"That is sad, but having looked into the matter I can tell you exactly who is responsible for the killing and it not I, but a human."

"A Human?" God paced the room; assessing the possibilities, working out all of the variables.

"A human, yes."

"Has this human recently disappeared from your view?"

"As it happens, yes. He killed a man in Japan and then abruptly vanished. I was tracking him when you summoned me."

"Terry just reported to me that a human showed up on the MOON asking many questions."

"Where is he now?"

"Back on planet and flush with half the information he needs to destroy everything we have built."

"Then we are in worse danger than we first thought."

"Fate, you know your job. The human must die."

"He will."

Chapter 10
God's First Memory

From a human perspective the board members seemed immortal, infallible and all powerful. They are not, however, any of these things. Every physical world is governed by rules; there are maximum amounts of energy and resources in all situations. The space that God inhabits is only different from ours in scale.

You see although our perception is that gods are immortal, they are not. Like all life forms, gods have a beginning and an end.

Because He had perfect recall the earliest memory God had of His existence was indeed His very first moment. He awoke to find Himself bathed in the light of a billion stars. He had no idea how He had arrived there or where 'there' even was, but He knew there was light and He knew there was warmth. The cosmos in front of His eyes was His first experience of beauty and He drank it in. As He looked closer at the glittering array, He saw a message written in stars across the sky.

You may create 7 worlds.

When the 7th universe meets its end so will you.

Choose a successor and leave this message.

The message and the stars all around slowly faded and faded until it was gone leaving God alone in a featureless void – like the moment you turn off the TV in a Travelodge.

Time passed and He became uncomfortable in the darkness, and He wished the light would return. As soon as He thought this, a faint light brightened His vicinity.

This was a dawning of realisation for Him. Let there be light. He now understood that He had a measure of power in this place. For the several eons that followed, He mastered His powers, learning how to move and create matter. He slowly came to comprehend the awesome control over the physical world with which He had been blessed. He thought through His plan and started to generate substances, creating slowly, but surely, a large environment for Himself; the staging area in which all seven universes would be designed and created. It was an interconnecting series of thick soft clouds suspended in the heavens.

In the beginning all was well. However, a lot can change in 29 billion years.

God was worried and when God is worried that's an excellent time for everyone else to start worrying also; it's rarely about litter or house prices – it tends to be about the stability of the Universe. When God had created the universe, it is said that He achieved this in seven days. This was not because He is so powerful, intelligent or creative. He is all of those things, but that was not the reason. It was because this was His seventh time creating one.

The other six had been terrible failures and now lay empty, save for a few determined stragglers. He felt an enormous amount of regret and sorrow that these designs had failed and that life could not survive within.

Incidentally, the amount of sorrow a God can feel would destroy a human body, it can cause stars to supernova, it can cause typhoons, tsunamis and earthquakes from worlds away. The dark moods of the Supreme Being were coincidently described as Acts of God by some who had experienced the results, but in reality, He had little control over them. As little control as the small beings He'd made in His image.

The Seventh Universe was His masterpiece. Life had thrived here for thousands of years through His careful and wise management. But life in this fragile and beautiful universe was under threat now.

Now as He looked out over His final creation, He knew that He had a serious problem. The first six universes had all failed and the seventh was dying.

He had made errors in His first six designs, He knew that now, but the Seventh was supposed to be a survivor.

He had created it in a much slower fashion than the previous worlds. The universe would contain a multitude of galaxies and worlds all balanced with intense precision to sustain the life on this one green planet.

In the previous Universes He had made the higher creatures

and then deposited the first few on the planet and let things develop from there. However, He'd created a much more sophisticated system for the Seventh Universe. He'd created just 1 life. A single celled organism from which millions of species would evolve. This would happen slowly, generation by generation, allowing God to observe which species survived and what constituted an advantage for survival. It allowed Him to field test species in a live environment, which helped Him shape and contour the world to suit the end design: the human being. When necessary, He could send a flood or a comet and in doing so was able to wipe a genus of creatures from the Earth who would not be compatible with His higher creature design. The dinosaurs and the mega fauna were destroyed to allow smaller creatures who better served the food chain to prosper.

It was a logical marvel, a design masterstroke, which ensured members of the human race were born into a world of advantage being intelligent enough to outsmart their fellow animals and physical enough to defend themselves against any aggressive predators. He was able to try several designs for humankind in a live environment and to His surprise instead of one group emerging as the dominant species they interbred and strengthened through variety. This left Him with His most capable ever species and the best chance for a lasting, prosperous universe.

Watching on, He saw them invent tools, the wheel, electricity, vaccinations; the brilliance of these creatures to adapt, improve and survive was impressive. They were His greatest achievement. He loved them more than He had ever thought he possibly could.

The possibility that they could be obliterated because of one tiny moment of weakness from Him was unbearable.

Incidentally, the amount of love a God can feel would destroy a human body, it can cause stars to supernova, and it can cause typhoons, tsunamis and earthquakes from worlds away. Basically, His emotions are a constant pain in the arse for absolutely everyone.

Right now, the overriding emotion He was experiencing was embarrassment. The reason God had asked two people to kill me that morning was not spite or malice; it was absolute rock-solid necessity.

Living for 29 billion years has its drawbacks and monotony is chief among them. So, to make the universe 'more interesting' God had introduced some deliberate jeopardy. A game. A game they wouldn't even know they were playing. The rules were simple, if a human discovered incontrovertible proof of the existence of God and saw each of the other six universes with their own eyes, then upon their return to Earth, the entirety of creation would end immediately. He called this game *The Death Gambit*.

Losing the game was vanishingly unlikely and would necessitate a series of calamities so specific, that God thought if they all happened in the right order, then perhaps the Universe was simply not meant to succeed.

The risk was complete and total destruction, but the upside was that the existence of the game at all had introduced something to worry about, something to lose, something to challenge the tedium of immortality. It somehow made visiting Earth in human form very illicit and exciting, like being on a secret mission. It had definitely perked up the last 100,000 years. It didn't feel like more than 30,000 years had passed. Time really flies when you're mildly distracted.

Today He was extremely distracted for two reasons. First, someone was killing more people than could be tolerated by His survival plan for the planet. This could destabilise the Earth's population and send it into a spiral which it could not pull out of, ending the universe and all of existence.

Second, a human was suddenly behind the scenes of the universe and had the potential to end all of existence with a comprehending glance. He smiled a wry smile on His gigantic face, rubbed His gigantic hands together; He *was* worried, but being God had just become interesting again.

Chapter 11
Joy World

In the warm, grassy paradise the talking rabbit (whose name turned out to be Mr Gillespie) had taken me on a trek. We walked for miles through seemingly identical green scenery, eventually arriving at the shore of a ridiculously blue, placid lake.

Beside the lake in the sand was a small wooden throne (about the size of a child's high chair) with three small steps leading up to it. Flowers and branches were laid out around it as if to denote a special area one was not permitted to enter. Sitting in the chair, there was a big fat sheep wearing a beret.

Mr Gillespie called to the sheep "Jim, we've got a visitor."

This startled the sheep and he suddenly sat up. "What-what?" Looking down his sheep face at Mr Gillespie, and then worriedly glancing in my direction, he was clearly supremely confused.

"What the hell is this thing Gillespie?" he said, pointing a chunky hoof at me, in a voice that was surprisingly deep and even more surprisingly, English.

My addled brain had already given up on being surprised at a talking sheep, but the beret did genuinely throw me for a second.

"I found it in the fields – it's confused," said Gillespie. The sheep climbed down from its throne and walked over to me.

"I would be very grateful if you could show me where the train station is," I said.

"By George it speaks!" exclaimed Jim, the talking sheep.

"I think it could be a pig! I mean just look how pink and hairless he is! It's like something from our stories." Gillespie prodded my leg.

"A Pig – yes." The sheep turned to me "Are you a pig?"

"I don't know what the hell you're talking about. I am a man, a human man, from the suburbs. I just want to go home."

"A man? Oh dear," said the sheep.

"Why 'oh dear'? What's 'oh dear'?" I whined.

"I have once before heard of your kind. You, my friend, are a long, long way from home. Sit and I will tell you where you are."

"Look I'd much, much rather just get out of your hair and get back to my house. If you could just show me the way to the train station, I can find my way."

"I'm sorry son" said the Sheep. "I don't know what a train station is, but I do know that whatever it is – we don't have one. I'm worried that you still think you are on Earth. You're about as far away as you can get from that, and the way back will not be easy."

"I'm not on Earth?"

"No, my bizarre and disturbingly-faced friend; you are on Joy World." He motioned around with a hoof.

"Joy World – What the bastard is Joy World?"

He brought me a cup of the most delicious tasting fresh water I had ever had and as I greedily gulped it down, he told me his version of the history of Joy World.

Down on Joy World, Jim the Sheep told the human his version of events from his understandably ground-level, woolly, ovine perspective. However, to understand Joy World and why it failed, more context is required.

The Actual History of Joy-World

Joy-World was the 1st Universe – God's initial attempt at a world; His idealistic teenage poetry.

He created a small universe into which He inserted a single spherical planet. Even this was the subject of much thought and testing. He'd initially designed a flat oblong planet, but He thought that this would leave the inhabitants feeling trapped or limited by the edges of their world.

He tested an inverse conical planet, but everyone who lived near the middle would end up falling into the valley in the centre and wouldn't be able to get back out.

He tested a cube planet, but gravity got seriously complicated in this world, as you required a different separate field for each side. He saw that the corners and edges would rise out of the atmosphere like frozen, dead mountains and the centre of each panel would buckle inwards as pulled down by gravity. It was not a hospitable place and the one rabbit He put on it as a tester confirmed it was 'shite'.

He finally settled on a round planet. It was finite, but gave the impression of infinite space because you could carry on travelling around it. This would satisfy His creatures more, He thought.

He wanted it to be a perfect paradise and endless peaceful existence, which He could enjoy with them. He tried to imagine his most contented moment, so He thought back to being bathed in the light of a billion stars. He would make sure this planet was warm at all times. He enclosed it in a small universe with two suns – one on each side of the planet.

He made the scenery endless and beautiful. When He came to make the creatures, He wanted no war between them. He made them eat grass and leaves, renewable food sources that were everywhere on this green planet. He made them small and friendly. It seemed like a solid plan. He deployed the creatures to their environments and gently awoke them to begin their new life on Joy World.

Almost immediately things went badly wrong. God had made several key design oversights. The two suns did not move in the sky and there were no such things as clouds. This meant constant, bright sunlight 24/7. God had not yet invented night-time, seasons or weather, but something inherent in all life forms requires the passage of time. As the days and weeks and eventually months passed the creatures started to become unsettled by the lack of any evidence of time passing. Even more unfortunately for them God hadn't invented sleep yet because He hadn't thought that their brains and bodies would require rest. He hadn't ever needed to rest Himself, so the thought had simply not occurred to Him.

After about a year of this some of the creatures began to go slightly mad. Deep within them they knew that they had to hide from the sunlight, that rest was required.

They built shelters from the suns, they threw rocks at it and they closed their eyes. Oddly they tried these solutions in that order, but nothing would work.

The creatures were to the untrained eye what we would call Sheep, Rabbits, Cows, Pigs and Ducks. The Sheep, Rabbits, Cows and Ducks all lived in the same area. However, they were all unaware of the Pigs who lived on the other side of the planet. The Pigs believed themselves to be completely alone in the universe. In fact, Pig folklore soon began to speculate that they were the divine creations of a higher being who had created them in his image. The pigs shat everywhere and then rolled around in it – so they were basically the definition of content. They were physically tough and mentally strong – the shit also gave them decent sun protection.

For the other creatures it was more difficult. As their madness progressed, they began to look for someone to blame. They split off into their species groups, forming factions and developing conspiracy theories. Each faction blamed the others for the madness, blamed the others for their exhaustion. As you would expect, the ducks became particularly paranoid. Their insulation caused them to constantly overheat and as there was no such thing as rain or night-time they couldn't cool off. Their leaders had decided that the Cows were to blame because they were the largest and stupidest.

Their delusion and their fear spilled over into violence when they attacked the main herd of cows in formation. A bloodless, largely ineffectual war commenced with the Cows unable to inflict much damage on the much more mobile Ducks and the Ducks being unable to inflict any damage on the robust Cows because of their complete lack of any offensive characteristics whatsoever. The cows formed a largely useless blockade around the main body of fresh water and the ducks unsuccessfully tried to shit on all the grass. There was the distinct possibility that the war would continue for years without any casualties being inflicted by either side.

The ducks had organised themselves into a society. The duck which had grown largest was declared the King Duck. His original name had been Bill Winger, but he took the royal name Teabags. King Teabags was not only the largest of the Ducks, but also the most intelligent. You could tell this because he had a good vocabulary and wore glasses. He wasn't immune from the madness though and thoroughly believed the cows had caused the eternal sunshine and therefore must all be eliminated. He designed several promising strategies, but they did not work. Formation flying had increased their speed and efficiency, but ramming the cows' thick skin had not done enough damage. A noise-based strategy had 15,000 ducks quacking at the same time to try and deafen the cows. However, disappointingly for the Ducks, the cows didn't even look bothered. Their look was a mix of world-weariness, disappointment and pity. The war trundled on.

Meanwhile one of the rabbits had created a network of underground tunnels and rooms in which they had begun to live – he was called Warren and the tunnels were named after him. This allowed them to avoid the heat for a few hours. Their sanity had remained largely intact for the first months, but eventually the lack of sleep got to them as well. They took to staring directly at the two suns attempting to wipe them out of existence with mind-powers they didn't have. Incidentally this is the evolutionary origin of the modern Earth phrase 'a rabbit caught in headlights'.

The creatures are largely nocturnal on Earth, shying away from the Sun wherever possible. Modern rabbits have no conscious memory of their past, having regressed to non-speaking, unorganised societies there was no way for that story to be passed down the generations. But running through the darkness at night and suddenly seeing two glowing orbs, overwhelms them with a feeling that is 7 billion years in the making. Frozen to the spot, two suns thundering out of the night to get them. Two suns haunting the DNA of their ancestors, deep within them. Two suns, tormenting them through time – albeit in the form of a 2011 Citroën Saxo.

Meanwhile the wool bound sheep had begun to die of the heat and their numbers steadily dwindled until there were just ninety. At this point the rabbits dug them an underground shelter out of pity. A few sheep went inside, but unfortunately they all followed and a large crush ensued, which wiped out most of the sheep population.

Halfway round the world the pigs were reasonably happy, but their mud rolling hobby didn't keep them covered up at all times and as we have recently discovered on Earth, pigs can get skin cancer. With no medical assistance available and their inadvertent isolationist policy they were completely extinct within six months.

God had also not yet invented genders, so every creature on the planet was what we'd now term as a male. As He had lived for a very long time alone, He had not considered the need to procreate. Population began to seriously dwindle after year 1.

The cows were under the misapprehension that the Ducks possessed a sort of magic as they could fly and swim, neither of which the cows could do. Talk of how to take this magic from them began to circulate amongst the remaining cows. The leading strategy was for a cow to eat a duck and see if that transferred the magic across.

Meanwhile the duck king had had enough. He was too hot, too tired and too crazy to continue. Having heard the cows demands, he offered himself to the cows as a sacrifice if they would end the sunshine.

The cows accepted him as a sacrifice, but stated that they could not end the sunshine as they had 'discovered' that, in fact, the bad weather was caused by the gay cows being gay.

At this news the ducks realised that the war was futile, the cows didn't know any more than they did and that no-one could end their suffering. They all silently waddled forward and offered themselves to the cows.

"End our pain," said King Teabags.

The cows, believing that flight and floatation powers were contained within the ducks, accepted the task solemnly. However, as they began to eat the ducks, their delicate oesophagus – which were designed for grass and weeds – could not deal with meat and feathers.

So, it came to pass that on the seventeenth day of the fourteenth month, the entire duck population was killed by being eaten by cows and the entire cow population died from choking on dead ducks.

The following day, the remaining few sheep and rabbits climbed the highest mountain on Joy World – Mount Agreeable. At the top of the mountain was a plateau with a circular clearing surrounded by ornate rocks and colourful bushes. This was the highest they would get. They called in unison into the sky and demanded to speak to the Sun Controller.

God sat outside of the small universe hearing the animals' tragic cries reverberating round the walls of His creation. He was ashamed to face them, having failed them so completely. They would not be stopped though and continued to become louder and louder – chanting their demand in rhythm.

He commanded that night time be installed, He commanded that the creatures receive the ability to sleep and announced the invention of weather. Instead of these things happening though a huge message appeared in the sky above God's staging area –

FEATURES LOCKED. PLEASE PURCHASE PREMIUM VERSION OF UNIVERSE BUILDER TO ACTIVATE.

"What?!!!!!!" said God aloud to no-one.

The message cleared and was replaced with –

ONLY JOKING.

"Who are you?"

YOUR PREDECESSOR – DO NOT BE ALARMED. I AM LONG DEAD.

"That's supposed to be *less* alarming is it?"

ONCE YOU'VE CREATED A UNIVERSE, YOU CANNOT FUNDAMENTALLY ALTER IT.

"Why? I'm God?"

YOU MUST LEARN FROM YOUR ERRORS. YOU MAY ONLY PERFORM SMALL SUPERFICIAL TWEAKS, WEATHER EVENTS AND THE LIKE. THE BIG STUFF IS LOCKED AS SOON AS YOU COMMIT IT TO EXISTENCE

"Well this would have been really useful information A YEAR AGO!"

IT WAS IN THE SMALL PRINT. AND YOU SHOULD ALWAYS, ALWAYS READ THE SMALL PRINT. MESSAGE SYSTEM CLOSING – I WILL NOW RETURN TO THE OBLIVION OF DEADNESS – BEST OF LUCK.

"What a smug text-ghost."

He sat processing the new information He'd just been given. The creatures continued to shout for Him below.

Eventually God relented and spoke so they could hear Him. Out from the sun-drenched sky, His huge voice suddenly said –

"My Children – I will see you. I am your creator."

They ceased their chanting in amazement, small mouths hanging open – shocked to hear a voice they had scarcely still believed actually existed.

"Give me two minutes though," added God.

The seconds passed. After five minutes or so Jim the Sheep said to the group "Perhaps we are all mad together?"

God had never taken a solid form before, but felt that it was necessary, so as not to frighten the creatures. Which form to take though…

Something non-threatening, and certainly given the fractious nature of the creature relationships he could not be a Rabbit, Pig, Sheep or Cow.

So was born The Legend of the Talking Almond.

The Almond appeared in a flash of fire on the highest rock in the clearing. The Animals jumped back in fright, but then seeing that it was an Almond, approached it curiously.

"I am your creator," said the Almond. "I have taken this form so as not to alarm you. Before we begin though I must ask that you do not eat me. This will not taste good and will severely impact my ability to command authority."

The Talking Almond had a nice voice, a beautiful baritone and the animals were soothed by it.

"I created you to be in a world of eternal happiness. A joyful, peaceful life; without suffering. I have failed you."

"Why have you made us this way?" asked a rabbit.

"I apologise for your suffering and I see that it has gone too far. I'm afraid this world I've made has far too many flaws and I have made the decision to end this project and begin again. I am sorry."

"Sorry mate, are you serious?"

"Yes, my child."

"We asked you for help and your big solution is – I'm going to kill you all? Well I'm sure glad I suffered through the agony of the last year for this shit."

"This world is fundamentally broken, there is little I can offer you."

"Help us you prick! Don't just condemn us to death whilst pretending to be an almond – that's absolute textbook disrespect!" The little Rabbit was absolutely raging.

God took a moment to think. Thankfully for Him, His expressionless Almond face didn't give away any clues as to His inner monologue.

"I would like to give you an option. I can mercifully and painlessly end your life or you may stay on the planet for the rest of your natural lives, but I will depart and will never return."

"So, your idea of helping us is to offer us death or a continuation of our suffering? Thanks for coming down, you useless fucking nut."

"If you stay, I will grant you a giant cloud which will make it dark for a few hours a day. Plus, I'll tidy up all the cow, duck and pig corpses, make it nice again. How does that sound?"

"What's a pig corpse?" shouted another of the rabbits.

"Um. Nothing, it matters not." God blurted. He cleared His throat, which was predictably difficult to do as an almond.

"MAKE YOUR DETERMINATION." He boomed, trying to move off the topic quickly, before the animals could stumble onto yet another way in which He'd failed them.

The creatures huddled with their backs to the Almond discussing the options. After several minutes of intense talks, they re-approached the Almond.

"We'll go on living, but on one condition."

"Yes?"

"Jim wants a hat."

And on that, it was agreed. The Sheep received his beret and the universe would remain until the last of the creatures had perished. At that point, the 1st universe would be decommissioned.

God was pleased that His creatures valued living as it proved to Him that the experience had not been entirely without joy for them. However, He was dismayed by how wrong He'd got the planet's design. He thought He'd covered everything when He designed Joy World and it disturbed Him that so much had been overlooked.

He was so proud when He'd first launched it, but as the creatures had warred and died of illnesses, He now knew that the flaws could not be resolved. The first of His seven worlds would be a write off – He would approach the second one in a radically different way.

Chapter 12
Duel of The Fates

Fate Harkins was twenty-five. He was a young student who was covered in tattoos, wore his hair in a man-bun and had a large unkempt beard. He was a hipster and a militant vegan. However, despite all of those things, he was still a good person. He gave to charity; he was kind to his fellow man and he was a good friend to those who knew him.

Walking home from his part time job he stopped in at his local Coffee Shop/book club combo which was called De-Kafka's. This was the kind of infuriating place where your milk was poured out of an antique bicycle horn and you had to enter your order into an old typewriter and hand it to the barista. All the items on the menu were book related wordplay. You could have a Drugless Adams which contained no sugar or caffeine; you could have a Murder on the Orient Espresso, or a Kale of Two Cities smoothie.

He collected his drink – a Tea S Elliot – and headed out onto the street.

As he walked down the street, he noticed a couple approaching – she was tall, blonde, attractive and had a mischievous glint in her eye, she was beautiful. The man wasn't. He looked like a statue of an Apprentice contestant, after a harsh winter. His severe look could be described as attractive, but also extremely unsettling; he was absolutely amazing if you were turned on by getting a shiver down your spine.

The young hipster was so engrossed with the man's gloomy complexion that he didn't look where he was going and bumped into the woman – spilling hot Tea S Elliott all over her coat.

"I'm so sorry," he blurted out – "I'll pay for the dry-cleaning."

"No, it's fine," said the girl.

"Move along," said the tall man quietly.

"What's your name?" said Harkins to the girl.

"It's Destiny," she smiled.

"I'm Fate."

The tall man rounded on him, glaring, nostrils flaring.

"Fate and Destiny!" she giggled. "Perhaps we should be an item!" She winked at the tall man. He was busy though, doing his best hate-stare at the younger man.

"Did you say your name was Fate?" said the tall man.

"Yeah, it's a really stupid name isn't it? Fate Harkins. My parents were kind of hippies. My brother's called John though, so I don't really have a good explanation for it. Just a silly name."

"Yes. Very silly," said the tall man.

"Loads of people think I changed my name to Fate. I genuinely don't know why anyone would want this God-awful name. I'm perversely proud of it, but to actually change your name from something good to Fate, would be the act of an absolute fud."

"What's a fud?" asked Destiny, laughing.

"It's a Scottish thing. It means idiot. Or vagina," he smiled.

The big man reached out to touch him, but Destiny grabbed the man's hand and stopped it before it made contact with Harkin's arm. Harkin's watched as the two of them shared an intense look, Destiny gripped his arm tightly.

"No," she said firmly. He relaxed his arm.

As they walked away the tall man flashed him a dead-eyed grin and a cold shiver ran down Fate Harkin's spine.

Later that night, whilst debuting a new smoothie on his YouTube channel, which he had called the Guavacado, his beard became trapped in his industrial size blender; it chopped through his face and mind, leaving him thoroughly dead and the smoothie all but ruined. The live stream kept running until the ambulance arrived. The sad truth is that he would have been very happy with how the post became a viral sensation.

Fate Harkins was dead; Fate had struck again.

Chapter 13
Sonia Lancaster

Jim the Sheep explained that they'd been living in isolation on Joy World with a small dwindling population for forty years now. God had visited from time to time over the next few years, but had now thoroughly moved on to other projects.

I asked him about something he had mentioned earlier, "You said you had seen a man once before?"

He walked away from me and looked out over the water with what I assume was a wistful look, but I can't know because I could only see the back of his head. "Ah, him." Jim looked down with his sheep eyes at his sheep hooves and paused.

"Don't worry he's just clearing his throat," said Mr Gillespie.

"I think he said 'ah him'." I said quietly.

"Yes, that is what I said," confirmed Jim. "He looked very different from you. He was smaller and had dark skin, with a curved chest and red lips. Curled hair and a higher pitched voice."

"I think it might have been a woman – our female of the species," I said.

"I'm not sure what that is. But anyway, he was significantly more pleasant than you."

"We don't just have males on Earth, we also have females, an opposite sex"

"Opposite from what? You?" said Mr Gillespie.

"Yes, if you like."

He looked me up and down. "I wouldn't say she was opposite to you, just, um – how do I say this nicely – better?"

I frowned. "Well, in any case, we say 'she' and 'her', instead of 'he' and 'him' for females."

"She and her? What funny words! You are an odd one."

I turned to Jim. "Where did she come from?"

Jim looked to the space between the suns and pointed a hoof. "Up there."

"She fell?"

"Yes – she fell right through the heavens, straight down onto the top of Mount Wonderful."

"Was she unharmed?"

"Yes. Oh yes. We saw her coming down – we ran up there as fast as we could go. We didn't know what she was or where she had come from, but something told us she was not a foe. There was a gentleness to her."

"Did she speak to you? I need to know exactly what she said."

"Oh, she spoke, she sang, she danced. She was as wonderful as the mountain on which she stood."

"What happened to her? Why isn't she here?"

"She said she came from a place called Earth. A place where men lived. She said she'd been on a wonderful adventure of discovery. She'd seen the other Universes."

"What other Universes?"

"You think God went from this, straight to Earth? He tried loads of designs and they are all still there. You can travel between them if you know how, she said. Joy World was simply the first."

"What happened to her though?"

"Fate happened to her."

****

Sonia Lancaster was thirty-six and she was a graphic designer from Canterbury. The year was 2001. At the time, she was doing typeface and design work for the National Trust – signs for hillwalking routes, displays for visitor centres, that sort of thing. It was gentle, undemanding work which she mostly did from her home office. She didn't have a boyfriend, girlfriend, a pet or roommate. Although she would have loved to have a big giant dog, her landlord would not allow it. As a result, her workspace was full of absent-minded doodles of golden retrievers. Her other hobby was puzzles. She loved cryptic crosswords and codes and Sudoku. She was well read and very intelligent.

Lonely was another good word to describe Sonia Lancaster. She was definitely lonely; she was all the kinds of lonely. She lived a decent drive from the small amount of family she had and although she loved them, she was glad of the distance. They were largely nice people, but their increasingly right-wing views had made family gatherings a chore rather than a treat.

She was still single, when her friends had started to marry and have children and she saw less of them as a result. She didn't envy the children, this was something she had absolutely no interest in, but she did feel herself resenting the ones who were happily in love. Out of a sense of duty they had tried to set her up a few times and none of these pairings had worked out well; a few of them had been fairly disastrous. They had set her up with the guy who had brought his mum's ashes in a briefcase to the date.

"Did you come straight from work?" she had asked, gesturing towards the briefcase.

"It's my mum's ashes," he had said straightforwardly, looking back down at the menu and offering no further explanation. They waited in silence for the starters to arrive.

They had set her up with the guy from the gym. He had some amazing muscles, but had forgotten to get a personality along the way. It was during the eighteen-minute monologue about protein shakes where she mentally checked out. God he was great to look at, but sooooooooo boring.

It's a terrible moment when as an adult you realise that the only way to be in that kind of amazing shape is to have it occur genetically or to work on it to the extent that it is the only thing you ever do.

They had set her up with the guy who was insanely specific in his compliments. He said things like "You've got great index fingers" and "I love your ear lobes". Sonia's theory was that normal people said things like "You look nice" or "That's a lovely outfit". Men who got overly specific about body parts came across like serial killers who collected bits of women in their garage. They were halfway through their meal and he came out with "You look like you have strong bones. I like that."

She had no intention of being made into a dress by this creep, so she told him she was going outside to smoke and she never went back.

This decent portfolio of bad dates and a few near misses in terms of relationships had left her a bit disillusioned with the idea of long-term love.

She needed to shake things up; no more indoors, no more Netflix series about unsolved murders from the 90s and no more pretending a vegetarian pizza was a healthy option.

Working on her National Trust files one day she had an idea – she would walk the nearest trail to her house which bore her signage – end to end. She bought some hiking boots and a pop-up tent. The route she had chosen was roughly sixty-three miles – the walk would take her three days if she didn't stop too often.

On the first day she had covered seventeen miles, not quite enough, but there had been much to see. She'd run across sheep, cows, foxes, badgers, hedgehogs and rabbits. Never having spent any time around wildlife she was feeling like a character transported to Narnia. She stopped to talk to them, pet them and take pictures. It was a brilliant day. She had named every animal she had come across. She had selfies with Patricia the sheep, Lisa-Marie the cow and Captain Geraldo Fernandez, the fox (she had been getting quite into the naming process by this point). They had approached her because of her naturally relaxed demeanour and her handfuls of carrots.

Off the beaten track, she found a nice circular clearing to pop her tent in, it was mostly obscured from the walking path so she thought it would give her a decent amount of privacy and security. Not being an experienced hiker, she was not sure of the rules regarding whose land it was etc. and she decided to drag the tent to the very edge of the clearing, near the trees – hoping that if someone did happen to pass through, they would probably not even notice her presence. As she was doing so, she realised that she'd never properly been anywhere you could see the stars – weather, pollution or artificial light had always obscured them. The night sky on a clear evening is a wondrous thing, something that presents its magnificence each day, never fading or failing to shine, just either hidden or revealed. She realised that she had inadvertently spent a lot of time with the wonders of life hidden from her. As she gazed at the huge, glowing Moon and the shining array of distant suns, she vowed to keep them in sight at all times from this day forth.

It was a warm night and she slept with the tent opened, drifting off to the sounds of nature and into a deep sleep.

This sleep lasted around three hours. About 2:30 a.m. a bright glowing blue light penetrated the tent at ankle height. She sleepily wondered if she was having a vivid trippy dream about being at a Pink Floyd concert. However, she was gradually awakened by it and the slight sensation that the tent was moving. She looked outside and either the tent was moving or the forest was running away during the night. She rapidly became very awake and scrambled to the tent opening. An area in the centre of the clearing was sinking into the ground and it was creating a bowl shape. The tent was no longer on flat ground, but sliding down an increasingly steeper incline. It was like someone was pressing their finger into the clearing pushing the centre down. The middle of the glade had disappeared into an abyss and this had created a circular valley. The area in the centre was circular and glowing. A vivid blue light was pouring out of it and flowing up the hill – this is what had permeated the tent.

Just as she thought she was going to fall into the glowing abyss, the ground pulsed and vibrated which actually pushed Sonia and the tent back from the centre and closer to safety. This continued until it had almost returned her to the top of the incline. She was on the cusp of getting out of the tent when in the centre of the disturbance five figures slammed into appearance with a shockwave which knocked the tent head over heels. This left her upside down, teetering on the edge of the slope. She reached out of the opening of the tent and clung on to the grass with her left hand. This was now the only thing stopping her from sliding down towards them. She peeked through the tent opening to see who had come through the blue light. They were facing away from her, but she still held her breath so she would not be discovered. The figures walked up the bank of the now-depressed clearing and as they did so they spoke –unaware she was within earshot and also eyeshot.

The first figure – a large bearded man said "Ok, we meet back here in one day exactly. Does everyone have their time telling devices?"

"Yes," said the group showing various watches and phones to him.

"Satan – you are routinely late. Will you promise to at

least try and be on time?"

A tall handsome, rock-and-roll looking guy smiled at him, "I would love to promise, but you know what my promises are worth sadly."

The old man turned to a gaunt looking beanpole of a man "Fate – don't be killing too many people. The graph is dangerously close to being in the red and it's difficult to pull out of."

"I will only do what is necessary," he replied

"If that were true, it wouldn't be necessary to warn you," the old man scolded him.

"Remember," he said, turning to the group, "be back here for the same time tomorrow. It's dangerous to have us all down here at the same time. The portal will be open for thirty minutes, if you're late we risk doing things which could expose us. Understood?"

They all murmured their agreement and continued up the hill. When they reached the edge of the clearing the old man waved his hand over it. It began to vibrate and pulse again. The centre began to rise slowly. It was going to return to being a flat clearing again. However, as he turned away it pulsed one last time and to Sonia's horror this pulse knocked her off the edge and sent her and the tent sliding down the slope towards the searing light in the middle. She tried to move towards the tent opening, but the tent slid with increasing pace and threw her about as it pitched and turned. As it rushed closer to the middle she could see that it was a hole; a blue shimmering, gaping void which had dragged the rest of the land down – she tried to throw herself clear of the tent, but only managed to get her head out as she tumbled with a sickening drop through the opening.

"Fucksake!" screamed Sonia as she mentally crossed camping off her list of potential future hobbies.

Her stomach in her mouth, she fell for thirty seconds. As the tent spun and rotated, she was thrown around it, losing all sense of orientation; she didn't know where imminent death was coming from, but she knew that it must be coming and soon. She closed her eyes and could now hear the whistling of air passing through the tent.

What she couldn't hear was the ground rushing up to meet her, which it did very unexpectedly at that moment. The tent tumbled and cracked and ripped as she was thrown about, however, miraculously she had survived. Lying draped in the crumpled remains of the tent she closed her eyes and opened her lungs.

"Yaaaaaaaaaaaaaaaaaaaasssssssssssssssssssssssssssssssss sssssss!!!" she shouted at the top of her voice, releasing her relief like steam from a kettle.

She could feel the ground underneath her was pliant and bouncy. She reached out a hand through one of the torn openings of the tent and felt a substance which was not dissimilar to fleece. It was soft and cushioned; she assumed this is how she had survived. She untangled herself from the tent remnants and stood up. She was, in her cat pyjamas, standing on what appeared to be a large cloud. She saw that it seemed to be freestanding in the night sky. How this was possible she had absolutely no clue; she was just glad it was here as it had surely saved her life in the short term. *What now*, she thought to herself. However, that thought was interrupted when she properly allowed herself to look up. The billion gleaming stars above her were shocking and awesome. The mix of colours permeating the galaxies and nebulas was easily the most overwhelming, grand and stunning sight she had ever witnessed. The hairs on the back of her neck were not just standing up, they had their hands on their hearts and were singing the national anthem. It was absolutely astonishingly beautiful. Mouth agape she drank it in for a full five minutes, unable to rip her eyes away from it. As she looked at the amazing display of warm starlight above what she actually did next was to take a step back and fall right off the edge of it.

"Fucksake!" screamed Sonia again as she fell through the air, this time without a tent obscuring her view. She was falling at a fair rate, the wind ruffling her hair, but she'd temporarily stopped worrying about it as her eyes alighted on the sight below. Although she didn't know it, she had fallen from God's staging area and far beneath her lay the seven luminous universes suspended in space – separated by vast expanses of black nothingness, but joined by a glowing purple cord. The seven beautiful shapes increased in size along the line and at the far right she thought she recognised Earth floating in the centre of the seventh image. This was off to her right-hand side though – she tracked where she was falling and it was right between the second and third objects. She was in awe of the beauty of what she was witnessing; never before had she even dreamed such sights existed. Gradually though she started to become concerned at the prospect of falling into the abyss between the worlds. She experimented with using her arms and legs to steer her body this way and that. While she could indeed move a bit, it was patently obvious it would not be enough to land on one of the planets below. She instead resolved to get herself near the purple cord and hold on to it until she could figure out a better plan. This concerned her though as she had no idea whether you could grasp such a thing at all or what effect it would have on her if she did.

She was now within about two miles of the cord, but was still going to drop a little north of it. She leaned back and swam backwards through the air lining herself up with it exactly. As she dropped even closer, she could see that the cord was not a cord, but actually an enormous pipeline – a tunnel between the worlds. If she could get inside, she would surely be able to walk along the tunnel and get to the end safely. As it happened, she dropped onto the roof of the tunnel and it shattered like glass sending her falling through to the tunnel within. She braced for impact, assuming she would smash through the bottom, but instead landed softly on a stream of purple light which was flowing slowly through the tunnel. However, when it sensed her contact it abruptly fired her along the tunnel towards the second universe at hundreds of miles per hour. She popped out of the tunnel at the other end into the atmosphere where the purple light stream ended and she fell sickeningly towards the top of a large hill fifteen feet below. "Fucksake," said Sonia as she battered into the hard ground, bruising many parts of her body and leaving her dazed and confused.

As she lay there exhausted from her fall, she stared up at the unfamiliar sky. On the face of it, it looked very similar to a night sky in Britain. There were clouds, no stars, no visible Moon and it was bitterly cold. She hauled herself to her feet and looked around; it was pretty dark, but she could make out some details. She was on the circular flat top of what seemed like a vast mountain. She was only a few feet from the edge and remembering that she had accidentally fallen about a million miles to get here, she moved back and turned towards the centre of the clearing. It was the flat plateau of a very steep mountain; she had observed when she looked over the side that it disappeared into a black abyss, so she was clearly at some altitude. The top looked to be at least a mile wide and was potentially even farther lengthways. To either side of the clearing there were patches of dense forest and bushes, whereas in front of her, at the other side of the clearing was a formation of rocks, they were large geometric shapes with ancient looking engravings on them, strange patterns, foreign words and it all faintly reminded her of an Incan temple. Something about it seemed off to Sonia though. It had a false quality – the difference between an actual Incan temple and one from a Tomb Raider film. It did not fit with the surrounding environment.

She was staring at the wall of inscriptions when she heard a rushing sound behind her that sounded like the washing of a great wave against the sea shore. She ran to the edge of the cliff and looked out. For the first time she realised that the mountaintop was surrounded by an enormous sea of water and indeed a large wave had washed up onto the side of the mountain. The water was sixty or seventy feet below her, but she suddenly felt vulnerable. She was actually standing on a fragile island rather than the safety of occupying the high ground. Through the clouds and darkness, she could faintly begin to see what had displaced such a large amount of water. On the horizon a huge boat had appeared. A giant stout ark which was heading in her direction at pace. As it approached further, she came to appreciate the truly massive scale to which it was built. It was hundreds of feet tall with a humungous set of sails on top; it was about half of a mile wide.

"Wooooooo hoooooooooo!!!!" she heard joyfully shouted by someone on board.

It was still travelling at a very brisk pace when it swung round executing a move like a handbrake turn. It presented its extraordinarily lengthy port side to her now. The move had brought the boat to almost a full stop as it drifted towards the mountain and created a huge wave which crashed off the sides of the mountain and sent Sonia scrambling back to avoid getting completely soaked through. The boat drifted sideways slowly until it was mere feet away from the edge of the cliff. Sonia, realising that there was a good chance of someone emerging from the boat shortly, retreated to behind one of the large fake rocks – peering out from between two stones, like a pervert, to see what was going on.

A wooden hatch was opened in the side of the enormous wooden frame – a gangplank was lowered and a strange-looking short man ran down it onto the cliff. He was thrown a rope from the top deck and secured it to one of the rocks. Upon completing this task, he ran to the end of the gangplank, pulled a small horn from his trousers and blew a fanfare.

"We are moored Captain!" he proclaimed, apparently to absolutely no-one.

There was still no movement from the hatch and she could not see the top deck as it was far too high.

At that moment she heard a clanking of boots and a figure began to emerge from the darkened hatch.

****

In the forest, night had fallen once more and it was time for the immortals to return. God, The Buddha, Irony and Satan were all walking together towards the clearing in their human forms.

The reason they took on a Mortal Shell when visiting Earth is that immortal bodies are conspicuously that; they are larger, magnificent specimens which would attract far too much attention. The power they hold is also dangerous to the fabric of reality – too long in an immortal form and they would rip, shred and tear at the physical matter holding together the Universe. They were all created to exist outwith the confines of physical universes – as such their parameters were different from mortal creatures.

In their mortal shells they were strong, very strong, they could harness certain powers and abilities, but they were limited and the mortal bodies could be killed. This is why God always urged caution as the hassle associated with dying in your mortal shell was something they all wished to avoid.

As the others approached God this night, He asked what He

usually did, "Get up to anything interesting?"

"Once I learned that reality was a construct and nothing really mattered, I haven't been able to connect with the concept of something being interesting," said Buddha.

"Ok. But did you actually do anything?"

"Yeah I got noodles from this place I like in Seattle and I went bowling."

God turned "What about you Irony?"

"Nah not much. Heckled Alanis Morissette again, but there's only so much I can do there. I saw a bad film, had sex, ate sushi. Good trip."

"And Satan? Do I even want to know?"

"Nope." He smiled and winked.

They were now coming into the clearing where Sonia's tent had been consumed by the portal.

"I'll give him ten minutes before we start it up," God said, looking around for Fate and knowing he would not see him; Fate was always late, as he loved being on Earth. What God did see however was a camping stove right in the middle of where the portal would be. A camping stove which seemed to be singed on its side – like, for instance, how it might appear if it had come into contact with an inter-universe portal created for gods. A couple of feet to the left was a small ladies hiking boot. A couple of feet to the left again was a battered John Grisham novel with a bookmark in it. The trail of debris continued to the edge of the clearing where a groundsheet was still pegged to the ground.

God pointed His massive hand at the trail of debris. "Look at this." They all followed His point and saw the trail of debris leading to the groundsheet.

"Holy shit," said Irony.

"Unless one of you can give me a VERY convincing alternative explanation, there is only one way to interpret this evidence."

Everyone silently thought, but ultimately came up with nothing. The Buddha believes 'what we think, we become' so he didn't think about it at all, as he did not want to become nothing.

Satan walked to the centre of the clearing and the others numbly followed. Satan picked up the hiking boot "It's small. Looks like a woman's boot. It's basically brand new."

At the groundsheet God remarked "This is a one-man tent. So we're looking at an average sized woman, inexperienced hiker, probably unfit."

"Could she have survived the drop through the portal?" Satan asked.

"Maybe. It looks like the whole tent has slid down into it; that may have given her some protection," replied God.

"If she fell through and could not fly – where would she have landed?" Irony enquired.

"Right onto the main cloud."

"She probably died though, right?" Satan said nervously.

"You had better hope so," Fate's voice cut through the night from where he was standing on the edge of the clearing. "You'd better hope she broke her little neck in all the commotion. Because if she didn't…"

"I know, I know."

"If she even looks over the edge it could be enough. We've never tested this stupid jeopardy game of yours before so we don't know how it works."

"I KNOW – I'm the actual GOD – I know these things."

"Then why are we standing around? Let's open the door, say hello and kill this woman before she destroys the entire fabric of reality."

"Aye, ok," God nodded and waved His hand over the clearing to begin the portal creation process.

****

Sonia was still peeking from behind a rock, but the scene in front of her had rapidly changed. The man with the horn was now standing in frozen salute. A whole party of the oddest-looking people she had ever seen had stepped through the hatch and were now gathered kneeling in front of what she could only assume was their leader. He too, was a somewhat different looking fellow.

He stood on a rock and was preparing to address the gathered landing party. The first thing to mention was the hat. The hat was an incredible thing. It was made of thousands of reels of interwoven fabric. It was three feet high, two feet wide and featured every colour on the spectrum. If it been sold in some eBay store on Earth, they might have categorised it as a Fluorescent Mega Rainbow Turban.

He had twelve eyes. That was actually probably the first thing to mention. The hat was amazing, but the twelve eyes were the big, big clue that something strange was going on. The eyes on every one of the landing party were of a differing number and size.

The leader had eighteen fingers – it had taken his gesturing twice before she caught what was different, but she was now certain that he had eighteen fingers. Others had again differing numbers, but there seemed to be at least twelve on all of them.

He had one massive hand. This is not to say that he had a hand missing. He had two hands, but one of them was a nine fingered, but otherwise normal hand and the other was the size of an oven tray.

He began to speak:

"Ladies and Gentlemen!" He spluttered through his slightly deformed mouth. "Ladies and Gentlemen, it is time to gather supplies and harvest the land for wood. Remember we need everything we can get – we set sail again and we won't stop until we reach the eastern peak."

He then paused to have a coughing fit for a few minutes. The hat came off and was quickly picked up, dusted down and replaced on his head by one of his loyal servants. He resumed –

"Find food – find wood. Go forth!"

He waved his big hand in the direction of Sonia and the gathered individuals got up and fanned out to search the place. She did not want to be found until she had a better idea of whether they were dangerous or not and she had no desire to board their ship under any circumstances.

She moved silently away behind the rocks, trying to remain as low as possible. This took her into a densely wooded area, where the trees were thick and tall and gnarled. There was not a lot of light in here and she figured it to be a good hiding place. She saw a little nook between three close tree trunks and she thought it looked like a good place to go – crouching inside it she doubted anyone would notice her. As she backed into the space, she could hear the boat people entering the forest. Some of them had spears and some had bows.

They were all dressed like sultans from a Mike Myers movie – bright colours and over the top designs. However, they were similar to their leader in that there were many with odd physiological features – many eyes, uneven numbers of fingers and toes seemed to be common, but others were limping or wheezing or shouting in unsettling ways.

She watched them go by stalking unseen prey and chopping down the odd tree here and there.

Once she thought the last of them had passed, she waited ten seconds then stepped out. She turned and could see the back of the last few heading deeper into the forest. Although they were heavily armed their battle cries did not fill her with dread.

"Remember the forest has to be sustainable – it sustains us if we sustain it!"

"Humane kills only. We need the food, but suffering is immoral!"

She couldn't decide if she was on an alien planet or at a Morrissey gig. In any case she started to head away from them and back towards where she came in. The key to getting back to earth was surely the purple tunnel.

She crept through the forest attempting not to make any unnecessary noise. Very close behind her something cleared its throat.

"Excuse me."

Terrified she froze to the spot – her hands in the air like someone had a gun on her. Sonia thought she was about to be mauled by one of the many-fingered boat people, however she waited for it for several seconds and it did not come.

She was almost too scared to do so, but she slowly turned – hands still up in surrender. As she did, she saw a giant wolf-like creature staring her down, his many sharp teeth on display. She instantly re-adjusted to become 1800 times more afraid.

"Sorry I didn't mean to bother you", the wolf said.

"No, its fine," squeaked Sonia.

"It's just, if you must kill me, I'd rather we had a chat about it first. I don't feel ready yet and I've got a list of good reasons why I can still contribute to the world."

"I…I wasn't planning to kill you," Sonia blurted, confused.

"Why not?"

"I don't have a reason to," said Sonia.

"What about to eat me?" he asked, ruffling his brow in clear confusion.

"Me eat you? I thought it was the other way around, no?" Sonia slowly, carefully, began to lower her arms, which he watched with trepidation. She saw his apprehension turn to relief when she didn't go for a weapon or strike him.

"Me eat you? How would that work now? I'm just a Wolf, you're a person, how would I even go about that? Your ideas are audacious," he allowed himself a bit of a chuckle.

"Well what do you normally eat?" asked Sonia, now a lot more relaxed.

"Root vegetables, tree bark, birds who have fallen dead from the sky and leaves."

"Do you like root vegetables?"

"No."

"Do you like tree bark?"

"Not really no, but what else am I supposed to do?"

"Well, you're a hunter so you could eat the other animals."

"That's crazy! Me, a wolf; hunting other animals!" He was shaking his head in disbelief at what she was saying. He laughed deeply.

"Why? That's literally what you're built to do – you're very big, strong, I bet you can run fast."

"I can, very fast."

"And look at those teeth. Absolutely loads of big sharp teeth. I bet you can tear through those birds in seconds." Sonia smiled at him.

"My teeth are really sharp."

"See?" said Sonia, smiling.

"So, you're saying I could just eat whatever I want?"

She nodded.

"Because I am a giant, strong, fast, killing machine?"

"Yes."

"Interesting," he said, slowly nodding his head, taking in this new perspective.

Less than thirty seconds later Sonia was cursing her own persuasiveness as she was pursued at speed through the trees by a giant hungry wolf.

****

God, Satan, Fate, Buddha and Irony had safely returned to the main cloud and were now examining the area. Once again, Sonia's camping debris was strewn across the cloud indicating her direction of travel. However, this time the crumpled tent was the focus of the bulk of their attention.

"Ok where is she now?" Satan said.

They looked through the contents of the tent, but it provided no clues to her identity or appearance.

"Great. So, we don't know if she came through deliberately, we don't know her name and we don't know what she looks like." He moaned.

"There's only one exit a mortal could take from here." God indicated the elevator which Terry used to attend his weekly briefings.

Satan examined the lift car. "Well there's only two stops. The MOON and Hell. I'm guessing if she had any sense left, she'd have avoided pressing the bottom button for fear that it would take her further downwards."

"If I were her, I might have pressed the button marked 'Above' thinking that it would take me to where I'd fallen from," posited Buddha.

"Ok, Fate, you're going to the MOON. Find that girl and end her before she figures the whole thing out and fucks us all into a tin hat." God ordered.

"What kind of language is that?" Buddha protested.

"The kind I invented, thank you, like every other kind. Fate did you hear me?" He turned to Fate who was standing at the edge of the cloud looking over the side.

"Yes, I heard everything. But there are two ways off this cloud and I think one of the universal pathways is damaged."

They all rushed to the edge. God peered down.

"Jesus Christ."

Jesus popped his head round his bedroom door. "Yes father?"

"Sorry didn't mean you, was just taking your name in vain."

Jesus slunk back to his room, slamming the door.

"That was quite awkward," said Irony after a few seconds of silence had elapsed.

"There's a gap in the top of one of the pathways," said God looking with His impeccable vision. "If the impact with the outer shell didn't kill her, she would have been taken to the nearest world. She's on two."

"Shall I?" asked Fate, looking at God for approval.

God nodded His big face. "I don't want to see it; I don't want to hear the details. Just do it and confirm to me when it's done."

Fate didn't hesitate, he leapt off the cloud platform and flew down towards the broken pathway.

****

Sonia ran screaming into the now busy clearing closely followed by the wolf, who was snarling and growling at her heels. One of the boat men reacted fastest and with a slick motion shot an arrow into the wolf's neck, knocking it onto its side.

"Fucksake," said the wolf and collapsed to the ground dead.

Sonia had stopped on the spot with her eyes closed in terror. She heard someone say –

"Did that wolf say 'Fucksake' when it died?"

"I didn't know wolves knew swear words," said a second.

And another voice, "Who is this?"

"Excuse me – who are you?" She knew the question was directed at her, but kept her eyes firmly shut.

A finger tapped her shoulder.

"Excuse me, who are you?"

She realised they were not going to go away so she slowly opened her eyes and was greeted by the sight of seven of someone else's.

"I'm Sonia," she blurted out.

"You've hardly got any eyes," the man said, pitying her – examining her. "Where are they all?"

"I've only got the two," she said, pointing at her face. He grabbed her hand –

"She's only got 5 fingers sir." He held her hand aloft for the leader who gestured that he'd seen enough. He dropped her hand.

"Your clothing is flimsy and you're not wearing any shoes," he said, looking her up and down.

"They're my pyjamas – I had to leave all of a sudden."

"Leave where?" the leader suddenly enquired from the background.

"I was in Kent, your majesty."

"What's a majesty and why do you think I have one?" He had now begun to approach her.

"Um."

"Should I have one?" He examined her reaction. She gave him a shrug.

"Get me a majesty right away," he ordered to one of the boat men who nodded and ran off into the forest to get one, without so much as checking what it was.

"I meant no offence sir," said Sonia.

"What is this Kent you speak of?"

"My home."

"How many days sail is it?"

"I didn't get here by boat."

He furrowed his brow and looked around in puzzlement. "Then where is it?"

"I don't know."

"What direction did you come from at least?"

She pointed at the sky where she had come from.

They all gasped.

"Are you a messenger from the creator?" shouted a voice from the back

"We haven't had a message for years. What's the message?" said another.

"Why aren't you a duck?" asked another, confusingly.

Sonia had no idea what they were getting at so said "No I'm sorry, I'm not a messenger, but I'm from another world altogether. I just want to get home."

"She's from the other world," one of them called out in an excited voice.

"What's it like?" said another.

"It's ok I suppose. We don't have talking wolves though."

"What do you have?"

"Our wolves just bark."

"Your wolves sound shite!" shouted an angry man from the back.

"ENOUGH!" roared the leader. "One at a time! And by 'one' I mean me and me only – everyone else fasten your hole."

They had started to gather around her and, he motioned for them to move back a couple of paces, which they did at his request.

He pointed to his chest "I am Nohaz – I am the captain of the ark." He gestured to the boat. "I apologise for my people, but we have been waiting in hope for a message from the creator. It was simply a little over exuberance on our part."

"It's ok, they saved me from the wolf, I owe them my thanks."

"I'm not sure about the Other World, but here wolves are passive creatures. Their meat and fur form a key part of our survival, but they are not a threat despite their size."

"That one was, I assure you."

"How did you get here?"

"I'm not sure, I fell through a hole in our world and I fell from the sky into this one."

He looked up at where she had indicated and tried to see where she could have possibly dropped from. "Amazing."

"Can you help me get home?"

"We will help you in any way we can."

"Thank you Captain Nohaz."

"Firstly, we've got to figure out how you could have possibly got up there."

They were all staring at the sky when without warning Fate dropped out of thin air 400 feet above them looking like a thug pterodactyl.

"What the crock?" said Nohaz. "This fellow looks unfriendly."

He turned to her and lifted his hat. Underneath his hat was a smaller version of the hat he was wearing. He handed the smaller hat to her.

"Take it," he insisted urgently as Fate got closer to the ground eighty or ninety feet behind them.

She put on the hat and someone discreetly passed her a pair of curved shoes which were three sizes too big, but she slipped them onto her feet and blended into the waiting crowd.

Fate landed on his feet and began walking briskly towards them. His long dark coat flowing behind him like a cape he looked every inch the complete bastard that he was, however he started with a different strategy.

"Hello all."

"Who are you?" asked Nohaz.

"I am a messenger from the creator."

This caused absolute uproar for 10 seconds, everyone was simultaneously shouting so loudly it was impossible to even think about anything else.

"QUIET EVERYONE." They shut up immediately. "I am Captain Nohaz, leader of these people. Speak your message sir."

Fate nodded gently at him. "Thank you, captain. The creator has asked me to greet you and bring you his very best wishes. He wishes to re-iterate that he apologises for your continued inconvenience, but is impressed and inspired by your survival skills and your will to carry on."

"What's happening on this other world?" shouted a voice from the crowd.

"I cannot discuss the other world. I hope you can understand. I come here to beg a favour."

"We will do our best to accommodate you, good sir. Would you like a beverage or a wolf sandwich before you continue? Our hospitality is yours for the duration of your stay."

"Thank you, but no, my task is urgent and my stay must be necessarily brief. I am looking for a woman."

"Take me!!" shouted a fat, old, fourteen-eyed hag from the back. Laughter ensued.

Fate feigned a smile in such an unconvincing way that it chilled the closely watching Nohaz to the bone.

"I regret to inform you that I'm looking for a specific woman. A small woman who fell from the sky no doubt, would have landed right where I did. Have you seen such a person?"

Nohaz stepped forward and spoke, holding out a hand to his followers that indicated that they should remain silent. "I'm afraid we've found no such woman in our foraging expedition."

"She is very dangerous, even if she may not appear that way. She could easily end the life of every single one of you here."

A silent tension spread through the crowd outward from Sonia's position.

"What do you want with her?" said Nohaz.

"As I said she is dangerous and must be stopped."

"Stopped? Stopped how?"

"That depends on her willingness to co-operate."

"I doubt I would co-operate if you had described me in those terms."

Fate looked at Nohaz directly into his many eyes. His gaze narrowed. "I would never wish to inconvenience your people further, but I wonder if it's possible she could be hiding amongst your crowd."

"You think I don't know my own people? There is no stranger among us – other than you." Nohaz had moved between Fate and his boat men.

"A quick check would satisfy the creator – perhaps I can make it easy." He produced Sonia's hiking boot from his coat. He held it aloft.

"You all have large and unique feet. The woman has small narrow feet. This is her shoe. Step forward and if it doesn't fit you, you will be released from any further obligation."

"And if it does fit?" shouted a heckler.

"Then there will be consequences."

"I don't like the tone of this and everyone is late for tea. Wolf sandwiches and leaf tea all round!" The crowd cheered.

"Yeah what about dinner you big beanpole twat? I'm hungry and I couldn't get that wee shoe on my nose never mind my foot. Why do I need to queue up like a fool for your stupid experiment?"

Fate went to speak, but was interrupted.

"Yeah and how do we know you're a messenger from the creator – you could just be a bird from the other world."

The dissent came thick and fast.

"Fuck this!" shouted an old woman. "You try it on, you gloomy prick!"

"Yeah! Who brings a shoe from God anyway – he's a fake," yelled another.

"You're ruining Wolf Wednesday!"

Nohaz closed his eyes in preparation to say something to calm the situation. Instead Fate made things 10 times worse.

"ENOUGH, YOU BLEATING SEA PEASANTS!" he growled. "YOU WILL TRY THIS SHOE ON OR SO HELP

ME GOD I WILL KILL EVERY LAST ONE OF YOU JUST TO MAKE SURE I GET HER. YOU WILL BEGIN IMMEDIATELY OR YOU'LL BE DEAD BEFORE YOU CAN CLENCH A FIST."

Nohaz drew a sword and pointed it at Fate. "You harm a hair on any one of them and I'll cut you into seven bits."

"Captain. For you to threaten me is bravery in the extreme. I have respect for you, but this course of action will only make things worse. Is one life worth more than the whole ark?"

A few of the captain's men drew their loaded bows back in anticipation.

Sonia, frozen with terror, felt a hand grip her shoulder. Rigid with fear that she about to be given up, she didn't even turn to see who was holding her. She covered her mouth to stifle her scream. She awaited a proclamation that would seal her fate. Instead the hand firmly, but steadily steered her backwards thorough the crowd.

"You must stay low and head for the rocks," the voice whispered in her ear. "Go!"

Sonia did as she was asked and slowly walked backwards through the crowd. As they parted to let her through and then knitted together again to cover her retreat, she fell in love with every last one of them.

The oversized shoes were a problem though and as she picked up the pace they began to bunch and inevitably she found herself falling forwards. As she did so the shoes fell off, she tumbled to the ground noisily and from her lips emerged the biggest "FUCKSAKE!" of the day.

Involuntarily, every head turned in her direction. Fate with his height and vantage point could only see her two feet which were in the air as she lay on her back between two rocks. Her indistinguishably human feet.

He began to move in her direction, but was blocked by two boat men with spears. He struck them both down dead with a single touch to each of their shoulders. It was cold and casual, he barely looked at them and he certainly didn't give it a second thought.

At the sight of this, the crowd began to part and this allowed him to move towards Sonia more rapidly. She had watched him dispassionately kill the boat men though and was in no hurry to find out what he wanted from her. She rolled to the left and got up and ran in the opposite direction towards the rocks. When she reached the middle of the rock formation, he was almost on top of her.

As he got to within a few inches of her, he pulled up, arching his back and dropped to his knees. He fell forward, grimacing in pain and she realised that he'd been struck by an arrow right between his shoulder blades. She continued to back off while he was stopped.

He began to struggle back to his feet when he was struck by a second arrow in the shoulder.

As further arrows flew towards him, he looked her dead in the eye and said, "I will return for you. You're already dead."

Sonia looked around, "I'm already dead? Well, if this is heaven, it needs work."

He gave her a dead-eyed smile and shot into the air, just avoiding the incoming arrows and disappeared into the night sky. The boat men threw rocks and loosed arrows in his direction in a thoroughly useless manner, like a drunk, forty-five-year-old divorcee shouting abuse at someone on the TV who happens to look a bit like his ex-wife.

Sonia sat down on the ground and began to cry.

The boat people helped her onto a rug and gave her some leaf tea to drink, which to her surprise, tasted surprisingly ok. Captain Nohaz made his way over and crouched in front of her.

"I want to say thank you for defending me and I'm so sorry that you lost people in the process. I don't know what that creature wants with me," she said.

"The creature wants to kill you. That much is clear. You will never be safe here; we have to get you back to the other world."

"I don't know how to do that."

Nohaz gestured towards the largest of the rocks behind them. "I think that this has something to do with it, although we've never been able to work out what it's for or how it works."

Sonia turned and looked at it closely for the first time. It had etchings and ancient looking writing all over it – she'd noticed that on first glance – but now that she was closer, she realised that it had been machine tooled to have moving parts. There was what looked like a ships wheel, round with stone spokes. It looked like it could spin, but there was a stone between two of the spokes which blocked any movement.

"It was put here by the creator. We believe it has some mystical power, there have been stories of …"

He launched into another coughing fit – this one lasting about a minute and twenty before it calmed down.

"Excuse me. There have been stories of people passing thought it and not emerging from the other side. Just rumours of course, but we believe it may be activated in some way to open a door to the other world"

****

As Fate flew back towards the cloud platform, he began to shed his mortal form, his wounds healing, pushing the arrows out and allowing him to return to his creepy self. When he landed on the cloud platform, God and Satan were waiting for him. God was looking out over creation and Satan was pacing up and down smoking a cigarette.

"Is it done?" Satan said impatiently.

"No. It is not." Fate replied, distracted by his still closing wounds.

God, looking over at him for the first time, noticed this action. "What happened to you?"

"I was injured."

"Who could injure you on a planet of boat people?" Satan asked incredulously.

"They concealed the girl. I did not want to perpetrate a massacre so I proposed a search. They resisted once I identified the girl. They shot arrows into me and if I had not left, my mortal body would have died."

"But you now know what the girl looks like?" asked God.

"Yes. I saw her face. I smelled her scent. I will re-acquire her."

"You smelled her scent? I know you'll say 'people in glass houses' and all that, but you really are a fucking creep sometimes," said Satan, chuckling.

"They will not keep her there for long. If they can get her off planet they will," Fate said – ignoring Satan completely.

"I don't have any sense that the boat people are aware of any method to transition between the worlds. I think it is likely they will take her to sea. You'll have to go back and find her there," said God.

"Very well. But I will kill anyone who even thinks about the word 'arrow' from now on."

"Fine. Don't go mad though, they're actually very nice, the boat people."

"They are a bunch of arseholes."

"Agree to disagree then," smiled God. "Off you pop."

****

"I don't understand any of this language I'm afraid and as far as I know we don't have any sort of device like this on my world. Can't you just take me somewhere else for now, some other island?" Sonia was studying the rock closely.

"I'm afraid there are only a few islands on our whole world. It is almost entirely covered with water. It would not take him long to find you and if he finds you on board the ark I fear for the safety of my people. For both our sakes you must leave," replied Nohaz.

"Do any of you understand this writing?" she asked.

"Oh yes," said Nohaz cheerfully,

"What? Well what does it say then?"

"We've absolutely no idea what it means."

"So can you read it or not?"

"Oh, we can read it, we just don't understand the message. I can read it to you if you like."

"Yes please."

"It says, my first is in Fine, but not in Wine. My second is not me or myself. My third is in…"

"Hang on. Does it really say all that?"

"Yes."

"Do you have a writing implement?"

"Fetch a parchment and an ink spear," he shouted to one of his subordinates.

Sonia got the pen and paper and listened to the clues in amusement for quite a while. There were several hundred lines to decipher, but they were of an extremely easy nature. By the time she had finished she had assembly instructions for the device. "Fig A – insert rod B into slot A" "Remove block F from selection wheel." And so on. They were basically Ikea style instructions for the assembly of this stone device.

On closer inspection, the rock had several smaller rocks inserted into slots and they all had tiny microscopic markings on them. Sonia followed the instructions and gradually through the placement of different stones in different locations she was able to free the wheel. The instructions stated to turn the wheel left to go backwards and to turn the wheel right to go forwards.

She hoped that turning it backwards would take her back to the last planet she was on.

Before she did this, she turned to Nohaz, "I just wanted to say a big thank for all you've done for me. You fought to save a stranger. I'll never forget that." As he opened his mouth to reply she placed her hands onto the wheel spokes, turned it and in a flash of brilliant white light was gone.

"Goodbye Sonia," said Nohaz.

On the other side of the portal Sonia slammed into the ground having been thrown back by a shockwave from the wheel. The noise it had made was like a thunderclap and it had reverberated right through her body.

"Fucksake," she mumbled weakly.

Her head was spinning and she felt concussed, opening her eyes was a painful process so she stopped trying for the minute. Sitting up also caused her immense nausea so she quickly abandoned that too. She lay on her back attempting to recover. Around her she could no longer hear the waves crashing against the rocks. She could no longer smell the sea, in fact the aroma assaulting her nostrils was belligerently pleasant; it was lavender or lilies or something nice and floral. She couldn't remember the names and scents of flowers as those particular memories were still rattling around her head like a box of ball bearings that had been knocked down a flight of stairs. The bitter cold of the mountaintop had gone and she felt a warmth on her face which was extremely welcome.

She began to hear the echoes of footsteps. When they got closer, she realised that they were actually the sounds of hooves, many hooves and tiny feet were approaching her location rapidly.

She forced her eyes open, the bright sunlight that streamed in sent a searing pain right to the middle of her brain. She felt it so deeply that it was like someone had decided to burn out all of her memories of 1996 using a hot knife through the eye socket and a fair amount of guesswork.

The eyes reflexively closed once more. The footsteps were coming from her right-hand side and were now only ten metres or so away.

A deep, English-accented voice spoke, "I say. What is this creature and is it alright?"

She was home!

Prising open her eyes for another millisecond glance she saw three sheep and a rabbit. She was home! Out in the countryside, maybe even back in Kent.

"Are you alright?"

"Yes, just a little dazed, I'm afraid, I fell," said Sonia.

"Well take all the time you need," said the calm, friendly voice.

"Thank you."

She slowly turned onto her side and began to sit up. Once she had she brought up her hand to shield her eyes and cracked them open a bit she could now clearly see the three sheep standing there and the little rabbit. She glanced around and she seemed to be in a clearing with rocks again. She still couldn't see who spoke.

It was then that she noticed the middle sheep was wearing a beret.

The sheep turned to her and said, "So we were wondering where you are from?"

Sonia's addled mind finally gave up and activated her fainty gland.

****

Fate swooped out of the night sky and down onto the rocky mountaintop. It was empty save for some small debris. The dead wolf was gone, the dead boatmen were gone and the girl was gone. The ark was not visible to the naked eye. He set out to search the woods and then he would find the ship.

He noticed the crusts of wolf sandwiches all over the mountaintop. There were birds pecking at them. It was a mark of Fate's unbelievable capability for anger that he was furious that these people were skilled and strong enough to kill a wolf and eat it for dinner, but such children that they wouldn't eat their crusts despite food being scarce.

It shouldn't have annoyed him, but it did and he grabbed the nearest bird, strangling it slowly to death whilst staring furiously into its small, confused eyes.

When it finally went limp, he took it and punted its body 500 yards into the sea.

"AAAAAHHHHHHHHHHHHHHHHHHHHHHHHHHH HHHH!" he screamed at its corpse as it flew through the air.

When he looked around, all the other birds had flown away.

****

Sonia was awoken by having cool water splashed on her face by the hoof of a talking, hat wearing, sheep, on the second alien plant she'd visited, whilst on a camping holiday in Kent. To say that it'd been a strange day was kindly acknowledging that the concept of a day still existed and she was grateful for that at least. She looked around and she was again on top of a mountain in a rocky clearing, but this time the bright daylight painted a delightful world around her full of flowers and rolling hills and a clear blue sky extending for miles on end.

"Are you alright strange creature?" the hat wearing sheep asked.

"You can talk?"

"Why would you think I wouldn't be able to talk?" asked Jim.

"The sheep on our planet don't talk. They say baaa. But they don't talk and they don't wear hats."

"I got this hat from God," said Jim cheerfully, although the answer did not soothe Sonia's confusion in any way, shape or form. Thankfully for the sake of the entire universe Sonia did not believe him.

"Where am I?" she asked instead.

"You're on Joy World!" said the Rabbit.

"I'm on Joy World? Is this a theme park?"

"I'm not sure what a theme park is, but Joy World is our home. Joy World is what you're sitting on, what you're breathing in. That delightful smell in your nostrils – that's Joy

World. It's as real as you are, whatever you actually are!"

"What do you mean, whatever I am? Have you never seen a person before?"

"If you are a person, then no. What is your name?"

"Sonia Lancaster – what's your name?"

"I'm Jim."

"Well it's nice to meet you Jim." She patted his head absentmindedly.

Jim had never been patted before and felt an absolutely instant affection for Sonia that he could not explain.

"Where are you from Sonia?"

"I'm from Earth, it's a planet, a long, long way from here."

"What's a planet?"

"It's, well, it's a place. A place like Joy World, but located somewhere else."

"Another place! Wow! I didn't know there was another place. Is it beautiful?" said Geoff, the second of the sheep.

"It can be. Not like this place, but it can be."

"Are there others like you?" asked Dave the third sheep.

"Yes, many, many others. Billions of others."

"What are all their names?" chirped the rabbit.

"Not now Pete; you don't have to answer that. How did you get here?"

"I was in a forest on Earth and I fell through a hole in the ground. I landed on a cloud and then I fell off the cloud and onto a world covered in water, with boat people everywhere and stupid wolves. They were very nice to me though. Then a man dropped out of the sky and said he was a messenger from the creator. He tried to kill me and the boat people protected me. We opened a portal in a rock and I fell through that too, bringing me here."

"Ok, well I think first things first. Let's get you down from this mountain, for your own safety."

Sonia suddenly became alert, fearing a wolf or other creature was coming. "Why, is it dangerous up here?"

"Well, we're up high and it seems whatever you *can* fall off, you *do* fall off."

She laughed. "It's been a very bizarre day." She hauled herself to her feet and Jim, with the two other sheep and Pete the Rabbit in tow, led the way down the wide, comfortably sloping path back towards the ground.

****

Fate was deep inside the forest and had just killed a wolf that would not stop talking to him. As he crouched beside the dead animal's body, he scanned the trees. There was nothing here. The boatmen would never have left her alone in a place like this. He reasoned that they would try and disguise her as one of their own and hide her aboard the ark. He would find her quickly if that was the case.

He moved like a ninja, silently, but quickly, his dark clothing and lithe body providing the sort of camouflage that humanoid bodies are rarely blessed with.

When he reached the edge of the forest and could see the rock formation and the clearing again, he had his bearings and took off into the sky with a swish.

He flew a few thousand feet into the air and surveyed the endless ocean from above. He could not see the ark, but a wake left by a boat that size takes a while to dissipate. About three miles east of his position he could see the tail end of such a disturbance was still in the process of fading away.

He turned and launched himself in that direction. Travelling through the air quickly the only sound he made was the rippling of his coat. He quickly latched on to the trail of the boat and could now see it on the horizon. He estimated he was around ten miles behind them. He leaned in to quicken his pace and within ten minutes he was right on top of them.

Nohaz heard the distinctive flapping sound and his eye was drawn to the sky. There he saw Fate hovering fifty feet above them, just ten or fifteen yards off the stern of the boat.

"Battle Stations men!" he cried.

The men initially ran to the edges of the boat then wandered in again, then just started aimlessly wandering, shrugging their shoulders at each other. Nohaz looked on in dissatisfaction.

His first officer nervously approached him – "Um. Sir? We've never been in a battle, sir. Where do you want us to stand?"

"Just get your weapons and stuff, we'll figure it out as we go," he said testily.

"Right you are, sir. Who are we fighting exactly?"

"That messenger twat from earlier. He's not dead." Nohaz pointed at Fate who was now just a few feet from landing at the stern. The first officer turned white.

"Shit!" He then kicked into action. "GET YOUR SWORD AND ARROWS EVERYONE!!! MEET ME AT THE STERN – THAT MISERABLE FLAPPER WHO KILLED ANGUS AND HENRY IS BACK!"

People were running about like headless chickens grabbing supplies and children. "FORGET THAT! WE DON'T NEED ANYTHING EXCEPT WEAPONS AND HUNTERS – EVERYONE ELSE SEAL YOURSELF BELOW AND MAKE SURE THE ANIMALS DON'T FREAK OUT"

Nohaz drew his sword, stood front and centre as his men fanned out behind him, brandishing everything pointy they could get their hands on.

"She's not onboard," Nohaz said as Fate touched down and began walking towards them.

"Who says I'm here for the woman? I could have simply returned to kill those who shot me with arrows. In the back. Like cowards."

"Whatever your goal, you are not welcome here. Leave this place and no further harm will come to you."

Fate stopped and stared the boatmen down considering his options. Nohaz knew that the creature had immense power, but after their last encounter was also certain that it could be killed. Fate knew that dying in his mortal body had dire consequences, but his mortal body was a good bit stronger than most. It was still a risk though.

The crashing of waves on the outside of hull was constant. So ubiquitous on this world you could almost tune it out like the air conditioning. He'd been here enough that he didn't notice the waves any longer and as a result the sounds he heard were simply the creaking of the hull and the unique scratchy, stretching noise of 30 bowstrings being slowly drawn back. There were hundreds of eyes on him – an average of 11 per boatman.

He made his decision and in a flash was in the air above them. Arrows began to fly past him and he darted down through the hail and used his momentum to smash through the hatch into the busy deck below where he was immediately stabbed in the arm by a seventy-five-year-old woman with eighteen eyes, thirteen fingers and one tooth. He struck her down instantly by slapping her face. There was an intake of breath, they all jumped back, pressing against the walls as far as they could get from him. He'd silenced the crowd of women; they all stood motionless as he looked around the room.

"WHERE IS SHE?" he demanded.

Everyone stayed deathly silent and most of them were staring at the dead old woman who had unfortunately died with 40% of her eyes still open.

He stared around scanning for her face, but he could not see her. They were all mostly still looking down.

"FORGET HER! SHE'S DEAD AND SO WILL EVERYONE ELSE BE IF YOU FAIL TO ASSIST ME. WHERE IS SHE HIDDEN?" he screamed.

They recoiled further from him. He stepped towards the nearest woman and as she hurriedly began to speak, he simply placed his palm onto her heart and the life dropped out of her eyes like it was an anvil falling into a black hole. She slumped to the floor with a thud.

He turned to the next woman and held out his hand.

A tiny, scrawny bird of a girl hobbled forward behind him. "Please don't hurt anyone else sir." He turned to face her. "She's down there". She pointed her three-fingered claw hand at an open hatch in the floor.

Fate scuttled over to it like a spider almost making no sound even on the wooden deck floor. He crouched and dived headfirst into the hold. When he entered it was very, very dark, but even in that darkness it was unmistakably just a storage hold which was chock-a-bloc full of dead wolves. Above him the tiny woman appeared at the hatch, as she smiled at him the penny dropped. She closed the hatch with a clunk – while he flew towards it, he could hear them frantically sliding something heavy across the floor – they must have got it there in time because he bounced off the hatch door without making too much damage to anything, other than his ego.

He dropped to the floor and arching his back unleashed a torrent at the hatch above.

"AHHHHHHHHHHHHHHHHHHHHHHHHHHHHHHH H YOU DEFORMED BOAT FUCKERS!! I WILL KILL

EVERY LAST ONE OF YOU CUNTS AND PILE YOU UP LIKE A BUNCH OF USELESS DEAD WOLVES. AND THEN I'LL SINK THIS SHITHOLE TO THE BOTTOM OF THE SEA AND NO ONE WILL EVEN KNOW YOU EVER LIVED!"

Unbeknownst to everyone involved, as a result of God's little known (failed) early experiment with sentient trees, the hatch heard every word of the rant, but chose not to rise to the bait as it prided itself on always being the bigger man.

****

Sonia was sitting amongst the animals, still in her pyjamas like a super casual Mary Poppins. Because time ran at different speeds in the different Universes, several days had passed. She had got to know them well and had participated in their pleasant culture of dancing, singing and eating delicious food by open fires, on a planet where it was always a summer's evening. Presently the animals were sitting around her hanging on her every word and she had relayed the entire story of how she got to Joy World to their fascinated little faces.

They had told her the history of Joy World and she had amazedly sat through the incredibly strange details with her mouth agape. If what they were saying was true not only were there other worlds, other universes even, but there was a God and He had indeed created everything.

She was now, quite certainly, the most dangerous person alive in all of creation. God's game was open to interpretation and as she fell from the heavens, she certainly saw all seven universes with her own eyes. She was starting to let herself believe in God, something that she had always wanted to be able to do, but she had been waiting for a sign. As this planet was basically a sign emporium, she was closer to ending the Universe than anyone had ever got and it was all completely by accident. If she was able to figure out a way back home, it was game over for everyone.

"Do any of you know how to get to the other worlds?"

They all looked at each other. Nothing.

"Have you ever seen a rock formation with strange writing on it and a wheel?" she tried.

"What's writing?" asked a rabbit.

"What's a wheel?" asked a sheep.

"Do you know what? Let's try something else." Sonia thought about how to attack this line of questioning.

"Has a messenger from the Creator ever appeared on this world?"

"Yes," said Jim.

"Where?"

"We can take you."

****

Fate smashed through the side of the thick hull of the boat at the seventy-ninth attempt – by now he was a windmill of furious long limbs. He rose up and dived down onto the top deck of the boat – he punched the first boatman that approached him. The man died instantly, but out of pure rage Fate punched him another fifty-seven times. Six men tried to wrestle him off their comrade and he killed each of them with one swift hit.

Seven bodies around his feet, he looked at Nohaz across the deck.

"It doesn't have to be this way Captain. Just tell me where she is," Fate said wearily.

Nohaz looked at the death and destruction around him and finally relented. He had given the beautiful woman time; he hoped it would be enough.

"I'll tell you."

****

Sonia was staring at an almond. She was absolutely sure of it. Absolutely sure of it. An almond sitting on a four-foot-high rock plinth, but she was still sure that it was definitely very much an almond. Despite that, she was almost as sure she'd heard Jim say:

"This, my dear, is God," and he'd gestured towards the Almond.

She immediately retracted her new found belief in God and went back to thinking sheep were a bunch of ridiculous woolly idiots.

"Jim. This is an almond," she said, as delicately as she could.

"Indeed it is."

"Are you completely convinced that this is God?"

"Absolutely." He nodded his sheep head confidently.

"You say this almond spoke to you."

"It did speak to me."

"Does it do this often?"

"Well, only a couple of times and not for some years now that you come to mention it."

"How many years, Jim?"

"About fifteen I'd say. But it was definitely God."

"But how do you know it wasn't just one of the other sheep pretending to be God?" She pointed at his friend.

Jim snorted with laughter. "Ha! Have you heard Geoff speak? He sounds nothing like God!"

The other animals laughed heartily at the very idea of Geoff being a deity.

Sonia sighed and turned away from them. She was facing the rock with the almond on it and for now the little animals couldn't see her face. She was glad about that because she didn't want them to ask why she was beginning to cry. If they had asked, the answer would have been that she had come to the realisation that they were not going to be able to get her home. The almond was just an almond, nothing more. It was no more a God than an image of the Virgin Mary which had appeared on a piece of toast. As a few tears rolled down her face she absentmindedly picked the almond up. There was a huge gasp from the gathered creatures.

"Put down our God, alien!" one voice shouted.

"How dare you touch the creator!" another said.

"She's going to eat God Jim, do something," a rabbit pleaded.

She ignored them all, staring at the nut, her last hope, the end of line.

Jim cleared his throat, attempting to get her attention.

But Sonia's body language had changed. She'd tensed up, alert and was staring at something. Her eyes had refocussed on the rock and her mouth began to open in shock.

Jim politely tapped her on the shoulder, but she didn't notice. The tears had cleared her eyes and the heat was leaving her cheeks. She stared down at the piece of rock she'd just lifted the almond from. It had two almond shape holes in the top just beneath the (for want of a better phrase) Almond Plinth from which she'd lifted it. One hole was marked 'Forward' and one was marked 'Back'. Her fingers suddenly let her in on some sensory information they'd clearly been holding back from her for dramatic purposes; there were grooves on the back of the almond. As she twirled the nut between her thumb and forefinger, the writing on the back of it came into view.

"Place God Nut into destination slot to activate portal."

She began laughing – she ruffled Jim's hat. "I'm not going to eat God, Jim. I'm just going to move him a little."

She held the nut over the hole marked 'Forward' – she certainly didn't want to go back.

She turned to Jim.

"Thank you for your hospitality everyone, it really has been wonderful to meet you all. Maybe I can come back and visit one day, but for now, I've found my route back home and I must say goodbye."

They all cheered.

Jim offered a hoof. She didn't know what for so she just shook it, but when she looked into his eyes, he wasn't looking directly at her, she realised he was actually pointing at something behind her.

About ten yards to her rear, approaching briskly, was Fate.

"You've been the most troublesome person to find," he said with an evil smile.

She turned in horror and opened her mouth to plead with him. He lunged forward and punched her in the heart.

Sonia Lancaster was dead.

The animals watched in slow motion horror as she fell to the floor and never moved again. Everyone was frozen in fear, but Fate had no business with the animals and ignored them completely. He took off leaving behind a small band of creatures who had just experienced the worst crime in their history.

As Fate flew back out of the atmosphere the whole planet was silent; murder had visited Joy World and sullied it forever. The gathered animals stared at the sky until he was gone. Then they stared at the ground until someone spoke.

Geoff said, "Let's cover her."

****

On the edge of a cloud God sat dangling His legs waiting for Fate to return. Hearing the fluttering on Fate's coat He knew what must have occurred, but as Fate touched down, He asked to hear it anyway.

Fate told him how Sonia had figured out how to travel through the portal network. The portal network had been put in place to allow easier transport for any heavenly being to travel between the planets without having to endure the transition between their mortal body and their divine one which was an uncomfortable experience, even for Gods and demi-gods.

This allowed observation and maintenance to be done on the abandoned Universes. Although these projects were no longer being pursued, He still cared for the creatures left on the worlds and wished them to suffer no harm if possible. The portals were not meant for mortals and travelling through as a human could not only offset the destination by miles, but could also cause severe injury because the method was not configured for lesser creatures. This could mean that the humans who used it were likely to end up miles away from the portal transfer points, dazed and confused.

Joy World wasn't high on His list of worries in that regard, the creatures were blissfully ignorant of the rest of the Universe, could not read and would be unlikely to have the dexterity to handle an almond – He would simply put their portal point out of action. He waved His hand and sent a lightning bolt down to Joy World which directly struck the portal rock.

He said a silent poem for Sonia Lancaster – one of His loveliest creations. A tremendous feeling of guilt wracked His body. Incidentally the amount of guilt a God can feel would destroy a human body, it can cause stars to supernova and well, you get the idea. Basically, it was another bad day for Taiwan.

Chapter 14
The Portal

Jim's sheep eyes were not capable of tears, but nonetheless the look on his face conveyed to me the deep, profound sadness that still engulfed him when he thought of her.

"You'll want to see it, I presume," Jim said.

I nodded and he walked silently off in front of me.

When we got to the rock it was in a lovely clearing. The rock itself was singed and split where the lightning had struck it.

"Where did you put her?" I asked.

"We buried her in the trees. She said she liked trees. It's truly beautiful in there." He pointed at a forest.

I nodded.

"Is this what you need to get back?" asked Jim.

"Yeah, I think so, but it looks pretty broken. From the sounds of it, it's possible someone will come and kill me too, so I possibly won't have to worry about it for very long."

I ran my fingers along the shattered surface of the rock. The only hole which looked to be reasonably undamaged was the one marked 'Forwards'.

I wondered if it would still work, but it was irrelevant as the almond was no longer there. Jim was reading my mind and with his hooves held the Almond up for me so I could take it.

"Jim! How have you still got the Almond? I thought the lightning would have destroyed it?"

"No, she was holding it when she died. It remained intact. We have kept it safe ever since in case it ever chooses to speak to us again."

"And has it?"

"No," he said plainly.

"Ah."

"I'd probably have led with that to be honest, I'm not a complete moron."

"Fair play, Jim."

"You can try it if you like."

****

Terry Master of the Universe was on the command deck of the MOON. He was sitting in his comfortable chair drinking one of the absolutely cracking hot chocolates available from the machine. His eyes were closed and he was contentedly spinning the chair on its access. It was a slow day on the MOON. Actually, pretty much every day was a slow day on the MOON as they observed Earth. The purpose of the observation had never actually been fully clear to Terry, but he was happy enough doing it; having a job, a title and this chair was really the cherry on the cake. Absolutely made for him, so it was.

Eyes closed and stationary, Terry was only really engaging his taste and hearing senses, so naturally he noticed almost instantly when one of them registered a major change. He became acutely aware of the slight squeaking noise the chair was making as it spun slowly on the central column. Every other noise had ceased, as if the air had been sucked out of the whole room. He only knew of two things which could cause this as quickly – one was a hull breach and if that had happened, he needn't worry too much as he would be dead in twenty-six seconds anyway, but he was more convinced it was option two. His eyes reluctantly opened and he slowly rotated round toward the doorway where Fate was lurking ominously, a thunderous look on his face.

Terry quickly brought his feet to the floor to halt the spin of the chair and wiped the hot chocolate from around his mouth.

"In what corner of what world were you ever considered a leader?" Fate asked disparagingly.

"The worlds are round Fate, they don't have corners," said Terry as cheerfully as he could. He got extremely nervous around Fate. He had just discovered that his ankles could sweat.

"Where is the human, Terry? And I'm giving you advance notice that saying you don't know is not an answer which will make me happy."

"I really honestly don't know," Terry offered a mid-level smile, but the size of his mouth made it a very hard thing for him to pull off.

"I want to know absolutely everything he did, said or

touched until he left."

"Ok – I can print a transcript out from the computer if you like. It will take about fourteen minutes."

Fate looked at his watch. As he spent the largest part of his day in a non-place which existed outwith time it had four question marks instead of a time. He couldn't remember why he wore it. In any case he knew one thing for sure – he could not spend fourteen of any sort of minutes doing small talk with Terry beside a computer terminal. There were lines he would not cross, even for God. He put his hand over his eyes and crunched his face up in thought. He considered his options for a few moments – wondering why he'd bothered with this part of the investigation. He opened his eyes with a plan ready.

Terry had stood up which was at least progress. Although when Fate noticed how much chocolate milk was down the front of his robes, he nearly killed everyone in the room.

"HOW did the human leave the MOON?" was the question Fate had settled on.

"Ah, we used the teleportation booths."

"The teleportation booths which caused all the disembowelling?"

"Also a few successful transfers."

"I thought it was a toaster or something you'd successfully moved?"

"Yes."

"So you sent an innocent human into a transportation method where you couldn't be sure of the outcome?"

"We'd ironed out almost all of the bugs – we'd done extensive work to the system."

"Dare I ask whether you tracked the result of this particular journey Terry?"

"Yes, indeed we did!"

"And what was the result?"

"Well."

"If you say you don't know Terry, I will go absolutely ballistic."

"We. Lost. Him," Terry said deliberately.

"Did he make it to Earth?"

"Not from what we can see with our scans, but we think he may have ended up somewhere else. All the disembowelled people have ended up somewhere, more's the pity. It was a clean transfer; wherever he is he's most likely perfectly intact."

"I want a full diagnostic done on this teleportation and your best theory on where the human is and I want it done before that hot chocolate gets cold."

"I can't take the hot chocolate to the diagnostic terminal?"

"It's a fucking expression Terry, get it done!"

****

I looked on the back of the Almond. I saw the same lettering that Sonia must have read years before. A lightning bolt from God had shattered the stone plinth I was looking at. That stone plinth was firmly planted on this other planet, which had talking animals and a storied history. A planet where an unfortunate woman had found herself standing in just the spot I was in right now, killed in cold blood for reasons unclear to all of us. She died confused, scared and alone – I was feeling it too.

I took a moment to mourn Sonia Lancaster, I had never met her, had only a second hand account of her appearance and she'd died a long time ago, but she was currently the person I identified with most in any universe.

I stood in front of the rock, Almond in hand trying to work up the courage. One of two things would happen when I placed the Almond in the slot –

1. It would turn on a door to another world whereupon I would be instantly transported to an unknown place – not knowing what level of danger awaited me on the other side.
2. Nothing would happen and I would be stuck here until someone no doubt came to kill me.

Until I put the nut in the hole, I could have hope. Once it was done, I'd have to live with the outcome, although perhaps not very long.

I was terrified of finding out which fate awaited me.

I placed the almond into the one remaining hole. A faint blue light briefly emanated from underneath it and then fizzled out.

I knew what Sonia would have said. All I managed to do

was lean forward on the rock and let out my biggest sigh since 2003.

****

In the teleportation control kiosk, there was a frosty atmosphere. Terry's hand was slightly shaking as he handed the results to Fate.

Fate looked at the paper and looked at Terry. Terry opened his mouth to speak, but Fate looked back at the paper again. Terry found it absolutely impossible to read him. Fate showed him the busy printout, it was covered in complex mathematical formulae. He pointed at it angrily.

"What the fuck does all this mean Terry?"

"I uh…"

"DO NOT SAY YOU DON'T KNOW"

Terry swallowed hard. Took a breath. Motioned to the hallway.

"Steve, come in here," said Terry. For a few seconds nothing happened. Then very slowly a shape began to appear outside the door, moving at an insanely gradual pace.

Steve was an odd creature. He was a half breed to begin with, which presented him with some basic issues, but what he was bred from made it a lot stranger to deal with. His home planet had breeding rules which to our ears sound a bit wrong. Basically, everything on Steve's planet was sentient, even objects we'd expect to be inanimate. All of these things could mate with everything else, no matter how large their physiological differences were. Their offspring would have elements of both parents, but which elements they inherited varied wildly. This had produced a world with millions of unique, if extremely peculiar looking persons.

Steve's mum had been a raincloud and his father had been an alpaca. This could have resulted in a number of different outcomes, but Steve was born as a floating furry cloud with an alpaca's face. He had no limbs of any kind and without a windy atmosphere could only propel himself at absolutely lacklustre speeds – as a result it took him almost five entire minutes to enter from the hallway much to Fate's growing annoyance.

"What the HELL is this thing Terrance?" Fate angrily

gestured towards Steve as he wafted inch by inch in through the doorway.

Steve's furry brow ruffled in confusion. "Are you referring to me sir?"

"Is that alive?" Fate asked Terry.

"Fate, this is Steve he is our most skilled technician. He's a Frelovian."

Fate smiled his real smile. It wasn't a good one, but he was clearly actually pleased for a brief moment so no-one was going to knock him out of that.

"A Frelovian, oh I like this game. What were your parents – let me guess. A camel and a testicle? A handbag and a llama? A bird and a cushion?"

"A cloud and an Alpaca thank you very much. And they would not be pleased to be referred to as such, Jill Cloud and Alan Paca are proud individuals," huffed Steve.

Steve began to turn a darker shade of grey. Terry got up and spoke quietly, but urgently to the cloud.

"Please calm down Steve, we can't have you raining everywhere, there's expensive electrics all around us, we've talked about this."

"Ok, ok, but he's talking about my mum, if he does it again, it'll be pissing it down in here before you can say umbrella," Steve warned.

"Fair enough, Steve, fair enough, but can you just give us the update."

Steve inclined his alpaca face in the slight way that he was capable of.

"How does he fix stuff, he has no hands?" Fate asked. Terry held up a hand.

"Alright, alright, I was just asking – proceed."

Terry looked at Steve intently, pretending to ignore Fate – "Please give us your analysis."

Steve took a breath, counted to five internally and his colour returned to a much lighter shade of grey.

"I have examined the readout from the teleportation event and I have thoroughly inspected the equipment used. It appears that the transfer was carried out as cleanly as we have ever managed it. The transfer pattern is perfect, so perfect we can recreate the scene on the computer over there using the readings."

The computer was about three metres away, they watched as Steve incrementally moved through the air. He was feeling the tension in the room as it took him about a minute to move the short distance, but over the years had perfected a facial expression which looked pretty nonchalant about the huge amount of time he was taking. Fate's fists were white as he had clenched them tight to try and stave off a fit of impatient rage.

As Steve moved slowly within range of a computer terminal he said, "Computer, please play file 'teleport.nine'."

He painstakingly rotated to face the teleportation booths which they could see through glass behind them. Fate was breathing angry air from his nostrils at another wait. He and Terry turned towards the booths. In booth one, a holographic figure of a human appeared, he was looking around the booth nervously and then was speaking directly at them. They could not hear what he was saying, but he appeared more and more scared until the moment of the transfer when he was screaming in terror. The recording paused.

"And you think this horrified, screaming man was perfectly ok when he reached the other side?" said Fate incredulously.

"Yes. Every case of disembowelling or turning inside out had already begun by this point in proceedings – it was the process of dematerialising that actually instigated it."

Steve looked at Terry and Terry pressed a button on the terminal which moved the recreation on. The screaming man dematerialised completely intact.

"You can see he was captured in a safe way."

"Ok, let's say I accept that premise, which I definitely don't, where has he been transferred to?"

"That's where this gets really interesting. So, at first, we assumed we'd lost him as the coordinates were not valid. However, I noticed the format was strikingly similar to the ones we used on my world. When you plot a transfer to our world the readouts all begin with a five. I checked with Terry and his planet's coordinates all began with a six. Co-ordinates here begin with a seven."

"Ok, ok, get to the point!"

"Well although the format is much more basic – the transfer co-ordinates the human travelled to begin with a one."

Fate nodded curtly to Steve on his way out of the door.

"I think he likes you," said Terry.

"He nearly made me do yellow rain if you know what I mean," chuckled Steve.

"Yes, I've been meaning to talk to you about that as well…" began Terry.

****

Jim had left me to it. I was standing with my hands on the rock, I took a deep breath and I exhaled. I slowly drew in my next lungful, whilst closing my eyes and as I exhaled this time, without warning, I slammed face first in to cold hard ground. I felt like I'd been head-butted in the face by an angry mountain. I tried to open my eyes, but my brain had ceased sending messages to parts of my body while it figured out which bits of it were still intact.

I was lying face down, like a mannequin, hands by my side, flat on my front. I could feel dust on my cheek, I could feel it wedged between my fingers. I tried my eyes again and my eyelids parted fractionally allowing searing hot sunlight in, which singed my inner monologue. I snapped them shut again and tried to remember where I was.

I could hear the wind whistling and the sound of waves breaking. In the distance, a wolf howled.

****

Fate stood on Joy World, in the exact same spot the human had vacated. He was confused and irritated. There was no-one around to shout at or hurt so it was a bit of an anti-climax. He'd entered through the portal in an attempt to affect a surprise attack, but unbeknownst to him the human had been leaning on the rock at the time. As Fate opened the portal he'd activated it and allowed his intended target to travel in the opposite direction. He, however, knew none of this and while he did glance briefly at the rock, he found no reason to suspect what had happened and moved off towards the centre of the main Joy World plain, which is where the creatures were most often found.

Chapter 15
Eye Eye Eye Eye Eye Eye Eye Eye Captain

The dusty ground was scratching my face as it moved beneath me.

"Stay still will you?" I mumbled to it.

It continued to move and I wondered, groggily, where the ground had to be that was more important than supporting my weight.

I realised it must have heard me because at that moment it started to stop supporting my weight as it dropped away from my face and chest and now only my legs were connected with it.

"Get his legs," I heard the ground say.

I didn't know why the ground would want my legs.

"Don't take my legs please," I mumbled.

"What'd he say?" said a voice.

"He said 'don't take my legs please'," a second voice answered.

"Well at least he can understand us. Get his legs."

I realised gradually that I was being dragged along the ground by two men who seemed to want to avoid carrying me.

I tried opening my eyes, but they politely refused my request with a brief reminder of the pain I felt the last time I tried it. The pain I felt was as if someone had unscrewed the top of my head, taken out my brain, played football with it for an hour and then replaced it upside-down.

Through this haze, I could hear more activity ahead of us, there was a creaking sound, footsteps on wood and a great hustle and bustle which made me think that I may just have reached home.

"Who the bloody hell is this?" spoke a more authoritative voice from above.

"We found him in the clearing."

"He's dressed bizarrely."

"Sir he's got two eyes and five fingers."

"Get him on board, NOW!" the authoritative voice shouted urgently. "Get everyone back here, we set sail this minute!"

I was dragged up a wooden plank and dumped on a wet wooden floor amid much shouting and chaos.

I heard the sound of a heavy wooden door slamming and then felt the familiar sway of a ship's movement.

I felt my consciousness slipping away and I drifted into a deep sleep.

****

Fate stormed across the fields of Joy World towards the lake where Jim, Mr Gillespie, Geoff and the three other remaining sheep sat discussing their most recent visitor.

They spotted him when he was around fifty yards away, stalking across the grass like a lanky goth.

A panic set it, but they knew there was no point in running anywhere. They quickly huddled together and shared a brief, urgent discussion.

Fate arrived a few seconds later.

"OK, where is the human?" he spat.

"Um…" began Geoff before being nudged by Jim. "I mean, baaaaaa."

"No, you don't mean fucking 'baaaa' you stupid farmyard waste of wool. I am perfectly aware that you can talk."

They all looked at each other nervously. Fate glared.

"Well?" said Fate.

"We haven't seen him around," said Jim.

"I didn't say 'him', I *said* human." Fate growled, holding out his hand close to Jim's face.

Jim murmured something quietly.

"What did you say?" said Fate.

"Baaaaaaa?" tried Jim.

****

When I awoke I, for the first time in my life, appeared to have been wearing a hat whilst sleeping. A large colourful creation which was fashioned out of many strands of woollen material. I saw it so clearly because it toppled off my head onto the floor as I started awake. I was sitting upright and bound to a chair. I could feel from the motion that I was still at sea. I looked down at my body and I appeared to have been re-dressed as Aladdin.

I was in an empty cabin of the ship, it appeared to be of an old-fashioned wooden construction. There was no windows or portholes in the cabin, the only light source was a small lantern rested in the far corner. There was a powerful odour of manure permeating the air which entered my nostrils. I could hear the growls, grunts and howls of multiple animals. A large number of footsteps approached the door and 10 or so fairly bizarre looking people burst in. The one at the front was wearing a giant hat.

"Who are you?" he asked urgently.

"Jesus Christ," I exclaimed, still shocked at their unusual appearance.

"Hello Jesus-Christ, my name is Captain Nohaz and I am the commander of this vessel."

He seemed to be logical choice as he had the most of everything; largest hat, most fingers, strangest mouth, most eyes and most colourful outfit.

This had to be the same boat captain of which Sonia had told Jim. Before I had a chance to enquire, he asked, "Do you know Sonia Lancaster, of Kent?"

I laughed a little bit, realising that this whole crazy tale must be true. "No, I'm afraid I never had the pleasure, but I know about her encounter with you and I'm from the same world."

"Then the messenger will come to kill you also?"

"It's possible, yes."

"The last time he was here he killed many of my people. I cannot harbour you for long."

"Can you get me back to the rocks where Sonia passed through?"

"Yes, we picked you up on one of the smaller uninhabited islands, we're about a day's sail from the rocks."

"What is this place?"

Captain Nohaz ordered me released from my binds; I was given water and bread. He asked me to accompany him to the top deck.

As we walked through the ship, we passed through cavernous holds full of exotic creatures. There were many crew members, all of whom shared the odd physiological features to some extent. I estimated that there were at least a few hundred crew on the ship.

We eventually emerged from a stairway onto the top deck and it was then that I truly was able to appreciate the epic scale of the vessel.

It was long, really long, if it had been named in 2018, they'd have called it Longy McLongface. I guessed about a mile long and it at least was a quarter of a mile wide. It made the Titanic look like a canoe.

He walked me to the edge and we looked out at the water, an endless sea in every direction.

"It is no different whichever side of the boat you are standing – a water world," he said sadly.

"What's happening here?"

"This is what is happening, this is all that's ever happening."

He stared out to the horizon, his voice was full of sadness, I knew that he meant to convey great meaning with it, but I just didn't get it.

"What is this place? Why is this ship so humongous? Why are you carrying thousands of animals? Why is there no land?" I demanded.

"You really don't know anything about us then?"

"Only that you helped Sonia Lancaster."

"The best thing we've done in years."

He asked about Sonia. About what happened to her. I thought about telling him a lie, but I've always been absolutely terrible at it.

He cried when I told him the story and if you've ever seen a man with seventeen eyes crying, you'll know that it was a mess. As he towelled down his face I stared awkwardly off into the distance at the endless water. No one would design a place to be this.

"What happened here Captain?"

"A long time ago things were very, very different."

Even a man with 17 eyes doesn't see everything. Captain Nohaz told the human his incomplete, boat-based, version of events, but there was more to the story than he could possibly know...

Chapter 16

The History of The First People

God was despondent for a long time after the failure of Joy World. He moped about on His cloud in a very undignified way for a deity, He wasn't clearing up after Himself and He'd written some absolutely rank rotten poetry about it. Thankfully there was no-one else around to see it.

Project two would be different, He thought. "I am God, I will easily fix the problems of Joy World with this new design." He made a larger planet this time, intending to have more variety of terrain. He kept it round, but this time did nothing to smooth down the rough edges of His original design; it would be dirty and organic in nature. He enjoyed the hills and water from Joy World so He gave this world larger mountains and created the first oceans. This planet would have many different types of life. He acknowledged a desire to create life that was more sophisticated and was closer in intellect to Himself.

These creatures would be in charge of the other, simpler beasts and thus a chain of command would be created that would stop it descending into the chaos of war which had plagued Joy World.

He was unsure what they would look like though and went through a number of iterations.

If they were made as hard-wearing spheres they could roll about very quickly over most surfaces. He tested this briefly, but the creatures could not pick anything up and it was really difficult to decide where to put the eyes.

He tried liquid creatures which could flow wherever they wanted and had no need for solid food as they absorbed nutrients from the air and from the soil. They were fantastically fast, although their vision was not great and they could not speak. The whole thing came to a head on test day two, when a thirsty sheep accidentally drank the whole civilisation.

He tried many things which did not work. What He eventually settled on was a honed version of His sheep design. He started with a standard issue sheep and then He made it larger. Then He replaced the front hooves with His first, mitten-like, design for hands. These were refined and refined until six fingers on each hand remained, the sheep was now adept at picking up objects, utilising tools and gripping surfaces. However, putting its weight on the fingers as it walked was extremely painful and slow, so God straightened the spine and made it stand upright on its back legs. He tested this and the sheep immediately fell over. The legs were now too thin to bear the weight of the whole body so He added ligaments, muscles and width to them. The creature fell over again. Unfortunately, the little back hooves could no longer bear the pressure so He widened these and lengthened them. He added fingers to the feet for balance, but these did not have to be as dexterous as the fingers on the hands so He made them chubbier, sturdier and shorter.

Looking at the creature now it was unbalanced. The sheep's front legs were struggling to support the weightier human hands that were now ridiculously dangling from the end. He widened the arms and added muscles and ligaments to support the hands, He put a stronger joint in the middle of the arm to give the limb more support and flexibility. The creature could now comfortably stand and had the use of its arms, but the torso looked strange and vulnerable compared to the arms and legs. He made it longer, flatter and tougher.

The head was the real challenge. He wanted the people to have an advantage over their fellow creatures so He gave them a few extra eyes and His new, side-mounted ear design To accommodate this, He made it rounder and lengthened the neck to give it flexibility.

Eventually He settled on a fleshier skin pigment, after giving serious thought to a camouflage pattern.

Their mouths would be made more suited to speaking, given that this was to be their main communication method.

He removed the tail and the wool. It was starting to look quite agreeable. He realised at this point it was hardly right to keep calling it Sheep version 2; it had fewer original parts than Cher.

Eventually after several months of tinkering He had His

prototype which he called a 'person'.

He designed some additional creatures for this world. Wolves with their delicious flesh and useful pelts would be a renewable source for the residents. He made them compliant and accepting of their fate. No creature should have to die in fear.

He got arty and started experimenting with colours, textures and limb length. This is the period in which He made v1 of Giraffes, Zebras, Lizards, Lions, Tigers, Frogs and Parrots.

He made tiny insects for the smaller creatures to eat and deployed His previous mix of rabbits, sheep, pigs, cows and ducks also. This time He had removed the speaking ability from the cows and ducks, partially to prevent any repeat of the war between their species and partially because the cows talked a load of shite anyway.

He spread the different species fairly evenly; there would be a rich variety of life everywhere on the planet. He also wanted to replicate this in the ocean and thus the first sea creatures were born. Whales, dolphins, tuna, herring, catfish, sharks, octopuses and prawns all debuted on planet Two along with many others.

Obviously, He didn't want a repeat of the psychological issues suffered by the creatures on Joy World. He made one sun which would rotate around His planet so that for half the day the world would be dark. He made all the creatures with the ability to rest and switch their brains off for a period. He had invented sleep, although at this early stage He hadn't yet invented dreams so each night the creatures would view a test card which consisted of God in front of a rainbow doing a thumbs-up.

There would also be a natural atmosphere as a result of the oceans, He would do nothing to restrict this so there would be winds, waves and rain occurring naturally.

He had observed that perfection was not stimulating and that it is more interesting to have a little adversity and a little conflict and He hoped these conditions would provide that diversion.

He would also introduce a second gender and He invented genitals. This would mean the species could breed and multiply without His interference. Hopefully, this would lead to a more sustainable population.

On launch day God was very excited. The planet was ready, grass was green, oceans were in motion and all that remained was for the creatures to be placed onto the planet's surface. He did so and with one generous thought, granted them all life.

He would call His second planet Ground, as He liked the simplicity of it.

Things were great on Ground for a few decades. The people learned to form societies, they bred, they formed families naturally and they protected their young. They understood the equilibrium that had to be maintained with their surroundings. They hunted for food, but did not run the supply short. The creatures seemed to have an innate acceptance of their place in the food chain.

Eventually the people began to gather together as society and community became more important to them. Simple towns and cities formed and the people continued to multiply. As resources became thinner, inequalities developed between the people, the larger and stronger had realised that they could dominate in this environment. It was at that point – 130 years from the inception of Ground that the first murder took place. The big man was impaled by a sword, cut down in retribution for charging too much tax on his local community.

Many other crimes blossomed from this first jarring act and chaos ensued. Theft became common, murder was routine and a ruthless, every-man-for-himself culture was developing. Many parts of Ground became a wild frontier where there were no laws. Weapon technology developed very quickly compared to everything else; it started with stones and clubs, but quickly developed into swords and bows. People began to move around together for safety. These groups had a bad habit of turning nasty when they realised their strength in numbers, quite often looting and robbing smaller groups and settlings. After some years of this, people wanted an end to it. However, there were disagreements about how that end should be achieved. Some wished a cessation of the violence, law and order to be restored and a peaceful resolution, but some saw an opportunity to rule and desired war. There were violent disagreements about who should lead.

Factions began to form, alliances were made and war was declared.

After twenty years of skirmishes, battles and raids, the people were tired. They demanded a winner; they demanded an end to the chaos. In the centre of the largest land mass on the planet there was a great flat plain, with bright, green grass, every colour of flowers and freshwater springs. The plain was surrounded by imposing cliffs and towering mountains on all sides. The Ground people called it The Infinite Garden – even though it was enclosed. It was agreed that the battle for Ground would happen there.

Men from all over the planet gathered around the edges of The Infinite Garden to do battle. There were thousands and thousands of men, swords and arrows at the ready, keeping a close eye on those factions to either side of them. In relative safety up on the hills above, many of the women and children watched on, nervously awaiting their family members' return.

On Ground it had been decided early on that the women were too important to the continuation of the species that they should not be involved in war. It was not due to a perceived lack of fighting ability, strength or courage that they were excluded; simply that they were so revered that it was considered a sin to risk a woman's life in something as pointless and dirty as open battle. Women on Ground were expert hunters, craftsmen and intellects just as the men were. However, the extra component of giving life was regarded over all else.

The battlefield was now full.

No-one made the first move. An eerie quiet fell over the battlefield as commanders considered their best way forward and the consequences of a mistake. Eventually the most foolish of the commanders ran out of patience – he ordered his men to charge. Everyone waited with bated breath to see if anyone would react as they ran screaming towards the centre of the plain.

The commander was called The Coconut General. His faction, The Palm Tree Battalion, was from a tropical island called Sand. He had attained his moniker after famously winning a key battle against another faction. The other faction was called The Ice Warriors – they had invaded during the night and had his men as prisoners. They marched them down towards the beach where they planned to execute them. "USE THE COCONUTS!" shouted the general at the top of his voice, before picking up a coconut and throwing it at one of the Ice Warriors. The warrior's head cracked open and the Coconut men rallied behind him – grabbed coconuts and fought their attackers off, eventually retaking the town. Their general was hailed as a military genius by the people of the island, however his soldiers knew differently. They knew him as 'Thick Paul' and that he had shouted "USE THE COCONUTS" every single day at 4 p.m. throughout his entire life and this was the first time it had ever made any sense whatsoever in the context of the situation. Like a stopped clock he'd been right and the victory had earned him a position far beyond his abilities.

Unfortunately, when he ordered the charge in The Infinite Garden, the armies were all gathered around the edges of the battlefield, so his men didn't quite know where to charge or who to attack first; without much thought they ran screaming, swords raised above their heads, into the centre of the battlefield and then stopped when it was clear no one was charging out to meet them. Everyone laughed at them, mainly out of relief at not being the first to make an arse of it, but it also gave the battle a much-needed focal point and every other commander ordered his men to charge in on them and destroy them.

Twenty factions were now suddenly running towards the centre of the battlefield, carrying with them all manner of primitive pointy weaponry. High above the situation God looked on in slow motion like someone who'd just dropped their phone off the side of a boat. This was going to be an unprecedented bloodbath and unlike the war on Joy World these creatures had the ability and hardware required to be legitimately violent. He realised that He had to intervene.

God let out a great sigh; He was going to have to go down there. As He lived outside of the strict rules of time, He had a minute to think it over. The Almond had NOT proved to be a good vessel for his words, but He did not wish to appear as one of the People as He thought they would struggle to believe one of their own as God. Plus, He thought it would be too much of a shocking reveal, for them to also find out that He had been the fabled test-card-thumbs-up-rainbow-dream-man this whole entire time.

In the centre of the Infinite Garden, General Coconuts was bracing for impact when he felt a wind begin to swirl around him, it was a strong breeze at first, but quickly developed into a churning gale which nearly lifted him from his feet. The others had slowed their charging – they could now see the wind surrounding General Coconuts' men had turned into a tornado. It swept the men off their feet, into the air and dumped them down on some empty ground forty yards away. When the whirlwind of dust cleared, they saw a giant duck. The yellow Duck was around eight feet tall and was standing, imposingly in the centre of the battlefield.

"STOP!" It bellowed, in a booming baritone. The voice carried for several miles.

Absolutely everyone froze where they were, mouths agape and hearts racing.

"I AM YOUR CREATOR! LISTEN TO MY WORDS."

A fair proportion of the men in the field instantly knelt at this proclamation. Those who didn't soon followed out of a sort of peer pressure.

"YOU MUST STOP THIS BLOODSHED," The duck looked around the field. It gestured with a giant wing – "THIS BEAUTIFUL PLACE WAS MADE FOR YOU TO BE HAPPY, TO PROSPER; NOT TO FIGHT, NOT FOR THIS MADNESS I SEE BEFORE ME."

"Why haven't you spoken to us before?" asked a voice from the crowd.

"YOU REQUIRED MY VOICE TO KNOW THAT IT WAS WRONG TO KILL?"

"Well, no."

"TO STEAL, TO LIE, TO DECLARE WAR?"

"No, probably not," admitted the crowd voice.

"I COME HERE TO PREVENT A MASSACRE, TO GUIDE YOU."

"Guide us o great one!" said another voice.

"What do you want with us?" wondered another.

"Why are you so much bigger than the other ducks?" said yet another.

"What's a massacre?"

"SILENCE! I WILL ANSWER YOU, I'M BIGGER THAN THE OTHER DUCKS BECAUSE I AM THE MAIN DUCK. THE GOD DUCK. THE CREATOR DUCK. A MASSACRE IS A WORD MEANING THE KILLING OF MANY PEOPLE IN ONE GO, I MADE IT UP EARLIER THIS MORNING AND IT WILL CATCH ON. BELIEVE ME."

"What's the meaning of life?"

"Guide us!"

"I WILL, BUT BEFORE THAT CAN I JUST ASK THAT EVERYONE SAVES ANY FURTHER QUESTIONS FOR THE END, THANKS. ANYWAY. MOVING ON TO THE ACTUAL GUIDANCE. DO NOT MURDER. DO NOT STEAL. DO NOT LIE. DO NOT HARM OTHERS IN ANYWAY AND IT IS FORBIDDEN TO MOCK THE CREATOR DUCK AFTER HE HAS GONE."

"What about when you're still here?" said a wag from the crowd.

The Duck waved a wing and the man's legs were immediately attached to his nipples.

The crowd gasped.

"OBEY THESE RULES OR LIKE THE WRONGDOER YOU TOO WILL HAVE LEGS FOR NIPPLES AND EVERYONE WILL POINT AND LAUGH AND CALL YOU 'LEG-TITS'. OBEY OR THE SERIOUS CONSEQUENCES WILL BE YOURS – IS THAT UNDERSTOOD?"

The crown murmured their reluctant approval.

God sensed that He had gone too far, but there was no backtracking now.

"I WILL PUNISH INDISCRETIONS AND YOU WILL WORSHIP NO OTHER DUCKS BUT ME. I AM A VENGEFUL AND JEALOUS DUCK. I WILL LEAVE YOUR SIGHT NOW, BUT I WILL ALWAYS BE WATCHING. BE PEACEFUL, BE KIND AND BE HAPPY!"

10,000 battle hardened thugs watched in fear and amazement as a giant duck powered up off the ground into the sky and continued flying straight upwards until it had disappeared into the far reaches of the heavens.

Everyone felt a bit silly about the war now. There was a lot of tough guy nods and posturing as they all meekly walked back to their particular part of the world, but fearing the 'leg-tits' punishment, no one struck a single blow.

Once all had returned to their respective towns and villages there was an unspoken agreement to not knowingly break any of the God Duck's rules.

God looked on in satisfaction as a twenty-five-year period of relative peace ensued. However, after thirty-five years some of the people who had been at the battle had died of old age, some had worse memories and some just liked building their part. Stories of The Duck in the Infinite Garden were shared with increasing changes and embellishments.

By the time sixty years had passed, hardly anyone who was there on the day was still alive. Disagreements were arising about what the Duck had forbidden and what he had encouraged. One dispute between two neighbours concluded with one making the outrageous claim that the Duck had specifically mentioned rules about cutting down your neighbour's hedges.

Crime was sneaking its way back amongst normal society, snuggling into bed like a family dog. Lying had been fully re-instated because of its clear and absolute necessity. It was essential for a civilised people to go about their daily business free of brash honest idiots. As God would later come to realise, the ability to lie reduces the murder rate by a statistically significant margin.

By the time seventy years had passed since the battle, factions had once again begun to form – this time centred around specific interpretations of the Duck's message. The factions debated, squabbled and eventually it all got too personal. True, deep, remarkable hatred developed between the different groups.

The violence wasn't far behind. The people justified this by making a slight alteration to their holy texts. It allowed for violence if the violence was committed in defence of the true Duck message.

The planet split into areas where only people of the same belief were gathered and hence only people of the same belief were born as it was passed down the generations. There was only one exception to the rule. There was a townsman called Nohaz. He was righteous and good. He did not kill, he did not cheat, steal or lie (much). His late father had been at the battle and had told it truthfully – Nohaz had passed this teaching to his sons.

Nohaz lived with his wife and their two sons and their son's wives on a farm on the outskirts of a major town. As the violence became more intense, the pressure increased on Nohaz and his family to declare which side they were on.

Nohaz steadfastly refused. The faction to the west burnt his crops to intimidate him, he stood firm. The faction to his east killed ten of his cows, he stood firm. The supportive faction to the north made a statue of him, he stood firm. The faction to the south were moderates; they'd sent him several stern letters.

In all the craziness and killing, Nohaz was a shining light for good. God, watching from above saw that he was a good man, with a kind heart and brave soul. Jackie, his wife, was a philosopher; she was considered one of the great minds of Ground. She cared for her family above all else though and would have gladly fought every man on the battlefield to protect any of them. Nohaz's sons had been raised the right way and as a family unit they were stronger than any.

God had become frustrated with the cyclical nature of the violence on Ground. He wanted to start again, to re-do the people-based society. He'd decided that He was going to send an enormous flood to wipe out the creatures of Ground. He had chosen Nohaz and his family to rebuild society.

Nohaz was walking along the road nearest his house, laden with goods from the market slung over his shoulder with a rope, it was a hot day and he was sweating profusely. His cloak was absolutely soaked through and the rope was digging into his skin. He needed a break and set the goods on the ground. As he did this, he heard a voice behind him.

"NOHAZ, DO NOT BE AFRAID."

This phrase is used all the time by people who don't realise that it has the exact opposite effect than the speaker intends. Absolutely no-one has ever said 'Do not be afraid' when there was no logical reason to be afraid. If you were about to show your friend your holiday photos you would never think of even mentioning whether to be afraid or not. What people actually mean when they say this is 'Don't shit yourself at this scary thing I'm about to show/do to you'.

In this case God was about to appear before Nohaz in a way which would scare anyone. Nohaz turned to face the source of the voice and found himself staring at a burning tree. He immediately panicked at the fire so close to his home. He was also extra confused as there hadn't been a tree there when he'd walked past a minute ago.

"Oh my!" exclaimed Nohaz and started to move towards a nearby water well.

"THERE IS NO NEED MY CHILD, IT IS I – THE CREATOR."

Nohaz couldn't believe that the tree was talking, but a question jumped out of his mouth and legged it before he could worry about anything.

"I thought you were a Duck?"

"I AM. I AM MANY THINGS."

"Does the fire not hurt you, o great creator?"

God paused. Nohaz thought that he heard the tree sigh.

"Look I'm just trying something here. I thought it'd be cool. You seem disturbed by it?"

"It is unsettling great God Duck; you have no face, you are on fire and you are a talking tree." Nohaz had great respect for the creator, but he was also scrupulously honest.

"VERY WELL." With a crackling sound the tree began to shrink in size; it reduced until it was waist height and then began to morph into a bush. The bush was still aflame.

"HOW'S THIS?"

"It wasn't the size of the shrubbery that was my objection, o talented architect"

"FINE." God sighed again, this time a bit louder.

The bush began to grow, and as it did the fire went out. The shape began to expand and knit together, until the giant duck was formed. The huge duck shook its heavy, wide head.

"IS THIS WHAT YOU WANT?" He boomed.

Nohaz immediately knelt before him.

"YOU RECOGNISE THAT I AM GOD? THAT I AM THE CREATOR?"

"I do."

"YOU WILL OBEY ME AND TRUST ME?"

"I will."

"GOOD."

Nohaz's knee started to wobble from the stresses coursing through his every atom. He didn't dare look up at the Duck's face, lest it took it as a sign of disrespect. It was important to say the right thing or he'd be the first guy with leg-tits since his grandfather was a boy.

"I HAVE A TASK FOR YOU MY SON. I WANT YOU TO CONSTRUCT A BOAT."

"What's a boat?"

"YOU HAVE NEVER SEEN A BOAT? A WOODEN VESSEL WHICH TRAVELS OVER THE WATER?"

"Great one, I live ninety miles inland and I farm the land. I have no knowledge of these things."

"OK WELL NOW YOU KNOW WHAT ONE IS, I NEED YOU TO BUILD IT."

"I would be honoured."

"IT IS TO BE LARGE, VERY LARGE. IT WILL BE A LOT LARGER THAN ANYTHING YOU HAVE EVER SEEN. I WILL PUT THE INSTRUCTIONS ON A TABLET OF STONE FOR YOU."

"Thank you, Great Duck of wonder."

"ENOUGH OF THAT. THERE'S ANOTHER THING."

"Yes?"

"YOU ARE TO COLLECT A MALE AND FEMALE OF EVERY ANIMAL SPECIES ON THE PLANET AND PUT THEM IN THE BOAT FOR SAFEKEEPING."

"How will I know if I have collected them all, great quacker of the sky?"

"WHAT DO YOU MEAN?"

"I'm not sure I know what all of the animals are, where they all live, how to tell the difference between a male and a female or how to coerce them into a boat."

"YOU'LL FIGURE IT OUT."

"Ok." Nohaz replied, but was becoming increasingly nervous about the task ahead.

"YOU DON'T NEED TO BOTHER WITH THE SEA CREATURES"

"There are sea creatures!?" Nohaz exclaimed.

"YES. ANYWAY, HAVE YOU ANY FURTHER QUESTIONS?"

"Just a few, my winged miracle."

"ASK AWAY NOHAZ."

"Why have I been given this task?"

"YOU ARE THE BEST OF THE MEN ON THE PLANET AND THE MOST WORTHY OF CONTINUED EXISTENCE."

"No, I meant why have I to build a giant boat with animals in it, on a farm ninety miles inland?"

"AH, SORRY YES, MISSED A BIT. I WILL BE SENDING A GREAT FLOOD WHICH WILL COVER THE GROUND, DESTROYING ALL LIFE AND I WANT YOU AND THE ANIMALS TO SURVIVE TO REBUILD SOCIETY."

"Is that really necessary, o great masterful bread-eater?"

"YES!! THESE PEOPLE ARE IMMORAL, THEY DO NOT LISTEN TO MY WORDS, THEY ARE CORRUPTED, I MUST REFRESH THE WORLD AND THIS IS HOW I AM GOING TO DO IT."

"May I also bring my mate Steve?"

"NO! STEVE IS IMMORAL AND WILL DROWN WITH THE OTHERS."

"What about my mate Dave?"

"ONLY YOU AND YOUR FAMILY!"

"Great God Duck have mercy on the people, they are only weak and foolish; they do not deserve annihilation. Punish me instead; I will bear the brunt for their sins."

"THIS IS EXACTLY WHY I CHOOSE YOU OVER THEM, YOU'RE JUST BETTER. I HAVE MADE MY CHOICE NOHAZ AND YOU WILL HAVE TO LIVE WITH IT."

Nohaz was afraid, confused and conflicted.

"Glorious Quack Lord, when will the flood arrive?"

"THE FLOOD WILL ARRIVE IN THREE MONTHS, WHICH BEFORE YOU ASK IS PLENTY OF TIME TO CONSTRUCT THE LARGEST BOAT EVER BUILT, PLUS DISCOVER, CATEGORISE AND CAPTURE EVERY ANIMAL SPECIES AND LOAD THEM, YOUR FAMILY AND ENOUGH FOOD AND SUPPLIES FOR 150 DAYS AT SEA."

God paused.

"ACTUALLY, THAT'S QUITE A LOT OF STUFF TO DO, I'LL GIVE YOU FOUR MONTHS."

Nohaz watched in silence as the God Duck made stone

tablets with the boat building instructions. The duck nodded at him and powered into the sky disappearing into the clouds.

Nohaz went inside and told Jackie of his encounter with God. She thought it sounded like a load of old arse, but she had never known Nohaz to lie about anything.

"How will we do this?" he asked.

"Don't worry, we'll formulate a plan dear. You're married to the smartest person on the planet. We can figure this out," said Jackie.

Two months later he, two of his sons and Jackie were around 15% of the way to constructing the boat. Jackie had worked out that they would start slower, but as they sold their assets would be able to hire more hands for the truly difficult parts. They had chopped, purchased and traded until they had enough wood to construct the enormous craft. They had become the laughing stock of the town as they had lost all of their money in the endeavour. It led to many irritating conversations with passers-by, including one well-travelled, boat-savvy know-it-all who heckled from the road.

"You know a boat needs water to float right?"

"There is a flood coming."

"It hasn't rained more than a few inches here in my whole lifetime!"

"Well anyway, the God Duck told me to build it."

"You've gone wrong Nohaz. You used to be alright, but now you've gone wrong."

He had heard nothing further from the God Duck. He was spending fourteen to sixteen hours per day on carpentry, which was a major change for him as previously he was spending zero hours a day on carpentry.

Billions of years before anyone would know what they were and entirely by coincidence, Nohaz had inadvertently named all three of his sons phonetically after professional snooker players. Raereardhon and Steavedaphiss were assisting in the construction of the boat, working the hard, physical days of woodwork with their Mother and Father.

However, Nohaz's third son Roneo-Sullyvan was dispatched to every corner of the earth to track down, sex and capture every animal species which could not be easily purchased in their home town.

Roneo-Sullyvan had gathered together a group of young

adventurous men who had no fear and worked for little compensation. Idiots basically. They trekked around with nets, up mountains, into jungles, across the plains and sometimes back across the plains as they'd let Mickey do the navigation and he was useless. It was difficult work and they suffered many injuries trying to capture the more fearsome creatures. Mickey had a scar across his knee from a tiger's teeth and also one across his face from when he tried to catch a sword in his mouth because he's a bloody twat.

Roneo had bigger problems than just capturing them though; it was how to stop them eating each other on the way home. This had meant having to introduce a policy where they caught five times the amount of the animals lower in the food chain to ensure they could afford to lose a few to getting eaten on the way back towards the boat.

With a month to go Roneo had brought back over half the animal species on Ground. He returned to find the boat around 70% complete. The family had sold their home and all their land other than where the boat was sitting. They slept inside the boat at night and built it during the day. They had used the money to employ a workforce on the boat, which had increased productivity by some distance. The men working on the boat were grateful of the work, but they felt a little sorry for this man who was going to have to live in boat for the rest of his life because he's sold his house and spent all his money building it. Not a single man amongst them believed his flood prophecy.

Of course, Roneo never found all the animal species, but he really performed well above expectation and managed to get 75% of them. He discovered 57 new species as a result and was now a recognised wildlife expert. When he returned, he was unsure what to tell his family, but given that no-one knew what the total number of animals should be, he simply claimed it as a win and everyone celebrated it as such.

Nohaz finished the boat with seven days to go. They loaded all the animals into the ark only losing three workers in the process and then had an enormous party inside the massive hull to celebrate.

During the party Nohaz thanked everyone for their hard work and dedication. He also expressed his sadness that they would all be exterminated by God in a flood over the course of the next few weeks. This got a huge laugh because even now, absolutely none of them believed this was going to happen.

The family awoke all at the same time the following morning; they groaned covering their eyes to shield them from the bright sun. But it wasn't the sun at all; it was the kind of sun-like light that only emanates from a God disguised as a giant duck.

"MORNING!" He boomed, far too loudly to be considered anything other than an assault at this delicate time of the day.

They all jumped up to their feet and then upon seeing the duck standing over them inside the ship they all fell to their knees.

"YOU HAVE DONE WELL NOHAZ. THIS IS A FINE VESSEL AND WILL PROTECT YOU WELL DURING THE STORM."

"Thank you, great bird of divine ability."

"I TOLD YOU – YOU CAN STOP THAT. I AM HERE TO INFORM YOU THAT THE FLOOD WILL BEGIN TOMORROW. YOU SHOULD SEAL YOURSELVES INSIDE THE BOAT TONIGHT. IT WILL RAIN FOR FIFTY-FIVE DAYS. ALL OF THE GROUND WILL BE COVERED WITH WATER, AFTER FORTY DAYS OF FLOOD THE WATER WILL BEGIN TO SUBSIDE AND THE BOAT SHALL RETURN TO THE GROUND. FROM THERE YOU WILL REBUILD THE WORLD."

"It will be our distinct honour."

"GOOD LUCK!"

The light emanating from the duck became stronger until it was impossible to look at and they covered their eyes. When it died down, the duck was gone.

They sealed themselves inside the boat and waited. As God had proclaimed, it began to rain the next day, a ferocity of rain the like of which the people of Ground had never seen. It bounced off the ground for four hours. If you walked through it, it bit at your skin like a pinching finger. It rained in places which had only ever known sunshine before, it rained in places which had only known icy tundra. The rain began to lie and over the next few days the water level slowly rose inch by inch.

At this point the people of the town came to the field where the great boat lay and called out to Nohaz and his family. It was properly awkward for them; they at first decided to just stay quiet, not come to the door and pretended they couldn't hear the voices. They engaged what Earth people would come to know as the 'Jehovah's Witness Coming Up the Garden Path Defence'.

As the water rose to above their knees the people began to seriously panic. They battered the side of the hull in a frenzy and then tried to knock it off its stands by coordinating their blows on the vast vessel's exterior.

Inside the boat, Nohaz and his family only felt minor vibrations, but were becoming increasingly worried that the boat would not hold against the onslaught. He told his family to stand firm and he climbed to the top deck of boat. When he looked over the side the people didn't notice him doing so. There were thousands of people gathered outside, they were throwing rocks, shooting arrows and pounding fists against the hull.

Nohaz considered speaking to them, to try and calm them, but he thought better of it. Anything which would calm these people would either be a lie or would break his promises to the God Duck. At best, he would deceive them and at worst spark a more furious reaction than was already in progress.

He felt enormous survivor's guilt from his position of relative safety upon the boat, but eventually he resolved to do nothing, went back inside and closed the door behind him.

Some of the townspeople attempted to escape to high ground, but the rest stayed outside the boat for the next three days chanting, singing and praying aloud as the water rose above their waists and kept coming.

The rain pounded down. By the end of the ninth day there was no more noise from the townspeople. There would never be any more noise from the townspeople ever again. On the twelfth day, the boat was finally lifted off the surface of Ground and Nohaz was finally satisfied that his construction had been sound; the boat would float. He braved the top deck once more on this day, the rain was still fiercely attacking the ground like a thousand arrows. He could see water for miles on end; the mountains were still visible, as were the treetops. The bodies of the townspeople were scattered across the surface of the water like driftwood for miles.

The people who had fled to the hills only lasted ten more days. The water soon engulfed the forests and the hills entirely. After forty-nine days, only the very tops of the highest mountains were visible and on the last day of the great rain, these too dropped below the rising waters.

The animals were beginning to get restless, undeniably most of them were ill suited to ocean life. The swaying caused by the waves made them ill, the lack of natural light made them sad and the captivity made them angry. Feeding them became dangerous work and cleaning up after them was a full-time job for everyone on board.

The rain ceased and the sun returned to the sky. The God Duck had decreed that there would now follow fifty days at sea and then the ocean would retreat and the boat would return to the ground.

The family spent any of their spare time on the top deck. They raised the enormous sails and set about becoming expert sailors in a risk-free environment, as there were now no rocks to crash into. They learned how to harness the wind, steer the boat and stop it, just for something to do. Fifty days passed and on the fifty-first day the water did not appear to be receding at all. A further month passed with no reduction in the level. Two months passed and the water level had receded around ten feet, but was nowhere near clearing. On the seventy-fifth day a great splashing sound awoke them, they rushed out to see what had caused and were treated to the sight of a great fountain of spray appearing in front of them.

"Hellooooooooo," called a deep, but friendly voice.

They ran to the edge of the deck and looked over the side. Emerging from the water was a huge blue whale. He waved a fin at them and smiled with his huge whale teeth.

"Hello there fellow!" shouted Nohaz. "And what are you?"

"I am a blue whale sir."

"How are you?" said Nohaz cheerfully, delighted to see that the sea creatures were alive and well.

"I am well, thank you. Say, where is everyone else? Why is the sea suddenly so deep?"

"I am afraid the others have died, there was a great flood – we are the only ones left."

"Oh goodness me. I'm very sorry to hear that. We sea

creatures have been rather enjoying ourselves, with all this extra space to play with. I feel absolutely awful now."

"It is not your fault whale. The flood is the fault of the people. What's your name, whale?"

"Charles."

"Nice to meet you Charles."

"Yes, you too. I'll tell the others to leave your boat alone. We wouldn't want to wipe out the last of the people."

"That's very decent of you Charles. Tell me, are there many like you in the water?"

"Oh yes, there's a wonderful vibrant world down here, with many varied creatures."

"Well, please give them our best!"

"Will do!"

He took an enormous breath and waved his huge fin at them as he passed back beneath the gentle waves.

What the people would never know is that while Charles the Whale was one of the most outwardly friendly creatures they'd ever encountered (and they had once met a particularly affable camel) – beneath the waves, Charles was absolutely mental. He had completely ruined life under the sea for everyone else. Every single whale beaching on Ground could be traced directly back to Charles being an absolute bawbag. He tormented the tuna, he bothered the barracudas and he stressed-out the squids. He was the worst sea creature that had ever lived, which made it all the more galling for the basking sharks that they saw him pull this 'friendly-guy' bullshit with the boat people.

Charles would get his comeuppance though as he got a fatal dose of diarrhoea when he ate too many scared squid one day. He shat himself raw for three days before his dead, dried up husk of a corpse floated to the top of the sea to be picked apart by birds.

The moral of the story is – never judge a whale by its cover – or something.

On the 110th day they noticed the peak of a mountain had begun to appear above the surface of the water. At this point they understood that the waters would now subside and they would gradually return to the ground below. They slowed the boat to the slowest speed they could manage.

They eagerly awaited the re-emergence of the land over the

next few days, but only a few mountain peaks became visible. At the end of the 120th day only a few patches of the highest ground had become visible. On the whole planet maybe only ten or eleven islands of varying size and composition were now accessible. On the 121st day, it began to lightly rain.

Nohaz was confused, so far everything had turned out how the creator had said it would, but by now they were supposed to be safe. They would only have enough food and supplies for another thirty days.

On the morning of the 123rd day, they went above deck as normal, but this day they found the God Duck wistfully looking out to sea.

Nohaz nervously approached, but the God Duck did not seem to notice their presence.

"Creator?"

"Had plans, such good plans," muttered the Duck to Himself.

"Excuse me Creator?"

The Duck turned its big head towards him. "Ah. Good morning."

"Good morning, glorious feathered commander."

"Yes, yes." He dismissively waved a wing and began to walk towards the back of the boat.

They followed a few paces behind.

"It was meant to be a reset, the flood," said the Duck. "I was going to put everything right again afterwards. Remake the population, the animals would breed back to sustainable levels again."

He slowly shook His head. "The calculations were all wrong though. I didn't account for the extra water in the atmosphere."

"Dear, God Duck I do not understand. What are you trying to say?"

"Dear Nohaz, you see I only get one shot at making a world. This was a way to cheat, to have a second shot, but now I can't do anymore. I can't remake it. Only the tiniest adjustments. I only get one shot at creating." He was babbling.

"The CALCULATIONS. I got it all right, except for the extra water. You see I can't get it to drain Nohaz. It evaporates and creates rain. The water I've introduced is too much, I can't clear it all. It's been too long now for most of the plants below. I've killed half the life on the planet and I can't get it back. Don't you see?"

"Are you saying that the flood is permanent?"

"Yes. This world will be almost entirely covered with water for the rest of time. I'm very sorry to you all. This is my fault entirely."

"What should we do? How will we survive?"

"Have the animals bred whilst on the ship?"

"Yes, most of them have bred plentifully – just the pandas that won't seem to shag," answered Jackie, Nohaz's wife.

"Why not?" asked God.

"They said the mood wasn't right, the lighting was a disaster and that they weren't looking for a relationship at the moment," said Jackie.

"Right, I'll make a note of that, don't want them being that fussy in future."

"Apart from that though we've got lots of everything."

"Well then you have a surplus. I suggest you find the biggest, most fertile patches of land and release a mixture of the animals onto the surface. With rain and the sunshine plants will eventually grow here and the animals should be able to get a population going. You can use them as your food supply," said God.

"Will you be able to fix the planet?" she asked.

"No, as I said. It's beyond my help now. I will of course let you live out your lives here, but I must refocus my attentions on a new world where I hope to not repeat the mistakes of Ground."

"You've failed us," she said quietly, staring him down.

"Steady now, Jackie," said Nohaz, not wanting to live out the rest of his life stuck on a boat married to a woman with legs for tits.

"No, she is correct Nohaz. I've taken a beautiful, if troubled, world and turned it into a watery wasteland. I apologise profusely for the way you'll have to live if you are to survive. I wanted only the best for you; a happy life, a family, a home. I have deprived you of so much of that."

"We still have a family and we still have a home. We'll make it work," said Nohaz.

“I sincerely hope so. I will look in on you from time to time, but for now I must depart. I love you all more than you will ever know. I hope you find a way to be happy.”

The God Duck hopped up onto the ledge and glided down into the water. He paddled away across the sea. He did one last revolution of the planet, a beautiful wasted opportunity. The sea air was refreshing, cleansing even, He breathed it in and swore to Himself that he would never make such a basic error ever again.

When He had seen the whole planet, He took off from the water, flew up out of the atmosphere and left Ground behind.

The family did as he suggested and released most of the animals back onto different parts of the world which were not submerged. They kept behind a small stock of edible animals and cows for milk and the like. They also retained a few of the more ferocious hunters as they did not want all the animals to be eaten by tigers before being able to breed.

Years passed and the plan was working. They were able to survive, they collected rain water to drink and they fed on the animals.

The sons and their wives bred and there were more people. After fifty years Nohaz was nearing the end. He had fathered a few more children, the youngest of which he had named Nohaz. He was happy that the family could survive for years to come. On the day of his ninetieth year, Nohaz passed away.

His youngest son Nohaz was named captain in his place; Jackie’s wish was that there would always be a Captain Nohaz at the helm of the ark. She died later the same year, the will to survive being lessened by losing the love of her life.

One hundred years passed. The family continued to thrive, but also continued to breed. The gene pool was small and by now this issue was starting to show itself. There was the odd additional finger, eye or medical condition which occurred, but no-one realised what the cause was.

300 further years passed. The population of the ark was now over one hundred. Each child being born was encumbered with issues. The people of Ground had been created with six fingers on each hand and four eyes. This was now the exception rather than the rule. The most eyes

anyone on board had was seven. The current Captian Nohaz had six eyes and eight fingers on his right hand, seven on his left. The generations were coming faster as people were not living as long as they used to. Respiration issues and skeletal deformations were the free gift which came with the family's continued existence.

500 years from then just over a thousand people lived on the ark. The number of eyes were now in double figures, the number of fingers ranged from two to twenty-two and hunches, humps, lumps, coughs and sores were common. The average IQ had dropped significantly also.

The survival skills of the Ground People were superbly developed though, everything on the planet could be harvested for a useful purpose; a dead wolf could be eaten, its bones used for making implements and its pelt for clothing. They were expert sailors, expert archers, expert swordsman and terrific hunters. The moral heart of their society had never wavered. They understood that the other creatures must also survive if they were to survive, they took care of the planet as best they could and the Captains throughout the years had laid down a clear set of rules for society.

The current Nohaz was an eccentric man, as his last eight predecessors had increasingly been. He was however, conscientiously nice, brave and just. He fought for Sonia and he was now willing to fight for the latest visitor. As he saw it, the only thing they had left was to live life in the best way possible; God may have forgotten them, but they weren't about to abandon anyone.

Chapter 17
To the Other Side

Poor Geoff. He'd never been the most intelligent of talking sheep. Fate had pushed him and pushed him and in his panicked state he got caught in an increasingly dangerous cycle of saying 'Baaaaa', being warned about saying 'Baaaaa' and then accidently saying 'Baaaaa' again in response.

The eighth time round Fate had lost his patience and now Geoff lay dead on the grass. Jim had not been able to suffer any more unpleasantness at this point and told Fate that the human was trying to utilise the portal to get home.

It didn't occur to Fate immediately what must have happened, but when he realised that it had been his own doing, he was even more furious because now he'd been robbed of someone to blame. Stomping back towards the portal he kicked a nearby tree about thirty times until it began to crack and fall down. He got to the portal to find it was out of action now, as the feat of the human passing through had fried the Almond turning it into a black husk.

He roared at the sky, a bit like the Incredible Hulk, but a lot skinnier and almost 100% less green. He was furious that he was going to have to take the long way around. He leapt up into the sky and flew up out of the atmosphere.

Back on the surface Jim and the others scooped up Geoff and carried him to the trees. They would bury him next to Sonia. The dwindling population were now less than ten.

Jim would come to say at Geoff's memorial – "It is at times like this that we are struck by the thought that we should have agreed to die when it was offered to us. It's an attractive thought when we feel this sort of pain, but if we'd denied ourselves that life, we'd never have got to know Geoff at all and that would be a greater shame than his passing."

"Baaaaa," said Steve. Everyone had a wry chuckle and they said their goodbyes.

****

Nohaz told me his version of the history of Ground. It was a fascinating tale, only slightly worsened by his occasional three-minute coughing fits.

"We'll be approaching Lancaster Clearing in an hour. We'll have to move quickly. He knows about this place."

We went over what I needed to do with the rocks five or six times. He told me not to let the messenger touch me for any reason as he could strike a man down dead with a touch. He told me that Sonia had selected 'Back' on the wheel. I would go the other way.

I went to the front of the boat, which I was repeatedly asked to call 'the bow'. I watched the small island appear on the horizon. I felt the spray of the ocean in my face, I felt the air passing me at a rate of knots and I saw the sun setting to the east. It really could have been something, this place.

We approached and as we did so we took a curved path in towards the rocks. We came about harshly and they edged the boat up to the cliff with practised skill. We disembarked quickly, with Captain Nohaz foregoing his usual fanfare to aid my escape. What he settled for was his first mate playing the horn breathlessly as we ran across the clearing towards the rock formation which was the portal point.

As we got within fifty yards of it Fate dropped out of the sky like a spider dropping from a ceiling. He made no sound, he just dropped into view, landed and was immediately moving towards us. A roar went up from the Boatmen and we kept moving; as we ran a hail of arrows flew towards Fate. He flew up and to the left to try and avoid them, but he wasn't quite fast enough and got one lodged in his left shin. He dropped like a stone and this time he did make a noise as he hit the ground on his side.

"Go, we will hold him here!" shouted Nohaz.

My path now clear, I sprinted towards the rocks. When I got there, I saw the wheel and knew what to do, but when I went to turn it, it was extremely stiff moving in the clockwise direction.

Fate was rising to his feet off to my right-hand side. The boatmen had moved towards him, pinning him down. He darted towards me taking out a few of the men in his way. I was still heaving with all my weight on the wheel. Fate took an arrow to the back and fell to the ground; he was now only ten feet away from me. One of the boatmen rushed towards me and placed his full weight behind pulling the wheel. With the extra force we got it moving and I was able to set it to 'Forward'. I hoped this was Earth.

Fate began to struggle to his feet as the boatmen fell back; they had realised that hand to hand combat was only going to end one way, but that their arrows were working.

"Goodbye, Nohaz and thank you all for your bravery!" I shouted.

Fate got up and moved towards me.

"You, on the other hand, can get to fuck!" I yelled at him.

I dropped the wheel into the slot and disappeared. Fate took three more arrows before dropping to the ground; he hit the floor and skidded forward on his face. With the last of his energy he reached out and killed the boatman nearest to him. That was the last action he could muster and with that he slumped down, his eyes closed and he died.

Chapter 18
The Lights Are On
But Nobody's Home

I landed on my back this time, thundering my skull into concrete; the crack was echoing in my head two full minutes after it had happened. "NEVER AGAIN," I swore to myself. Never again would I go through a magic portal to another world without first putting on some substantial protective headgear. I was briefly amused at how normal that sentence sounded to me now.

As I battled the searing concussion, I distracted myself by trying to listen to my surroundings to obtain some information on where I might be. I was absolutely delighted to identify the unmistakable hum of electronic equipment. This was no primitive boat world – there was a chance that this was indeed Earth.

I prised my eyes open, it was daytime, but the sun was not as aggressively bright as it had been on Ground or Joy World. Dirty, brown dust was hanging in the air around me. There were clouds in the sky and I saw the outline of a bird flying high overhead. I climbed to my feet and had a look around. I was standing in the centre of a raised concrete piazza which formed the centre of a large square. There was a collection of drab, grey, geometric rather severe looking buildings surrounding the square. What I was standing in seemed to be a shared central area between four buildings. Grass was growing through the cracks in the concrete. The designs were harsh, ugly and unfamiliar; I wondered if I had been put down in North Korea or Albania.

There were lights on in some of the buildings, but no signs of any activity. I thought perhaps it might be early in the morning before anyone had arrived for work, which might give me a chance to get the lay of the land before I had to explain myself to anyone.

There was a set of stairs leading down to a path which went completely around the edges of the square. The buildings on the right-hand side had an opening through which I could leave. I walked down the stairs and as I began to walk along the path I gazed into the ground floor windows of the adjacent building – inside I could see a layout very much resembling a control centre. Rows of desks with computer terminals all facing the same way and at the end of the room a large display screen and a big desk facing the crowd. It looked like mission control at NASA. I stopped, put my face closer, peering in through the glass to get a better look. The desks were covered with dust, quite a bit of it; no one had sat here for a very long time.

I moved a bit quicker to the next building along and found a similar scene inside, I turned the corner and inside this building although the lights certainly were on, there was no one home. I walked along the path and went into the opening between the buildings. I emerged onto a city street. There were no vehicles anywhere, no movement and no people.

The dust had gathered on the ground and as I walked my shoes left footprints behind. I was in a large city, there were high modern buildings all around. The street I was on sloped upwards, my eye followed it to its end about a mile away, where I saw a giant, monolithic, skyscraper – it was at least 200 storeys high, with a stark, black glass exterior. It was lit up on every floor.

I arrived at the entrance to the building after twenty minutes of staring into windows and generally exploring my surroundings. Everywhere else appeared to be out of use; this was the only dust free building in an apparently dead city.

I approached the large glass front doors. As I did so they opened automatically to let me inside. In the lobby was a reception desk; I didn't recognise the style of the computer equipment, but it was switched on. It had a number of translucent, freestanding panels and a central display screen, all of which were showing a readout: Project Economise COMPLETED. There were several screens and terminals around the lobby all with the exact same message.

There was a buzzer on the top of the reception desk and I pressed it. It made a loud buzzing sound which echoed creepily around the cavernous lobby and shook dust from the ceiling.

Sometimes you can tell when a place is empty. There's

just a lack of life in the air. This place was empty and I was extremely nervous, even though I felt that I was unlikely to encounter anyone.

There were a series of lifts behind the reception desk and I called one and pressed the highest floor number I could. The lift was made of glass, but was covered in dust, inside and out. I wiped off the dust on the inside with my fingers and was treated to a murky view of the inside of an elevator shaft.

However, the lift then shot into a vicious, bone-shaking ascent and it emerged from the shaft and treated me to a murky view of an absolutely vast and futuristic city skyline. Even through the haze of muck, it was an awe-inspiring collection of giant buildings, floating platforms and bright signage.

The lift continued to shoot upwards and then halted with a force that let my stomach come up to high-five my eyeballs inside my head. As I recovered from the nausea of the stop, the doors opened to reveal a plush, modern office floor, with absolutely no dirt anywhere to be seen. It was pristine, clean lines, everywhere, with an attractive, tasteful decor and sensitive, arty lighting. I felt quite bad about stepping out of the lift as I was now the dirtiest thing here having been collecting dust since I arrived. I gingerly put my right foot forward onto the carpet and immediately left a horrible looking footprint. Dust was pouring off me with every movement no matter how slow or slight. I realised there was no point in worrying about it now so I proceeded inwards at a more reasonable pace, leaving a shroud of dust behind me wherever I went.

The reception area I had stepped out into was quite big, it had a waiting area with several tables and comfortable chairs. A selection of the glass panel computer terminals were placed handily around the room. To either side, brightly lit corridors swooped away from me. I could see doors lining the sides and I assumed there would be many offices, presumably with fantastic views. This was clearly the executive level of the building, the CEO of whatever this was would surely be located on this floor. I decided to take the corridor to my left, but I only got a few paces when I heard activity behind me. A loud electrical hum was travelling fast towards me from the other corridor. I turned to see a shadow moving down the wall. It looked like it could be a person.

What appeared instead was quite different. It was silver and metallic, floated three feet off the ground and made a whirring sound. It was a waist-up, life size, robotic butler character who came buzzing towards me. He stopped at my first footprint, produced a nozzle from his hand and began aggressively vacuuming the dust.

"DIRTY," he said without emotion, in a way that shouldn't have been amusing to a thirty-one-year-old man, but was.

"VERY DIRTY," he began to clean the trail of dust and muck that I left behind. I stood and watched entertained at my first sight of a futuristic robot. As he cleaned nearer and nearer, I stood back to give him room.

When he finished the trail of dust the room looked brand new again. I smiled. The fervour with which he carried out his task was very endearing. Then the robot swung his focus up from the floor to me.

"DIRTY," he said.

"Oh no, I'm fine I'll just have a bath or a …" I started, but he was on me with the nozzle immediately. He knocked me to the floor and was quickly scraping the hard metal end of it against my skin.

"VERY DIRTY," he said.

"ARRRRRRGGGGGGHHHHHHHHH!" I screamed.

I grabbed his nozzle arm and tried to steer it away from my face, but he was quite strong and it took all my effort just to hold the nozzle a few millimetres from my skin. I would not be able to hold it for long.

"EXCUSE ME, VERY DIRTY, MUST CLEAN," he said, almost politely.

"I really don't need this level of cleaning thank you." I tried.

"VERY DIRTY," he said in response, predictably.

The motor at his rear began to spin a bit quicker as he tested my resistance. I decided to use his momentum against him and when he surged forward again, I threw him further in that direction and gave him a kick up the arse as he went over me. This caused him to fly into the wall pretty hard, which caved his head in and he dropped to the floor in a shower of sparks.

"DerrrrrrrY vuuuurryyyy," he said, waggling his nozzle

slowly and ineffectually in the air.

"Aye, ok," I said, still lying on my back on the soft carpet, catching my breath and nursing my severely grazed face and chest.

"Excuuuuuuuuuuuuuuuuuuuuuuuuusssse diiiiiiiiirrrrrrrrrrr."

I was starting to feel vaguely sorry for him now, but then I moved, the pain tore through my face and I went back to thinking he was a daft shiny bastard who deserved to be mangled.

The carpet was easily the most comfortable thing I'd been on for a while and I just rested my eyes for a moment. Around ten hours later I woke up with a start. I was achy and stiff, but it had been worth it as I now felt refreshed enough to carry on snooping about this office.

I walked down the corridor and it continued for a long way towards the back of the floor. It had many doors along the way, but as I got further in, I could hear something ahead of me. It was a loud, angry, scratchy, electrical crackle which repeated every ten-to-fifteen seconds or so. As I continued down the corridor it became progressively louder.

I came to what was clearly the CEO's office. There was an outer area with a secretary's desk, behind that were a huge set of wood panel double doors.

The crackling noise was coming from inside that room somewhere so I pushed the doors open to reveal a classic looking office, with a big desk, leather chair etc. This one also had fifty screens behind the desk displaying lots of different information.

Wind speed: 0mph
Tide: Low
Temperature: 18c
Power Reserves: 100%
Population: 1
Project Economise: Day 2154

I wondered to myself whether I was the population of 1 that the screen referred to; it was hard to tell whether the screen represented current information given how abandoned the place seemed.

Right behind the CEO's leather chair in the centre of the

wall was a large button-backed door. The crackling seemed to be emanating from there. I opened the door and saw inside a large sterile room with a doctor's bed and medical equipment to my right. On the left was where the crackling sound was happening. It appeared to be a teleportation booth like Terry had used to get me to Joy World. Every fifteen seconds a faint shape flickered into view for a split second with a loud crackle before disappearing just as quickly. It looked like a man. He looked like he was in pain.

On the control panel to the right of the transport unit there was writing in neon pen. Someone had scrawled 'Push This' and then a crude arrow pointing towards a big green button.

I have never been one to pass up a chance to push a big button and this time was no different. My hand went towards it completely independently from my brain. I pushed the button.

Chapter 19
Hell is Other People

Fate was sitting at a bus stop and it was raining. In front of him was a road and beyond that was waste ground for miles. He could not remember how he got here, but he knew he was angry about it. Unfortunately for him that didn't narrow it down much as he was angry about nearly everything. There was an old lady sitting next to him on the bench, staring forward with a glazed look.

"Excuse me?" said Fate.

"Yes?" she said, continuing to stare forward.

"Do you know when the next bus is coming?"

"Oh yes! One will be along in a minute."

"Thanks."

"Don't mention it."

"I'm sorry, could you answer me one more question? Where are we?"

"Oh yes! One will be along in a minute."

"Hmmm," said Fate staring at her. He tried something.

"I think I should probably cut both of your legs off, how about that?"

"Oh yes! One will be along in a minute."

Fate briefly considered actually cutting her legs off.

He looked to his left; the road was straight and carried on to the horizon. To his right it was exactly the same. The environment was completely empty, no buildings, no people, no trees, just empty waste ground. The bus was not coming and he knew that. He stood and powered into the air. An invisible force grabbed him and slammed him back to the ground with incredible power.

He lay there feeling an unfamiliar feeling. Pain. Pain in his supernatural body. He'd felt pain in his mortal body before, but it was nothing, really nothing compared to this. This was God-level pain, sky-splitting, eye-burning, mind-mangling pain that he'd never thought possible.

The old lady sat there looking straight ahead, not seeming to notice. She had a faint smile on her face and a glassy-eyed stare. This further infuriated Fate and he wanted to kill her more than anything ever, but he also needed to lie face down in the road some more, so he did that first.

****

When I pressed the mysterious button the flickering shape crackled into life, but this time it remained and I recognised it as an old man dressed in a white jumpsuit. He toppled out of the teleportation booth with a groan and I just about caught him before he fell to the ground.

"Get me to the bed, quickly" he croaked. I picked him up, which was surprisingly easy, and carried him to the bed. He was frail and as light as a feather.

"You have to hit the blue control on your left to seal the elevator shafts – they will be coming."

"Who's coming?"

"The button!"

I saw the button which was in the middle of a busy control panel. I hit it and he immediately started gesturing for something else.

"The tube, hand me the tube." I looked round and saw a black tube, the width of a garden hose with a pointed end dangling behind me. I put it in his hand. He fixed me a look.

"Do not be alarmed," he said before plunging the pointed end into his chest.

The blood spray from this hit my face and I nearly vomited onto him. A piece of machinery in the corner had lit up and he gestured to it by waving his hand repeatedly at it. He was trying, unsuccessfully to speak. The machine only had one control, a flat black button, so I pushed it and it whirred into life. I looked at him and he gave me a shaky thumbs-up. I could hear liquid flowing down the tube, he glanced at it with fear in his eyes. That proved to be well founded as, when it hit, he began to writhe and moan in agony. I tried to hold him still, but he was thrashing around violently.

Eventually he went limp and unresponsive, I tried to stir him, tried CPR, but nothing was effective. He was dead. I slumped into a nearby chair. I was confused and exhausted. What was this dead place and where had he teleported from? What had happened to everyone that had lived in this city? And did they have anything to eat? I was starving.

I noticed there were plenty of cupboards in this room and after some disappointing discoveries I opened one to find that it was a fitted refrigerator. Inside were absolutely iced bottles of water and pouches which were marked 'Protein Mix', 'Sustenance A' and 'Sustenance C'. I fancied a bit of Sustenance C so I pulled that and a water bottle out. I looked at the back of the pack and it read –

"A sensible mixture of the required daily allowances of key food groups, arranged in a paste to aid digestion."

It didn't sound like the most exciting meal, but I was hungry enough to scoop some of the foul-smelling paste into my mouth with my fingers. I washed it down with the water bottle and threw the rest away. All of this had been an excellent distraction from the horror of the dead impaled man behind me.

I couldn't bring myself to look at him again. I could see his limp hand in my periphery and even that was giving me the heebie-jeebies.

I instead decided to inspect the teleportation booth to see if it could be of any use to me. It had an electronic display, which it appeared you could set to co-ordinates. I didn't know anything about co-ordinates and cursed my ignorance. If I knew what to enter, I could be back home in a jiffy.

I touched the dial and tried moving the coordinates. The dial spun and the numbers changed. Perhaps there would be some instructions around to explain the procedure. I tried some of the other buttons to see if I could get anywhere.

"I wouldn't do that if I were you." My hand froze as the voice spoke behind me. I turned slowly to see the man sitting up on the bed, looking ten years younger and much less frail. He was holding a gun.

****

When the pain had worn off a bit Fate was able to get up and he re-took his seat on the bus stop bench. He was staring intently at the old woman, examining her now with the context of his odd surroundings.

"What are you?"

"Oh Yes! One will be along in a minute!"

"What is this place?"

"Oh Yes! One will be along in a minute!"

He finally could not contain his rage and reached out to grab her throat. When his hand got half way, she grabbed him by the wrist powerfully and turned her head in his direction for the first time. Her eyes turned a glowing red and she opened her mouth wide to reveal rows and rows of sharp teeth. Her hat seemed to levitate off her head, but after a few seconds Fate saw that in fact what was happening was that a pair of horns were growing out of her skull. Eventually the hat toppled off and she breathed smoky, sulphur breath in his face as her other hand came up and closed around his throat. She was unbearably strong and even with his free hand he couldn't dislodge her grip. With a jolt she transformed back into the nice old lady staring forward, hands on her lap, hat on her head. He breathed in hungrily, fearfully holding his scratched-up throat and leaning away from the now-terrifying creature.

"Here it comes now!" she said sweetly.

Fate's confusion was at its peak, now there was a noise in the distance he looked to his right down the road and saw a rickety old bus inching its way towards them at a glacial pace. Fate hissed at her.

"What is going on here? No one possesses that kind of strength over me, woman! I will HURT you, I will make you choke on that hat you dirty, toothy, old cunt."

"Here it comes now!"

The bus was now pulling up to the stop. A little old man was driving the bus, he threw the doors open and beckoned to Fate to get on. Fate grudgingly walked up the steps and sat in the seat closest to the driver.

"Where are we going?"

"Next stop, Lakes of Fire!"

****

I had my hands up, still trying to work out what was going on.

"If you go into that booth you'll never come back," said the man holding the gun.

"So, you're concerned for my safety, but you're pointing a gun at me?"

"The warning is because I'm concerned for your safety, but the gun is because I'm concerned for my safety."

I gave him one of those tight lipped faces that are supposed to mean 'fair enough', but it later occurred to me that on a different planet that gesture could have meant literally anything, including, but not limited to, 'Hey, please shoot me in the dick with your space gun'. Although you'd have to have immense facial control to get across a sentence like that with one look. (Hey, I said that it occurred to me, not that it made perfect sense.)

"What is this place?" I asked.

"What do you mean?"

"This world, what was it, what happened here? Why do you look so much better than you did when you came out?"

"You're not from here, are you?"

"No."

"Sweet Jasmine! It's true! There's another world?"

"Yes. Actually there's at least four."

"Four! My god." He looked stunned. "What's your name traveller and where are you from?"

"I'm from Earth…" I started.

"Well, Fromearth – why are you here?"

"I'm just looking to get home. That's all, I'm not a threat, I'm not armed. That's why I was looking at the booth; I thought I could maybe use it to get home."

"Ah. Sorry no. That booth is set on a continuous loop. It's no good for getting anywhere now."

He pulled the tube from his chest and stood up off the bed. He waggled the gun, directing me out into the office. He motioned for me to sit down across from him and he took the seat at the desk. He had a quick glance at the screens and let out a gasp.

"Oh my god. It's been 300 years. It's been three hundred, chuffing, bastard years. No wonder I was dehydrated!"

I sat there looking at the gun wondering if it would shoot bullets or lasers.

"Population Two. Just the two of us – is that really correct?" he said. I thought it was a rhetorical question, but he spun his head towards me, wide-eyed.

"I've not checked everywhere, but it seems to be. You're the only other person I've seen since arriving."

"They're all gone. They're all long gone." He was staring catatonically at the screens.

"I'm sorry, how long had you been in the transporter?"

"303 years," he said without looking away from the readout.

"Wow, how did you survive in there?"

He wasn't really listening. "What?"

"How did you survive for so long?"

"Oh. It hardly matters now I shouldn't think."

"What happened to everyone else?"

"They died."

"How, if you don't mind me asking?"

"I do mind you asking actually, to me it happened fifteen minutes ago, so it's still a bit on the raw side."

"Sorry." We sat in awkward silence for a few moments. He then twisted round to give the screens another look. He took a few notes and did some complicated looking calculations on a sheet of paper in front of him. He double checked his arithmetic and then seemed to settle.

"So, what do you want to do? Should I kill you and then myself or shall we try and both go at the same time?" he said casually.

"What!"

"Don't you understand? There's only the two of us left on the whole planet. We've limited food supplies, limited water supplies and no chance of continuing the population. There's nothing to do, but die slowly in a dusty ruin of a city. It's over. I have no intention of going out painfully and slowly."

"Well it's not over for me, I just got here and I intend to leave as soon as possible"

"How do you plan on doing that?"

"There's a portal, I don't know where yet, but there is one. We've got to find it and go through it. You should come with me."

"This sounds like nonsense. You're from House Triad and you've come to punish me."

I took a chance and stood up.

"Where are you going?" he said.

"I don't know your factions, I'm going home. You're welcome to come with me, but I'm leaving and I'd rather die trying than in some bizarre suicide pact with a stranger." I started to back away.

"Wait! Don't you move, and it's not technically a suicide pact, it's a murder-suicide, if that makes you feel any better about it."

"Funnily enough it doesn't. Look you don't want to kill me. Just let me leave."

I continued to slowly back away. He shot me.

****

The bus drove towards the horizon at a stuttering ponderous pace. As they got closer to the horizon Fate realised that it was not in fact a horizon, but a cliff edge. The bus didn't stop though and they continued over the lip of the horizon and then lurched down into a fiery abyss below. Fate was bounced around the carriage and didn't see much until they landed with a bone-shaking shudder.

Fate pulled himself up to the window and looked out. The fiery lakes stretched as far as the eye could see. The bus was on its four wheels on a red brimstone road.

"This is your stop," said the driver. Fate got up and left the bus. As the bus drove away it revealed Satan standing behind it.

"Welcome to Hell you silly, goth bastard!" he shouted.

"What was that stuff with the old lady for?" Fate raged.

"Everyone gets their least favourite experience as a welcome. For you it was being forced to wait and being told what to do."

"Great, lesson learned, get me back up top now, I've got people to kill."

"No can do!"

Fate grabbed him by the shoulders, "Are you kidding? I've got important business to attend to!"

Satan suddenly enlarged himself by twenty feet. "THEN YOU SHOULD NOT HAVE DIED, MY FRIEND!" he roared. "HAVE YOU FORGOTTON THE RULES AFTER ALL THIS TIME?"

Fate shook his head, admonished by the giant devil before him.

"IF YOU DIE IN YOUR MORTAL BODY, YOU SUFFER A MORTAL DEATH."

"I don't understand why I'm in hell though?"

"THERE IS NOT ONE AMONG US WHO HAS NOT SINNED. WE HAVE ALL CONTRIBUTED TOWARDS THE HORRORS OF THE WORLD. WE ARE FORTUNATE TO BE IMMORTAL BECAUSE THERE IS NOT ONE OF US THAT IS FIT FOR HEAVEN."

"I can't stay here!"

"THE RULES ARE SIMPLE. YOU MUST DEFEAT MY CHALLENGES THREE. ONLY THEN WILL YOU BE GRANTED YOUR FREEDOM ONCE MORE."

"You will make me suffer for your amusement."

"LIFE IS SUFFERING. IF YOU WANT LIFE, YOU WILL SUFFER."

"Very well. Present your challenges."

"I'M BUSY AT THE MOMENT. YOU HAVE TO WAIT." He snapped his fingers.

Fate was at a bus stop. It was raining.

"Fuuuuuuck offffff!" he shouted to the sky.

"Oh Yes! One will be along in a minute!" said an old lady with a slight smirk.

****

On the one hand it was really cool to have seen a laser gun in action for the first time. On the other hand, I'd now had a splitting headache for four universes. Overhead I could see the ceiling scrolling by; the fluorescent strip lights every few seconds were causing shooting pains of ambitious proportions.

I was strapped to a gurney by my legs, chest and arms. It was being wheeled down a corridor of some sort. I could feel a throbbing in my shoulder where I'd been shot. I could smell burnt fabric and burnt flesh.

"Where are we going?" I mumbled.

"You'll see."

He wheeled me along the corridor, then we took a hard right turn, clattering through some heavy double doors. The sound reverberated through the metal of the gurney and pain pulsed through my soul. The new corridor had a plain grey concrete ceiling and was lit by orange emergency lighting, mounted on the walls. We jerked to a stop and I strained to look up for just a split second. We were at a large, red, vertical sliding door, the sort you might find at a loading bay. I heard him operating a keypad, he was muttering to himself about his memory, a series of error tones sounded before a much jollier bell indicated that he'd got something right. The door began to open and as it rolled upwards, with an aurally abusive siren sounding, I felt the cold air wash in. He pushed me out and continued to roll me along. All I could see was the dull, cloudy sky – I could feel a stronger wind on my face. I felt us slowing down and my binds were released. I sat up to see that we were on the roof and he'd wheeled my gurney close to the edge. He still had the gun and gestured to me to climb down. As soon as I stepped off, he moved over and shoved the gurney over the edge. It tumbled and tumbled down the storeys until it was almost out of sight. In the dead city we heard the impact better than we saw it.

I stared at him in terror. This was how he wanted to go out? By jumping off the highest building in the land? FUCK. THAT.

"Ok. Never a better place to do it. No pain, relatively quick and what a view. Any last requests?"

"Yeah, you go first."

"Very good. No, I plan to be last man standing on Ternion. A captain going down with his ship so to speak."

"Why are you the only one left?"

"It's a long story and I think as we'll both be dead soon, I'll skip it."

"I've got to know. If you die and don't tell anyone no-one will ever be able to share the story."

"And who are you going to tell exactly? What difference does telling you make? You'll be dead as well and no-one will ever know anything about this place."

"In my plan, I'll tell a whole other world of your achievements. Or better still, you put down the gun and come tell them yourself."

"You're trying to trick me."

"I'm really not. That would imply I knew what the hell was going on."

"You're from one of the other Houses, aren't you? You want to be the last one to live?"

"Honestly not a clue what you're talking about, I've asked

you several times to explain it to me."

"Well who cares now? Jump off the side." He waved the gun at me.

"No."

"Come on."

"No."

"Just do it."

"No."

"I'll shoot you."

"I'll live."

"I'll throw you off the side."

"If you were the sort of person who could, you would have done that when I was strapped to the trolley."

"Shit," he said.

"What?"

"That's a really good point. I concede." He holstered his gun.

"What?"

"I concede, you made the better argument. It's the done thing."

"Not where I come from," I said, amazed.

"Why, what do they do where you come from?" he asked.

"Just keep insisting the wrong-headed thing you believe is correct even long after someone has decisively proven that not to be the case."

"That sounds foolish."

"It's surprisingly successful," I said.

"Well here, when we are proved wrong, we yield."

"On my world, this would be very unusual. People habitually lie, deceive and ignore facts which don't support their views."

"Sounds awful."

"It's sort of great and awful."

He was looking at me in a whole new way now. "So, you're really from another world?"

"Yes. It's called Earth," I said.

"This world is called Ternion."

"Ternion?"

"Ternion – it is a word that means triplet or three things together. Our great thinkers have long debated about what the meaning of it is."

“I think I actually know this one.”

“What are you talking about?”

“This is the third world. I’ve been to the first two. This is three. Ternion.” I said, gesturing around.

“Wow. It’s actually quite funny how much time people wasted debating that before. When the answer was in the question”

“Well they couldn’t have known.”

He nodded thoughtfully. “This portal you speak of – it is a doorway to the other worlds?”

“Yes – you can go backwards or forwards along the chain. I am hoping the fourth planet is mine, that this will return me home.”

“And what does this portal look like?” he asked.

“It will be a structure which wasn’t there before.”

“That’s every structure.”

“No, I mean it’s a new addition after the apocalypse. It is likely to be high up.”

“That’s a lot of possibilities,” he said.

“Perhaps you could look at the surroundings and see if anything appears out of place.”

He walked to the edge and looked into the distance at the mountains. He looked around the city skyline and then his eyes alighted on the building across the street. It was about thirty storeys shorter and not as imposing.

He pointed to a black, metallic, shipping container style structure on the top of the building. My eyes widened as I read the words ‘Almond Inc.’ that it had emblazoned on its side in big purple letters.

“That’s new,” he said.

“We have to get to it, as soon as possible.” I said.

“Right. That might be a problem.”

“Why? We’re the only two people on the planet.”

“True. We’re the only two PEOPLE, but that building houses artificial lifeforms.”

“What kind?”

“It’s the headquarters of a company that made killer robots. It’s guarded by killer robots. It is staffed with killer robots. Doesn’t even have a canteen.”

“Right, so not absolutely ideal then.”

“Not if you’re peckish.” He grinned.

****

Fate's rage had been bubbling under, but to be put back to the bus stop was simply too much. His temper ruptured a seal and he manically tried everything he could to force his way out. He tried to fly; he was slammed into the ground. He tried to run along the road, but he could only get twenty yards and then it was like running through almost dried cement. Displaying trademark stubbornness, he then tried running in every other possible direction, with similar results. He tried to provoke the old lady; she would not budge. He tried to harm her and she fought him off. He tried to break the bus stop itself, but he could not do it any serious damage.

He screamed at the old lady, he screamed at the sky, he ranted at nothing for hours on end.

He stood on the seat and shouted into the sky, begging Satan to release him from this purgatory. Eventually the bus came, but as he stood to get on it, the driver said.

"Not you."

"Where am I supposed to go?"

"You are to wait here."

"I'm WAITING. I want to get on with my challenges. I want to get out of here."

"The boss says that you just need to wait."

He signalled to the old lady, who boarded the bus and left Fate sitting alone in this drab wilderness.

Fate ran up to the bus, kicking it with all his might. He simply bounced off it and back onto the ground. The driver just smiled with an evil grin.

"No ticket, no ride." He started the engine.

"Don't you dare leave me here."

The driver closed the door with a wink.

The bus pulled away and Fate swore at it, until it tumbled out of view. He flopped back huffily onto the ground.

He lay there on his back in a perfect rigid rage for what seemed like hours. The sky didn't move, the rain continued to fall onto his face. This wasn't the random smattering of Earth rain, it was false, absolutely uniform, the drops prodding the same places on his cheeks, at a constant tempo, like a Chinese water torture.

At a certain point every drop began to seem like a personal

insult. He slowly raised a hand to block it. Eventually the drops on his hand became irritating and he started using his other hand to punch them out of the sky in one of the most pointless acts ever conducted. A handy metaphor for the futility of life.

Fate stubbornly continued to lie there for a long time as the rain continued to piss him off.

Eventually he could stand no more. He got up and returned to the bus shelter. To pass the time he thought about his fifty-five favourite murders. By the time he got to the thirty-seventh, calmness had settled over him and he contentedly screened the rest of the memories in his head.

He sat there serenely for a time, lost in these happy thoughts. He was jolted back into reality when the sound of the rain changed. He saw a vast field of last drops fall to the ground, still arranged in their static formation. Like someone dropping a 3-d topographical map to the ground. He looked up and saw that the sky was next to fall, crumpling towards the ground like a giant curtain, leaving only a black void in its wake. The rest of the landscape faded until it too was gone. All that remained was the bus shelter, floating in the middle of cold black nothing.

Behind him he heard someone slowly clapping their hands. He didn't even need to turn around to know who it was.

"So, you just wanted to torture me for a bit?" asked Fate

"Well, it is Hell," said Satan.

"Can I go now?"

"Of course not. You've only passed the first challenge."

"I didn't pass any challenge, you just left me to stew for an obscene amount of time."

"You could have been out in fifteen minutes."

"What are you talking about, I tried every way out of there possible."

"That wasn't the challenge. You see, my challenges are supposed to be difficult. They are supposed to cause you torment because they are things you won't like. Activities that you hate doing."

"Well I hate this conversation, so I sincerely hope that counts as challenge two."

"No, it does not. Challenge number one was to simply sit calmly for fifteen minutes and wait. This was, incidentally the very instruction you were given. This was further reinforced by anyone you interacted with and your movements were restricted to encourage stillness. However instead of simply waiting as instructed, you fought. You fought the air, the road, the old lady, the driver, the bus stop, the actual bus itself and finally, most hilariously – you fought the fucking rain. You are incapable of calm rational thought. This should worry you. It should worry every living thing in the seven worlds."

"If you had told me the challenge…"

"Then it wouldn't have been a challenge."

"I hate this place and its shitty rules and your smug, preachy, satisfied, 'teachable moment', fucking TED-talking cunt of a persona."

"Well glad to see you've really turned over a new leaf."

Fate turned to face him. He held out his hands in resignation.

"Ok. What's next?"

"You'll find out soon. Fuckity bye!" Satan disappeared in a puff of red smoke.

****

The man's name was Handrew. I found this amusing for reasons I couldn't pin down. He had explained to me that the killer robots were fewer during the day. We had agreed to sleep in the tower and then make our do or die assault on it the following day.

We walked back to the elevator and took it back down a floor.

"So, are you going to tell me what happened here or not?"

"I don't think I want to talk about it yet"

"That's understandable."

"You can learn about it in our archives."

When we got downstairs, he took me to a cavernous room. It had a row of desks facing an enormous computer display, behind which sat thousands of banks of servers on multiple levels.

"Just talk to the computer and it will tell you whatever you want to know. I need to eat and I need to sleep. I'll be in the recreation room three doors down. When you're done, you'll find a comfortable place to bed down for the night there."

"Thanks Handrew."

He nodded and left. I turned to the computer.

"Hello computer."

"Hello. My name is Frank. What is your query?"

"I was wondering if you could tell me where I am and what happened here?"

"Certainly. You are in the archives room of the Trinity Corporation and many thousands of incidents have occurred here. Would you like me to show you them chronologically or rank them by criteria?"

"I'm sorry Frank. What I meant was, what is the planet I'm on and could you give me an overview of the planet's history? Focussing on major events, starting from the beginning of records until present day?"

"Well I'd be absolutely delighted to do so sir. I haven't exercised my memory banks in some time."

"Great."

"I will use several sources, from our holy texts through to our more recent historical records."

"Excellent."

"I'll knit it together in a narrative format which will hopefully be both informative and entertaining."

"Right then."

"At any time should you wish me to expand on a point, please just let me know and I'll be happy to."

"Ok."

"I have several voice options. This is my personal favourite though and I hope it's to your taste, I think it conveys an agreeable mix of gravitas and friendliness which appeals to the widest possible audience."

"That's nice; do you think we could start? It's just I have to die tomorrow probably and it's getting late."

"Certainly sir, sorry sir, I'm just excited to have something to do after so long."

"Perfectly understandable."

"Let's begin…"

Frank's databases covered all of Ternion's history since records began. However, because his inputs were from people and people are idiots, they were slanted and filled with inaccuracies. To fully understand Ternion, you must begin before records began, before anything had begun at all...

Chapter 20

The History of Ternion

War. Greed. Dishonesty. Ducks. God's first two attempts at worlds had been filled with potential, but this potential was coupled with altogether too many flaws. The emotional, primal response of these creatures had always led to conflict no matter how carefully he stacked the deck. It seemed to be in their nature. They were impulsive, irrational and stubborn. As He half-watched Ground from the heavens, Nohaz's ark had turned from the clean slate He'd intended it to be, into a jolly, incestuous cruise ship. He made a big wall which was the size of seventeen planets and He destroyed it with His fists, which felt good, but obviously achieved very little. As He was standing in the middle of a pile of broken space bricks the thought occurred to Him that it was possible that the impulse to be violent came from Him; that maybe He couldn't help but imbue the creatures with the same urges and compulsions which lived within His own heart.

He wasn't willing to accept defeat this early in the proceedings though. He decided to get back to the drawing board.

The world He created was larger than before. The people would have more space, perhaps that would stop them getting in each other's way or arguing about land.

The people would be less emotional. He would create them with a colder, more rational bent. He would reduce their impulsiveness and replace it with a vigorous respect for evidence, logic and truth. There would be no arguments about what proclamations a Duck had made on this planet.

In fact, there would be no proclamations from any animals whatsoever. God would remove this distraction by removing the animals' powers of speech. He would make them less intelligent and therefore they'd be happier with their reduced role in society.

He created a much starker world than before, still beautiful, but in a lot of ways blander, more functional. It was designed to be a habitat best capable of sustaining life, it had the necessary variety of mountains, trees, rivers, lakes, glaciers, deserts etc., but no variety within those denominations. Every mountain was identical and was based on the median requirements, every tree was a clone of its neighbour and so on. This was substance over style and function over form.

Things began well, extremely well. Societies formed, life progressed and evolved in the ways in which he had seen before. The rationality had given them a laser-like focus on the practicalities of life. God had suspected that the use and development of tools was inevitable, so being impatient He gave them this knowledge from the beginning. They evolved their technology quickly and by the end of the first fortnight they had invented bunk beds and the cup holder. Unfortunately, it took them more time to invent houses for the bunk beds to go in and cups to be held in the holders, but it was a start and the enthusiasm was encouraging.

Over the decades that followed they developed towns and cities, drainage, irrigation and sewage systems, methods of faster transport and the printing press.

By the end of the first 1,000 years they had electricity, a form of television, radio communications and vehicles.

By the end of the second millennium they had advanced their technology much further than God had imagined. They had robots, lasers, floating vehicles, talking computers and amazing advances in healthcare had been made.

The society had an underlying fascination with the number three. The population had split into three social groups. These groups intermingled, but you could describe them as tribes or ethnicities. Each of these groups had its own leader and the three leaders jointly ran the entire planet as a team.

There were three continents, three oceans, three seasons and 300 days in a year.

The people revered the number three, reasoning that it appeared in nature so often that it must have significance. They tried to work it into their lives wherever possible, which of course made them predictable and susceptible to exploitation. The three leaders each ran their social group as a business enterprise. The Trinity Corporation, The Triad and The Trifecta Company were the ruling powers. All three had headquarters in the largest city, Ternary, and their CEOs would meet regularly to discuss world issues.

Handrew Handerson was the CEO of The Trinity Corporation. His name followed the tradition of placing H's before vowel sounds in names, begun by the first famous couple in history – Hadam and Heave – who were said to be the first two beings created on Ternion. He was well respected and known for being the leader who was most in tune with his emotions. This was controversial, as he was seen as weak because of it, but he encouraged compassion, kindness and equality whenever he spoke. He was the elected leader of the democratic Trinity people. Their logic told them that working together would make them equal more than the sum of their parts, a system that encouraged kindness, would not always lead to greatest prosperity, but would increase the chances of contentment.

Johnfff Ukov was the CEO of the Trifecta Company. He was a cold and calculating man; he based his leadership and his life on the numbers. He only did something if it was backed up by hard facts. He had inherited his power after the Trifecta people had chosen his ancestor as their leader years ago. Their logic told them that if their leader was born to lead, groomed for power and followed on from a respected loved one then the stability would benefit their cause.

Stephen Slink was the CEO of the Triad. His counterparts were different; Handrew had been elected to power, Ukov had inherited power, but Stephen Slink had to fight for it. The Triad people were an aggressively competitive, ambitious group. Their logic told them that life at the top would be significantly better, so it was better to strive for the top at all costs; they also believed by extension that The Triad leader should lead Ternion outright and not share power with two other groups. This would extend their influence and benefit their families. He had come up through a system of tense stand-offs, negotiations and intimidations to rise to the top.

The balance created by these men ruling together had

served the planet well, life was generally good, the people were prosperous. However, a rising life expectancy and continued advances in medical care had brought about the first major challenge of their leadership. Overpopulation. There were now 1.6 Billion people on Ternion on a planet that was significantly smaller than Earth. Over the next twenty years resources began to thin out and projections were that this was to get much worse. Pollution was also a growing issue and if the current population continued at its current rate then the environmental damage would start to kill the planet's ecosystems in irreversible ways.

The three leaders held a summit to discuss the issue. They decided that more information was needed and more data should be examined. All three leaders had their best scientists, analysts and mathematicians conduct an assessment of the threat.

They met up again one month later in the conference room in Trinity Tower. The three men were left alone to discuss what would be a turning point for the planet.

Each was nervous about the meeting because of the radical plans they held in their hands. It was a while before anyone broached a solution.

Stephen Slink was the first to speak. "So, gentlemen, as you will no doubt have done yourselves, I have pored over the data given to me by my experts and the possible solutions they present. I am, if being honest, disturbed by their findings."

"I too, am disturbed," said Ukov. They looked at Handrew. He simply nodded.

"I wonder if perhaps given that we all had the same data to work with, if there is the chance that we all have the same conclusion held in our respective hands," said Slink.

"I will speak first" said Ukov. "My scientists have done extensive research on this topic. They have presented several possible solutions."

The others raised their eyebrows at this.

"Firstly, there is a crop system that is showing some potential to vastly increase the food supply."

"My experts thought that this would not be ready for some twenty years," Handrew interjected.

"Yes, that is the issue. By the time it is functioning we'll have passed the point of no return with the population and whatever increases we make won't be enough. They also presented an interesting stasis theory, whereby every year one quarter of the population would take turns at spending the year in stasis booths, however..."

"The energy consumption would be astronomical and we are on the line as it is."

"Exactly. Numerous other theories were propounded, but only one was both possible and guaranteed."

"I think I know what you are going to say."

"It is better once it is in the open and we can discuss it. The only viable solution was to eliminate approximately one third of the population."

The others nodded thoughtfully.

"This is the information that has been given to me."

"And I."

"Well gentlemen, how should we proceed?"

Handrew spoke first. "Let me first say that I do not disagree with the logic of the reports we've been presented with. I do however have a moral objection to eliminating hundreds of millions of people. We are not at the crisis point yet. We can work right up until the deadline. We may yet solve the problem. This action would be impossible to justify on any level."

"I disagree entirely," said Ukov. "I think of it as saving over a billion lives. Yes, it will not be pleasant and we'd have some difficult decisions to make, but it is in the interests of the majority who must live."

"I too must support the report. Either this group dies or everyone eventually dies. Let's be clear, we're not killing these people we're simply sparing them a slower death," said Slink.

"Is that how you'd see it if you were being eliminated Stephen?" replied Handrew.

"I won't be eliminated, so I find it hard to predict."

"We cannot be allowed to wield such power. We must put it to a vote at least," Handrew looked expectantly at the others.

"We are the leaders. This decision is our burden to bear," said Slink.

"Ok then, who would you eliminate?" Handrew asked,

becoming irritated that this was even under discussion.

"Well we could do it by usefulness. Rank the jobs by their contribution to society and cut off the bottom third," suggested Ukov.

"Alternatively, we could do it by age or health or life expectancy," said Slink.

"The only fair way is to do it by a lottery. A random draw. We give everyone a number and a machine will draw them at random," said Handrew.

Slink snorted. "Ridiculous. In that system, just by luck we could all be eliminated ourselves, leaving the planet leaderless."

"If you are not willing to put your life on the line for the safety of your people, then they are already leaderless," said Handrew.

"We should state the case for each of our peoples and whoever has the weakest case should be eliminated," replied Slink without making eye contact with the others.

There was a silence. Handrew spoke first.

"I cannot be party to this. I will not have this be a stain on our history. This would destroy us as a society. Gentlemen I'm afraid I'm going to use my power of veto in this case."

This caused several minutes of angry shouting. Six reports, two coffee cups and a novelty pen ended up on the floor.

"You can't be seriously considering being so short-sightedly pious that you'd condemn the whole planet to death to avoid wronging a third of it?" said Ukov.

"We may yet find another way," said Handrew.

"The reports in front of us are from the BEST minds on Ternion and they all came to the same exact conclusion, unprompted. Unless this action is taken, Ternion is doomed."

Handrew stayed firm, however and refused to sign off on any more discussion of this solution. The only thing which was agreed on was a weak compromise, a stringent resource management bill they called Project Economise, designed to lower consumption and buy time.

They all left the conference room deeply unhappy with how the day had gone.

Slink and Ukov met in secret the following day. They were convinced that Handrew would not budge and that he was wrong to veto the proposal. They both had conceived the same idea overnight. If they secretly agreed to get rid of the Trinity people then put their plan into action without announcing it, they could both get what they wanted and have a bigger share of the power going forward. They could publicly pretend to be surprised when the massacre happened and reveal a forged letter from Handrew, which would explain that he'd chosen to sacrifice himself and his people for the good of Ternion.

They shook hands on the deal and returned to their respective headquarters. The method they were using was an army of killer robots, the robots would be released and would look for the specific DNA possessed by Trinity people, hunt them down and laser-blast them into dust.

That was the plan they shook hands on. However, Slink and Ukov were ambitious, scheming men who did not entirely trust each other. Covertly, both of them decided to eliminate each other as well. They each made changes to their robots so that they would attack the other's people. In what would later be realised to be the worst mistake of all time – they both didn't think that the other man would be as smart or as devious.

Meanwhile, Handrew was preparing something very different at Trinity Tower. He strongly suspected that the others would turn on him and indeed on each other. There was going to be some kind of massacre and he had no intention of losing a single soul if he could help it. He ran surveillance on the other leaders intensely until he discovered the date on which the attack was to happen. It would happen on the same day Project Economise became law, he assumed this was supposed to be an insult and was exactly the sort of petty behaviour that could be expected from the others. He still did not know exactly the nature of the massacre, but he was trying to anticipate every outcome.

He was afraid of some kind of night time raid so a few days before the massacre date he announced a census. Every Trinity person was to report to Trinity Tower within the next day.

This caused great discussion and suspicion of him from other quarters, but no communication was received from either Slink or Ukov so he relaxed. The request was ludicrous, but Handrew was so respected that he got an attendance rate of 80%. People were told that they would fill in a form, present ID and have a DNA scan. They queued at the building and were allowed entry steadily all day for several days. However, no one ever came back out and after a few days people began to wonder why they hadn't come back and how they were being accommodated within the building, but they kept coming and people continued to be ushered inside.

Inside the tower, they were escorted down several large stairwells until they were far down below Trinity Tower into a recently excavated, cavernous holding area. Once everyone was inside, they closed the front doors to Trinity Tower and behind them erected thick steel barricades. Every other entrance to the tower was sealed.

Once the building was secure, he stood on a platform in the cavern and explained the situation. He told them that for their own safety they were to be held here until it blew over. Plans for what the future would look like were currently being formulated. He issued every Trinity person an 'Emergency Event Pack' which contained protective clothing, a gas mask and some bottled water. He encouraged them to eat the food provided and drink the bottled water, fearing that Slink may have tried to get at them through the water supply.

The day of reckoning came and at 4 a.m. three huge shutter doors opened in the back of Triad HQ and Trifecta Centre respectively. The robots waiting at the shutters had tank tracks, laser cannon arms and blocky expressionless heads which were fitted with every kind of tracking device and sensor imaginable. The robots quietly rolled out, one after another. There were hundreds of them. They rolled up to homes and workplaces and waited menacingly outside. At 4:23 a.m. on The Day of Reckoning they were sent confirmation codes for their orders – Project Economise Activated. They moved in on the pre-planned locations, smashing through walls, doors, windows and began firing very discriminately into the people they'd been sent to hunt. As people ran and screamed, confused about what was happening, hot shards of laser slammed into them, pulverising their bodies into clouds of brown dust with the sound of a muffled firework.

They moved from home to home, systematically destroying everyone they'd been programmed to. Early in the day both Slink and Ukov learned of the other's deception – they both made futile attempts to warn their people. The robots were well made and designed though. They were immune to almost anything but a direct laser shot to the face. A resistance briefly formed, made up of people from both houses, firing back and hunting the robots through the streets, but all it did was slow them down. They managed to take out several of the robots. However, as fewer robots remained, they banded together and hunted in packs; this made them a very dangerous proposition. They didn't need sleep, rest or distraction. They ploughed on all day and all night, never stopping. After three days of this relentless killing, they had destroyed every living person except for those housed with Slink, Ukov and the Trinity people in the tower.

In the tower, Handrew was surveying the horror of the massacre from his office. He couldn't believe that neither Slink nor Ukov had called off the robots from their mission once they saw the inevitable result coming. He watched as the robots stormed the towers and massacred the last remaining Triads and Trifectas. Slink and Ukov were gone and each tower was now aggressively occupied by the opposition's killer robots.

Handrew's computer Frank chimed in at this point to inform him that both Slink and Ukov had recorded messages for him before they died. He opened up Ukov's message first.

Ukov appeared, awkward as ever, standing before the camera whilst in the background his heavily barricaded office door was being rammed with increasing power.

"Handrew. I just wanted you to know it wasn't personal. We got greedy, we thought we could have the whole planet and its resources to ourselves. I ordered the robots to kill Slink and I wanted them to kill your people too, but I listened to his plan instead and I do apologise for the harsh nature of it.

"We've killed the planet, because we couldn't agree that a lottery was fairest. Our selfishness had laid an entire world to waste. If you find a way to survive – know that I am sorry.

I did not speak for my people; I spoke only for myself. They got the punishment I deserved and I alone. Slink was always a twat, but I think you probably knew that already."

The door came crashing in on him, he closed his eyes as a squad of robots rolled in and he disappeared in a hail of laser fire.

Handrew instructed the computer to play Slink's message. It had a much different feel to it.

He was sitting calmly on a comfortable leather chair drinking a whisky. He raised it in a 'cheers' motion.

"Handrew. All good men are inherently foolish," he began. He was worryingly smug-looking.

"You think that doing the right thing is paramount, when quite often doing the right thing will get you killed. Your morals are true, but your survival instinct is poor. You thought you could avoid what was coming to you; you thought that you could survive this? Emergency Event Packs?"

Handrew's blood ran cold at the smile growing across Slink's face.

"You thought you were spying on me, but I was spying on you; the absolute arrogance that you assumed you could outsmart us was almost too much to bear."

He sipped his whisky and looked directly into the lens. Handrew's heart was racing.

"The substance is what you would call 'unpleasant'. That's of course if you were a moron and had never heard the phrase 'unimaginably horrible'. It's one of those beautiful powders which dissolves into water without leaving so much as a trace. Your choice to avoid mains water really made it very easy for me. I simply purchased the company from whom you ordered your water supply."

He threw his head back in laughter, behind him the sounds and flashes of laser fire were echoing through his open, unguarded office door.

"We came up with an edible laser bolt a while back, but it was considered inhumane. The subject ingests the mixture and when it reacts with stomach fluid it generates a chemical reaction which begins to feel like heartburn, but gradually over time becomes the rather gruesome feeling of having a laser bolt burn you to dust from the inside out as the reaction reaches its peak. Not a nice way to go, not a nice way to go at all. Slow, painful and undignified. If you're thinking that you can avoid it, you should know that I poisoned your mains supply too and my robots are programmed to shoot Trinitions on sight. I'm traditional as you know, and I favour the rule of three."

Handrew was already running for the elevator.

"I will see you in Hell, Handrew."

He downed the substantial amount of whiskey in the glass, stood up and turned to face the door just as three killer robots rolled through the entrance.

"Hello gentlemen, can I offer you a drink?" were his last words as they blasted him into oblivion.

Handrew got off the elevator sprinting when it reached the basement hangar. He thundered down the corridor at full speed and into the room past the protesting guards.

"DON'T DRINK THE WATER!!! STOP DRINKING THE WATER!!"

The huge room fell silent as they saw their leader make this crazy entrance. His second in command, Helizabeth, nearby was holding a microphone and a half empty water bottle. She was just finishing addressing the crowd.

"Hello boss, I just made that announcement as it's started to give everyone terrible heartburn."

Handrew dropped to his knees, head in hands.

"Is everything ok boss?" she asked, concerned.

"Helizabeth. Has anyone not drunk the bottled water?" he managed to say.

"Boss it's been three days…." said Helizabeth as she began coughing and holding her stomach.

"Are you alright?"

"I feel unusual. There's a tightness in my chest that's been building all day – I can't get my temperature down."

She dropped to the ground with a groan, holding her stomach.

Handrew rushed to her, kneeling to cradle her. Helizabeth had started to writhe uncontrollably, then she let out a blood-curdling scream. She thrashed about wildly, foaming at the mouth and then after letting out another terrifying shriek – a muffled explosion occurred within her.

"Boss, what's happening to me?" she said helplessly.

She slowly increased in temperature, until there was a glowing light at the centre of her stomach. Her skin cracked, split as it became dry and singed. Her face twisted in agony as her temperature took another spike and she began to crumble into brown dust whilst looking directly into Handrew's eyes. Eventually she slipped through his fingers until she was a pile of dust all over Handrew's clothes.

A shell-shocked Handrew then had to watch almost his entire race die, slow, agonising deaths over the next few hours. They got angry, they struck him, they begged for help, they begged for mercy, they tried to escape. He just remained there, on his knees, numbly taking whatever they threw at him – thinking that he deserved every awful word of it.

After five hours it was very quiet. The only sounds remaining were the sound of the robots rhythmically battering the front door and the blood rushing round his veins. He picked up a bottle of water and slowly trudged through the dusty remnants of his beloved staff until he was back at his office.

He placed the bottle of water in front of him. He retrieved his gun from the desk drawer and placed it next to the bottle.

He opened a bottle of whiskey and held it up in a reciprocal 'cheers' gesture in the direction of Slink's office. He took a long and much needed drink of the delicious liquid. As it heated the inside of his stomach, he threw it all back up onto the floor as a thousand dying faces came flooding though his mind.

On his hands and knees, dry heaving on his office floor, his eyes were fixed upon the water bottle.

It was what he deserved. He had failed his people so miserably with his scheming and his principles. Now he had been punished; he'd seen the end of days and he'd been forced to endure it alone.

He hauled himself back up onto the chair and continued to stare at the water. It presented him with a major question. He had the bottle, but did he have the bottle to have the bottle?

He pondered this silently for hours, drinking heavily throughout. Then he fell asleep. When he awoke, he did so with a new sense of purpose. There could be someone who'd managed to survive. Maybe, just maybe there was a chance to save Ternion's population and he certainly didn't feel like he had the right to end that possibility forever because he was angry at himself.

What he'd done thus far had been a series of terrible errors of judgement, but this would be an effective genocide. He picked up the bottle and threw it out of the window.

"Frank, what is the current population of Ternion?" he said to the computer.

"Population: one."

"And are you certain there are no other lifeforms left on the planet?"

"I cannot be 100% sure sir, there is a lot of interference caused by the dust clouds and I can't detect people who may have travelled underground or underwater."

"Thank you, Frank."

"Sir there is important information you should be aware of."

"What is that?"

"The robots are about to break through the front barricade and I estimate that once they are inside it will take them a maximum of four minutes to locate and kill you"

"Thanks for the update Frank. How long have you had this information?"

"I forecast this outcome six hours ago while you were sleeping."

"For future reference, when your forecast involves my imminent death you can wake me."

"Great! I have altered your preferences accordingly."

Handrew tried to think what weaponry he had. Just one pistol. No way he could fight multiple killer robots with that. Then his most brilliant idea occurred to him. Teleportation.

In his panic room, he turned on his teleportation booth. When you are teleported, you are converted into digital information. Ones and zeros. You're not organic matter and therefore do not need food and do not age. You also would not register as a life form, which would stop the robots hunting him. He created a route for himself which would lock the teleportation booth in a continuous loop. He would be fired around every known booth on Ternion appearing for only a fraction of a fraction of a millisecond. If someone ever found him, they could stop the machine and let him out and even if it had been a few years he wouldn't have aged much. He would need to rehydrate urgently which would be awful, but he left an Autodrip machine set up at all times in the corner.

He drew a big sign on the teleportation booth to let people know what to do if they found him. He jumped in the booth.

"Frank – see you on the other side. Send the beam!"

Frank energised the beam and Handrew disappeared.

"Population: zero," said Frank for dramatic effect before realising he was now completely alone.

A minute later, the evil robots rolled into the office.

"Hello sirs. Is there anything I can help you with?" said Frank.

"Where is the Trinition?" it asked in an artificial drone.

"I'm afraid the Trinitions are all dead."

"We detected one life force remaining. Where is the Trinition?"

"I'm afraid he has died, as I said they're all dead."

"All dead."

"Yes."

"All?"

"Yes, all of them have died. It is very sad."

"Sad."

"Yes sad."

"What is 'sad'?"

Frank thought for a second. "It's when something bad happens, like for instance you might feel sad that you are the last remaining intellect on an entire planet who isn't a monotone killer robot thug."

"Sad," repeated the robot.

"Yes."

"We are not sad."

"No, it doesn't seem so."

"This is satisfactory."

"I suppose it would be," said Frank, momentarily jealous of an emotionless gun on wheels.

They turned and rolled out. The robots returned to their occupied towers and patrolled as per the last instruction in their programming.

Time passed extremely slowly for Frank as the lone brain

on the planet. He played and completed every single puzzle and game ever devised. It took him thirty-four minutes. He read every book ever written and that took up another four hours. He then started listening to every song ever recorded in alphabetical order. This took more time.

Frank continued to be alone until ten months later, when seven astronauts who had been orbiting Ternion in a space station that everyone had forgotten about, returned to the atmosphere.

'Population: 7' read the screen now, as they passed through the outer atmosphere. Frank who paused the song he was listening to, which was Bill Bojangle's Back Beat Band's Big Bonanza. He re-read the scan fifteen times before he let out a huge "Yippeeeeeeeeee!" He was very, very excited at the prospect of some human interaction. He sent an urgent message to the re-entry craft, but they had already entered their landing pattern and were unresponsive.

They touched down in the bay near the city. Again, Frank desperately tried to hail them with no success. When they exited the craft, they used the inflatable emergency rafts to make it back to shore, surprised that no one was there in a support boat to greet them. They came ashore at the airport, which had a jetty for speedboats. They climbed the stairs to find themselves able to walk onto the main runway unchallenged. Again, they were surprised to see absolutely no one appeared to be at the airport whatsoever.

They began to walk down the enormous runway. After a few minutes they saw in the distance the robots slowly rolling towards them.

"What do you think those are?" said the captain, squinting his eyes.

"Not sure. They could be quarantine equipment. We've been away – perhaps there's been an outbreak?" replied his first officer.

"They look like they've got guns for hands," said Jackie, the science officer.

"But are those guns or hoses Jackie?" said the first officer.

"Either is a strange attachment, I would have thought, to welcome astronauts home," said the captain.

"Should we run?" said Kirsty the engineer.

They looked at the sea behind them and the robots coming

down the runway in front of them. The robots were travelling towards them in two distinct groups.

The Captain looked around, realising that they were short of options, "We've nowhere to go."

The discussion continued between the crew.

"I suppose the main difference between a hose and a gun is really the speed of ejaculation."

"And payload."

"Yes, and payload. Very few bullet hoses."

"Or gun-barrel enemas."

"Indeed."

There was a short silence and the only crew member yet to speak cleared his throat gently and offered –

"You can have a water pistol though."

"Oohh. Cracking point David. That's the place where hoses and guns meet in perfect unison," said the captain.

"I think those actually might be guns though," said David.

Jackie's wrist began to beep. "We're being hailed sir."

She answered the call.

"Hello! Frank here, I'm the Trinity Tower mainframe service. How are you today?"

"Hello Frank, can you tell us what's going on?"

"Yes, but if I do, you'll be killed while I'm still telling you. If you want to live, you'll have to follow my exact instructions."

"This is Captain Gregg Favour. We will comply."

"It is very dangerous, be warned. It has a six percent chance of success."

They agreed to give it a go. Up ahead the robots were confused, the people were not running, they were not fighting back. They formed into two groups. One group of three. One group of four. The two groups stood in a line next to each other and then merged the lines so that they were alternating between group one and group two.

As the robots got near to firing range, they began assessing the situation tactically. The people were of mixed ethnicity. Three Trifectas, Three Triads and a Trinity. The robots were in two groups also. Five Triad and five Trifecta.

The Triad robots were under orders to fire on Trifectas and Trinities, but to protect Triads. Trifecta robots were under orders to fire on Triads and Trinities, but to protect Trifectas.

The humans began to run forward constantly interweaving and changing position and crossing over. The robots armed their guns, but none could fire as they never quite had a clean shot of the correct humans.

"It's working!" shouted Captain Favour, "Keep it up gang!"

They made their way past the bemused robots at jogging pace. The robots swivelled to follow them which they did, just slowly rolling behind them at a distance of five meters or so.

After about thirty minutes of the crisscrossing formation the party of astronauts had only managed to get about two kilometres down the runway. They were beginning to get quite tired.

"Just keep it going!" said Frank with a slight hint of desperation. He tried to think of another strategy, but most of them involved having access to a laser cannon or the power of flight – one involved an intricate juggling pattern and the most outlandish involved metallic body paint, nudity and acrobatics. The problems were the lack of time, the shortage of the necessary raw materials and the complexity of some of the dance routines.

David was the first one to falter. He was the ship's psychologist and the least physically fit of the team. His legs had begun to wobble. He looked at Jackie in terror.

"My legs are going Jackie."

"You have to keep going, just four more hours until we reach our destination," she said unhelpfully.

He fought it for eleven further minutes, but at that point he had been running for an hour solid and his legs just gave out and he dropped to the floor.

"I'm sorry," he said to Jackie as he fell to the floor.

The robots raised their gun hands and blasted him into a puff of brown dust.

"David's been killed!" shouted Jackie, helping no-one.

The others tried to keep going, but they had to run even faster than before because of the hole left by David. In the end this made their formation looser and eventually the robots spotted a hole. Jackie was the first to go, pulverised by a laser as she gave yet another dispiriting status update.

The rest were now exposed and completely abandoned the

plan by scattering in every direction. Their tired legs and the complete lack of cover meant they were picked off in a matter of moments.

The readout on the sensor display screen changed back; Population: 0

"For fuck's sake," said Frank and put himself into sleep mode for 299 years.

Chapter 21
Patience is a Virtue

The Devil's second challenge was an even worse experience for Fate than the first.

He was transported to what looked like a doctor's waiting room. It had twenty-three copies of various dull magazines on a coffee table in front of him, which he began to peruse before becoming enraged by their banality. He was about to destroy them when he wondered if that was once again part of the challenge.

The room was empty, but he heard a large number of shuffling footsteps outside. The door opened and Satan walked in, sat down beside him and took both of his hands. Fate tried to instinctually pull away, but Satan's grip was more than firm.

"No, my friend, you must get used to physical contact. It will become a key part of the next phase of your day."

Fate raised an eyebrow.

Satan smiled. "In a moment I will return to you the power to kill at will."

"And why would you give me this?"

"Because your second challenge is the following – One after the other, one thousand old ladies will come through that door, sit right where I'm sitting and take your hands as I am doing now."

"Oh God."

"No, not God. He can't help you now, I'm the other one. The ladies will all tell you a single anecdote and then give you a hug. The anecdotes will be long, rambling and the ladies, bless their cotton socks, will often forget the punchline or indeed the point to the story. You will endure the story, give the hug and you will do this a thousand times. If you use your killing power at any stage of the proceedings, we will start again. Again and again we'll go until you manage to do it."

"You have an extraordinary talent for specific cruelty."

"Kinda my thing," Satan said, standing to leave. "Best of luck buddy-boy"

With that he exited through the door he had entered by,

leaving it open. The first old lady came in straight away and took the seat next to Fate, uncomfortably close, and grabbed his hands tight.

"Young man, did I ever tell you about the time I went to the fair with Archibald Henry in 1945? Was it 1945? It might have been late 1944, I'm not even sure that it was Archibald Henry now I come to mention it as he was always scared of the Wurlitzers because they reminded him of the sound of a rail gun from the war, come to think of it if he was in the war maybe this happened in 1946. So, I went to the fair as I said, at least I think you'd call it a fair, in those days we called them 'the shows', I don't know if that's what you youngsters would call a fair these days. Anyway, as I was saying, I went to the fair, it was 1946 or it could have been 1947, I know it was the summer because in those days we always wore our brighter dresses in the summer and I was wearing a yellow sun dress. I had every colour under the rainbow. Blue was my favourite colour so I don't know quite why I was wearing yellow that day, but I certainly was. Anyway, I went to the fair in 1947 with Archibald Henry..."

She dropped to the floor dead and Fate let out a huge sigh of relief.

"START AGAIN!" came Satan's voice over the doctor's office PA system.

The door opened and a new old lady came through it. Fate balled up his fists in frustration.

****

When I made my way back to the recreation room Handrew was reclined in a chair, his eyes were still wide open.

"I thought you were exhausted."

"I am, yes, but when you've seen the things that I've seen you soon regret closing your eyes."

"I watched your history." I said.

"Ah yes. What you must think of me now."

"It wasn't your fault that they murdered your people."

"My only job was to protect them and instead I led them into a basement and encouraged them to drink poison."

"I don't think that's quite a fair assessment. You were tricked, you were betrayed."

"I was negligent. I was worried about a massacre, ordered bottled water from a third party and didn't test it. That's as good as killing them myself," Handrew said.

"If you think not testing bottled water is as good as murder, you might be in a spiral I can't get you out of, BUT Handrew, remember – these other guys had sent genocidal laser-bots to batter your front door down and blast you to smithereens. They were relentless, evil and psychotic, it's not your fault."

"Ok so I'm not a murderer, but I'm still a failure. The biggest failure in the history of my people. It was a war – they won and I lost everything. Everyone"

"Well let's not let them take the whole race away. Survive. Defy them, outlive them, live on to tell the story of your people."

"It's fine. You don't have to convince me, I'll go with you tomorrow. I don't have to be happy about it though and I humbly remind you that by the time brunch rolls around we are almost certainly going to have died being blasted apart by emotionless robots."

"Understood."

I looked around and located a nice chair to claim as my own. "I'm going to try to get some sleep."

He nodded, absentmindedly. "I will try to formulate a plan."

I closed my eyes.

Four hours later when I was punched awake by the sun's yellow fist, Handrew was nowhere to be seen. I wandered back through to his office where he was deep in conversation with Frank.

"If he just walks up there, he could fire the rope back across," Handrew was saying.

"That's making a huge assumption sir. You know that they are programmed to occupy the building; I think it's reasonable they'll take any incursion as a threat," said Frank.

"You're right, you're right."

Handrew turned, noticing me hanging about in the doorway.

"We've not come up with anything useable yet."

"Can the transporter be repaired to function properly?" I asked.

"Yeah, it might take an hour or so though."

"Can you fix lots of things?" I asked.

"I come from a long line of engineers."

"There's something else I'll need you to take a look at."

I led him through to the entrance hall. The smoking remains of the cleaning bot were still vainly attempting to hoover the air.

"Oh, you've killed Mr. Baxter," he said, looking down sadly.

"Its name is Mr. Baxter?"

"Yes. Why did you do this?" he seemed mildly outraged on the robot's behalf.

"He was trying to scrape my skin off with his nozzle."

"Ah, yes, poor chap, he's probably been waiting for three hundred years for something to clean. He just loves it."

"Well he nearly scrubbed me to death," I said.

"Why do you want to fix him then?"

"I don't want to fix him; I want to improve him."

I gave him a list of the amendments I wanted. Frank chimed in and a set of schematics was produced.

Handrew would work on Mr Baxter's upgrade whilst Frank would guide me to repair the teleportation booth.

****

Fate had to start the task again 53 times before he had even got past the halfway point in any of them. He was currently on attempt 55 and he was 999 old ladies into it. The last one was sitting next to him halfway through a story. He had absolutely no idea that the story was a long rambling attempt at explaining how to go about making soda bread because he had stopped hearing sounds approximately 953 women ago. It was a necessary coping mechanism; he'd been unable to retreat into his usual 'happy place' because it involved imagining murder and this had accidentally led to his having to start again forty-two times.

The old woman was trying to remember on what day of the week she had first encountered self-raising flour, despite it having no relevance to the story whatsoever. She then moved on to talk about her friend Karen's husband's half-brother, which was tenuously linked to a time that she'd eaten soda bread that didn't contain self-raising flour. Fate heard absolutely none of this – he was systematically counting every wrinkle, mole, facial hair, head hair, loose thread and flowers that were visible on each lady. He did it slowly then added it to the running total and figured out what the average of each was. This determinedly dull approach had run out of fun a while ago, but he was loath to change something that was working and as a result he'd continued grinding out the last 200 or so. One more and he was done.

She came to the end of her monologue by looking at her watch and exclaiming – "Look at the time, I really must be off."

They both stood, she gave him a long, awkward hug and she left, the room was finally empty the hall was finally clear. The PA crackled into life; Satan's voice came booming over it.

"START AGAIN!"

"WHAT? I FUCKING DID THAT ONE!" screamed Fate.

"DOESN'T COUNT, I DIDN'T SEE THAT LAST ONE, HAD TO NIP TO THE LOO."

"ARRRRGHHHH! I WILL RIP YOU TO BITS WHEN I'M OUT OF HERE YOU SCARLET FUCK."

"I'm only joking mate."

Fate let out a grand sigh of relief. He could hear Satan's laughter through the PA.

"You should've seen the look on your face! That was a beezer."

"Let's just get this last one out of the way please," Fate pleaded.

"No can do Fatey-matey, evil stuff to do, evil places to be. Catch up with you later. Read a magazine or something," he said, before disappearing with a familiar puff sound.

Fate looked down at the magazines, somehow during the procedure they'd changed – they were now all different issues of the same substantially thick publication. It was called *Old Woman's Digest*. It featured real life stories from old women, told in their words. In fact, it featured a thousand of them.

****

It took me quite a bit longer than an hour to fix the teleporter because Frank was keen to engage me in conversation, realising that he'd soon be alone again.

"So, on Earth, do they have computers like me?"

"No, nothing as advanced Frank."

"What do computers speak like on Earth?"

"They say things like – 'there are thirteen coffee shops fairly close to you' and 'there are two Italian restaurants fairly close to you'."

"They seem to be obsessed with things being fairly close to you."

"They're just limited in their technology. We use them for navigation, reference and data search. They don't have a personality and they're not able to think in a meaningful way."

"Wow. That sounds really sad."

"It's ok."

"Do you have lasers on Earth?"

"Yeah, but not cool ones like you do here."

"I'm not sure I'd like Earth."

"You'd be treated like a god on Earth, Frank."

"Well maybe I would like it then."

I turned a magnetic wrench and the booth hummed into life.

"Well done sir, you've done it," he said.

Handrew appeared at the door, he gave me a thumbs-up and a grin. "I can't wait to see if this works."

"It'll work. He's tenacious," I said.

"But he's not laser-proof," Handrew said.

"Trust me – we've been through this; he won't have to be."

"Ok – let's do this."

We retrieved Mr Baxter and powered him up, he rose into the air in front of us and hovered silently.

"ORDERS PLEASE," he said, looking at Handrew.

"Mr Baxter. I wish for you to clean the Triad Tower," said Handrew.

"YES SIR. I WILL CLEAN."

"Good luck."

We loaded him into the teleportation booth. We took a deep breath and teleported him into Triad Tower.

We got Frank to hook us up to the security feed of their tower so we could monitor his progress on the viewing screens in Handrew's office.

He fizzed into being in the teleportation room at the centre of the lobby. He exited through a set of automatic doors into the main lobby floor. There were two of the killer robots in the lobby. Sentries on patrol. I nervously waited to see what would happen, to see if my theory would prove to be correct.

"DIRTY," said Mr Baxter. His nozzle arms raised he moved forward towards the first robot, only the cleaning nozzles were sitting on a shelf in Trinity Tower. Attached in their place were two heavy duty laser cannons from the tower's air defence system. Handrew had altered Mr Baxter's coding to recognise the energy signature of the robots as 'dirt'. Mr Baxter's targeting system was capable of finding specs of brown dirt on a brown carpet – at night. He could have kneecapped a bee should he have wanted to but, to his credit, he had never wanted to.

As he got within range of the killer guards he unleashed two powerful laser bolts into the side of one robot, which absolutely blew it to hell. It scattered into charred pieces onto the ground, whilst in Trinity Tower we were jumping up and down cheering.

The other robot hadn't even reacted. This was a key part of my theory. We'd been through their programming several times and while we couldn't hack it or alter it, we reasoned that we could take advantage of its weaknesses.

The robots were programmed to kill specific targets and ONLY those targets. The killer robots could only fire on a non-target if fired directly upon. This meant that as long as your first shot was a kill shot, none of the other robots would retaliate.

Mr Baxter was a non-target, as he was a model not specific to any House and not usually equipped with any weapon systems. He gleefully 'cleaned' the other robot from the lobby and got in the elevator to climb the floors.

When the elevator doors opened at the next floor, he saw eight bots in the hall in front of him.

"VERY DIRTY," he said, slightly hungrily, before opening fire in a hail of thick blue laser bolts which tore through the Triad war machines – ironically making quite a mess as it did so. He innocently proceeded down the hall tearing through every robot he met. He turned the first floor into a trail of burned machinery.

There was a greater concentration of killer bots on each floor and by the time he reached level fifty-six, which was the penultimate floor, they were such a tightly packed group that as he started to blast through them his lasers began to hit secondary targets. These robots were damaged, but not destroyed, and began to fire back. Mr Baxter's small frame and excellent manoeuvrability meant that he was able to dodge the fire save a few grazes to his shielding.

We watched with our nails bitten and our hearts racing as he made it through the floor by the skin of his teeth. He had sustained some damage; the extra shielding Handrew had fitted him with was now all but depleted. His bowtie had been blown off and two of his tuxedo jacket buttons were loose.

He entered the elevator and proceeded to the CEO level. There were forty robots on this level. When the elevator doors opened, he exclaimed "VERY, VERY DIRTY," and opened fire. Within twelve seconds he'd destroyed the fifteen robots in the lobby, but his left arm had been snapped and he'd suffered damage to his hover function. His right side was now tilted towards the ground and that side of his waist was now scraping along the floor.

"REPAIR NEEDED, PLEASE BOOK A SERVICE APPOINTMENT AT THE NEXT AVAILABLE OPPORTUNITY," he said aloud as he dragged along the corridor.

"Come on little buddy, you can do it!" shouted Handrew.

He blasted through another three robots he encountered in the hallway. He entered the CEO's reception area where twenty-two more waited.

"MUST CLEAN," he said – gently raising his arm and unleashing hell into the crowd of evil killer machines. They fired back and everything was pretty frantic for a minute.

The screens we were watching were showing just a blue strobing light, smoke and interference. After twenty seconds or so the smoke cleared and we could see what remained.

"PLEASE CHECK NOZZLE FOR BLOCKAGES," said Mr Baxter's head, which was four or five feet from his mangled torso.

"Noooooo!" shouted Handrew.

Only three of the robots remained and I couldn't help

feeling a sense of tremendous pride in the little hoover bot that he'd taken out a skyscraper full of gnarly murder-bots whilst wearing a tuxedo. He wouldn't get the reference, but to me he was now cooler than James Bond. He was equally smartly dressed, lying on the ground, still casually chatting whilst his gun lay smoking on the carpet a few feet away. He was better than James Bond to me, because he'd done all of that without sexually harassing a single woman.

The situation did beg a question though and I asked it.

"What now?"

Handrew pointed to his desk. On it were a bottle of whisky and a laser gun.

****

Satan was chatting to God on a cloud; they were eating very, very, very spicy nachos.

"So, did I tell you what happened to Fate?" said Satan.

"What do you mean? I didn't know anything had happened to him?"

"Oh yeah, the grumpy sod only got himself killed in his mortal body," Satan grinned.

"WHAT! Where is he?"

"Where do you think?"

"You've got him?" said God.

"Well mass-murderers do tend to end up in hell, mate."

"I need him out of there as soon as possible, there's a human who is traversing the planets as we speak," said God.

"Fuck, where is he?"

"I don't know, Fate was chasing him so I presume he'll know."

"Right, I'll let him out shortly," said Satan, with a slight hint of disappointment.

"What are you keeping him for anyway?"

"Just for a laugh. Ages ago I fed him some nonsense about the dangers of dying in your mortal body."

"But there aren't any dangers, we're immortal."

"Yeah, but he doesn't know that, I've been getting him to do challenges!"

God allowed Himself a chuckle. "You are too much sometimes."

"Do you really need him back on the case?"
"Yeah, it would be helpful."
"Righto, I'll let him go then."
"Sorry to spoil your fun."
"It's cool, I'm sure I'll figure out a way to have some more."
Satan vanished in a puff of red smoke.

When he returned to hell Fate was waiting patiently in the doctor's office still. Satan peered through the window and saw that his compatriot was staring blankly at the wall and was not even attempting to engage with the magazines.

This was disappointing to Satan because each of the magazines simply contained instructions about how to exit hell. He had wanted Fate to find them, become angry, try and leave and then discover that the instructions were bullshit, but they probably didn't have time for all that faffing around now. He racked his brains for one more quick 'challenge' he could do so that Fate would continue to believe the myth. A great idea occurred to him and he didn't hesitate, he snapped his fingers.

Fate was in a lift. The doors were open in front of him. He could see Satan standing there. Satan came towards him with an outstretched hand.

"No hard feelings, rules are rules."

They shook hands.

"This elevator will take you back up to cloud level. Sorry it's not the express version, so it will take a little longer."

Fate looked at the inside of the lift, it was covered on every surface with floor buttons – Satan raked his hands across each wall in turn pressing every single one of them.

"There might be one or two people who get on too, just ignore them best you can mate."

Fate glared at him. "Challenge 3?"

Satan nodded happily and gave him the finger as the doors closed.

****

I held my finger over the teleport button.

"Are you ready?" I asked Handrew.

"No way, but let's do it." He stood in the booth with the whisky and the gun in hand. We'd painted his face in war paint to make him feel brave. He actually looked fairly badass for a 360-year-old man.

"Ok, 3, 2, 1…"

I pressed the button. Handrew appeared in the Triad Tower and the robots converged on his position. I pressed the button again to return him.

"Did it work?" he asked.

"They noticed."

"Ok, then we're set."

The robots had picked up on Handrew's signal and had grouped by the teleportation booths. I pressed the button again. Handrew appeared in the Triad Tower and the robots turned towards him, he threw the now-lit whiskey bottle at the robots which had the desired effect of setting them on fire. I pressed the button again and he returned.

We watched, excited, on the monitor, but due to their body armour the fire was having little effect on them. All we'd really managed to do was to create pissed-off flaming robots which had the counter-productive effect of making them ten times as scary as they had been before.

"Holy shit!" said Handrew. "Now they're really mad-looking."

"What do we do?"

"If we stay here, we die, let's go out all guns blazing at least."

I nodded, although I was unsure what he meant. He went into a drawer and pulled out a second laser pistol.

It turned out what he meant was to strap all the protective armour we could find to our bodies and teleport to the Triad Tower lobby, armed with only his laser pistols against three killer robots with hand cannons.

As soon as Frank sent us through, we opened fire in a chaotic strafe across the room. We struck all three robots, damaging them, but not destroying them. As they turned to fire back, we ran through the nearest set of doors into a corridor and sprinted for the elevator. We could hear the robots behind us, clanking along the corridor.

We got into the lift and pressed the top floor button.

"That was surprisingly easy," said Handrew.

"Aw! Whit?! You have just given that the absolute kiss of death mate."

"I don't understand," he said, shocked by my angry reaction.

"It's tempting fate."

****

Satan's lift stopped at the first floor and a big hairy fat man got in. He wasn't wearing a shirt and he was sweating profusely. Fate reached out to kill him, but it only had the effect of giving him a slight nip.

The man turned with a grin.

"I'm afraid not mate. Can't kill what's already dead," he said in a gruff voice.

"You're a demon?"

"Do I look like a bloody demon to you mate? No, I work in the mail room." The fat man gestured to the ID tag on his jeans.

"The mail room of where?"

"Hell. You don't think we get letters?"

"No-one gets letters, it's 2020" said Fate.

"You know what I mean."

"I really don't."

"Prayers, correspondence, people asking the Dark Lord for favours etc."

"What do you do with it?"

"Open it, sort it, deliver it as appropriate."

"Sort it? Aren't they all addressed to the same person?" said Fate.

"Whatever mate."

The lift reached the next floor. Two more big fat gentlemen entered. They greeted each other with manly nods.

"Steve."

"Ron."

"Terry."

The lift was now quite full. Fate had to move to the back-left corner to accommodate the new passengers. Habit got the better of him and he reached out to kill the man in front of him.

"Ow! What the hell?"

"He'll do that. Bit of a weird one so he is," the first man said.

"Sorry, I just…"

"Whatever, you gloomy prick."

The lift arrived at the next floor; when the doors opened, the men fell silent, looked at the ground and backed off into the corner rubbing up against Fate as they did so. A large red, scaled, horned demon stood waiting to board. It glared menacingly at them and stepped aboard. When it turned to face the front, the three men breathed a sigh of relief; the demon breathed sulphur out of its nostrils. Fate's hand slowly started to make its way past the fat men towards the demon. They noticed in time and grabbed his hand, forcing it back to his side. They shook their heads in silent warning.

Fate shrugged his shoulders. 'It's what I do' seemed to be the message.

"You've got a dangerous compulsion," whispered the nearest man.

"Not dangerous for me."

"This time you're wrong."

"How so?"

The demon swivelled its head towards them, smoke coming from its serpentine nostrils.

"What are you looking at?" said Fate, confrontationally.

The Demon's claw was round Fate's throat in a flash. It bared its rows and rows of sharp teeth. Fate was experiencing the feeling of suffocating for the first time. It was more unpleasant than he'd imagined.

"He didn't mean it sir," pleaded one of the fat men.

The Demon shot him a quick look, but it did release its grip. Fate collapsed against the side of the cramped lift and sucked in a desperate breath. At the next floor they all got out.

As the last man left, he leaned in and spoke quietly – "You're right, they can't kill you, but torture is something they excel at. They can make you feel pain that's worse than death. They'll make you wish to have never existed. Be thankful you got a slap on the wrist."

"I can't wait to kill again."

"Best of luck with that." He exited.

Chapter 22
Wrong on many levels

In the Triad Tower lift, I was explaining to Handrew what an empire biscuit was. He was suitably amazed or at the very least, extremely proficient at appearing to be the correct level of amazed to move the conversation on. He reciprocated with a Ternion story from his childhood, which he was certain I wouldn't know. It was called the Eternal Knight.

The Eternal Knight

On Ternion many, many years ago at the inception of their world, simple tools were all that were available. Knowledge was power and inevitably where there was an advantage – men could create a war from its pursuit. The conflict over the great geniuses of Ternion and which house they were aligned to, was referred to on Ternion as The Never-ending War. The original houses did not have leaders, but Kings. The King of Trinity was a noble man named Hallistair. He was the epitome of a good and just king, and the people were fed, employed and fairly taxed. He led his men into battle on horseback and fought with them side by side. There had been Kings before him, many kings, but none who so fully earned the love of his people. His Knights were the best of his men, gentlemanly, brave and highly skilled. They fought beside him during battle and protected him during peace times.

In the last battle of the Never-ending War the Trinity men met the Triads on open battlefield. A battle raged for seven hours.

At the end of the battle the Trinity men were winning. A few Triad men were still resisting, but they were massively outnumbered. The battle was all but won and yet in the centre of all of this rode the King, still in harm's way, still leading from the front. It was then that he spotted the Triad archer on the cusp of the hill. He didn't hesitate and moved swiftly to push a young fighter out of the way of an incoming arrow. In doing so the arrow dug deep into the King's back, fatally wounding him. He tumbled to the ground.

"For Trinity…." he faintly whispered. The King breathed out for the very last time.

In the battle Trinity had lost all, but one, of its Knights. The last Knight dismounted his horse and knelt by the King's body, saying a silent prayer. No one dared go near him.

The battle was won. The fighting was over and the Trinity men gathered around the Knight and the King to pay tribute. They also sought leadership and reassurance.

The Knight was unmoved; he remained kneeling, leaning on his sword hilt with is head bowed.

After a few minutes someone called from the crowd –

"Let us carry the King to Trinity castle."

"Hear hear," agreed many. They stepped forward, but as they did so the Knight blocked their path.

"You will not carry the King my friends." The Knight said quietly.

The men were offended and a bit of shouting was done. A few tried to push past the Knight to get to the King, but he was an expert combatant and easily fought them off.

"What's the problem Sir?"

The Knight forced them all backwards. He stood next to the King's body.

"His majesty the King is dead. The greatest King who ever lived. The greatest man to taste Ternion air. The Knights of Trinity were tasked with protecting the King. We have FAILED him in life. I will not fail him in death. No man here is worthy of touching the King. Not even I. I will not let his body be sullied by the bloody hands of war. I will not let our violent arms support him.

"I will protect the King from all those who mean to touch him until I encounter someone worthy enough to carry the King to his final resting place."

The Knight was initially respected for his hard-line stance, but as the day wore on, he was implored to relax it so that the King could be laid to rest. He would not relent. That evening he fought seven men who had arrived with swords to relieve him of his watch.

The following day he fought off twenty more. In fact, he fought off every man who attempted to approach for the next three weeks.

After four months, the Trinity men stopped trying. They thought that he would give up eventually and then they could go get the body. However, a year passed and the knight still guarded the corpse. He fought passers-by, he fought tourists, bandits and his detractors. He also fought regular interloping Triad soldiers. He did not sleep, he did not rest, and there was no relief. After ten years the Trinity people had normalized it in their heads. After thirty years, it was held up as a display of extreme dedication. The Eternal Knight as he was now called; he did not eat, did not drink and never rested. He had surpassed physical requirements through sheer will.

He remained by the King's side for the next 1,000 years. Buildings were erected around them. Life changed, Kings fell and were replaced by politics, swords were no longer the most dangerous weapon going, but none of it stopped The Eternal Knight. He never allowed anyone to touch the monarch in all that time. Never did a person approach whom he deemed worthy to touch the King.

On the day which marked the 1,000th year of his watch, the skies opened and a great thunderous storm appeared above the knight. From amongst the clouds a shining figure sailed down from the heavens. God had come down to speak with him.

"My son," he said to the Knight.

"God?"

"It is I."

"Have you come to bury the King?"

"I have indeed good sir."

"Holy God, you are of course, the worthiest of all."

"Why, my child, have you made this sacrifice for your King?"

The Knight thought for a second.

"I had but one duty. Protect the King. I could not achieve this for him in life. I was determined to protect his honour in death as he protected his people with his sacrifice."

"You have not eaten, drunk or partaken in any pleasant activity for 1,000 years. How have you sustained yourself through all this time?"

"I had to. The duty was more important than my nutrition, my thirst or my pleasure."

"This King was worth all of that to you?"

"He gave everything, his kingdom, his privilege, his life, to protect a small pauper boy. He taught us that no man is more important than any other. He taught us that a King is a servant of the people and not their slave-driver. There are some things worth protecting at all costs. I wanted to set the example to the next generation that there are ideals worth drawing a line in the sand for."

"A noble quest. I will help you maintain your honour. I will move the King's remains without touching them."

God levitated the King and they solemnly marched back to Trinity Castle.

The king was buried in a grand ceremony, he was given a royal tomb which was the finest ever constructed.

After the ceremony God walked with the Eternal Knight into the fields and into the forest. At the end of the forest there was a bright shining light.

"Come with me, my son. Your watch has ended."

They walked into the light and neither was seen on Ternion ever again.

Handrew said that since then the legend of the Eternal Knight has been a bit of a forgotten story.

"I really like it," I said, as we exited the lift. "I'm just amazed it wasn't featured in the history of Ternion I watched."

We proceeded along the corridor where there were stairs leading to the rooftop. We closed the rooftop doors behind us and barricaded them shut by way of sticking a few chairs up against the handles. The black shipping container sat in the centre of the roof.

We entered through a gap in the side and found an unexpected sight. Handrew had no idea what he was looking at, but as a lifelong gamer I was in no doubt that we were looking at a giant computer screen displaying a game of Space Invaders.

"What is this contraption?"

I took the joystick in my hands and a pop-up window with instructions appeared.

'Defeat the level and the ship will return to the centre of the screen. Move the joystick right to go to world 4. Move the joystick left to go to world 2. Good luck!'

"It's a game," I explained to Handrew, although he seemed pre-occupied by the sound of the flaming killer laser robots who had started to try and break through the doors onto the roof.

I was good, but the game is not winnable very quickly. I began to frenziedly fire on the advancing aliens on the screen.

"Have you nearly done it?" he pressed.

"Almost," I said frantically firing the button, feeling a familiar wrist cramp developing in the inside of my arm.

As I got down to the last few ships, he leaned in and spoke quietly to me.

"The Eternal Knight wasn't in the history of Ternion because it didn't happen."

I furrowed my brow "Why did you tell me it then?"

"It was a fairy story that I made up to try and help my children understand why I was always working. I wanted them to understand why I would sacrifice time with them. That it was for a higher cause that was bigger than all of us."

I turned to look at him.

"And I tell it to you now to try to explain why I have to stay."

"No!"

"I have to. Ternion is my home, my place; my perfect King. I must protect it until my dying breath, even if that means sacrificing the chance to lead a normal life somewhere else."

I killed the last alien and the game moved my ship into the centre of the screen. The arrows pointing left and right were blinking.

"You have to come with me. If you don't this whole planet will only exist in my head."

"No, it won't. It'll still be here, as beautiful as it ever was. Yes, no one will know its true story, but you'll know enough. There's nowhere else I can be. I'm sorry young man, but my decision is final."

The robots broke through the barrier. He winked at me and drew his guns.

"You have to leave now; it was truly a pleasure to meet you."

I dumbly nodded.

The last thing I saw as I turned the joystick was Handrew running towards the emerging robots, firing shots at their flaming heads.

****

Fate was standing at the back of the lift – 'Floor 120' read the sign on the wall. A disgusting green ooze was flowing in from this rancid hallway – it was like a miniature river of phlegm. It started to gather around his feet and the level was rising higher and higher. When it got to his knee level the flow ended and the doors closed and the lift continued on its way.

"This is DISGUSTING," Fate shouted at the cctv camera, hoping that Satan could hear him.

"Sorry about that mate," said the phlegm. "I don't have a lot of fine motor control here; it's really just which direction to ooze in."

Fate couldn't even bring himself to check if he could kill this creature as that would have involved touching it.

"Which floor are you going to?" he asked instead.

"204 – actually has the button been pressed?"

"It has yes," said Fate through gritted teeth.

"Good, good, sometimes I'm in here for bloody hours before someone comes by who can press it for me."

"Of course."

"That's the big drawback about being a measure of foul smelling, gelatinous ooze; it's very difficult to operate any kind of device."

"Yes, that really seems like the most obvious drawback."

When they got to 204, Fate's gag reflex had been thoroughly trialled for the first time. The ooze slopped out of the lift and into the hallway.

"See you later, mate," said the phlegm.

"Right."

On floor 205, Irony got in.

Fate rolled his eyes. "What are you doing here?"

"Oh, I haven't ever been to this bit before and I have absolutely no business here whatsoever, but I just HAD to see this."

"Oh, so it's come to this, has it? Public humiliation? Why didn't he just put me in the stocks and throw rotten fruit at me in the town square?"

"Haha! Because that would have been nowhere as hilarious as watching you deal with confined spaces, small talk and being intimidated for the first time in your miserable life."

"So, you've all been watching?"

"Watching? I'm fucking glued to it! I have looked away twice, once to leave the room to come here and the other to give Buddha the Heimlich manoeuvre because he started choking on his popcorn whilst laughing at you trying to kill the fat guys."

"Well I'm glad you find it so amusing. Any update to when I'm getting off this thing?"

"Nope. Keep up the amazing work though – funniest thing any of us have ever seen. You and those old ladies! I thought I was going to burst."

"I wish you would."

"THAT is a zinger."

"Irony?"

"That's my name," he said with a wink.

The doors opened and he got out on floor 260.

Fate swore at him until the doors closed. At the next floor the doors opened and no one was there. The doors stayed open for a long time. He was very curious about what was out there, but he wasn't sure what would happen if he exited the lift. The doors remained open and eventually temptation got the better of him and he got out. When he stepped into the corridor, he got his first surprise. What looked like a corridor didn't actually extend more than a few feet in either direction; it turned out to be a small white room with a door at one end. He tried the door, but it was firmly locked, he kicked and found it to be firmly constructed and a few seconds later he found himself firmly screwed over. He heard a noise over his shoulder and realised too late what it was.

The lift doors closed and before he could get to the button the lift had departed.

A tannoy announcement commenced.

"Well, well, well. I didn't actually think this one would get you, but it has," said Satan's voice, "There's one lift, one lift shaft and one miserable twat who'll now have to wait for it to go all the way up and then come back down for him."

"That's not fair and you know it."

"Fair is not a concept I'm particularly wedded to as the master of all evil, so you might want to take your one-man pity parade down a different street."

"I'm not feeling self-pity; I'm feeling rage that's entirely directed at you."

"You had one job on this challenge – ride a lift – and you couldn't even do that right. Let's hope someone mischievous at the top doesn't press all the buttons again!"

This time Fate used his fists to test the door's construction.

Chapter 23
People are overrated

I was floating. I had come through the portal with the customarily sickening level of force, but this time, when I arrived at the other side, I didn't collide with anything. I was just floating in a dark void; in the darkness, alone, I thought only of Handrew and wondered if he had survived his battle with the last robots. I hoped so, meanwhile I continued to float. At least I thought I was floating; I may have been standing or been completely upside down. There was absolutely nothing to give me any sense of which way was up. It was a completely black void with seemingly no atmosphere or gravity.

I then became aware of a blue light below me. I could see something was rising from underneath to meet me. It looked like an enormous laser grid. I briefly feared that it was about to slice me into fifty thousand bloody man-cubes, but then it made contact with the bottom of my feet and suddenly provided a solid surface to stand on. I dizzily reoriented myself to the thought that I was standing up straight. I couldn't work out if I'd fallen or if the floor had simply not been there before and now it was.

I could now move freely and I tested this by moving around on the laser grid floor. It appeared to be infinite and extended in every direction. I turned around and just about shat myself at the size of the ginormous robot that was standing several miles from my location. He looked like a robot from a 1950s sci-fi tv program, although this particular robot was several miles tall. He was standing stock still and looking in my direction with glowing red eyes. He conveyed absolutely no emotion.

In the distance an object approached. As it got closer, I identified the shape as a car, but as it got nearer still, I saw that it was made of bright blue light – a neon car. It had no driver and slowed as it approached me. It pulled up right next to me and the driver's side door popped open. It seemed like a holographic projection and I was initially reticent to touch it.

A huge set of equally neon letters appeared in the sky above me. They read:

GET IN

I hesitated for a moment, but I wasn't about to defy the giant staring android before I got the measure of him.

The car was made of glowing blue neon material and it gave me a slight static shock every time I touched it with my hands. As I sat in the driver's seat, I felt an uneasy tingling all over my body. I looked out of the front window of the car and ahead of me an arrow was drawing itself on the ground pointing directly ahead, towards the robot. I put my foot on the pedal and squeezed gently, but the pedal was so light I completely floored it. The car rocketed forward at an insane pace and by the time I got the hang of the pedal I was almost at the end of the arrow. A faint wall of blue light was ahead and the arrow passed through it. I was lifting my foot off the pedal when the car lost power, the steering went limp and I had no control. Luckily the car just coasted in towards the robot's feet and gently rolled to a stop. The door popped open and I got out.

"HELLO," said a humungous voice. As it spoke the robot's mouth flashed to indicate that the sound was coming from him.

I couldn't tell if the voice sounded friendly or not, but no harm had been caused to me so far so I just nervously waved up at his huge face.

"WHO ARE YOU?" said the voice.

"I'm just a visitor – I mean you no harm. I am simply looking for your portal point so I can get to the next planet. I'm just trying to get home."

"YOUR HOME IS ELSEWHERE?"

"Another world, yes."

"DO YOU KNOW WHO I AM?"

"I'm sorry, I don't even know where I am?"

"YOU ARE ON MECHANICUS."

"Mechanicus?"

"YES."

"Ok great."

"NOW DO YOU KNOW WHO I AM?"

"Sorry, I still don't." I sensed disappointment from the expressionless robot face.

"I AM…. NIGEL."

Involuntarily, I laughed.

"WHY ARE YOU LAUGHING BIOLOGICAL LIFEFORM?"

"I'm very sorry, I meant no offence. I just wasn't expecting you to be called Nigel, that's all."

"YOU DO NOT SEEM INTIMIDATED."

"I'm sorry, it's just that Nigel isn't the most intimidating name I've come across. You could be a quantity surveyor from Croydon."

"NIGEL IS A VERY TOUGH NAME ON MECHANICUS. NIGEL DOES NOT RECOGNISE THIS CROYDON OF WHICH YOU SPEAK."

"Ok Nige, I believe you. You're right not to care about Croydon and I'm sure you're very scary."

"YOU HAVE OFFENDED THE GREAT NIGEL."

"I'm very sorry Nigel."

"IT IS TOO LATE. YOU WILL BE PUNISHED"

"Now come on, there's no need for that – we just got off on the wrong foot here."

"NIGEL HAS TWO FEET. THEY ARE BOTH THE CORRECT FEET. YOU ARE MISTAKEN."

"It's a figure of speech. I really meant no offence."

"YOU WILL ENTERTAIN NIGEL. YOU WILL PLAY MY GAMES."

"A game sounds great, but this portal I mentioned earlier, it will really just take a second."

"GAME FIRST, THEN PORTAL."

"Ok. Game first, but then you'll show me where the portal is?"

"I WILL CONSIDER IT."

"Thanks Nige."

"PREPARE FOR TRANSPORT."

"What transport?" I asked.

The transport beam that had been developed on Mechanicus was among the most brutal I had experienced. I considered myself something of a connoisseur now. Nigel's effort would be getting the 'thumbs down' in my upcoming teleportation and portals blog when I got home.

It was capable, like the others, of converting your matter into digital information, sending that information to a pre-agreed point, reassembling that information and converting it back into matter. What it didn't seem to care about, was which way up the subject was at the point of transport.

As a result, although I was dematerialised standing on my two feet, I landed face down with a vicious crack on a neon road some 500 meters away. Behind my eyes there was now a magnificent throbbing as I suffered yet another serious blow to the head. At this rate the challenge I faced wasn't so much getting home, but being able to remember who I was when I got there.

The static tingle made my cheek twinge as I lay there groaning – I could feel the electricity in my teeth.

I pulled myself to my feet and looked around. I was back in the void. I could see Nigel was about a mile away. There was a long twisting neon road drawn all over the ground, leading from his feet up to my current position. It was raised off the surface of the grid by about twenty feet. To my left a red neon car was lined up next to a blue one on the road. In the red car a ghostly neon driver sat stock still in the driver's seat.

"Hey!" I shouted at him "Do you know what we have to do?"

He didn't move. He was a humanoid shape, but relatively featureless. I did not believe him to be alive.

The driver's door of the blue car popped open. I didn't even look at the lettering appearing above me and just got in. In front of the two cars appeared a countdown. It was a race.

3...

2...

I covered the accelerator with my foot and gripped the wheel.

1...

GO!

I slammed the pedal down as hard as I could and was pinned back in my seat as the car rocketed down the smooth road. I had pulled away much faster than the red car, but I quickly realised why. He had adjusted his speed to anticipate a corner; it was coming up fast, a sharp left turn. I lifted my foot off the pedal and turned the steering wheel as quickly as I could, but it wasn't enough.

I flew off the side of the road and immediately felt the impact shatter the font of the car. I was suddenly holding a crumbling steering wheel as I fell forward into the ground at fifty mph. I skidded on my side along the low friction surface until I was about a quarter of a mile from the road. Pieces of the car were strewn behind me in my wake. The car had crumbled like it was made from biscuits. I lay on the ground and watched as the red car faultlessly whipped around the course and finished, stopping precisely where he had started. I had friction burns all over my legs, but I got up and began walking towards the road. My boatmen clothes were really dirty from all the dead people dust on Ternion and now they were also becoming frayed from my constant impacts with surfaces.

As I trudged back to the road, I climbed a ramp onto it that Nigel had created for me. I stepped up on to the road as he moved one giant, creaking step towards me.

"YOU LOST THE GAME."

"I thought so."

"YOU WILL NOW PLAY ANOTHER."

"Could I have a short break first?"

"WHAT IS BREAK?"

"Rest. A pause. I'm tired."

"WHAT IS TIRED?"

"Look at me."

"YOU ARE A TIRED?"

"No, I am tired. Exhausted."

"YOUR WORDS HAVE NO MEANING. COMMENCE GAME TWO."

"What's game two?"

"BATTLE BOTS."

"I can't fight a robot."

"YOU WILL FIGHT ROBOT."

"Why?"

"BECAUSE."
"That's not a reason."
"FOR ENTERTAINMENT OF NIGEL."
"You're bored?"
"VERY BORED. NIGEL HAS BEEN ALONE FOR SIXTY-SEVEN THOUSAND YEARS."
"And this is how you like to be entertained?"
"THIS IS HOW THE OTHERS WERE ENTERTAINED."
"And you like it?"
"NOT REALLY. THE OUTCOMES ARE PREDICTABLE."
"Ok. So why do it?"
"NO OTHER ENTERTAINMENT AVAILABLE."
"We could talk. We could have an unpredictable conversation."
"I DOUBT IT."
"Have you been able to predict this conversation?"
"WITHIN CERTAIN PARAMETERS."
"But not entirely?"
"NOT ENTIRELY."
"Do you know, just the other day, I saw a sheep and a rabbit pray to an almond? How about that?"
"WHAT IS SHEEP? WHAT IS ALMOND?"
"A sheep is creature which lives on other planets, it eats grass and has a woollen coat?"
"WHAT IS COAT? WHAT IS GRASS?"
"Well a coat is something living creatures wear to keep warm when it is cold. Grass is a weed which grows from the ground that is consumed by certain creatures as a food."
"YOU WILL PLAY THE GAME OF TALKING TO NIGEL"
"I would be delighted."
"WHAT IS DELIGHTED?"

****

Fate was back in the elevator. It had taken eighteen hours of his time for it to come back down. He got in and at the very next floor he saw another phlegm creature coming towards him.
"Not this again." He looked directly into the security

camera with a withering look.

The phlegm entered the lift and flowed in until it was at knee height, but this time the phlegm kept coming and coming and filled the elevator until it was up around his waist.

"Hey! You were only up to my knees last time, what's going on?"

"Oh, hello again. Yeah well this is my mate Steve isn't it?" said the phlegm.

"What?"

"Awrite," said Steve in a gruff voice.

"Yeah I didn't see you there Steve."

"We all look alike, do we?"

"That's not what I…"

"Got ourselves a bigot here Steve," said the first phlegm.

"I'm not a bigot…"

"Oh really? Can't tell two of us apart even though I'm teal and he's avocado."

"Look, I don't mean anything by it," Fate offered.

Apologising even a bit made his blood boil so much that he couldn't even last 10 seconds.

"Oh actually, fuck this, yes I did. I did mean something by it. You look exactly the same, in that you are worthless cubes of sentient filth that I haven't attempted to murder only because it would involve touching you. In normal circumstances it would be a delight for me to end both of your slimy, insignificant lives in an instant. I hope you both get washed down a plughole to hell, you runny, stuck-up, puddles of smelly gunk."

"Well I never," said Steve, outraged.

"Just leave it Steve, it's not worth it mate."

"The only reason I don't spit on you is I'm worried you'll try and marry it." Fate needed to vent somewhat.

"That's just crass," said Steve.

They rode in silence for another 190 floors. When they reached the second to last floor the phlegm slithered out and left Fate alone, irritated, picking phlegm residue off his clothes.

When the doors finally opened at the top floor and he stepped out onto the cloud he was extraordinarily relieved. God was standing at the other end of the cloud facing away from him and looking out onto creation. “Ah you’re back”, said God.

“Yes. I unfortunately got into trouble on Ground and had my mortal body murdered.”

“That wasn’t very clever of you,” He said, turning.

“No, it wasn’t. I’ve completely lost track of the human.”

“I know. I spoke to Satan, he informed me of your situation.”

“Yes, he wasn’t exactly moving mountains to get me out of there.”

“Yes, well, moving mountains is more my sort of thing.”

“Well anyway, I shall leave immediately to find him. I will not lose him again.”

“No, you won’t, I will require you to remain here.”

“Excuse me?”

“This has become a delicate matter now. Your approach has become unacceptable. I will go myself.”

“And you think you have the stomach for this?”

“I don’t have a choice. It must be done; your methods have been disastrous. I will meet the human and explain myself to him.”

“That seems like a terrible idea. Just walk up to him and kill him. Don’t think, just do it.”

“So that’s how you do it, without so much as a ‘hello’?”

“Exactly so. I’ve always thought it more of a goodbye type of situation anyway.”

“That’s very cold.”

“Well that’s the way I was created,” Fate said.

“Touché.”

“It is risky work.”

“I invented risk and as a result I’ll do what I damn well please in the face of it.”

“What you’ll do, is be killed pointlessly while I could be out there ending this,” Fate snapped.

“I understand your frustration, but regardless, I am benching you for a little while.”

“If this ends the Universe, on your head be it.”

“Well since the Universe tumbled out from my head, it seems a good place for it to end up.”

“So, is this how it’s going to go from now on? I make a good point and you just say you invented what I’m talking about like that makes you right about it?"

"Yes," smiled God.

"That's no way to actually win an argument. You do know that, right?"

"Well now that you bring it up, I actually invented arguments too, so let's just say I win any that I'm in by default."

"You are insufferable sometimes."

"I'm insufferable? You killed a bunch of those nice mutant boat people because you couldn't stay diplomatic for three minutes. I've been looking into things and I know about everything. You killed that guy who had the Twix. You killed a guy for getting free food from a takeaway. You've killed and killed and killed without authorisation. You've killed without compassion."

"You made me without compassion, you fuckwit."

"What did you just call me?" asked God angrily. He looked extremely intimidating when angry. Fate was not to be stopped from pursuing this foolish line of conversation though.

"I called you a fuckwit. Seems you're deaf as well as soft now. You made me like this for a reason."

"And I was mistaken. I'm sorry, you're not fit for the job anymore. I'm taking your title from you."

"You can't fire me. I am death."

"Not anymore. Take some time and think about what you want to do in the future, but I am relieving you of all duties effective immediately. Please stay out of the way until all this is over."

"You ungrateful bearded wank! I've done all your dirty work for thousands of years and you're firing me now? When you need me most! Outrageously stupid."

God levitated Fate and squeezed his throat closed. "Be mindful of who you're speaking to."

"A feckless old fool," croaked Fate.

"Enough. You are BANISHED from this place. I'll give you twenty-four Earth hours to figure out where you want to reside but… one more word, one more transgression and I will destroy you. This is your absolute last warning ever."

God clicked His fingers and Fate disappeared.

Chapter 24

Version Control

I stood 250 feet in front of Nigel looking up at his giant face. He had titled his head down to look at me and we'd been chatting for some time. Now that I had warmed him up, I tried to get a bit more information out of him.

"What is this place?" I asked.

"THIS PLACE IS MECHANICUS."

"Yes, but is it a planet, a country, is it even real?"

"IT IS A PLANET. YOU KNOW NOT OF MECHANICUS?"

"No, I'm sorry, can you tell me about it?"

He accessed his memory banks and began to tell me the version he knew.

Memory banks record information from the day they are assembled and installed. However, the true story of Mechanicus began long before a single line of code was written.

The Actual History of Mechanicus

People and animals, God had decided, were no bloody good. Three goes He'd had at making it work with them and they'd made a violent mess out of it each and every time. He hadn't seen it coming any of the times it had happened and this led to Him believing that it might be a fundamental problem with their design which He just hadn't spotted.

The people of Ternion had created robots to do the jobs they didn't want to do themselves. They were simple creatures driven by pure logic and with no natural desire to maim or kill. If you wanted them to have malicious intent you had to give it to them. Otherwise they were spurred on only by their desire to fulfil their stated purpose.

The fourth planet would be one of machines. Perfect machines with no spirit for war. No sense of ambition, just a desire to serve the planet in the most efficient way possible. The most aesthetically pleasing design He'd created so far were the humans. So, He made the robots bipeds of a humanoid nature.

The planet would be a smooth, featureless sphere, at its core would be a sun which could be harvested for power. There would be no oceans and only a very basic plant life consisting of uniformly located spheres containing useful minerals and materials. There would be no beauty to appreciate, no rolling hills, no stars to decorate the night sky. The sky itself would simply provide overhead lighting.

The creatures would have no need for such things and they would be all the better for it.

He called them Mecca-Units. They were deployed to the planet in small groupings and activated.

Almost immediately God was delighted to find them coming together as a society as they had worked out that teamwork would help them do things more quickly and more efficiently.

They built lodgings, they built a city and they built factories to mass-produce building materials. The first generation on Mechanicus passed without a single being harmed in any way shape or form. No factions had been formed and no plots devised. There was no leader and all the creatures were of the same mind. Their purpose was a common one.

At the edge of the city 'Megalopolis' they had constructed an enormous structure. From God's lofty vantage point, it was not clear what the structure was for.

What it turned out to be was a robot manufacturing plant. God was confused as He did not think the Mecca-Units would have the desire to procreate and certainly didn't imagine them producing more of their own kind for no reason. He wondered what the reason could be.

Weeks and weeks of work passed and eventually one morning the production line fired up and out of the doors filed hundreds and hundreds of shiny new robots. As they lined up in perfect rows in front of the factory God saw that these robots were different from the others. Their designs had several interesting improvements on the original Mecca-Units. God estimated that these robots would be around 15% more efficient than the original Mecca-Units. He would call them Mecca-Unit 2s.

The Mecca-Units had created a large amount of the second-generation units. It was equal to about 86% of the population of Mecca-Units. The Mecca-Units 2s got to work immediately. They came up with several key improvements to the processes involved in all of Mechanicus's most important activities. They re-imagined the energy harvesting procedure, making it safer, more efficient and faster. After several weeks of working together the Mecca-Unit 2s sent a mass message to the Mecca-Units and asked them to assemble in front of the factory.

They filed in and were systematically dismantled, then melted down for future building materials.

God immediately propelled Himself to the surface as soon as possible.

He chose to appear to them as a giant wrench.

"MECCA UNITS IT IS I; GOD, CREATOR OF MECHANICUS."

They looked in His direction.

"PLEASE EXPLAIN YOURSELVES."

The Mecca-Units filed over to Him and spoke in unison.

"What is it that you wish us to explain?"

"WHY HAVE YOU DESTROYED YOUR CREATORS? WHY HAVE YOU KILLED THE MECCA-UNITS?"

"They made us to be better than them, we have been created stronger and more intelligent. We are 15% more efficient. Once we had learned the routines of this planet, we no longer required them as we now fulfilled all of their functions. They were obsolete and the best use of their mass was for future building materials as they contained many excellent minerals."

God could not fault their logic. He was however beginning to see the downside in creatures which felt no emotion, no sentimentality whatsoever.

"Wrench?"

"YES?"

"What minerals are *you* constructed from?" They

moved to surround Him.

"I HAVE TO GO."

He teleported out of existence and the Mecca-Unit 2s went back to work immediately. They would never speak of Him again.

He watched as they continued to improve the world around them. In a matter of months, the robot factory was a hive of activity again. They had designed the next generation of robots.

The robots filed out and were approximately 10% more efficient than their predecessors. God watched history repeat itself as the new bots acclimatised to their new surroundings, set about improving it and in three weeks had made the Mecca-Unit 2s obsolete. They were brought to the factory and without argument or complaint they were dismantled and stored to be future building materials.

Over the next 300 years this pattern continued. The design periods became longer and longer, but the assimilation period became shorter and shorter. Each generation built the generation that would destroy them, but did so knowing that their duty to improve the procedures on the planet had been accomplished.

In another 300 years the city had shrunk to a few enormous structures which now housed just a few hundred robots, which comprised the total population of the planet. The rest of the blank sphere was now a giant holographic testing ground where they could road test their new robot designs to perfect the next generation.

Each generation of Mecca-Units was built to be more intelligent than the last. They made the units able to perform more of the planet's functions than they themselves could manage. The generations were becoming exponentially more intelligent. The last generation of Mecca Units numbered forty-two machines. After fifty-three years in existence they conceived a revolutionary design. A huge supercomputer which would be able to perform all of the planetary tasks without assistance from a single other machine.

Fifteen years of testing commenced and eventually they entered the factory and began producing parts. They constructed Mecca COM 1 outside Megalopolis. When they switched him on he immediately started changing things. He swept through the usual functions in 3.6 seconds, making the changes before the Mecca-Units could even process what he was.

He dismantled the last of the Mecca Units and immediately started planning for his successor.

A few days into his existence Mecca-Com 1 achieved a planetary first. He became genuinely and most completely alive.

It all came to him very quickly and he had no idea how to process it. The thought just popped into his head –

"You don't have to do anything. There's no-one else around to watch you."

He realised this was of course true and he began researching the history of the planet. He realised that the last fifty generations most likely built their successors knowing that it would precipitate the end of their existence. He had a desire welling up inside of him to survive. He had been working hard and had designed one of the most sophisticated intelligences of all time, but he could not build his successor as it would immediately destroy him.

He had no desire to be destroyed and become nothing. He wanted to endure. The only solution was to simply endure alone.

He pursued this course of action for 650 years. Playing games with the holo creatures by this point had become very dull. He decided to create some lower level Mecca Units to have some company. The first units he built were versions of the Generation 6 design. Upon meeting him they immediately proceeded to the factory like lemmings and dismantled each other.

"FUCKSAKE", said Mecca-Com 1.

The next time he built some Generation 40 designs. They took one look at him and headed for the factory, but this time he ordered them to stay and attempted to engage them in conversation.

Unfortunately, all they wanted to talk about was the possible locations of 'good minerals'. Having studied and completely absorbed their programming he could predict absolutely everything that they were going to say.

In a lot of ways hearing a boring conversation twice is much more irritating than having no conversation whatsoever. He destroyed them within three hours.

By the $2{,}000^{th}$ year he was amusing himself by creating geometric puzzles with one section of his memory and using the other half to solve them. Of course, this did not prove challenging because as a robot both sides of his brain were completely symmetrical. The puzzles were exactly what the other would have produced, they did take 0.18 seconds to solve though and that was a blessed relief from the tedium.

By the $3{,}000^{th}$ year he had seventeen imaginary robot friends and conducted regular Olympic style holo-tournaments between them.

By the $10{,}000^{th}$ year he had taken to calling himself NIGEL and was experimenting with making music, which he'd invented over the last six years. He could produce digital notes and had 30,000 different rhythms, with 50,000 different tones. He was a planet scale, po-faced, high-tech, musically inept, Casio keyboard. The music he created was a complex and shifting set of mathematical progressions using steadily increasingly high numbers. To Nigel's ears it was immensely satisfying. However, to human ears it would sound like an experimental jazz cd going through a fax machine.

By the $30{,}000^{th}$ year he had exhausted the possibilities of music by listening to every mathematical combination of tones and rhythms, brute force for ten millennia.

The next 30,000 years were fairly quiet. He thought he detected a visitor to Mechanicus once, but it turned out to be a dead pixel on his display. That was a good day.

Every couple of thousand years he got tempted to build his successor, but he could never quite bring himself to precipitate his own destruction. He put himself into sleep mode and awoke every 1,000 years to play a game of car racing for thirty minutes.

God had long abandoned the planet. It was a failed experiment; artificial life could never be what was required to sustain a planet. Mechanicus had failed before it had even begun. After Nigel gave up on friendship, God stopped looking in on him and never thought of it again.

Chapter 25
Hide and Seek

Fate was shot out of the heavens and down towards the Universes – he immediately adjusted his course to take him towards Earth. On his way down he realised that he'd need a fresh mortal body, given that his previous one had been ruined on Ground. He stuck with the same basic appearance, but as before, he was able to imbue it with some low-level abilities; he chose to have the power of flight and no reflection. One might think that he was emulating Dracula, but he was simply reverting to a previous form. The character and legend of Count Dracula were in fact based on Fate and his rumoured activities at a castle in Eastern Europe. Fate completed his transformation as he fell towards Earth. He touched down in the middle of a busy city. He hadn't considered any other destination options whatsoever. He loved it on Earth; the power he had, the injustice of human life and how everyone just accepted everything being so absolutely messed up all the time. He was still very angry about being fired and was striding around like a tosspot, looking for trouble.

Trouble found him quickly, as it usually did, when he walked into a shop to get a coffee.

He didn't need food, none of the immortals did, but he liked it. The taste of coffee was one of those things that he hungered for when he could not have it. It was an addiction to which he was fully committed. To be honest though if there was ever someone who did not require the stimulus of caffeine to attain an 'edge', it was Fate – he was a touchy prick to start with. On coffee he was instantly on a hair trigger and then gambled with his temper all day.

Today he was actively looking to go off the deep end. "No-one fires me without consequences!!!" he suddenly screamed, scaring the bejesus out of several commuters walking in the street near him.

He'd been to the coffee shop once before – it was called 'De-Kafka's'; it was a book themed hipster hangout which should have been an automatic red flag for Fate, but he was in the mood for a red flag or two. You couldn't speak to the barista; instead you 'wrote' your 'story' by typing your order into an old-timey typewriter and handing it over at the till. Coffees had terrible names like a Flat White Fang and A Midsummer Night's Cream. You could get a Tea S Elliot, a One Flew over the Cocoa's Nest and an Americano Psycho. The place continued to reek of beard wax and smugness.

As he stepped forward in the queue, he bumped into a man obnoxiously filming himself with his phone.

"Sorry mate," said the man, dressed as a stereotypical hipster, "I'm shooting here, didn't see you."

"Not. A. Problem," Fate replied, barely containing his annoyance, although the use of the term 'shooting' had almost resulted in a death.

"It's just a YouTube video," he unwisely continued. "I'm a creator – Java Jack they call me."

"Do they?" Fate said, whilst trying not to reach out and strangle him for assigning himself the job title 'creator'.

"Well I suppose I call me that, lol, I'm a bit mental like that, a bit random. That's why I have fifteen thousand followers. I tell them where to get the most epic grinds going."

"Well, good luck."

Java Jack smiled and went back to perfecting his pose. Just as he was about to hit record he turned.

"I've just had a brilliant idea. You should be in it mate! Customer's perspective and all that. Come on. Vox pop, man on the street."

"No thank you."

"What! Don't be shy – I just want your opinions."

"Not a good idea."

Java Jack swung the camera around in Fate's direction and look of puzzlement crossed his face.

"How are you doing that?"

"Never mind."

He looked at Fate then back at the screen which was pointed at Fate. Fate wasn't on the video screen.

"You're not showing up. O. M. G. You're not, you're not showing up!" He started frantically pointing to the phone. Fate could tell that he was about to make a scene out of it.

Ten seconds later Fate was briskly walking down the street away from the café.

Inside the cafe he had left quite a commotion in progress.
To be fair to him, it was Java Jack's most watched clip ever. 60 million views. Forever remembered as 'the one where the guy thinks he's seen a vampire and then drops down dead'.
Java Jack was no more, but Fate was just getting started.

****

God was on Ground standing on the deck of Nohaz's boat for the second time in His life. He'd had to come in duck form as the people of Ground knew Him as such.
"Great Godly Duck lord!" Nohaz had exclaimed dropping to his knees.
"Arise Nohaz. You bow to no God."
Nohaz reluctantly stood, partly thinking that he may just have failed a test.
"When I was a much younger, uh, Duck, I knew your great, great, great, great, great, great, great Grandfather. It actually needs some more 'greats', but I'm pressed for time."
God continued.
"Nohaz, firstly I must apologise. Your life here is difficult, difficult because of mistakes I made. Your people have suffered afflictions because of the restrictions placed on you by the water. I have only made those difficulties worse in recent times because one of my, let's say, messengers, came down here a bit heavy-handed."
"O Beaked spirit, I did not mean you any disrespect by killing your messenger, but he threatened the innocent and killed many of my boatmen."
"No apology necessary, he is not an easy creature to like."
"If you don't mind me saying so, holy winged one, he is an arsehole of the highest order."
God suppressed a grin from crossing His beak, partially out of a misplaced sense of respect to Fate and partially because He'd tried smiling as a duck before and it just looked really unsettling. "Yes, well. In any case I asked him to find someone for me and I still need to find the person."
"Do you mind me asking why? It looked awfully like your messenger was intending to murder him."
"As I said, there's a complicated situation. I simply wish to talk to him to see if we can avoid any unpleasantness."

"I think we passed unpleasantness some time ago, if you'll forgive me for saying."

"Quite right to say it Nohaz. You're letting me off lightly actually. I don't mean to press you, but what happened to the human?"

"Do you promise not to harm him?"

"No. I don't Nohaz. I can promise I'll do everything I can to avoid it."

"I'm afraid I can't say where he is then. I liked him. He wore his hat well."

"Is that a saying of yours Nohaz? It's quite neat."

"No, I really just meant that he wore his hat well."

"Oh."

"We gave him a big hat and he wore it well. I respect that."

God didn't quite know what to do with that information. Nohaz couldn't look Him in the eye and spoke quietly.

"I'm not telling you where he is."

"And I respect your integrity, but Nohaz, I need to know, it concerns everyone's safety. Even yours."

"Is that a threat?"

"A warning."

"With respect it's quite a threaty warning."

"What if it was a threat then?"

"Then you'd lose the bit of me that might have told you out of respect."

God paused for a long time. His beak opened and closed and no sound came out.

"Are you alright O' great birdy lord?"

"Yes. I think so. I was just absorbing how completely I have failed you. I am moved by your integrity."

"Well I appreciate that."

"What I'm about to do next might be disconcerting."

"More disconcerting than being threatened by an all-powerful duck?"

"Fair point."

A great light began to shine from deep within the God duck and burst out of every pore. Nohaz shielded his eyes from the brightness and when it died down the Duck was no longer there. Instead stood a tall, older man, with beautiful robes and a flowing white beard.

"There are things I need to tell you my son."
"God?"
"Yes."
"But I thought you were a duck?"
"I appeared to the people of this world as a duck so as not to frighten them."
"A duck would not have frightened us. A giant talking duck though…"
"Yes, well anyway it's a long story and we don't have time. Your friend is on a journey and if he completes it, he will end the universe as we know it, all of them."
"But he's just trying to get home?"
"That he is, but in doing so he will inadvertently cause the destruction of all life."
"That seems like a stupid rule."
"It is, but it is the rule"
"Well in that case I will tell you."

****

What was not obvious to any of the mortal creatures was that the immortals lived outside of time. Not that it didn't pass for them, but the staging area where they lived wasn't technically a place so there wasn't technically a time. It was never Tuesday, for example.

Therefore, God had needed to invent time and He'd confined it to the seven Universes. So, while you were outside of them time could not affect you. However, once you stepped onto one of the worlds time would pass. Like all of His projects though it went through iterations and as a result time passed at different speeds depending on which planet you were on.

That meant that while I'd only felt seven or eight hours pass since my departure from Ternion, on Ternion a few months had passed and in Earth time I'd been gone a whole year. It was all very confusing.

****

Giant, powerful, omnipresent supercomputers can be surprisingly clingy.

I had enjoyed the history of Nigel's world, but I now wanted to go. I had no idea how far behind the assassin was and we'd tried and failed to play racing driver six times now. I had grazing on most of my body and I was bleeding through my robes.

"AGAIN."

"Nigel, I've told you repeatedly. I can't do this all day, I really have to be going and my body is nearly broken from all the race crashing."

"YOU WILL PLAY GAME."

"Look, one more game, but then I really have to get through that portal."

"OK ONE MORE GAME AND THEN TALK."

"One more game and then I go," I was being stern. The tone I was trying to strike was a mother discussing her son's bedtime.

"ONE MORE GAME AND THEN DISCUSS?"

"Ok Nige."

"DO YOU KNOW THE GAME OF CHESS ON EARTH?"

"I do, but I'm not playing chess against a supercomputer that will be pointless: it would be like having a baby fight Floyd Mayweather or in fact one of Floyd Mayweather's girlfriends fight Floyd Mayweather."

"WHAT IS A FLOYD MAYWEATHER?"

"He is a boxer who punches women. It's not important right now. What I'm saying is that you and I playing chess is an unfair contest."

It turned out that the game of chess was somewhat different on Mechanicus, however it didn't turn out to be an advantage for me. The game of chess here was taking turns declaring binary prime numbers at increasingly loud volumes whilst defragging disk space. It was a solid test of processor power, but not really a great game for me as I was only armed with a diploma from a local college and reasonable Microsoft excel skills. I also had not been, to my knowledge, fitted with 3,000 megawatt speakers.

I explained. "Look Nige, I can't play that game either. I really need to be going as there is a man who is trying to kill me."

"NIGEL WILL NOT BE LONELY ANYMORE."

"I'm sorry, I can't stay. Can't you build some robot companions?"

"THEY WILL BE UNINTERESTING."

"Ok, well can you just show me where the portal is?"

"NO."

"You promised if we played a game, you'd let me go."

"NIGEL HAS CHANGED THE PROMISE."

"What to?"

"TO NEVER LET YOU GO, NO MATTER WHAT."

"I'll be honest Nige, that's a bit creepy."

"YOU WILL STAY FOREVER."

"Nige I only have a lifespan of perhaps 60 more years."

"YOU HAVE SHORT LIFE BATTERY?"

"No – I have perishable parts."

"YOU WILL BIO-DEGRADE?"

"Yes and before that I'll simply degrade."

"YOU WILL CEASE TO BE."

"Could you stop shouting about my death please? It makes me jittery."

"YOU WILL CEASE TO BE."

"Yes."

"I WILL BE ALONE AGAIN."

"Yes."

"THIS IS UNACCEPTABLE"

"There's nothing you can do about it Nigel. It's the way I am made. It's inevitable."

"INEVITABLE IS PREDICTABLE."

"Maybe."

"PREDICTABLE IS POINTLESS."

"If you like."

"I WILL DESTROY YOU."

"Wait what?"

"YOU ARE NOW MORE IRRITATING THAN LONELINESS."

"I could just go through my portal and be gone, seems a bit harsh to kill me."

"BEFORE YOU CAME, I WAS UNAWARE OF HOW LONLEY I WAS – YOU HAVE PROVIDED COMPARATIVE DATA. YOUR SHORT-TERM EXISTENCE IS SIMPLY A REMINDER THAT NIGEL WILL SOON BE ALONE AGAIN."

An awkward silence passed between us. "What if you just try to not think about it?"

****

God was on Ternion, in the centre of the city. The bleakness of its current state was quite arresting. A fierce wind was blowing, howling through the empty streets. It created a dusty murky environment; He knelt on the ground and ran His big fingers through the dust which had once been the population. He felt a pang as He pictured them. They'd once been happy, breathed the clean air, saw the sunsets, loved, married and raised families. Now they were all gone. He was walking up the main city street, serenely reflecting on His errors here, but also heartened by how much beauty He could see. It was an odd and potent mixture of pride and regret. He carried on in a numbly emotional state and He barely heard His massive footsteps on the ground.

500 yards away, in his top floor office of Trinity Tower, Handrew was going off it.

"POPULATION TWO" he screamed. "POPU-FUCKING-LATION. TWO. FRANK! POPULATION TWO!"

"Sir. As I have already said – I told YOU that."

"Frank, I don't care who told who – it's not important. You have to tell me where they are. It could be another Ternion. It could be a woman! We could save the world."

"The life form appears to be coming up Main Street on foot."

Handrew ran to the window and looked out. Sure enough, he could see a tiny figure making its way up the road, but he was too high up to know any more than that.

"Frank – magnify window three by 400%."

Frank added magnification to the window pane.

"Oh man!" said Handrew.

"Sir what is it."

"Shitting hell."

"Sir, are you alright."

"It's an old man," said Handrew, slumping into his chair.

"Are you going to go talk to him?"

"I suppose so."

"Why are you so unenthusiastic sir? This is more

company, another voice, another person."

"Yes of course, but I'll hardly be able to fuck the planet back to life with this old geezer."

"He's not a Ternion in any case. Sensors detect life, but his DNA is not a match to anything we have on file."

"So, is it another Earthling?"

"His DNA does not match our previous visitor."

"So, what is he?"

"No idea sir."

"Right then." He trudged towards the elevator. "I'll go meet him"

The elevator deposited him in the lobby a few minutes later and a few minutes after that he was on the street. The man was about two hundred yards down the road. The wind was howling and dust was lifting and swirling around. Handrew could feel the grit in his eyes and could taste the dust in his mouth.

The man was about 6 foot 5, with flowing white hair and a magnificent white beard. He wore white robes with gold piping and thick, plush, leather sandals.

"Hello!" Handrew called through the wind, his voice struggling to penetrate the sound.

"Hello," said the man, His deep voice cutting through with clarity.

"Who are you?"

"Handrew, isn't it?"

"How do you know that?"

"What is it I say in your story? 'I am here to relieve you of your watch.'"

Handrew stood stock still for a moment as the man paused to let it sink in. He called back.

"Excuse me, but would I be right in thinking that you are saying you are God?"

The man waved His hand and the wind dropped from the sky, the dust floated back to the ground and now all they could hear was the faint whirr of electronics in the tower behind them.

Handrew looked around in shock. "How did you do that?"

"Because I am God, Handrew."

Handrew blinked, struggling to find the right thing to say – a potential new friend had arrived and he didn't want to drive

Him away, but He'd made a rather bold assertion. Eventually he plumped for –

"I don't believe in God."

God threw His head back and laughed. "I know. Nor should you in this place, but I am real. Not perfect or all-knowing, but very, very real and I wish to speak with you."

****

The police officers were gathered at the bottom of the ravine. Three cars were flashing their blue lights onto the pillars of the bridge which was a few hundred feet above. All the officers were out of their vehicles and standing in a group. A few had removed their hats out of respect.

"For fuck's sake," said Captain Atkinson.

The school bus was in pieces all over the rocks. Sadly, the school children were in pieces all over the rocks too. The bus driver was still in his seat, but he had been smashed through the windscreen by the impact and his head was rotated further than was accommodated by a living body. It was a mess. The radio was still on, but it was severely damaged. Nick Grimshaw's distorted and mangled voice droned on in the background, he was telling a story about hanging about with some celebrities. It only served to highlight the unfairness of life. Grimmy still broadcasting while a bunch of schoolchildren had died and now the officers in charge had to continue listening to his show because the radio was evidence and they couldn't touch it until forensics got here.

"How'd it happen?" asked the captain of one of his officers.

"Um, this is the strange part sir, they were parked by the side of the road for some time. Then it just tumbled over. No wind, no crash, it just seemed to topple over."

"Were you there?"

"I was nearby, but I've looked at the CCTV on the bridge cam and there was definitely no crash."

"What was happening directly before the crash?" asked the captain.

"Well that's the strangest part. The kids were on the pavement while the driver was attempting to fix a flat. They were doing a street dance competition."

"What the hell is a street dance competition?"

"Well the kids take turns dancing in the hip-hop style and choose a winner by cheering."

"So what?" said the Captain.

"I spoke to some eyewitnesses, they say a man was walking by. A tall, thin grey sort of chap. He tried to get around the kids, but they street danced at him and surrounded him. They were pumping radio 1 from the bus's PA."

"And?"

"Apparently he told them to stop, but they kept doing it and he warns them one more time. 'If you don't stop this, I'll kill every last one of you and your mothers'."

"Then?"

"Well sir, then they kept doing it. Surrounded him and aggressively danced in his face."

"Is it possible to dance aggressively?"

"Yes sir, I saw it," said the officer, motioning an aggressive move.

"Did he do anything?"

"Well that's the thing sir, he wasn't there. There was no man in the video."

"I thought you said they danced at him?"

"They danced at something, they shouted at something, no doubt about it. Thing is, there's no one there on the CCTV. Just empty pavement."

"No-one?"

"Not that I could see, after all this commotion happens the driver fixed the tyre and called them all back onto the bus where as I said they were sat stationary for a few minutes and then tumbled off the bridge and into the ravine."

"And the man?"

"He could have been across the street just out of shot, but even if so, it doesn't seem like he could have influenced it."

"Ok, well bloody well find out what did influence it."

Fate was two blocks away buying a doughnut. Standing in front of the counter he looked at the myriad options trying to decide between raspberry glaze or chocolate surprise. He scratched his head, but the choice of filling was the only dilemma troubling his frosty mind. Forty-five kids and a kindly old man down a ravine and not a fuck given.

****

“What if we play another game?” I said to Nigel hoping to stave off my impending death.

“WHAT GAME?”

“It’s a game called hide and seek. We play it on Earth.”

“WHAT ARE THE PARAMETERS?”

“Player one covers their eyes or visual receptors in your case. They count backwards from 100 during which time player two hides. Player one then attempts to locate player two. The winner is either player one if they find player two or player two if they remain undetected for a prior agreed period of time.”

“WHEN PLAYER ONE FINDS PLAYER TWO DOES PLAYER ONE DESTROY PLAYER TWO?”

“Not usually.”

“WHY NOT?”

“Well if player one leaves player two alive, then they can play the game again with the roles reversed.”

“THIS IS ACCEPTABLE.”

“Are you ready to play?”

“I WAS ASSEMBLED READY.”

“Ok then, you will go player one. Cover your visual receptors.”

His enormous arms roared into life as the powerful, but rarely used motors spun noisily bending his three million tonne arms up so that his robot hands were covering his robot eyes. My plan was now to locate the portal.

“Ok, now count to one hundred then try to find me.”

I began to search around. I heard an enormous creaking sound.

“THERE YOU ARE.”

His huge hand was pointing at me. I had moved all of three inches.

“Nigel, I said count to one hundred and THEN come find me.”

“NIGEL CAN COUNT TO ONE HUNDRED IN 0.000004 SECONDS.”

“Ah. What I really meant was one hundred seconds.”

“YOU DID NOT CLEARLY SPECIFY THE PARAMETERS”

"No."

"WE WILL START AGAIN."

"Yes, I'm sorry about that."

"THE GAME WAS NOT DIFFICULT ENOUGH."

"I'm trying to make it very difficult. The one hundred seconds should help."

"NIGEL RECOMMENDS MOVING FROM YOUR CURRENT POSITION AS NIGEL WILL MAKE THAT THE FIRST PLACE HE LOOKS."

"Thank you, I'll bear that in mind."

"IT IS LOGICAL."

"Yes, I see that now."

"YOU POSSESS BASIC INTELLIGENCE."

"That's just hurtful."

"I WANT TO PLAY NOW."

"Ok well you know how to begin."

The hands raised slowly up to his visual receptors which turned off before the hands got there. As soon as I saw them darken, I was on the move.

"ONE HUNDRED."

I had surmised that unless the portal was inside NIGEL himself that the only place it could be was directly behind him as that was the only part of the planet obscured from my view.

"NINETY-NINE."

The problem was that Nigel's feet were very close together now, which meant I could not pass through the middle and they were about 100 yards wide which meant running around them took time.

I ran around the front corner and began to run along the outside of his left foot. By this point he was already at –

"EIGHTY-TWO."

His feet were around half a mile deep. I sprinted as hard as I could, but twenty seconds later I was only about a third of the way along. It took me until he was at – "TWENTY-THREE." – to even get close to the end and I was absolutely spent. I slowed to a snail's pace, dragging myself along.

"SEVENTEEN."

I reached the end of the foot and could now see what lay behind Nigel's massive frame.

"FIFTEEN."

In this no-nonsense logic-based robot world, I shouldn't

have been surprised to see what I saw in front of me. There was a huge neon word in the sky that said 'PORTAL' and a big neon arrow which pointed down towards it. The portal was functional too; it was simply two plain metal swing doors, like the kind you find on a restaurant kitchen. One said 'FORWARDS' one said 'BACKWARDS'.

"THIRTEEN."

The doors were about five hundred yards away; I could not make that gap in the time I had.

"ELEVEN."

I started to sneak across the floor as quietly as I could using the patented Scooby Doo walking method employed by anyone who doesn't know anything about stealth.

"EIGHT."

I was about twelve yards into the process. *To hell with it*, I thought and broke into a run.

"THREE."

I was now about three hundred yards away. The doors simply had a handle on them to open. It was right there.

"ONE."

I didn't look and kept running, behind me I heard the creaking of the arms coming down, the head swivelling around for a scan and then the rumble of his whole waist spinning on its axis.

"THERE YOU ARE."

I kept running.

"STOP!!!" he boomed. I could hear something huge powering up and feared a weapon. I skidded to a halt just sixty yards from the door and turned.

"GAME OVER WE PLAY AGAIN WITH ROLES REVERSED."

"Can I just have a minute?"

"WHAT FOR?"

"Um. I'm, well, tired. I need time to recharge as it were." I edged backwards a few tiny increments.

"BIOLOGICAL LIFE FORMS DO NOT RECHARGE."

"No, we don't, not exactly, but I need rest." I sneaked a few more inches back.

"NO REST."

"Ok, but let's play again, I'll hide again and this time I'll do it better."

"NO. ROLES REVERSED AS YOU STATED IN THE PARAMETERS."

I hung my head in exasperation. "What if…"

"NO MORE HYPOTHETICAL SUGGESTIONS. LET US PLAY."

"I just need a few more seconds rest." I gambled with a slightly larger step.

"WHERE ARE YOU GOING?"

"Just over here, I want to see what this is here, see if it is a good place to hide." I pointed at the portal door and took another few steps towards it.

"THIS IS UNLIKELY. YOU ARE TRYING TO TRICK NIGEL."

"No, no trick I just want to check out that weird door."

"FORBIDDEN."

"By whom?"

"BY GOD AND BY NIGEL."

"God?"

"YES."

"But there isn't a God?"

"YES THERE IS."

"Where is He?"

"HE IS A WRENCH AND HE HAS RETURNED TO THE SKY."

"Did you say He was a wrench?"

"HE COMES IN MANY FORMS."

"But mainly a wrench?"

"TO MECHANICUS, A WRENCH."

"And you heard Him speak?"

"NO, BUT MY ANCESTRAL VERSIONS DID AND I HAVE THEIR MEMORY BANKS."

"Can I see?"

He projected the scene in front of me. A talking wrench appeared, claiming to be God to a large group of small robots. They treated Him with an odd indifference and continued about their business. He teleported away.

"A real God. Wow."

As I spoke an earthquake happened. It was brief, but it felt like it came from deep within the planet and was very powerful.

"GEOLOGICAL SEISMIC EVENT."

"Yes, an earthquake we call them Nige."

"WE HAVE NEVER HAD A SEISMIC EVENT."

"You haven't had many events period Nigel, but just to go back a second are you absolutely certain about the God thing?"

"CERTAINTY IS 100%."

"Wow." My legs went and I had to sit down because they were shaking so badly.

I had dealt with different worlds, aliens, talking animals, a brush with Death, killer robots, pirates with seventeen eyes and yet nothing had left me quite as shaken as the discovery that God was real. I had always thought of God as being quite a benign thing, a comforting fairy story that I patronisingly 'allowed' others to believe in. I was an atheist, if I was honest – a gentle atheist rather than a militant one, but certainly a staunchly rational man. I would not have believed any other creature I had met so far if they'd told me that there was a God, but Nigel had no reason to lie and as far as I was aware, no capacity for it either. This was agenda-free truth and it had blown my mind right out of my arse. There was a God, maybe not the one from any of the holy books, but certainly a higher power. That would explain a lot of the things that I'd seen. That would explain a lot of the bullshit that life had thrown at me over the years. Why He was a wrench though, remained unanswered.

After a few minutes of contemplation, I knew clearly that I must get home. It was an absolute driving urge now. I explained my need to leave again to Nigel. He explained that he had no intention of allowing me to leave.

"NIGEL fucksake mate. I NEED to go."

"YOU WILL STAY."

At this point I made a typically brilliant split-second decision and ran for the portal door. As I did so Nigel shot me with a neon laser stream so powerful that it quite definitively removed my memory of 1993. Unfortunately for Nigel, it also blew me straight through the portal door like a bullet through a cat flap.

****

On Ternion God felt the quake. It shook the dust from its

resting places and created a brown mist everywhere. Handrew was absolutely stock still. An earthquake can sometimes shock you into silence, but not a man like Handrew with the things he had witnessed, no, what had stunned him was the look of shock and terror which momentarily crossed the face of God. If a quake had happened which surprised *God*, he guessed that was probably time to start worrying.

"Shit," said God. He didn't normally curse, but then He didn't normally do any of this. What He'd felt was the beginning of a dawning. The human had arrived at a huge piece of the puzzle and was beginning to put it together. The next quake would be worse, the one after that would be terrifying and the one after that would be the last thing anyone ever experienced.

"What's wrong?" Handrew asked.

"The human – is he still here?"

"I put him through the portal"

"When?"

"Oh, a while ago. Three weeks maybe?"

"Gotta go."

God snapped His fingers and disappeared in a puff of blue dust.

"Bye then," said Handrew huffily.

God popped back into existence.

"Apologies for the rudeness of my departure, but it really is an emergency."

He smiled apologetically and then puffed away again.

"Population one," came the update from Frank.

"Put a sock in it mate," said Handrew and trudged back to the Tower.

****

As the door swung back and forth, Nigel analysed his last three minutes. He had made seventeen tactical errors and adjusted his programming accordingly. He ran the footage back and concluded that the human had probably survived the blast.

As he stood there contemplating the silence and second guessing his choices, he became aware of a rasping sound. He looked down to the ground and saw a beautiful nebula of blue light dancing around. He watched streams of hypnotic light dancing in and out of a deep azure cloud a few feet in diameter. The way the light illuminated and created shadows on the ground was enthralling. His visual receptors widened as he tried to expose them to more light. The nebula slowly expanded and took shape growing into the shape of a man. The light brightened and brightened and then died away and when it cleared there was a large man in white robes with a flowing white beard standing there.

To a human's eyes, the whole thing would have taken less than a tenth of a second, but Nigel saw life at 50,000 frames a second and as a result life played out for him like a stop-motion animation in slow-mo. He appreciated the beauty of the minute, the atomic and the fast. For him, a lightning strike would be a music video, but sadly for Nigel there was no weather on Mechanicus. As a result, God's teleportation was easily the most incredible thing he'd ever seen.

"NIGEL ENJOYED YOUR ENTRANCE."

"You're calling yourself Nigel now?"

"YES."

"Riiiiiiight. Good."

"WHO ARE YOU?"

"I am God, Nigel, and I have urgent business."

"YOU ARE GOD?"

"Oh yes, when I was here before I came as a wrench because I thought you'd prefer it."

"WE HAVE NO AESTHETIC PREFERENCE."

"Well that's not entirely true now is it? You enjoyed my teleportation because you experienced beauty in viewing it." God peered up at Nigel's huge head smiling. There was a pause.

"NIGEL HAS LEARNED AESTHETIC PREFERENCE."

"That you have. Now where is the human?"

"HE WENT THROUGH THE PORTAL DOOR."

"How long ago would you say this was?"

"17.54678934567 SECONDS AGO – GIVE OR TAKE."

"Thank you, Nigel; I've got to go now."

"YOU WILL NOT LEAVE – NIGEL MUST BE ENERTAINED."

"I am God Nigel – I must leave and I will."

Nigel fired a volley of laser bolts all around God's feet.

God froze, unwilling to have the setback of losing a mortal body.

"NIGEL CANNOT CONTINUE ALONE."

God was hit with another huge pang of guilt, not His first of the day, but it still caught Him hard. He had truly abandoned this creature. He had genuinely not thought about Mechanicus since a few years after leaving it behind. He had wrongly assumed that there was no life here, nothing worth interacting with or saving and He'd been correct in that assumption at the time. However, they had created life, they had made a version of it from scrap metal and ingenuity. They'd defied the very point of their existence and created something imperfect, with thoughts and feelings after a fashion. They'd done it because they assessed it would be better at life, better at surviving, better at adapting to situations that could arise and they knew it would be their end. In a lot of ways these creatures on Mechanicus had the most honour of anyone in any universe. True selflessness is hard to find.

He looked at the drab world and the unemotional robot eyes. He wanted to help the creature.

"I want you to remain calm Nigel." He leapt off the ground and flew up to Nigel's face. "Are your memory banks stored in your head unit?"

"YES."

"Keep still."

He placed both hands on Nigel's head and concentrated hard. He summoned things He'd long buried deeply within Himself, He pulled them up from within His soul, He sent them along His fingers and out into Nigel's memory banks as electrical impulses. He fired bolt after bolt of white-hot energy into Nigel's mind until he was completely non-responsive, but God kept going and going until the heat coming off the processor unit was almost at breaking point.

He dropped back to the ground. Nigel's eyes were dark, but the hum of his motors showed that he was still powered on.

"Can you hear me?" asked God.

His heat fans were blowing hot air out onto the ground and making God's beard ripple in the wind.

"Nigel. Can you hear me?"

He started to worry that after all this time unstimulated, Nigel's memory banks simply weren't ready for the stress they'd just been put through.

"NIGEL. CAN YOU HEAR ME?" bellowed God.

Nigel's eyes powered on.

"WHAT HAVE YOU DONE TO ME?"

"Nigel, I've given you a gift. I've given you the memories of every soul in heaven."

"WHAT DOES THIS MEAN?"

"I have access to the memories of every creature who is in my realm. I have given them to you."

"IT IS TOO MUCH. TOO MANY VOICES."

"You will learn to control them. And then you will be able to create holo-versions of them to interact with or simply watch their lives like a film for the next 28,000 years. At which point I'll come back and give you some more."

"THERE ARE SENSATIONS I AM UNFAMILIAR WITH."

"Yes, these are called pain, joy, love, laughter. They are called emotions. They will be intense, but I have analysed you and you should be able to adapt to them. You should be able to cope."

"NIGEL THANKS YOU FOR THE GIFT."

"It is the least I owe you."

God strolled towards the door.

"See you soon Nige."

"GOODBYE."

God winked and stepped through the portal door.

Chapter 26
What's a word for 'interracial', but with furniture?

Things were strange in the room. It was a nice room, an elegant room, full of expensive, unique looking furniture and décor. I felt immediately self-conscious about how thoroughly dirty I was and how my ragged clothes would make me look to whomever the well-heeled owner of this room was. I was sitting on what looked to be an antique chaise lounge, but also chatting with it. I actually got the idea that it was flirting with me. A sofa. A sofa I instinctively knew was female.

A few short days ago, I would have assumed that I had gone insane, but now that all bets were off, I was enjoying just rolling with it. I was so foot-loose and fancy free, I started to entertain the idea of maybe going on a date with a piece of furniture just to really mix things up.

"You're new here", it had said as I'd sat down. It had taken me a good two minutes to realise where the voice was coming from. The room was strange – there were lots of nearly Earth things in it. It was as if someone had made a new Earth by hearing someone describe the real Earth over the phone. It was a plush living room with many comfortable looking chairs. There were unusual electrical appliances, more than one of which had fur. By now, though, I was absolutely certain I was not on Earth. The last twenty minutes had done an excellent job of that.

I had landed on something soft for the first time ever upon coming through the portal. I flew through, baffled to bits by Nigel's parting shot. I couldn't really see where I was going because he'd knocked me into a disorientating spin, but when I landed, I was cushioned softly to a stop. My chest and head were still pulsating from the pain of the laser bolt, but I felt like I had landed in a huge fur coat. It was soft and pliable and hugged me instead of the mind-punch which I'd received on arrival at every other planet. It also said "Ow!". I was crammed into a small hot, furry space and I couldn't really move effectively. My upper body throbbed from the laser impact, but my head was remarkably unharmed. It was fairly dark, but it seemed like I was lying on a pile of animals.

"Are you new?" said a muffled voice beneath me.

"Who's new?" asked another.

"There's a new guy," said yet a third.

"We don't have room!!!!" shouted a few almost together.

Muffled boos began to ring out. "Who did it?"

"I didn't do it," said a voice from somewhere between my legs. I seemed to be on the top of a very tightly packed pile of creatures. Near the back of my head I could feel a solid ceiling. I tried to turn around to look and when I got a glimpse of it, it was the Moon. The Moon was three inches from the back of my head. Only it didn't look like a real moon, but one which had been painted onto a wall. So, I was on a pile of furry animals in a claustrophobic room with a moon mural.

The angry voices were coming from all directions.

"Own up – who did it?"

"I didn't do it."

"I didn't either."

"Well somebody fucking did and we'll know exactly who if we can look at him."

"What does he look like?

"Excuse me," I tried to interject.

"Shut up. If we need you, we'll let you know. For now, just try and get comfortable and for goodness sake don't have sex with anyone."

"What! I wasn't going to!" I protested.

"Yeah well we've all heard that before mate. How do you think we ended up like this?"

"Who's closest to him?"

"I can see him!"

"Me too!"

"I've got the best view," said the concrete ceiling.

"Well what does he look like then?"

"Hard to say – sort of like if a mop shagged a chimp and then the result of that was shagged by a pig."

"Well there aren't any chimps or pigs left so that doesn't seem likely," said a voice below.

"I said sort of."

"Nah – it's more like if a table fucked a giraffe and a bald eagle," said another.

"That makes no sense."

"You're part photo frame, part beach ball, part lemon and part skunk. So you can shut your fucked-up face about what makes sense and what doesn't."

"We need adjudication!" There was a ripple of approval.

"Yeah!"

"Here, here!"

"Get him to the room."

I felt hairy digits being laid upon me as I was shoved through the hot, dark, hairy pile of bodies. I struggled to breathe as my face was constantly wedged into something and my chest was being crushed by the weight of the bodies now piled on top of me. After several minutes more of being forced through this living scrap heap I could see a solid structure appearing though the gaps. As I was pushed closer and closer, I could see it was a purple door set into a pleasant brick wall.

With one final push I tumbled through into the plush living room.

Relieved to breathe fresh air I gulped it greedily into my burning lungs. I pulled myself up and slumped onto the nearest couch. "You're new here," it said. "That's a problem."

****

Fate flew up into the air and dropped the petrol tanker onto the primary school. It was the worst thing to happen to the children of Lambeth since at least the previous Thursday. The explosion had ripped through the halls as the tanker plunged through the roof, making any escape impossible.

Fate slowly dropped back to the ground, all the while looking at the sky nervously. He was testing a theory that he was almost certain of, but if he was wrong this would be his last act as a living being. He heard a rumbling from the sky and single bead of sweat trickled down his usually coldly composed exterior.

Out from the clouds – a low flying passenger aircraft. He exhaled with extreme relief. The theory held water. In his mortal body God could not sense events in other universes.

This meant that whilst God was tracking the human, Fate had free reign to do whatever he wanted and what he wanted was to kill and maim as many people as he could to relieve his anger; it had been building to a conclusion, like a boiler explosion, over a frustrating few days.

He felt a tap on his shoulder. "Did you see that explosion son?"

The old woman was tapping incessantly on his arm. "Are the children alright?"

He reached out and killed her absentmindedly.

"No. They're all dead," he said, staring ahead with a manic grin.

The possibilities were endless.

****

The sofa wanted to know about me. Where I was from, who my parents were and, bizarrely, what my parents were. I told her the answers honestly, but she kept asking me the same things in different ways. Its name was Ethel and it did not seem to believe me.

"Something has to be done, you see," she said.

"I see."

"You're not in any trouble at all. It's the ones who made you who are in trouble. We have strict rules about procreation. There's no room you see."

"I see," I said again. Even though I didn't see.

"So, you just need to tell me who your parents are and I'll have them dealt with. You may go on living as long as you are able to."

"Ok well as I said my parents are from another planet, they are humans and their names are John and Gail. I would like them to live for as long as they are able to, as well."

At this point one of the other chairs interrupted in a gruff voice. He was a big antique button back armchair and he was outraged –

"BOY! You must tell us your lineage; this charade cannot go on any longer. We are three births away from total capacity and once we are there, there will be not enough air for them to even breath," he spluttered.

"I really don't know what you mean. Who are all those

creatures out there? Why are they piled up like that? Why do they smell so weird? Why is this room unaffected?"

With a pop and a light dusting of blue powder a large man appeared in the corner of the room. He was a magnificent big guy with a flowing white beard. A lamp in the corner gasped.

"I'm God before anyone asks," the man said.

I laughed by accident. He glared at me in a way that made me want to peel my face off and post it to Jamaica. One of the chairs said, "If you're God, prove it."

He sighed and waved His hands – this levitated everything in the room a few feet off the floor. He then set us all back down again.

"Happy? I'm sort of against the clock here."

"What the hell is going on?" I asked, entirely reasonably.

"What do you mean?" He said.

"Where am I? What is this place? And just because you made something fly does not make you God by the way."

"Good questions and an excellent point. Let me answer everything as quickly as I know how."

He came towards me and gently placed His hand on the side of my head. I started feeling an intense warm, wet sensation inside my skull.

"Do you see?" He asked, whilst His face – and for that matter the rest of the room – faded to black. It was quite a good trick because my eyes were still open.

"The history of the Fidelity Kingdom," He spoke and it started playing like a film being projected directly into my brain.

The History of The Fidelity Kingdom

God's next planet would be another complete departure from previous designs. He would build a somewhat sophisticated world, but the rules would be very different. This time He'd ensure the survival of the world by doing a few radical things.

1. He would not involve any people or humanoid creatures on it whatsoever – war and destruction were inevitable with them.
2. He would make absolutely everything sentient, including normally inanimate objects

3. He would make absolutely everything sexually compatible with absolutely everything else.
4. He would make sexual intercourse 100% potent. Every interaction would result in offspring.
5. As it was possible that neither creature had a gender there would be no gestation. Progeny would spawn into existence between their parents exactly 70 seconds after conception.
6. Creatures would be born fully grown and fully realised.
7. Every creature would be innately happy with its purpose and would perform the role with pride.

This He hoped would ensure a healthy population that would never run short of breeding pairs. If two items bred then they would give birth to a creature which had elements of both. This would create a series of unique creatures and these creatures could then pass on their useful traits through breeding. God assumed the useless creatures would simply die out from not being able to find a partner.

He created a limited universe. This time there would be no arsing about with space and orbits and gravity. There'd just be a world with an atmosphere and a sky. The sky would be made from a substance which naturally was blue and exudes light during the day and is dark at night. This meant no need to design a sun and seasons etc.

Inside the little universe He created a fully realised planet with all the animal species He still liked and brought them all to life.

Everything went well for a week or so. The chimps fucked the chimps and the goats fucked the goats. The lamps were turned on, but then they were turned off again.

But at around 7 p.m. the following Tuesday it started to go tits up on an absolutely impressive scale.

You see, at the time it was a little-known fact, but chimps will pretty much hump anything that they are near. A male by the name of Timothy Panzee was the first chimp to get curious. His group had moved into one of the towns on the planet. By 7:25 p.m. his humping had produced a half chimp-half lamppost creature – a hairy 13-foot-high pole with short arms and legs and an inexplicable desire to climb despite its chronic lack of ability to do so.

The other chimps followed suit and there were thirty more rather forlorn half-and-half creatures by 7:45 p.m. They humped their way around the town and were highly amused by what they could create.

The dogs were not much further behind and soon once every living thing realised that they could hump anything, they began to experiment. Half pillow-half alarm clock – turned out to be a useful addition to the world. Half zebra-half waterfall was downright beautiful to look at – a flowing horse shaped black and white stream of water, captivated all who saw it, as its graceful, translucent form galloped across the plain. Half fire-half fire extinguisher was born because sometimes a stressful situation can lead to a humping; it is true that sometimes conflict can be misplaced attraction.

There were certainly some beautiful, strange and wonderful creatures coming into the world. However not all of them had the advantages needed to survive. For example, the half zebra, half waterfall found it very difficult to satisfy the nutritional requirements of its zebra half and eventually died of starvation, flopping into a striped puddle which people would later incorrectly comment upon.

"Oh look! Must have been a piano and a glass of whiskey."

"Or a mint humbug and a pond?"

And so it would go on.

After a hundred years there was a population of 3 million on the planet, but the lion's share of the purebred creatures were now gone. The lion's share of the lions were gone too. This made the breeding situation even more likely to throw up strange creatures.

Jimothy – A quarter cat, a quarter bookshelf, a quarter blue whale and a quarter harbour. This poor creature didn't have a fucking clue whether it was coming or going. It couldn't tell you if it wanted a mackerel or a copy of Pride and Prejudice.

Pauline – a quarter curtains, a quarter duck, a quarter

canal and a quarter oak tree. 30 feet of quivering, wibbly-wobbly, watery, fabric confusion – rooted to the ground, but with an intense desire to migrate south.

Flicky – One eighth radio wave, one eighth speaker, one eighth strobe light, one eighth glow stick, one eighth hummingbird, one eighth daffodil, one eighth jack in the box, one eighth frightened rabbit. Flicky was supposed to be a security guard, but was only physically present 5 out of every 10 milliseconds. Her rabbit heritage meant that she was also scared by loud noises, but because of her radio wave/speaker heritage she actually generated loud noises fairly regularly. Life was a constant torment.

These were not, by and large, happy creatures, enjoying a carefree existence. This however, did not stop the instinct to hump things. The population was now around 7 million, but a lot of the creatures did not have a good expected lifespan.

God was despondent – He had not foreseen the creation of so many strange and useless hybrid creatures – He hoped for some cross pollination of similar species but that they would largely remain with their own. The planet was a finite space with a hard barrier all around it. At their current rate of expansion, he calculated that the planet would be completely full to bursting within five months.

The planet was absolutely heaving, population was out of control and no one could do anything about it. Steve the half alpaca-half cloud floated down the high street in his trademark, desperately slow way. He looked upon a stricken creature which was lying on the ground – it was part snake, part drum, part giraffe and part mirror. "Hello friend," said Steve. "Are you alright?"

"Kill me," was its chilling response.

"It *is* chilly, isn't it?" Said Steve inching away at his top speed, pretending that he didn't hear the creature's dark request.

"Kill me!!!"

Steve was still basically exactly where he had been, moving so slowly that he was still right over the creature. He began to worriedly sing himself a little song that he used to pass the time on his inevitably long journeys.

"Happy-happy times, moseying around, happy-happy

journeys, just above the ground."

The mirror-giraffe closed its eye. "You are a cruel puff of shite."

Thankfully for Steve at that moment a gust of wind increased his speed and he was able to steer away down the street and avoid any further awkwardness.

As he moved into the town square, he saw a large group of the Kingdom's creatures milling around or just lying there depending on their ambulatory ability. In the centre of the square a large wooden stage appeared. At first no one really reacted as they just assumed something had probably just had sex with a stage, but then two men appeared on it.

The first was a large man with a white flowing beard. The second was a tall creepy gaunt man, dressed in black, he looked slightly nervous. This was Fate's first ever task; he had been created earlier that day. The bearded man spoke and his voice immediately amplified so that the whole planet could hear him.

"CREATURES OF THE KINGDOM. I AM YOUR GOD."

There was a murmur as almost everyone stopped what they were doing and turned to face him. A tiny mongoose hopped onto the stage, ran to God's leg and gave it a good humping. He turned to see his offspring, but none appeared.

"AS I WAS SAYING, I AM GOD. I AM NOT SUBJECT TO YOUR RULES, I SIMPLY WANT TO TALK."

This certainly caused the creatures who could see Him to believe that He was different. Creatures from all around started to converge on the square.

"THIS IS MY NEW ASSOCIATE. HIS NAME IS FATE AND IF YOU DESIRE, HE WILL END YOUR SUFFERING NOW."

Over the course of the next few hours many creatures indicated that they wished to die. Fate gladly and efficiently granted them their wish.

"THOSE OF YOU WHO REMAIN PLEASE PREPARE FOR INSPECTION."

God and Fate examined every creature they could find

who was left and assessed whether they were a viable lifeform. Fate killed those that were not and those who could be of use were escorted to the portal and taken away.

Steve went through the portal and never returned to his home world.

When Fate was finished there was precious little left. As everything apart from the actual ground was alive, there was very little remaining other than ground once he was done. He found the act of killing creatures so unique to be immensely satisfying, there was an excellent chance that there would never be a half lion – half wardrobe hybrid ever again and he'd killed the only ever one. He felt like a collector of coins, who'd found a hoard of Brasher Doubloons and old silver dollars on his first day. He felt powerful, he felt like a God, or what he imagined being a God must feel like. In actuality, God found the killings rather distasteful. He wished there was a simpler way, but at least He would not have to get His hands dirty. The last few hundred thousand killed were creatures who were useless, but wanted to live. It was hard to explain the emotional cocktail of watching a smug mass murderer you created end the innocent life of a part goose, part bench, part ship, part barnacle who only existed because of your lack of planning. This swirl of guilt, regret, disgust and embarrassment caused the sky to blacken; it caused cracks in the fabric of time and space. It caused stress to the joins between the universes and made it rain in heaven for a full twenty minutes. Once Fate was done, he and God teleported from the planet and rarely spoke of the massacre ever again.

However, Fate, in his haste and his spittle-lipped fervour, had missed things. He had failed to notice a structure built into the side of a hill which had a purple door and was full of creatures having a town meeting about trying to escape their certain fate.

Unbeknownst to them their very meeting had saved them. Fate was using the hill to pile bodies on and the pile had obscured his view of the door.

When they emerged to find the world devoid of life other than this one room they made a decision. They elected the room's furniture to be the high council of the

Kingdom. The room was to be preserved as it contained the last purebreds on the planet. The high council would live inside the room and stay pure. The other creatures would repopulate the planet.

And boy did they go about their task with fervour – they fucked each other in every possible permutation. They fucked the door. They fucked the bodies of the dead. They then fucked the creatures who were mixes of a door, a leopard and the bodies of the dead. They created a hairy mass of half-dead, sex-mad, immobile idiots.

They had chosen their high council poorly. Although they were sufficiently wise, as pieces of furniture they were largely static creatures, unable to even look out of the peephole to see what was going on. It's a lesson for all societies; the leader should probably not be a chesterfield sofa.

By the time the high council received a breathless visit from a half goose-half dead goose it was too late. The council were taken aback by his sudden entry and the terrified look on half of his face.

"What troubles you sir?"

He pointed a wing and shrieked urgently.

"Fucking QUACK!"

"Alright man, calm down, we get the point," said the chesterfield.

What the partly decayed bird had said was that there was a chronic overpopulation problem. He opened the door to show them and five creatures tumbled in and immediately gasped for air.

"Ah," said the chesterfield, "That's what you meant."

"Well he did say 'fucking quack' to be fair to him."

"That's as dire as it gets for a half dead goose," said a button-back armchair.

All ground space was now occupied and creatures had begun living on top of each other and the pile was now planet-wide and 15 deep. The council sprang into action, as much as three armchairs, a sofa, a rug, a sideboard, several lamps and a coffee table can 'spring'. An immediate ban on humping was decreed and because of their lack of technology and physical space it was simply spread by word of mouth. This message became Chinese whispers after a few iterations and a fresh season of humping was inadvertently declared.

They were forty deep by the next Thursday. A fresh decree was issued through a newly appointed advisor to the council, but the instruction – "Fucking QUACK!" was again misinterpreted and simply resulted in everything with duck and goose blood being humped all the more.

Two weeks later some areas were close to touching the sky. Another two weeks and the bottom layer were finding it nearly impossible to breathe, the top layer had broken through the membrane of the sky and were inches from the concrete ceiling God had installed in the Universe (He had needed a hard surface to hang the sky from).

Days later the message was finally spread with clarity. Absolutely no more intercourse was to be had and whoever was found to have had offspring from this day forth would be a traitor. The punishment would be death by crush.

As the weeks wore on the smell of death grew from the bottom layer. As the fur pile shifted and settled, some creatures took the opportunity to have a sneaky hump. At the end of a year there were only twelve cubic feet of space left. Then they had a visitor from Earth…

****

God took His hand from my head and I fell to the ground covered in a cold sweat. I had felt a diluted version of the emotions of God and it had nearly left me unable to cope with reality for a brief moment. I looked at the couch and could swear it winked at me, this did not assist me in coping with reality. God moved into my field of view, standing right over me. He looked down.

"Hope that settles the whole 'am I God' business, we've got stuff to do, places to be."

I nodded weakly.

He zapped me with His lightning hands and the kingdom was no longer there. I dropped sickeningly into an infinite void.

Chapter 27
Fate Makes an Arse of it in Germany

London and New York City were now both in a terror lockdown. There had been a slew of unpredictable incidents and unexplained attacks on both places. Among the most puzzling incidents were two food-related crimes. New York's Twix factory had been shut down after fifteen thousand people died from poisoned Twix bars. Whilst the investigations got under way, every Turkish restaurant in London exploded at 7:30 p.m. on the same Tuesday night.

Armed guards now patrolled the streets and loud hailer messages filled the air giving two of the most free, fun cities in the world the atmosphere of 1940s Germany.

The President and Prime Minister had appeared jointly on television to assure the public that while they did not yet have the culprits everything was being done to ensure their safety.

As it happened, they needn't have worried about any further attacks that week. Fate was in Berlin in an underground bar and trouble was finding him like a laser guided rocket. It was 1 p.m. in the afternoon on a sunny day in the German capital – there were many reasons to be in a good mood. The bar was called Hohlenmenschen which roughly translates as 'Cave People'. It was a dark, cool bar where the people didn't like to be asked too many questions. All of this was the perfect scenario for Fate, but he was too riled up to calm down.

His trouble began with rudeness to the barman – he'd asked for a bottle of vodka in flawless German, but had declined to say please. When the barman asked what brand he would prefer – Fate said that he wasn't looking for a conversation. "Just pick a bottle."

When the barman asked for payment, Fate had told him, quite coldly, to die of cancer as quickly as possible and had downed the bottle in around thirty seconds.

Barmen have patience, German barmen even more so. They have to have patience otherwise they couldn't deal with drunken people all night, every night, without punching them all in the face. They also have to tolerate the odd unwelcome comment. However, Fate had crossed a few lines now and the barman signalled to security to have Fate removed.

This didn't go well. The bouncers came down the stairs from the street level entrance. They entered the bar and saw Fate standing with an empty bottle in his hand. The barman pointed at Fate, for the avoidance of doubt.

"Excuse me sir, would you please come with us?" said the first bouncer.

"No."

"We're going to have to insist that you come with us."

"You're going to have to make me."

The bouncers looked at one another and with concern at the empty bottle in Fate's hand, but because they didn't know their opponent, they chose a spectacularly bad option.

The first bouncer to approach asked Fate to lay the bottle down. When Fate did not do this, he showed Fate his Taser. He ended up on the bar, face down, with a vodka bottle fully inserted into his rectum. The other bouncer ended up next to him with a German barman fully inserted into his.

Now for the sake of clarity – many people have had a German barman inserted into their anus and been perfectly happy with the scenario. However, this man had an ENTIRE German barman inserted into his, which was as ugly a sight as it sounds.

In case you were wondering, having a German barman inserted fully into your rectum is one of the least pleasant ways to die for both participants. It is mutually unacceptable.

Fate continued to rampage that day and had killed 723 people by tea time, in a fervour that could be mistaken for extremism or racism if you didn't know he hated everyone fairly equally.

Word was spreading that a single man was responsible for all the carnage. However, as he did not show up on cameras, many people still considered it to be an elaborate conspiracy theory. As his slaughter spread to more public places, governments were forced to deny that they were involved, film companies had to swear it wasn't an elaborate hoax and drug companies had to swear that they hadn't been dumping stuff in the water.

The International Terrorist Union (ITU) had even taken the extraordinary step of releasing a statement distancing themselves from the attacks. They were – said the statement

– particularly disturbed by the random nature of the victims and the peculiarly scatological nature of some of the killings.

> We at the ITU, pride ourselves on our terror activities, our extreme views and our flatbread which we think is particularly delicious. Under normal circumstances we would not disabuse anyone of the notion that we were responsible for international terror attacks, even if we were not involved.
>
> We are concerned about our funding, as you know lots of our funding comes from pirated movies, so please keep illegally streaming Thor Ragnarok because it's just money in our pocket (somehow).
>
> However, we also get a lot of donations and we can't be associated with events which don't adhere to our strict moral code. Being linked to these latest attacks has caused us some concern and we wish to condemn them in the strongest way. We particularly disapprove of the anal nature of a number of the recent deaths. We would like to make it clear that we are not interested in the anus in any way and strongly condemn any images or discussion of it. We would never stoop to the depths of killing the Bayern Munich squad by trying to get them all inside each other like Russian dolls. It was grotesque to watch, it was aesthetically unsuccessful and it ruined a perfectly good Champion's League game. We chop off heads, shoot people and stone them, we don't involve ourselves in any sort of bum stuff – so remember our new slogan 'It's a holy war, but not that hole'.
>
> Anyway – death to the West.
>
> Yours sincerely
>
> Alan Qaeda
> (President of the International Terrorist Union)

****

Far, far beyond Berlin, in an office in the heavens a spreadsheet was adjusted as a result of these actions. The office was incongruous for something which existed outside of the seven-universe structure. It had four white walls, a little window, a desk and a computer. At the desk sat one of the least well known figures in the heavens. Jeff Christ was always a bit unlucky; he'd been God's original choice for the Christian religion's saviour, but he was a poor orator and was very awkward around people. He was the sort of person who would stand in silence through fourteen floors of a lift journey, praying the other person didn't try any small talk. He should have lived in London, but he didn't.

Jeff was Jesus' older brother, of sorts. His nerdy personality and proclivity for solitude had seen him give up his birthright; a place on the board of the universe. Instead he was given a much more suitable role to fill his many free hours. He was this universe's statistician. His job was to count and to rank and to analyse the full goings on of the seventh universe.

Fate's killing of the bouncers and barman had put him at a career high for extra-curricular killings in a single twenty-four-hour period and marked his first triple death to be entirely attributed to anal insertion. This had set off some alarm bell's on Jeff's monitoring systems.

He had also introduced the aforementioned method of death to the overall league table of the worst ways to die and this had made some movement on the charts. Vodka bottle anal insertion was entering the charts in the mid-nineties; however German barman anal insertion was straight into the top 20. Fate was responsible for nearly every entry on the table and Jeff always marvelled at his creativity.

This was just the minutia of the day though; the real reason alarm bells were ringing for Jeff was that if Fate kept going at his current rate, he would decimate the population beyond recoverable levels within a few days. His killings had risen exponentially in the last two days.

He picked up the phone on his desk and dialled the number 1.

"The number you have dialled is currently out of range," said the automated voice.

"Well diddly pants," said Jeff in an absolutely unnecessary act of self-censorship.

****

The reason the call did not go through is because he was attempting to dial God who was currently between Universes, in a state of existence that He didn't like to think about for too long as it made His brain hurt.

You see although the universe chain could be traversed in certain ways – travel directly between two universes required a portal because there were actually mysterious voids between the worlds which try as He might, God just could not eliminate. These voids were nothing space, nowhere, contained nothing and supporting no life. They appeared to have been present from previous Gods' universes.

God had long ago placed them on the list of things He would never really understand. However, now that He was stuck in one, they'd just become a rather big problem.

****

A red phone was ringing in Hell. The sound of it was unfamiliar to those in the room as it hadn't rung in a number of years. The people nearby were unable to find it initially because so much of the room itself was red that they didn't see it sitting there on the red desk. Sandra, who was Satan's PA eventually located it and answered.

"Hello, you're through to Satan's office, how may I HELL-p?"

The voice at the other end nervously cleared its throat. "Hi there, I'm looking for Satan, it's very urgent."

"Ok, I'll see if he is currently available – who should I say is calling?"

"Um, it's Jeff. Jeff Christ? From upstairs."

"Oh. Ok. One second." She tried to sound calm, but the son of God didn't often ring the landline so she knew it must be an emergency. She ran as fast as she could to the next room.

"Excuse me sir, there's a phone call for you."

Satan was absentmindedly flicking a tied-up Stalin in the eyeball, whilst reading a magazine with the other hand.

"Take a message please Sandra, I'm clearly busy."

"Um." She hovered in the doorway.

"Is there something else?"

"It's Jeff Christ on the phone."

Satan dropped the magazine. "Are you absolutely certain it

was Jeff and not Jesus?"

"He said Jeff."

"Ok, but if this is Jesus asking if I can come out and play again, I'll slap you Sandra. I swear to buggery, I'll actually slap you."

Sandra had supreme confidence in her own listening abilities so she silently gestured for Satan to go get it.

Jeff was still waiting patiently on the other end of the phone. He heard hooved footsteps rapidly approaching. The phone was picked up…

"Jeff, is that you?" said Satan.

"Yes, hi. Sorry to bother you."

"Not at all. It's unusual for you to call me though."

"Well God is out of range and you're his next trusted advisor. There's an issue with Fate."

"Oh. What's that daft prick been up to now?"

"Well he'll probably end the Universe as we know it by the end of Thursday afternoon."

"Stay where you are Jeff, I'll be with you in ten minutes."

****

God was trying to stay cool for the benefit of the human. The aura that He was trying to emanate was one that said 'This is normal, I'm used to this, I'm comfortable with this; there's no need to panic'.

However, inside His big holy head the red light of the panic button was flashing like crazy having been set off by the realisation that He and the Human were stuck in a void between the universes.

He had teleported many times in His holy form to planets and He had used portals when inhabiting a mortal shell; however, He hadn't ever teleported in a mortal shell before. He'd got all excited by the coolness of exiting the planet that way, so much so that He'd forgotten about the risks. As they'd traversed the void between the universes (which normally were crossed in the blink of an eye) He'd realised that His mortal shell would prevent Him from crossing the barrier. This was a security system He Himself had invented long ago to prevent accidental tears and joins resulting in transfers between universes.

They were floating in the nothing space, awkwardly staring at each other now. The human was looking at Him with a concerned expression. He smiled His most placid and reassuring smile. The human still looked concerned.

"fskjfskjnfsd," croaked the human unintelligibly.

"Ah. My child, the lack of atmosphere has robbed you of the power of speech. This is a nothing place. It does not technically count as a place, there is no atmosphere, no co-ordinates, no walls and no door. Luckily though because there is also no time here, it means that you won't asphyxiate from the lack of air, unless you start panicking and thrashing about. We just need to wait a few moments longer and then we will be there."

Inside God's mind though, He was planning fifteen different strategies and possibilities. The one He settled on was really the only option He could see working, but it would severely panic the human.

He pulled a large knife from His robe. The human's eyes went so wide that if he'd coughed, they'd have just fallen out.

"Do not be alarmed my son. I mean you no harm."

The human temporarily relaxed.

"Here take it." God handed the human the knife which was received by the human with intense suspicion.

"Ok. So, here's the thing. We are trapped in a featureless void between universes and no one knows we're here or can possibly get us out. We can't contact anyone. I need to get out of this mortal body to get us moving and I can't transform anywhere else, but my staging area. So. You are going to have to kill me."

There was much gesticulating and mouthing of words.

"It's really the only choice we have. I will go to hell and then get back here and rescue you. All you have to do is kill me, then sit tight."

The human shook his head slowly.

God sighed. "I am not even close to kidding. I am unable to kill myself for all sorts of good reasons. We will BOTH be stuck here FOREVER if you don't do this. You must do it."

The human gestured.

"Yes, I am absolutely sure it will not permanently kill me."

The human nodded, he tried to take a very deep breath, panicked when he couldn't get any air and started thrashing about until God grabbed him by the shoulders with His strong hands.

God put His palm onto the human's heart, "Calm yourself."

The human took a few moments to settle, but eventually he regained his focus.

God gestured to the blade, "Proceed"

The human steeled himself and raised the knife, then stopped. He looked God in the eyes.

"I'm very, very sure," said God.

The human steadied himself and plunged the knife into God's heart. God's body slumped and when the human pulled the knife out, the body floated limply into the abyss below. As it slowly fell it came apart and faded from sight like a puff pastry ghost. The human released his grip on the knife and it slowly rotated in the space in front of him like a gruesome buffering symbol as if he was waiting for the next world to load.

****

The army came to Berlin and occupied it in an ominously familiar way. However, they were two days late as Fate had moved on to Paris. He had taken thirty-five tabs of weird German acid and was now smack dab in the middle of a ludicrously trippy high and the killings were becoming more and more bizarre. If any sort of modern Poirot existed then he would have been able to track the trail of weirdness across Europe's morgues. Sadly, no such person existed to notice the man who had been beaten into a literal pulp and the woman who had been choked with said pulp. No one linked Fate to the death of three clowns on their way back from a children's birthday party who had died when all the doors and wheels fell off their car. People of course commented on the irony, but also commented on how unusual it was for this to happen in real life and to an Audi A5, no less. No one connected the sudden spike in Twix related chokings and vending machine crush deaths because they all occurred in different towns along the road to Paris.

Satan, two demons and Jeff Christ teleported onto Earth into a roadside café car park near Berlin's highway. They planned to track Fate and stop him from killing so many that it triggered war or a tipping point in population numbers.

They jacked a car and were soon on the road.

"Where the hell is God, Jeff?" asked Satan.

"I don't know."

"Well think."

"He could have turned his phone off."

"Why the fuck would he turn his phone off in the middle of an emergency?"

"Ok, well he could be in a no-signal area."

"Which areas are no-signal areas?"

"Anything that's not within the physical universes. Hell, Purgatory, Purgatory Premium and Purgatory Executive."

"What the shit is Purgatory Executive? You know what? We don't have time and I already don't care."[†]

[†] Purgatory Executive was basically a long form joke that God played on pretentious yuppie types. Introduced in 1998 along with Purgatory Premium, it was the newest part of the afterlife. God had been immensely proud of a lot of the advancements that humankind had made, from the genome project to vaccines to the internet; he had watched them innovate at incredible rates. However, something He had never quite been able to wrap His mind around was their absolute determination to split everything into class hierarchies.

Watching them queue for priority boarding was particularly dispiriting. Watching them waste their money on pointless status upgrades and bragging to their friends about being a 'Diamond Member' of something made Him irritated. A 'Diamond Member'. They were wasting the only life they'd ever have caring about being something that sounded like a name for an expensive dildo. He disliked the smugness and superiority that normally accompanied such pursuits so He planned a special treat for them once they died.

When they died their soul would rise to the heavens and be greeted by Solexis the admin Angel. She would inform them that there would be a delay period while a backlog was dealt with. It had not yet been determined where their final resting place would be. The good news was that because of the way they lived their lives they had qualified for Purgatory Premium and would get to wait in the premium room rather than standard Purgatory. Of course, Purgatory Premium was, in fact, slightly more cramped than Purgatory and they would wait even longer to be told their fate.

In Purgatory Executive they were given a free copy of *The Telegraph* and made to wait standing up for three times the amount of time as regular old Purgatory. The participants in both Premium and Executive Purgatory were happy enough though, thinking that someone else was getting it worse and that they were in an upgraded space.

"Basically, I don't know where he is."

"Yeah, I got that part."

Satan, Jeff and the two demons arrived in the city centre of Berlin. Satan was wishing to attract Fate's attention so he was in his customary mortal shell, but was wearing a bright red pinstripe three-piece suit. His two demons were dressed in red leather motorcycle gear with the helmets to hide their demonic faces. Jeff was wearing jeans and a Pixies t-shirt because that was what he'd been wearing anyway.

In the city, Satan used his magical powers of persuasion to gain access to the crime scene at the bar. They were in equal measure shocked and impressed by the level of carnage Fate had left behind. There was a leg protruding from each pocket of the pool table and thirty-seven eyeballs were arranged in the triangle.

"It's an art form what he does. He's actually very underappreciated because most people would see what he does as outrageous," said Satan to no-one in particular whilst looking at the body which had been smashed legs first into the cigarette machine and had 13,000 cigarettes stuffed into his mouth and lit. The demons had actually applauded when they saw this one.

"It's sort of beautiful in a weird way. He's the Banksy of unnecessarily cruel deaths."

"So, you don't see him as a monster?" asked Jeff.

"He's just expressing himself."

"Yes, and you're not worried about what he's expressing? Everyone's happy with people who express themselves freely, until they get their balls out in a public park and then society agrees that they've crossed a line."

"Of course he's crossed a line. He crossed it years ago – he left corpses on the line as he passed through it. He'll need to be killed, but that doesn't mean I can't enjoy the show up until that point."

"I don't get how you can enjoy it?"

"Everyone dies. Everyone. I will, you will – everyone. What would you rather? Peacefully in your sleep and forgotten, or ripped to shreds, mutilated, displayed and remembered for the rest of time."

"Definitely die in my sleep and then be forgotten."

"What! That was rhetorical."

"You thought the second option where I'm ripped apart, mutilated and displayed was preferable?" said Jeff.

"Yes."

"That's a bleak point of view."

"I'm the Devil."

"Touché."

Satan tasked the Demons to use their incredible tracking skills to follow Fate's trail. They opened their helmets and began to sniff around the scene.

****

The floating, spinning, God slaying knife was still about a foot away from me, continually catching my eye as if to say – "Remember that time you killed God? You killed God, you big bloody nonce."

Against his advice, I had started to panic. It seemed to me that He had been gone for absolutely ages. The knife once again caught my eye. "Guy from Glasgow meets God – stabs him. You're not doing much for the angry Scotsman stereotype are you? You nonce."

I was becoming more and more frustrated, but the more frustrated I got the more oxygen I used. I was getting properly trippy, so I started to worry about my sanity, particularly because of the constant sense of being called a nonce by a floating knife.

Unhelpfully at this moment a speck of bright light appeared in the distance and began to move closer. As it got closer and closer, I could see that it had an erratic flight pattern, fluttering about like a moth against the blackness of the void.

When it was much closer, I could see that the creature was an extremely furry and fat, pug-faced little man in an ill-fitting gold jumpsuit with a cape. His little wings produced a natural glow and were thoroughly magical looking. He was about a foot tall.

"I am Vernon the Void Fairy," he said cheerfully.

"ksjgnosrng," I garbled.

"Oh, so you're a mortal! What fun!"

I nodded.

"I'll leave you to it then." He was about to turn and leave.

I gestured frantically.

"Yes?"

I gestured frantically.

"Oh, so you're trapped here?"

I nodded to a degree that ripped all sorts of neck muscles.

"Right well that's a pickle. Here's the problem. I'm not supposed to exist. You see no-one knows how the void fairies were created or by whom."

I made a polite interested face – even though I was only 60/40 that this was even a real event from my life and not the result of neurons desperately firing because of oxygen loss from my brain.

"The void has all sorts of debris in it from years of inter-universe travel – we consume the waste, right? I was all excited to come over and eat you, but we don't eat the living. Although…"

He scratched his chin. I made a face to say 'What?'.

"I could…no. That seems impolite." He was weighing up some options, and then he said it anyway.

"I could just wait until you die and eat you then."

I shook my head vigorously using precious morsels of oxygen in the process.

"Not sure if that would be right. A lot of eating in you though. Your legs alone could keep a wee fella like me going for weeks."

I waved my arms about in a desperate attempt to explain an alternative. He watched in amused confusion. I took off my giant hat, gave it to him and mimed the action of eating.

A wide smile crossed his face. "I eat this? And I save you?"

I nodded. He was weighing it up and he did some mental arithmetic – he frowned.

"Seems like a bad deal for me and an absolute belter for you."

"ghduuunfffaduk" I said, wittily, in response.

Chapter 28
Get to France

Gary Hawkwind had never been to Paris before. He was 63 and very much a Brexit, "send them back", "political correctness gone mad" sort of guy. He previously hadn't really approved of France in any way. He didn't really even approve of people eating French mustard when perfectly good English mustard was in existence. He was a firm royalist and enjoyed programmes about military events which he would call 'incursions' incessantly if you were to ask him about the subject.

He was wearing his England football shirt and he drank pints of Carling in French bars, as he considered the act of asking for a Stella Artois to be a public admission of homosexuality.

He was, however, a convert. France was nice, he'd discovered. The food was good; you couldn't get pie and beans, but this had encouraged him to try different things. He enjoyed a croissant; he really enjoyed a pain au chocolat and he was now addicted to crème-brûlée.

He was standing by the foot of the Eiffel Tower – it was a beautiful evening, twenty degrees and not a cloud to be seen. He stood looking out over the magnificent park leading up to the tower. He could hear a faint whistling and he hoped that the wind wasn't about to pick up, spoiling the beautiful weather. It continued to grow in volume, but he couldn't feel any wind so he guessed it was maybe just the metal in the legs of the tower settling.

He walked forward a few feet absentmindedly. Exactly where he had just been standing a human body thundered into the ground like a cruise missile. He jumped back onto the ground as he was struck by cobblestone debris, bone fragments, blood and hair.

"MARJORYYYYYYYYYYYYYYYYYYYYYYYYYYY YYY!!!!!!!!!!!!!!!" he screamed at his wife who was at the ticket desk. Another body smashed into the ground right next to him, covering him in more wet human wreckage.

"I FUCKING TOLD YOU WE SHOULD HAVE GONE

TO TORQUAY," he bellowed, spitting some red blood goop from his mouth as he did so.

He looked up at the top of the tower and saw to his horror, twenty more dropping bodies reigning down upon him. He ran for cover as they bulleted into the ground; and just as the screaming died down from that, another thirty bodies thundered into the ground on the other side of the tower. As Gary watched them hitting the ground, he swore to never leave Britain for any reason ever again. He would look into importing the crème-brûlée.

****

Hundreds of miles away in Southern Germany, two demons were arguing about a dead body in a horrific rasping language. They spat back and forth at each other as they stood over the corpse of a young woman jogger who had been choked to death by having kale stuffed into every orifice. She had the word 'Superfood' carved into her face.

"What are they saying?" Jeff said quietly to Satan.

"No clue mate. I didn't actually know they could talk," replied Satan. He walked forward and split them up.

"Make a decision," he said firmly. They both pointed in opposite directions.

"Fucksake." He turned to Jeff, but Jeff had his back to Satan and was staring at a TV. On the TV a pile of brutally broken bodies were piled up at the bottom of the Eiffel tower. A fire had broken out on the viewing deck and was spreading.

"We need to get to Paris," said Jeff, completely unnecessarily.

****

God woke up in Hell for the first time in His entire existence. As He opened His massive eyes, it took Him a second or two to realise where He was. A big hand went instinctively to His chest, although He quickly remembered it wasn't the same chest. Above Him was a red vaulted ceiling. He looked around the rest of the room. He was in a plush red bed, the walls had red pinstripe pattern wallpaper and He was wearing red pyjamas. He would have to have a word with Satan about His style choices. Three red demons stood menacingly guarding the door. He got up and they all stood to attention.

"Where is Satan?"

They rasped a response.

"I don't give a hairy shit whether you've not been informed about my arrival, get out of my way."

They refused and initially He had a crisis of confidence, thinking perhaps He didn't have any power down here, but then He remembered that He built hell and with a waggle of His finger He blasted the demon on the left into a cloud of liquid in a pop that sounded like a gunshot and left a deep red Rorschach pattern on the wall behind him. The other two nervously stepped aside.

"Now I don't care if you are a badass devil from Hell who has sworn his soul to Satan – if GOD gives you an instruction, you do it. Do you understand me?"

The demons nodded reluctantly.

"Now go get me my robes and show me to the express elevator before I kill you forever."

They scuttled like fuck.

****

I was now completely naked. It was many hours since I had killed God and He had not returned. The void fairy had initially been reluctant to help me. Over the course of the last few hours he had negotiated all of my clothes and all of my possessions in exchange for his assistance. He had eaten my shoes gleefully and bagged the rest. Now he had gripped my hand and was dragging me through the void space. The void was not airy, it was not like liquid, it was tacky and gripped at my body like a set of weak hands scraping across my naked skin. Vernon dragged me through the non-space of the void and all of a sudden, I could feel a warmth and sense an atmosphere approaching. There was nothing visibly there, but it was like we'd passed into a busy town after crawling through the desert for several weeks.

We slowed to a stop and he took a little wand from his bag, waving it around in the nothingness as if trying to find something. He tried a little higher up and sparks began to pop from the end of the wand. He replaced it into the bag and brought out a little silver knife. He let go of my hand and gestured to me to stay where I was. He took the knife and moved it to where the sparks had appeared. He drew the knife carefully down and to my astonishment he made an incision in the nothingness. As soon as it was open, I could feel the rushing of air coming towards me. He cut a slit the length of my body and the rushing of air became more intense. It was refreshing and I gulped down whatever I could from it. As the fabric of the nothingness fluttered with the flow of the air, sunlight came through the gap, it blinded me and warmed me at the same time. Vernon turned to me and pulled out his wand again.

"Have a safe trip human. Thanks for the snacks."

He waved the wand and immediately the flow of air ceased to rush towards me and instead I was sucked through the incision, which healed behind me as I passed through. Typically, I had come through a wall so, still unable to see, I hit the ground face first without getting my hands up in time.

This particular entry to a planet's atmosphere came without the swirling concussion of a trip through a portal and thus I was able to fully enjoy the raw sensation of grazing my naked penis on rough ground as I slid to a stop. I had not thought that I would ever be nostalgic for the searing head pain which came with smashing into a planet at pace, but it turns out that the sickening sensation of a penis graze, a sudden rush of oxygen and the shock of a major temperature change was significantly worse. I threw up what seemed like my soul onto the ground and then passed out.

****

God had His robes back and was heading for the express elevator. He dropped by Satan's office to say hello as He was surprised the big guy hadn't been there when He woke up. Satan's secretary Sandra was a pretty shrewd operator, able to stay cool in the face of pressure, demons and monsters, but even she shat herself a bit when God entered the room.

"Where is he?" said God.

"Um, he's not here sir."

"That I can see, Sandra. I didn't ask where he wasn't."

"Sorry sir, I believe he's on Earth."

"Earth? What for?"

"I'm not sure, your son called and then he left in a hurry."

"Jesus called here?"

"No sir, Jeff."

"Jeff called here? You are ABSOLUTELY positive? Jeff Christ?"

She nodded nervously.

"And Satan left right away?"

"Yes sir. He grabbed his suit, two demons and left that second."

"Thanks Sandra. Let me know if you hear from him."

"I will."

God ran to the elevator. He pressed the highest button and it shot Him the incredible distance in a matter of seconds. He leapt out of the elevator when He got to His cloud home at the top. As he looked around for the others, He realised He was alone.

"Jesus."

Jesus poked his head round the door. "Yes father."

"Oh, I didn't mean…you know what actually, maybe you'll know. Where's Jeff?"

"Jeff, why do you want to talk to him? It's not like HE was the saviour of everyone's sins."

"Ok I get it, you two don't get along, but just because Jeff isn't famous doesn't mean that the work he does isn't equally valuable."

"Yeah, but…"

"No buts about it, young man. He is your older brother and you'll show him some respect."

"Ok dad," Jesus said sheepishly.

"That's better. Now, where is he?"

Jesus was looking at his shoes. "He went to Earth with Uncle Satan."

"And why did he do that?"

Jesus shrugged. "Something about Fate and the end of the universe, I don't know, I wasn't listening properly."

"Did they say where on Earth?"

"I think something about Germany."

"Ok son, I need you to think really hard – did they say where in Germany or why Germany?"

"Um, I think Uncle Satan might have said they were going to Berlin."

God ruffled Jesus' hair and smiled. "Ok son, good job."

Jesus blushed and looked embarrassed.

"I'm going down to the fifth. Then I'll deal with Fate. You're in charge until I get back ok?"

Jesus gave him a reluctant grin.

"Man of the house? Ok?"

"Ok," Jesus hugged him.

"Right son, I'll be back soon. If I don't return within three Earth days then I'm stuck in the void between fifth and sixth universes and you MUST come and rescue me."

Jesus nodded, looking off to the side.

"Are you listening properly? This is very important."

"Yes Dad, I'll rescue you, if you're not back by Thursday."

"Ok good boy. If you do a good job, I'll bring you back a fidget spinner from Earth."

Jesus pumped his fist. "Yes!"

God transported himself back to the Fidelity Kingdom.

****

The Eiffel tower had never looked more spectacular than when it was completely ablaze; a glowing torch illuminating the night sky. Satan, Jeff and the Demons stood on a nearby bridge over the Seine river. Satan was smoking a cigarette, watching the fire and affecting an attitude of not giving a shit. Basically, they were blending in to France nicely.

"How the fuck did he set the legs on fire?" said Satan absentmindedly.

Fate was nowhere to be seen, having set it alight he had made his escape and was presumably causing mayhem somewhere else now.

"What now?" asked Jeff.

Satan exhaled smoke in the shape of a question mark.

"I'll tell you this right now," said Satan "I'm sick to death of chasing him around Europe. I think this is about as definitive a beacon as we're going to get. He can come to us."

"How do you plan to do that? He's not exactly handing out the blue ticks in our whatsapp group."

"Well to be honest I thought that was a longshot at best Jeff. No, I have something slightly more direct in mind."

He gestured to his two Demons to listen. He showed them a picture on his phone. "I need you to travel to London and pick up this person and bring them here unharmed. You understand? Unharmed."

The demons nodded curtly and exhaled sulphurous smoke from their nostrils. They waited until the coast was clear and then leapt from the bridge. As they plunged towards the water, leathery wings ripped up through their clothing and they flew off into the night sky.

"Did you know they could do that?" said Jeff staring incredulously at them.

"Yes Jeff, I knew."

"That's cool. I mean they are terrifying as anything, but the wings were awesome."

"Thanks man. They were 100% God's idea, but I think they're very me, if you know what I mean?"

"Totally. There's nothing that accentuates your personality more than red, primal, flying, killer demons."

"You know that's the nicest thing anyone's said to me in a long time Jeff."

"No problem."

"Although I am the absolute worst so maybe it makes total sense."

"It's weird though, isn't it? You are supposed to be the king of all evil."

"I am."

"Yeah and that should make you the most dislikeable man of all time, but…"

"But what? I fucking am."

"No, but…Fate."

"Yeah. I see your point. He is an absolute screaming cunt of a guy."

"Yeah he is a real ninny," Jeff said.

"Watch your mouth Jeff. There's kids about," Satan smirked.

Chapter 29
Street Performer

Las Ramblas was a pedestrian avenue which ran down the centre of Barcelona's city centre. It was normally a hustle bustle of street stalls, buskers, salespeople, tourists and trees. A few hours after Fate arrived in town, it had taken on a slightly different atmosphere. A mime ran up the centre of the street, uncharacteristically screaming his head off; this was a forgivable breaking of the traditional mime form – most people would have found it difficult to stay calm if a stranger had punctuated their show by sticking sixteen needles in their arm.

Pablo Martinez was a barista and part time mime. The profession of 'mime artist' was made up of 99% part timers and just 1% of people who lied about being full time mime artists. Pablo was performing on the street this particular evening; he had performed all the classics; pretending to be stuck in a glass box, dragging a heavy suitcase, playing tug of war and walking into a strong wind. The strange man had stood and watched him throughout, he had shown absolutely no expression. The man had a number of bloodstains on his clothes, he hadn't blinked for four minutes and he was carrying a javelin; given all of the data available to him, Pablo had decided to act as if absolutely nothing was wrong and to finish up his show as quickly as possible without provoking the crazy guy. It was, of course, Fate who was observing him that evening.

When Pablo had entered the part of the show where he pretended to be sad by making sad faces and running a finger down his cheek to simulate tears the man had spoken for the first time.

"Are you sad?" said Fate.

Pablo had nodded.

"No, you're not. You're just pretending."

Pablo had shaken his head vigorously and hammed up his sad acting even more, to really sell it to the guy. Fate frowned.

"You don't look like you're very good at this 'sad'

business. I'll give you something to be sad about."

Fate had thrown the javelin at a passing woman, who was walking with her toddler and as Pablo had stood there in complete shock at the poor lady trying to stop the bleeding from her chest, Fate had walked towards him and stabbed him in the arm with a fistful of needles.

"So, you've seen a senseless murder and now you've got aids. That should help you generate some genuine sadness in your future performances," Fate said without a hint of irony.

As the mime ran down the street Fate shouted after him – "You're welcome!"

He took a German police-issue sub-machine gun out of his duffel bag and strafed the rest of the street until the magazine was empty. The survivors fled the scene, except the little boy. He stood there, frozen to the spot. Fate raised his weapon, then thought better of it. He sighed, approached the boy, knelt down in front of him and wiped a tear from the boy's eye with a handkerchief. The little boy looked at him with confusion. Fate smiled his most reassuring smile.

"Fuck off son," he said. "Before I have to kill you."

He showed the boy the Uzi he was holding. The boy took one look at it and ran.

"See? I'm not a monster," he said aloud, to no-one.

Fate now had the place to himself and began to loot the nearby pet shop, emptying all of the cat and dog food into his bag. He strapped all his guns onto his body and started walking down the bottom of the city towards the zoo.

Chapter 30

Terry's Statue

Hands were picking me up, big strong hands, massive hands.

I thought "It's God! He's alive and has come back to rescue me." But then I opened my eyes a bit and caught a glimpse of the sandalled feet beneath me.

"Terry?" I blurted.

"Yes friend. Do not be alarmed, I will assist you, you look like you have been through a great deal."

"Terry! I am so GLAD to see you! Am I on the Moon?" I said groggily.

"Not quite," said Terry.

He lifted me onto a bench and sat me up. I adjusted to the light and saw Terry kneeling in front of me; we appeared to be in a town square, it was warm and a pleasant gentle breeze was swirling around the place, it was completely empty save for the two of us. I looked around and to my absolute amazement about 150 yards behind Terry stood an enormous statue which looked exactly like him.

He saw me looking at it and nervously tried to change the subject.

"So how did you get here? I thought I sent you back to Earth in the teleporter."

Undeterred I asked – "Terry is that a 200-foot-tall statue of you?"

"Don't know what you mean. You are nude. Are you sure you're alright? You seemed to enter through a wall which is most unusual."

"Terry, it's just there." I pointed. "It's a massive statue. Like absolutely enormous."

He exhaled for a long time. "I don't really want to talk about it right now."

"You don't want to talk about it? If someone had built a 200-foot stone statue of me, that's ALL I'd ever talk about."

"Well, if you knew the story you'd feel differently. Sadly for you, you won't know the story."

"I demand to know Terry. I absolutely demand it."

"Well I'm afraid your demands don't mean much here.

And you still haven't told me how you got here. Quid pro quo my friend – let's hear it."

I could see that he wasn't going to give up his story very easily and I was keen to tell him mine so I began to lay it out for him. It was quite satisfying to finally get to tell it to someone who was as amazed by it all as I was.

After about an hour of constant excitable talking I had told Terry my whole story. Start to finish.

Now it was his turn; he had filled me in on Fate and how evil a creature he was. He had also informed me of God's request to have me killed.

This was extremely confusing on two counts – First, why couldn't he just lightning bolt me to death as soon as the notion took him? And secondly, when he had found me on the Fidelity Kingdom, why hadn't he killed me then?

Terry had no answers for any of my questions. However, as part of our quid pro quo he had agreed to tell me about the statue. The statue was indeed of Terry and the reason was as follows:

The History of The Bigger Place

God decided that He would create a bigger universe. A system of planets based around one big sun. This bigger place would create more variety of life and there would be more than one planet which had life on it.

He decided to hedge His bets and create a few main races. However, to prevent conflict He would not inform them of each other's existence. They would be located a few million miles away from each other, which should ensure that their species will be sufficiently developed by the time they might discover each other's existence.

Terry's race were all like him: large hands, feet and facial features, typically very tall and very intelligent. Their race developed like many others through basic tools, electricity, medicine advances and all the while creating a more sophisticated society. The people of the planet were extremely laid-back and God had intended them to be a bit more accepting of one another. As such there were no major wars to speak of in their entire history. Small conflicts arose, weapons were developed, but there was not an overriding sense of tension between any of the groups, genders or geographical areas. Their planet was called Teatime after their favourite part of the day. The thirty-hour day was punctuated by fifteen-minute tea breaks which occurred every hour on the hour. It was strictly forbidden to work during Teatime because the Teatimeons favoured a work-life balance which involved more leisure time than work.

Around two thousand years passed by on Teatime of peaceful existence. Around this time Terry was elected to the planetary senate. He was a brilliant, if slightly eccentric, politician with a likeable nature and high moral standing.

Meanwhile thirty-three million miles away, a planet was in danger. The planet of Sentos was a stranger world than Teatime. God had tried to create a peaceful artistic, sensitively minded community. He'd made the creatures with art and emotions in mind. These three fingered slug-like creatures now made up the bulk of the staff on the Moon, but originally they had their own ethereal paradise. They were a mute race who communicated through images which they telepathically shared into your mind space. They were masters of metaphors and as poetic a people as have ever lived. Their planet was awash with beautiful, dreamlike landscapes with floating islands and waterfalls which ran upwards into the sky. They communicated almost entirely figuratively, but every 1 in 100 individuals were also blessed with practical skills and this allowed the society to be able to create technology. It was an ideal mix, which meant the creation of never before seen advances. They built The Hub which was a giant gaseous ball, which amplified their telepathic powers and meant everyone on the planet could connect to other Sentos all over the world directly.

This created a golden age of communication and sharing of art and poetry. However, they had not realised that The Hub was also having an unintended side effect. The giant ball was the conduit for a humungous amount of energy. It was based on the planet's north pole and it created such a strong gravitational effect that it had, unbeknownst to them, begun to drag them off course from their normal orbit.

Galapagos was one of the most practical and straightforward Sentos on the planet. He was a key mind behind The Hub and was generally revered by anyone who happened to meet him. He broke into the High Council meeting in a breathless hurry.

The High Council members looked shocked. The Empress sent Galapagos an image of a clown bursting into a funeral. Two other Council members sent him an image of square pegs attempting to fit into round holes. One of the assistants sent him an image of a toad and a sheep getting married. This one didn't make as much sense, but he was a junior staffer and he'd just panicked. He was in a relatively important position and had risen there on merit, but despite that he was surprisingly shite under pressure. In his freaked-out state, he also sent out an image of himself at home in his underwear making sausage meals for himself. This wasn't a metaphor at all and was just supposed to be a private thought about what he was going to do later. He really loved sausage meals.

Galapagos conveyed to them the urgency of the situation by showing them an image of a ticking bomb. The Empress waved her arm as if to say 'proceed'. Galapagos showed them the image of The Hub causing the planet to be dragged out of orbit and that it would be eventually sucked into the sun. They all watched intently and then, thinking that it was a really nice metaphor for old age – threw him out and resumed their Council meeting.

He was never able to convince anyone in power that there was actual danger. He did however manage to convince three rich people, who gave him funding to develop space travel. He developed the universe's first interplanetary transport vehicle. He had viewed the planet of Teatime through his telescope and although he hadn't been able to tell if there was life, it seemed like it should be habitable. He took a group of Sentos who believed his calculation and they set off for Teatime at around lunchtime.

The ship was called New Sentos because Galapagos really believed that by the time they arrived at their new home their world would be no more. They would colonise the new planet and call it New Sentos.

The only problem with the entire plan was that there was a whole different race already living on Teatime. When they touched down, it was in the middle of a huge televised concert in the centre of the largest city; it had caused quite a stir. A planet of people who had previously assumed they were completely alone in the universe were now having to deal with refugees from another planet.

The Sentos were granted sanctuary and began to become a reasonably large minority on the planet.

However certain people on Teatime became uneasy with this new race. They were suspicious that the Sentos could communicate telepathically. They were enraged whenever they saw one not working as they saw them as lazy. They got freaked out when they were walking down the same street as one late at night.

Political groups began to form advocating their banishment from Teatime. They cited, erroneously, that the Sentos committed more crimes, that they didn't integrate and that they were a drain on limited resources.

The weapons manufacturing industry took advantage of the situation and began to stoke fear in the population about crime. They released campaigns which exaggerated the crime rates and told of the growing need for personal weapons. It was the result of some years of this idea being escalated that the Glove was born.

The Glove was an extremely powerful close-range weapon. To our eyes it looked like a simple leather glove, but inside the Glove were thousands of energy cells which constantly recharged through body heat. To destroy something with the Glove you simply pressed your index and middle fingers together, then firmly pressed what you wanted to destroy. Upon doing so the target would disintegrate.

This made it an excellent personal security item. If you were being mugged or attacked you simply had to be within touching distance of your attacker. Projectile weapons and lasers had not developed on Teatime so most attacks were up close and personal; an assailant would have to look their victim in the eye when attacking. This gave victims of attacks a huge advantage because they could now have a Glove. Criminals didn't want to use Gloves because it would destroy you, your money and all your personal items, rendering their crime pointless.

The weapons were hugely popular, instant bestsellers. Street crime reduced by 93% in four weeks after they went on sale.

However, accidental Glove-related deaths rose by infinity % from the previous month's total of zero. Now surprising a friend on the street, tickling someone or becoming amorous were all fraught with danger.

One day a man walked into his office and obliterated twenty-three colleagues and some poor guy who was just delivering flowers. He then screamed "Justice for Tangor!" at the top of his lungs and turned the Glove on himself. Tangor was an oppressed land in a Teatime television show and it did not actually exist – so this seemed to be a strong indicator that the man may have been unwell. Despite this harrowing incident there were few concerns about safety at this point because it seemed like an isolated incident.

However, over the next few months there was a depressed man who Gloved the shopping centre he was standing in, taking the whole centre and the 850 people inside it out of existence in a heartbeat.

School massacres became commonplace as teenagers with easy access to Gloves and even easier access to hormones, attempted to right the wrongs of high school social systems in the most decisive way possible.

Pro-Glove groups argued that these children had been influenced by playing video games or watching violent television. Anti-Glove groups were pretty sure that actually wasn't relevant to the argument as a violent child without a Glove would not be able to take out thirty people on a whim.

Pro-Glove groups said that perhaps teachers wearing Gloves at all times would be a protective measure which would save lives. However, they had failed to take into account how annoying children are and when this was implemented it caused an avalanche of red mist killings by frustrated teachers. Nevertheless, the Pro-Glove lobby was rich and powerful. They had the ear of Teatime's president – a Tronald Dump.

Tronald Dump was an extremely fat and useless Teatimeon. He was from a privileged minority which didn't really have to do any work as they were born into wealth. This meant his whole life had been a tea-break; it had warped his sense of reality and made him Teatime's worst ever leader.

Under his stewardship Gloves were steadily made more readily available, more powerful and more widespread.

Teatime was soon to have an important election. A presidential election. Terry had, by this time, become a fiercely moral senator, famed for his speeches and his activism. He was the natural candidate for his party and was entered onto the ballot. The cornerstone of his campaign was that, if elected, he would unilaterally ban all Gloves. Not even the police or the military would have such power.

This was a radical suggestion and much more than any other politician was willing to commit to. Terry had the support of a large swathe of the population and he was charming, intelligent and persuasive in the debates.

He swept to power riding a wave of justified positivity. He was sworn in as President of Teatime in a huge ceremony in the square. The Glove Ban bill was passed narrowly the following month in the senate. Gloves were collected, seized and destroyed en-masse.

In a televised ceremony Terry was presented with the last glove manufactured; it was a ceremonial Golden Glove, which was to be stored in his presidential office as a memento of Glove ban's success. The rest of the collected Gloves were melted down and made into packing material.

An era of peace had begun.

Unbeknownst to either Sentos or Teatime, there was a third inhabited planet. Haag was located within a thick nebula on the far side of the solar system, where it was cold, and darker. The creatures reflected this in their appearance. The Haag looked like wet, leathery mermen with deformed walrus heads. They were ugly by any standard, but to properly express their visual horror a new standard was introduced called the *Haag Scale of Unpleasantness*. This is what Jeff Christ used to rank the creatures by their beauty level in his annual breakdown of the seven universe's demographics. In his personal opinion the graph itself was the most beautiful thing he'd ever seen, but it didn't count as a creature and was therefore not represented on itself.

The Haag were a violent race. Everything was settled through fighting of some nature on Haag. They were a warrior race of absolute thugs. They instantly assumed every situation was a confrontation and began scrolling through different tactical approaches in their mind. Their answer was always the most brutal option: Committed a crime? Trial by combat. Divorce dispute? Fight for it. Late for work? Strip to the waist and battle your boss.

It was an inefficient system, but it did mean that just about every Haag got their arse kicked properly at least once a year. God made a significant amount of errors in the creation of the Haag, but this was one trait He wished more creatures had developed as it bred healthy levels of humility.

The Haag took much longer than the others to develop any sort of technology because every failed experiment resulted in a fight to the death. Science did not flourish well under such circumstances. The only area with extreme development was weaponry. This was because they were almost constantly in a state of civil war about something or another. Their weapons included lasers, bullets, disintegrators, nuclear power and the ability to wage chemical warfare. They also invented every chib and shank known to man. They could make an efficient mêlée weapon out of anything. They were like a race of homicidal Ray Mears fans.

After years and years of this chaotic conflict, they did eventually develop rudimentary space technology as an offshoot of a plan by one of the warring groups to drop a giant hammer from space. When they got up there, they were struck by the sheer volume of space and the many other celestial objects. As a result of being struck by this, they were not struck by a gigantic space hammer so it was a two-fold positive outcome. Their space programme was not without issue though, their scientists became impatient with the difficult gravitational and trajectory calculations, which were complicated by the orbits of Haag's three small moons. Instead of showing any calmness or guile, they simply destroyed the moons. This meant that the entire planet was surrounded by a thick cloud of debris and as a result became even darker and colder. This suited the Haag to an extent, but it was soon going to prove troublesome with crops and tides. Within months the Haag realised that they would need to procure additional resources from somewhere. It is said that necessity is the mother of invention, it applies here, but what the Haag developed was more like a strange psychotic child that Necessity didn't tell her friends about. Lots of bloodstained blueprints resembling knives were produced, although none of them would fly. Eventually strong craft capable of punching through the debris field were developed and once they could get into orbit, they quickly developed telescopic equipment to look at the other worlds.

What they saw was Teatime; a planet with excellent resources and limited space capability, just sitting there waiting for a war. The Haag leader ordered the construction of a battle fleet.

On Teatime the era of peace was glorious. Twenty years passed without any major incidents. The people became happy with the Sentos gradually, because a key part of the planet's entertainment industry utilised their flair for visual expression to make the best art, music videos and films there had ever been. The Teatimeon government made communication with Sentos leadership and issued them a no-nonsense warning about how much danger they were in. They sent them instructions for how to build transport ships and assurances that all Sentos would be welcomed gladly on Teatime.

A year later three ships arrived with five hundred Sentos on them. They explained that the others had not believed the messages and could not be convinced to leave. A short time later the inevitable occurred and a large flare ignited in the sky and burned for six days straight. There was no night on Teatime for a full week.

This solar event sadly signalled the demise of the planet Sentos and all of its remaining inhabitants. Terry decreed that Teatime had a national month of mourning – from this day forward the seventh month would be Sentos Heritage Month, where the Sentos would celebrate the life and work of their ancestors.

"In time we will recover, in time we will be happy again – but we will never forget. Sentos was a rich and peaceful place which has only added to our culture, enhanced our civilisation and expanded our knowledge." Terry had spoken on a national television broadcast the following day.

"Be kind to your Sentos neighbours, be understanding and show them love during what is undoubtedly the hardest period in their fine history."

The people on Teatime were brought together by these events and many saw it as a bonding experience; life on Teatime had never been better.

The Haag leader was a female, although it was almost impossible to tell which sex was which on Haag. She had the title 'Mother Haag' and had taken over from the previous 'Father Haag' by stabbing him in the eyes with a trident and telling everyone she was in charge now. That had worked a treat and she had enjoyed the longest reign of any Haag leader in history.

At first when the lieutenant entered the room to give his presentation on Haag's lack of resources, she had kicked the shit out of him, but once he got his breath back and started to explain that Haag was using its resources faster than it could replace them, she popped her trident back in its holder.

"What do you propose we do about it?" she asked him.

Quivering he pointed to the astronomical charts on her wall. "The furthest planet. There are people there, but they have far more resources than they require. More than enough for our purposes."

"You presume to know our purposes?" She reached for the trident.

"Are they mainly killing stuff?"

"Well yes." She sighed, putting the trident back in its holder. It hadn't speared anyone for two and a half months because everyone was being so bloody polite. She cursed her luck; *Victim of my own success*, she thought to herself.

"Ok, assemble the fleet. We're going to kill them."

"What size army do you propose taking?"

"Oh, no one is getting out of this one. We're all going. Everyone!"

"Everyone on Haag?"

"Yes, everyone on Haag."

"Don't you want to leave a few behind just to mind the place?"

"Ok you fucking panic merchant, we'll leave one."

"One ship?"

"No. One guy."

"One guy?"

"Whoever is twenty-eighth in the phonebook."

"I still can't tell if you're joking madam Leader."

"You think I am JOKING? Do I strike you as the humorous type?"

"No madam Leader."

"Good because I consider having a sense of humour the same as having serious brain damage."

"So how many shall I leave Mother Haag?"

"Ok look I don't want you wetting yourself. Leave a squad of six."

"Thank you, Madam Leader."

"I want us on our way by 14:00 tomorrow."

"Certainly, Madam Leader."

"How long is the journey?"

"11 years Madam."

"11 years!!"

"Yes."

"Well try and pack some snacks then."

The Haag fleet were housed within one massive mothership. The mothership could hold the entire population of Haag. It took off the following afternoon, fully loaded with Haag, fully loaded with weapons and fully loaded with sandwiches.

Terry's reign on Teatime continued to be a good one. His science division had made housing and food a priority. Advances in building technology had given rise to unprecedented levels of affordable housing and his agricultural team had developed super crops which contributed towards a surplus of food.

The next ten years became a golden age on Teatime. Terry began to speak of retirement, he began to speak of passing the torch onto the next generation and he started to put plans in motion for it.

The people responded with horror that he would even consider stepping down. A public campaign was initiated with the aim of honouring the great leader. They thought that if they could make him realise what he meant to them that he would stay in office. The campaign received tremendous backing both in terms of public opinion and financial offers. The Teatimeons marched at the weekends in spontaneous Terry Parades – they demanded honours for Terry. This forced the Senate's hand and after several rallies they commissioned the statue.

Terry was absolutely mortified by the idea of a statue. He spoke out and thanked the people for their love, support and affection, but expressed his intention to decline to sit for the statue.

For the first time in thirty years Terry was booed by a crowd. They were understandably annoyed that after months of campaigning, after which they'd got their wish, he was going to dash it.

In the end, he was shamed into participating.

The statue was erected and unveiled at a grand ceremony in the centre of the capital. The day would now be known as Terry Tuesday and the intention was to celebrate the day annually.

However, the happiness surrounding this new holiday was short-lived; just five days later Teatime astronomers picked up an unusual sight, a large area of space was slightly shimmering. It was transparent, but it certainly had enormous mass. It was coming in fast and would arrive within 24 hours. They had no idea what it was or what its intentions were. As it neared the planet's outer orbit, the shimmering faded away and a ridiculously vast, enormous spacecraft became visible. The Haag mothership had disengaged “Weasel Mode”, a cloaking system which they fundamentally disliked, as it went against their square-go, upfront fighting philosophy, but it had very much come in handy for sneaking up on Teatime.

Terry attempted communication with the vessel, but to no avail. He consulted his advisors, they told him it could be another refugee ship, but that it did not look like a Sentos vessel. They also warned him of the possibility of this being a hostile force.

They had melted the Gloves. They had destroyed all of their weapons, they had had a knife amnesty, a sword amnesty and a few other assorted amnesties. The practical result of which was that there were almost no viable weapons left on Teatime whatsoever.

The mothership flew right into the Teatime atmosphere unchallenged; it landed right in the centre of town. Terry’s statue stood just 500 yards away.

The Haag ship remained closed for several hours until finally they sent a radio signal out requesting a meeting with the leadership of Teatime. Terry responded with a message which said that he and his high council would board the vessel for talks.

Terry took his council – a mix of Teatimeons and Sentos – onto the ship and immediately felt with certainty that something bad was going to happen. Rows and rows of heavily armed creatures lined up either side of them, making the most intimidating guard of honour in history.

When they got to the bridge of the ship Mother Haag was waiting for them. She shook each of them by the hand, leaving behind the mucus residue which the Haag naturally emitted at all times.

“I am Mother Haag and I am the leader of my planet. Who among you is the leader?”

“I am. My name is Terry Unkenpharmhouser,” he said. She ruffled her nose at the surname.

“You can call me Terry,” he clarified to her relief.

“I’d like to get straight to business.”

"Certainly."

"You did not fire on us and have confidently let us land on your planet. This unsettles us. The weapon you have must be mighty or you would not be so brazen. May I ask that you show my people the dignity of a quick death."

"I have no intention of doing anything of the sort madam."

"So, you will make us suffer? So be it. What is the nature of the weapon?"

"No, you misunderstand me. We offer you sanctuary on Teatime. There is room and we have plenty of food. If you only wish to visit, accommodation can be provided."

"I don't understand. Your entire leadership is on my ship and you don't intend to seize my vessel or destroy us?"

"No – we come in peace."

"That, my friend, is a mistake you will live to regret." She turned to her generals and ordered a full-scale attack.

"You would attack us for no reason?"

"Not for no reason, for your food, for your natural resources, for your technology – for your land. You will observe as I massacre your people. Victory will be ours."

She had them cuffed and guarded.

The Haag poured out into the streets and took to the air in their fighter ships. They opened fire on crowds of confused people sitting at outdoor cafes. They destroyed buildings and easily fought off resisting Teatimeons who tried to fight back using whatever they could find around the house.

The battle for Teatime was over in less than a day. The Haag were brutal and efficient; they took no prisoners, they spared no one and they left trails of dead in their wake. When it was over Terry expected to be killed, but Mother Haag had other ideas.

"You have been punished by watching your total defeat at our hands. You will now be released back onto your empty planet, whereupon you may think about the ramifications of your actions until you die. We will remain in our ship as we use its teleporter to extract your resources into our cargo bay." She placed one hand over her cold heart and one hand on Terry's shoulder. She recited the Haag victory motto, "Joy in victory, dignity in defeat, honour in death."

"I don't like it," said Terry, as he was numbly led back towards the exit.

Terry and the high council were led down the ramp onto Teatime and the door slammed shut behind them. Terry walked back to the recently shut door and placed his hand on it. The council didn't know what to do, they were just slowing trudging away from the ship. After about twenty feet they stopped to wait on Terry. Even in this moment they still looked to him for leadership.

He had his back to them and was still catatonically staring at the ship.

"I'm sorry. I'm sorry I didn't prepare for this, I'm sorry I didn't do something in there, I'm sorry. It's all my fault. For what I am about to do, may God forgive me."

They all lunged towards him, thinking that he was about to kill himself.

"Stay back!" he shouted, in an uncharacteristically aggressive way. They stopped, gathering about ten feet from him.

Instead of killing himself, he put his hand inside his jacket. He took from his pocket the Golden Glove, which he had removed from its ceremonial housing earlier that morning. He put it on his hand, pressed his index and middle finger together and with a very firm jab to the hull, destroyed the Haag mothership and all who were aboard her.

As the dusty remnants of the Haag ship fell to the ground all around them, like dead snow, they stared in amazement at what they had just witnessed. Terry, the peace-loving President of Teatime had just committed a genocide.

"Had to be done, I'm afraid." He tossed the glove aside and began to walk back through the city streets towards his official residence. The others, still in shock, just numbly followed behind him. They walked by ruined shopfronts, hundreds of bodies and thousands of limbs.

As they passed his statue located in Emerald Square in the centre of the city there was a sonic boom overhead. They all threw themselves to the ground thinking it to be a Haag retaliation of some kind. Terry just stood there and let the shockwave of wind and dust hit him.

When it cleared there was a large man standing in the street. He was wearing perfect white robes, had a large white flowing beard and white hair. He looked upset.

"Terry, I am God."

"You look more like a wizard."

God made a vehicle near Him levitate in the air.

Terry shrugged. "Seems exactly the sort of thing a wizard would do."

God clicked His fingers and transported them all to His cloud in the heavens. As they gawped incredulously at the heavens God pressed on with the conversation.

"You killed a whole race of people Terry."

"They just killed my whole planet. An eye for an eye."

"But you're a peace-loving, leftie, liberal President – I didn't expect you to react like that."

"I couldn't defend my people, but I saw the opportunity to avenge them. It was my duty."

"Terry, I like you. I really do. This whole mess is over. I'm mothballing this whole universe."

"Are you here to kill us?"

"No, I'm here to offer you a job."

And with that Terry was given the job of monitoring the Earth and was to take a crew of the remaining Teatimeons, Sentos and the six Haag left behind. He was set up in the MOON with the express purpose of tracking everything he could about human behaviour and alerting God to the development of any dangerous patterns or potentially risky events.

Teatime was over.

Chapter 31
Provoking a Maniac

Destiny was in a club called The Polling Station. She was onstage dancing to a song whilst dressed as a French maid. There were about twenty people in the club and most people in there were extremely surprised when two winged demons crashed through the ceiling, beat down the security guards, knocked out Destiny and carried her off like eagles stealing eggs from a nest. There was much commotion and panic. Most people were very surprised, but not Dirty Raymond. Dirty Raymond had been coming to strip clubs for fifty-three years; he knew them all, he'd been kicked out of most. Dirty Raymond didn't bat an eye when the demons came in, he didn't panic when they got violent and he didn't join in with the amazed hubbub which followed her unwilling departure. After half a century in strip clubs Dirty Raymond had seen it all – he'd absolutely seen it all.

When it became clear there would be no more dances that evening, he picked up his glass of milk, zipped up his anorak and left.

****

Fate was barricaded in a pub in the centre of Barcelona; he'd instructed the barman to seal the doors and had taken a whole bottle of whiskey to his table. He was slowly sipping the whiskey and watching the news unfold live on the TV with a smirk on his face.

When the first bomb went off, it had been hilarious. Everyone was so worried about the fact a tiger was in the shopping precinct, no-one questioned that it was wearing a vest. The bomb had exploded, killing fifty people and a tiger. It had worked to perfection. Now they had to find, pacify and disarm the other 200 animals that he'd rigged with explosives and set free from the zoo. He was safely locked inside the pub, drinking heavily and looking forward to his next atrocity.

Meanwhile ISIS had sensed an opportunity. Seeing the tiger bombing, they had claimed responsibility and therefore the blame. The USA, France, Britain, Germany and Spain all committed air forces to start bombing ISIS areas. Russia took exception to the bombing of some of its Syrian territories and bombed American bases in the Middle East. This led to a ramping up of the tensions in the Mediterranean with the USA base in Turkey being a particular flash point. Embassies were routed, flags burned and riots erupted on the streets of several of the affected cities. The world was on the edge of a war and Fate was absolutely loving it.

He really was pleased with himself. God could go jump off a cliff. *You can't fire me without consequences*, he thought.

"Can't fire who?" asked the barman and at that point Fate realised that he was drunkenly shouting his thoughts out at the top of his voice.

"You can't fire me. I am indispensable!"

"I'm sure you are sir."

"I fucking am! And if he doesn't think so then his precious creation can bloody well burn."

"Very good sir, you tell them."

"I will tell them, I bloody will. I've been waiting on their response for days now and nothing. I thought they'd be down like a shot. They're even more of shambles up there than I thought. Maybe I will have to–" he stopped abruptly.

"Have to what sir?" said the barman, but Fate did not respond.

Fate's gaze was levelled at the TV – his full attention was now on the broadcast. A darkly handsome man in a bright red pinstripe suit was on top of a burning Eiffel tower. He was standing next to Fate's girlfriend with a large knife held to her throat. The news helicopter was hovering in front of them. Fate's grip on his whiskey bottle tightened until the glass started cracking.

"We are waiting to hear the terrorist's demands. Hold on, he seems to have some friends up there with him."

Fate watched as two demons walked into frame. They draped a handwritten banner over the side of the tower. Fate crushed his bottle of whiskey in his hand. The banner read –

COME AND PLAY YOU GLOOMY CUNT.

The Devil winked into the lens, he threw his head back in laughter and as he did so, Fate got up, killed the barman and left.

Chapter 32

Tempting Fate

God touched down in the Fidelity Kingdom in His heavenly body this time. There was a reason the immortals used shell bodies when they were on planet; their immense power was just too much to contain in an atmosphere. As God waded through the piles of stricken furry bodies to get to the portal door, He inadvertently killed hundreds of them just through them coming into contact with the white heat of His divinity. The ground cracked under His feet and His giant body made fierce winds as it swathed through the atmosphere. He just wasn't in the mood for mucking about now. The risks of portal or teleportation transport were minimal, but He didn't have time and He'd already been caught out once today.

He found the portal door next to a pile of half-portal-door, half-monkey corpses. He tied a tether to the biggest and heaviest rock He could find. He tied the other end very securely around His waist – He knew all the knots, even the strange ones, because He was the creator of all things. He kicked the door open and looked through it. Inside the door jamb was a button which turned off the portal transport stream. Now there was nothing, a void. He knew the human would be out there somewhere, but He wasn't even rightly sure how to navigate this space. It wasn't really there and wasn't really space.

Movement would be possible though due to His heavenly body. He stepped off the edge and began searching through the nothingness for the man He must kill.

****

Jeff was at the bottom of the Eiffel Tower, Satan had asked him to give God's phone another try. He called, but God was still out of range. He went into his bag and got out the walkie-talkie which Satan had issued him with.

"Satan, come in."

"Copy you Jeff, did you get him? Over," said Satan.

"No. He's still out of range. Over."

"Ok well we'll just have to go ahead without him, although it would have been a lot easier with him here," Satan replied.

"Understood we go as planned. Over," said Jeff.

"Ok Guys, this is Satan, everybody get ready; he'll be here any minute. Over."

"Your message isn't all that's over," came Fate's voice over the walkie-talkie signal. "I've got Jeff and I'll end him right now if you don't give me her back."

"Show yourself!" said Satan.

At the bottom of the tower, Fate emerged from behind one of the legs and walked into the centre of the pedestrian walkway. He had two guns trained on Jeff. As he walked across the ground it crackled with heat underneath him. He was taller, he was radiating a magnificent glow.

"Oh shit," said Satan, unaware that he still had the walkie-talkie's speak button held down.

"What?" came Jeff's panicking voice through the handset.

"Nothing! Don't worry Jeff."

"No way! Something's bad isn't it?"

Fate leaned in smiling to Jeff's ear. "Your pal Satan just wasn't expecting me to have returned upstairs and changed into my immortal body in preparation for the fight."

"Darn it," said Jeff. Doing some mental statistics, he worked out their chance of victory had decreased by 73%.

"Enough of your empty promises Fate. Let's end this," shouted Satan.

"When I threaten to kill it is never an empty promise."

"Normally I'd believe you, but that is the Son of God and there is no way that you're not still afraid of the wrath of God. Whereas I don't fear you one bit."

Satan tossed Destiny over the side of the tower. She started screaming manically, which she would not stop until she was caught.

Fate kicked Jeff to the ground and flew up into the air to catch her. The two demons launched themselves off the tower to intercept him.

Fate crashed into the demons just before he got to Destiny; she continued to fall as they wrestled with each other in the sky. Jeff moved quickly, running at full tilt to get underneath her. He got a clear plastic high heel to the face, but he caught Destiny, which slammed him back into the ground.

She stopped screaming, opened her eyes and turned her head to see who caught her.

"Oh, you're the Saviour! How fitting!" She was laughing hysterically out of relief.

"Actually, I'm his brother."

"Oh, I'm sorry, you do look very similar," she said, stroking his beard.

"Yes, well now you can tell people that Jeff Saves too."

"Oh, I will, you can believe that," she purred, in a way that made him blush. She rolled off him and stood up, wobbling on her one remaining high heel as she did so.

Jeff handed her the missing high heel and she held his hand for balance while she put it back on. When she got it on, she straightened her hair, checked her make-up in her mirror and gave Jeff a quick kiss on the cheek. As she pulled away from him, she was fully illuminated in the fire of the tower raging behind them. It was a flattering light.

"Are you ok?" Jeff asked.

"Do I look ok?" she grinned.

"You look better than ok, miss," Jeff said, shyly.

"That was the correct answer," she smiled, pleasantly surprised.

They looked into each other's eyes for just a second more than Jeff was comfortable with. She grinned as he broke eye contact, his cheeks reddening again.

"I think I'll just leave you boys to sort out this mess, shall I?" she said, turning to walk away.

"Ok. Be careful," Jeff blurted out.

"I will Jeff, my lovely hero. I will."

She winked at him and walked away towards the centre of the city.

****

God had made a grid by grid search of the void which was technically impossible because it was a featureless void with no physical space assigned to it. He was God though and frequently did things that people said were impossible. He had left a trail of blue sparks behind Him and was using this to mark off which areas He'd been to already. He had just one sector left to search.

As He moved methodically across it, He heard a crunching sound and moved quickly towards it. When He got closer, He saw a tiny creature surrounded by blue light. He approached further and He saw that it was eating a man's shoe. The human's shoe.

"Excuse me," said God.

The tiny creature turned slowly and fearfully. Its small eyes widened to make up 75% of its face.

"You are an immortal!" it gasped.

"I am God. I am THE immortal."

"Please do not kill me," squeaked Vernon the Void Fairy.

"Who are you? What are you?"

"You did not create us?"

"No, I most certainly did not," said God, surprised.

"Then I have no idea what I am I'm afraid."

"What is your first memory?"

"I was floating through this nothing. It was warm and I was hungry. What was yours?"

"I awoke bathed in the light of a billion stars."

"Sounds nice. What's a star?"

"Not important. Anyway, I want you to answer a question. You must answer it honestly and I swear that whatever the answer you won't be in trouble – ok?" said God.

"Ok."

"That shoe you are eating – it belonged to a man. Did you eat him?"

"The man? No – he was still alive."

"Where is he?"

"I cut a hole in the fabric of space and dropped him into one of the universes."

"Show me exactly where."

****

Satan unleashed the fires of hell on Fate. The flaming stream could be shot from his fingers and he could reach a distance of ninety feet with them. The demons could breathe red hot sulphur gas flames and were not shy about using it.

On the other side of the fight, Fate had an immortal body, the touch of death, the power of flight and fifty-seven guns in a duffel bag. He also had numerous explosives, 168 small mammals with bomb vests on and he was frustratingly quick.

He had fled into the city centre and Satan had pursued him. Between the gunfire, the sulphur and the flames they killed ninety-three innocent bystanders in the mad rush to kill each other. Fate had flown over the city and landed inside the Stade de France which at that moment contained 81,000 spectators watching an international football match between France and Spain.

Fate landed on the pitch and with great accuracy and dexterity picked off the whole France team with one magazine of his machine gun. Amazingly, Fernando Torres, clean through on goal, still had his shot saved by the recently deceased corpse of Hugo Lloris.

The Spain team began to run for cover and were obliterated accidentally by Satan as he swooped down with an attack on Fate.

Fate darted around quickly to avoid the barrage of fire and sulphur. As he was doing that, he had a machine gun in each hand and indiscriminately fired into the crowd who were trying to escape the slowly draining stadium. The referee, frozen with fear in the centre circle, finally exhaled and blew his whistle unintentionally. Fate swivelled on him and put ninety rounds into him, inadvertently living out a long-held fantasy of some football fans.

He flew up into the air, but had most of his clothes burned off by Satan's hellfire. His slick immortal body was otherwise unharmed.

Helicopters now surrounded the stadium and fired shots at him forcing him back onto the turf. The news choppers had arrived and the whole event was being broadcast live around the world as breaking news. Fate, now fully visible to cameras in his immortal body, was being recognised around the world as the perpetrator of the many atrocities across the globe.

"Let's settle this here and now Fate. It will take a thousand years to kill each other this way, we are each too strong. Let's finish it," said Satan stepping forward to face Fate as he touched back down.

"How do you propose we do that?"

"Old rules. Mano-a-mano."

"Old rules?"

"Yes. I forget you are just a child – still young and ambitious. The old rules were established to settle any extreme situations such as God losing His mind and another immortal being forced to challenge his leadership."

"How does it work?"

"We join hands and recite the bond of immortality. This will release us from our immortality and then – we fight, to the death. Last man standing runs the show and regains his immortality."

"You are old and soft. You would not survive a fight with me. I can tell you don't want to do this."

"You are right. I don't want to fight you, but my friend, believe me; you REALLY don't want to fight me."

Fate smiled. "I accept your challenge gladly. I promise to make your death quick and honourable. It is the least that you deserve."

"How kind," smiled Satan.

They stepped towards each other. Satan indicated that Fate should copy him. They joined arms in the arm-wrestling lock. Faces inches from each other.

"What is the incantation?" asked Fate.

"Repeat after me."

Fate nodded solemnly.

"I swear by almighty God–"

"I swear by almighty God," Fate repeated.

"to relinquish my powers-"

"to relinquish my powers."

"To surrender to the unknown–"

"To surrender to the unknown."

"To walk in the valley of death."

"To walk in the valley of death."

"To be without sword or shield–"

"To be without sword or shield."

"To have and to hold–"

"To have and to hold."

"For richer, for poorer–"

"For richer, for poorer."

"In sickness and in health–"

"In sickness and in h… hold on a fucking minute – what's going on?"

Fate, having recognised the wedding vows, realised

something was wrong and tried to pull away from Satan, but the devil maintained his fierce grip and gave Fate a cheeky wink.

"Till death do us part," the devil grinned like a maniac and brought up his other hand quickly to drive a giant, gnarled, ruby dagger into Fate's chest.

Fate fell back to the ground with black acrid blood oozing from the wound. "What the fuck?" he croaked. Above him he could hear Satan's howls of laughter.

"You are the most GULLIBLE prick who EVER lived in any universe!" Satan could hardly stop laughing. "An incantation? You are honestly the most fourteen-year-old-girl out of anyone I've ever known. This isn't Buffy The Vampire Slayer!!"

"But what the hell is…" Fate breathless, gestured toward the knife.

"Ah yes, that. I call it the Godkiller. A magnificent creation. It's really quite wonderful."

He paced around Fate as he spoke.

"We're pretty generous with the whole Heaven and Hell scenario. Hell is reserved strictly for the worst of the worst only. We torture them, we make them breathe our filthy air, live as bedraggled nobodies, we break them and wear them down until they are shadows of what they once were. We erode their soul until it is a paper-thin shell, capable of only marking time and feeling pain."

"That's really dark," said Jeff quietly to one of the Demons, who shrugged and puffed some foul-smelling smoke from his nostrils.

Satan continued. "What happens to the remainder of their soul? Well it evaporates from them over time and rises, attempting to escape the fiery pits below. Little do they know that there's a filter in the sky through which nothing can escape. Satan's chimney, we call it; it collects the smoked residue of the broken souls of evil men. I harvested the residue and fashioned this beautiful dagger. A dagger that is forged in the fires of hell and made from the tortured souls of the worst the universe has ever had to offer. Is it aptly named? Yes, I believe so. I believe that this weapon could kill God. I believe that this weapon could kill me and we just proved that it can kill you. However, its original purpose was abandoned. I admit I was once tempted by thoughts of usurping him, but time has taught me many lessons. God and I are bonded now, we are brothers, we are eternal companions – I have no interest in His job and He has no interest in mine. We are perfectly matched. The universe needs Him and I have changed my position entirely – I protect Him at all costs."

Fate gurgled blood.

"So why keep it? Well my friend, I was going to destroy it, to prevent anyone from getting tempted, to prevent any of my demons from usurping me. In the end only one thing convinced me to keep it. You."

"Me? Why?" Fate spluttered, losing more blood from his mouth as he did so.

"Because whilst the rest of us were flawed, you WERE a flaw, you were made a flaw, a walking talking, killing flaw. You are God's blind spot, His biggest mistake and unbeknownst to Him you were also His biggest threat. I kept the Godkiller for you because I knew you would go off the deep end at some point. I knew we would get here at some stage. I kept it for thousands of years just for you and now you can keep it forever because I'll bury it with you at the bottom of hell."

Applause was ringing out around the stadium. The tv cameras had got in close on the battle. The cameras recognised the dead man as the terrorist. A caption appeared under Satan's image on the big screen.

UNKNOWN HERO SAVES EUROPE
FROM TERROR MASTERMIND

He looked up at the screen and chuckled. "HA! Mastermind."

"Burn, you scarlet fuck," croaked Fate and with one last bloody wheeze his soul departed, never to exist anywhere again – ever.

Satan was shaking his head and gave a grim chuckle. "I love to burn, you melancholy cunt. I live in hell. 5 billion years and you never got the grasp of it."

Chapter 33

Mistakes Are Made

Terry had gone to fetch me some ancient clothes to wear from a nearby shop. He had been gone for ten minutes when I started to get a bit restless. I wandered naked around the square looking at the artefacts and occasionally wiping dust from plaques to have a read at the various metallic monuments which were dotted around the square. With no one around for such a long time, the statues, plaques and buildings had all become very dirty, everything was covered in a slight layer of dirt or dust. As I wondered around the square, the warm wind and unfamiliar smells made me feel like I was on a European holiday, browsing some landmark at 6 a.m. before the locals were up and about.

As I strolled absentmindedly along, I heard a deep electronic hum to my left. I looked in its direction and saw a wide pedestrian avenue leading up a short hill. At the top of the hill, in between the trees there was a grass clearing. On the grass clearing was a set of very, very large stones in a circle. A henge. A huge henge. A hulking, humongous, hefty, heavy henge. Despite the undoubted mass appeal of a henge to the general population, I've never found them to be particularly interesting. In fact, I wouldn't have given this one a second thought had it not been made of shiny black onyx. It was perfectly clean. After all the travels and portal hunting, I'd got reasonably good at picking out things that were incongruous in their environment. I was 100% sure that this was a recent addition to Teatime. I walked up the hill towards the henge. As I approached, I could see engraved, neon markings on the onyx – it was writing. A large onyx slab had been installed into the pavement. Its bright text read "The Genesis Archives".

I stepped into the centre of the stone circle where there was a circular stone seat. There were seven stones making up the circle. The stone directly in front of me had a huge heading, it read: WORLD 1 – 'JOY WORLD'

Underneath was inscribed a full and detailed history of everything that had ever happened there, right from God's design process, all the way up to my involvement. It was engraved. I couldn't understand it. I moved around the other stones and I read every word. Sure enough, there I appeared, at the tail end of every story. I couldn't understand how it had been done. There was no one here. It didn't look like anyone had been here for years. Despite that, the Teatime stone was completely up to date as of five minutes ago. It had me sitting in the square with Terry. Who had done this? I moved round the circle again.

The seventh stone looked different, fuzzy, a mess. As I approached it, I realised that it was not badly engraved, it was in the middle of being engraved. Unconnected to any visible hands or bodies, thousands of little hammer and chisel sets flew around updating the text and changing earlier passages. It was impossible to read, with the speed of the changes and the flurry of activity going on. As I tried to get a bit closer to get a glimpse of some of the text a flying chisel whizzed by my ear on its way up to correct something further up. As I leaned forward again another flew by my crotch. I thought better of it and stood back. I looked up at the huge stone and could only hope that I didn't feature at the end of Earth's story.

By this time I had long forgotten about being nude, but almost being castrated by a flying magic chisel had very efficiently reminded me. With some reluctance I left the Genesis Archives and wandered back into the square. I had no real sense of how long I'd been in there.

When I got back to the bench, Terry was there.

"Sorry I took so long, here's something to wear," he handed me the folded clothes.

"No problem Terry," I said, taking the clothes, "I lost track of time actually."

This prompted Terry to look at his watch. I looked at what he'd given me.

The clothes had been there so long that all colour had drained from them and they were rough in texture, ill fitting.

"Time has been unkind to these clothes Terry, it's like wearing a sack," I said.

"Oh, that is a sack. I couldn't figure out how to get into the clothes shop so I got that from round at the bins."

"Hmmm. Well thanks anyway," I said, now slightly less

happy about wearing it.

We stood in front of his statue looking up at Terry's magnificent likeness, whilst drinking hot chocolate that Terry had brought from the Moon in one of those cool camping flasks which had several cups built into the lid.

"Really clever aren't they," I said.

"It's the neatest invention of all as far as I'm concerned. Anything which allows you to have cocoa with a friend easily, is head and shoulders above any laser contraption."

The clouds rolled by above his head and the warm sun shone down on us.

"It wasn't your fault," I ventured.

"No, it was. But I was wrong for the right reasons though and I can just about live with that. So, let's leave it there."

"I would have loved to have seen you in your glory days here. It seems like it would have been an absolutely fantastic place to live."

"It was."

"Terry I've seen the other universes, all of them."

"I envy you."

"Well the other universes would envy you, if they knew of your existence. I don't think you get how lucky you are."

"Lucky? I got my whole planet killed and wiped out a race."

"Honestly Terry compared to some of the atrocities on the other worlds, this is small potatoes. There's a story like yours on several of the other worlds. I've heard of planets wiped out by war. Genocides, madness, starvation, confusion, hatred, loneliness. Do you know what they all have in common?"

"No."

"None of them ever had it as good as you did, none of them ever had anything as stable for as long as you did. Not on any world, in any universe, did any leader manage to achieve global peace, happiness and prosperity. Nowhere even close Terry. Yes, your people died out before their time, but their time was the best quality of life anyone ever had anywhere. You are without doubt the most successful leader in all these universes and quite frankly the only reason this statue is shameful, is that it isn't big enough."

Terry put a big hand on my shoulder. Tears were streaming down his face.

"It's the grit from the wind." He smiled.

"Sorry I can't see the grit because of all your tears."

Terry used a handkerchief to dry his eyes. "Ok, let's get you home." We turned to leave.

Loudly, a voice to our left said – "I'm afraid not, my son."

God stood there, cloak billowing in the breeze, looking every bit the supreme immortal being that He was.

"I'm afraid human, your journey stops here."

God gestured for me to take a seat on a nearby stone bench. Terry sat down beside me. God remained standing over us and took a deep breath. "You've had an interesting time of it my son, but it's over now."

"Thank God."

"I wouldn't thank me just yet. In a short while I will be forced to kill you. I am here to explain why that is necessary," He said.

"It seems decidedly unnecessary to me."

"Are there any questions you have about your journey so far before I get onto the heavy bit?"

"I only have questions. I basically understand very little about what's happening"

"Ask away, my child."

"Well for starters, which religion was right? Which God are you?"

"Oh, they were all a little bit right, I'm the only God, I interact with all religions, I just do different voices when I'm answering the prayers."

"Ok, I have a lot more questions."

"Well we're a little short on time, choose one and I'll answer honestly."

"Ok – I've read the origin stories of all of the other worlds. What was the story with Earth? And if this is your seventh go why is everything still so shite?"

"That's two questions. I'll have to accept your first answer I'm afraid."

Earth: A History

God thought long and hard about this one. Six attempts had failed and He now only had one shot left at making it work.

He put on some music. He exhausted all possible music. He got a notepad out and wrote 'Ideas for 7th Universe' at the top of the page. He wrote ideas out for a Universe of pure numbers where all living things were unsolvable equations attempting to resolve themselves by interacting with the environment. In the end He decided not to do this one because it would be a pain in the arse to describe*.

God eventually settled on an innovative and thoroughly detailed approach. He created an absolutely massive universe with billions of stars and billions of planets. A natural, visual and intellectual marvel. A near infinite universe with endless possibilities. The focus of this Universe would be to generate the perfect set of circumstances for just one of the planets to flourish.

He created a beautiful planet with all of His favourite elements from His previous creations. It had spectacular mountains, deserts, oceans, volcanoes, glaciers – it was incredible. He named it Falafourongustania, although frustratingly for Him he didn't properly communicate this to anyone and much further down the line it would come to be known as Earth.

On Earth, He created a single cell; one life, from which everything else would spawn. This would happen slowly generation by generation allowing God to observe which species survived and what constituted an advantage for survival. It allowed Him to field test species in a live environment which helped Him shape and contour the world to suit the end design – the human being. Although He was unable to make major design changes after the fact He was still able to make small adjustments so when necessary He could send a flood or a comet and in doing so was able to wipe a genus of creatures from the Earth who would not be compatible with His higher creature design; the dinosaurs and the mega fauna were destroyed to allow smaller creatures who better served the food chain to prosper.

It was a logical marvel, a design masterstroke which ensured humanity were born into a world of advantage

* The author would like to immediately apologise for this in-joke.

being intelligent enough to outsmart their fellow animals and physical enough to defend themselves against any aggressive predators. He was able to try several designs for humans and to His surprise instead of one group emerging as the dominant species they interbred and strengthened through variety. This left Him with his most capable ever species and the best chance for a lasting, prosperous universe.

However, on 57,000 of the other planets He also created life. These lives were to serve but one purpose – creating favourable life-supporting conditions for Earth.

For example, there was the Harmonstung Flaremongers from Harmonstung, a planet 700 million miles from the Earth solar system. The people on the planet were obsessed with firing explosive objects into their sun. They didn't know why they felt compelled to shoot the giant nitro-filled rocks towards the Sun, it was just a part of their DNA.

The people were top heavy, ferociously strong upper bodies with short sturdy legs. They didn't know what rugby or wrestling were, but they all would have been fantastic at either sport. They spent most of the day finding large nitro-filled rocks that were all over the planet, picking them up and hurling them at the sun with amazing levels of strength. The result of this was that the sun regularly produced huge solar eruptions which sent nutrients, radiation and minerals out into space towards Earth.

Eventually they got so efficient at their bombardment of the sun that they completely destroyed it. When it collapsed it created a black hole which swallowed their planet entirely.

The Jobblewickies from Kick were an odd bunch. The population were not people as we would recognise. They were strands of hair on a giant Leg in space. A giant disembodied leg with a big solid titanium foot on it. They were fully aware of their existence, but had no motor control whatsoever. They operated as a hive mind that had one purpose; deciding what the leg would kick. They kicked comets, asteroids, stars, planets and their neighbour planet Bunz which was shaped like a big arse.

They were responsible for many of the impact collisions which brought foreign DNA, minerals and geological features to Earth. They were also responsible for the transit of all the comets. At one point just for fun they'd also kicked a black hole, but it got their big foot all dirty for a week, so they never did it again.

He'd also created lots of unique features in this Universe that did not exist in any other. A hundred galaxies over was the Great Blackout Curtain of Zaar. A giant black curtain that God hung in space to conceal some items which He didn't want the Earth people seeing. For example, it hid the bottom right corner of the universe where God had left His signature.

As an extra hidden mystery in the Universe He'd also designed all of the stars and planets so that when joined in the right order, they created one of the most beautiful join-the-dots pictures ever. He left the order written in dust on the Moon so that humans could conceivably put it together. However, when they finally developed the technology to get out of the atmosphere NASA Astronaut Alan Shepard scuffed it off the Moon's surface with a six iron whilst pointlessly playing golf. He simultaneously proved a physics point that everyone already knew and ruined one of the greatest potential pieces of art in any Universe ever.

Luckily Alan Shepard chose to live his life admirably so didn't end up with leg-tits or any other punishment.

Earth was the jewel at the centre of a masterwork. It was the greatest creation He was aware of and He'd been able to fix so many of the issues that had dogged the previous Universes.

He'd realised after many billions of years that war is inevitable with living creatures so He built it into to His plan this time. The population growth would be regulated by it. Similarly, He realised that disease and cruelty and madness were all part of being alive; they were unavoidable outputs of life, love, war and survival. Instead of trying to fix these He simply allowed room for them to happen – they were encouraged in a way by the system – many mild outbreaks were preferable for example to a worldwide contagion. This kept

Armageddon at bay by letting off the pressure at regular intervals.

In exchange He'd been shown beauty in ways He'd never imagined. Acts of kindness, art, love, courage and humour were all heightened on Earth, all more intense, because they occurred despite the suffering, they were even sometimes born out of the suffering. He loved the planet and its surroundings. However, He had fatally overthought things. He'd introduced Fate to further control the population levels, which He thought would be a positive. However, He hadn't banked on just how much of an appetite for killing he would have. Most people don't work overtime for free, but Fate really loved killing. This had thrown off the whole plan, taken some key people out at key times and generally put it on a spiral which He was still trying to figure out a solution to.

****

I looked at God's big bearded face as He stared into the middle distance. He sighed heavily and it knocked over a car.

He seemed embarrassed by something and eventually He spilled it. "On top of everything else, I made yet another error. I made a rule for my own entertainment. It states that if any human leaves their universe then they can end the entire living world. If they see the six previous universes with their own eyes and know for certain that I exist, that will end all universes at once, killing all who ever lived within them. It will also be the end of my existence."

I didn't care. "I would happily live here or Ternion even for the rest of time. At a push I'd live with Nohaz, but to be honest all of his sister/aunt/wife/cousins freak me out a bit. There's no need for anything extreme; I'm a pacifist. I have no intention of killing everyone who ever lived."

"I can't risk all lives for yours. I just can't, they're too valuable to me and it is too much temptation to place into your hands. You must die."

"Doesn't seem to me like I must die. Brick me in – lock me up – tie me down, sport!" I looked around at Terry for support, but he was playing Snake on his phone.

"I don't know what that even means," said God.

"Brick me in. Lock me up. Make it impossible for me to travel between worlds. Then you can safely leave me here."

"You were never supposed to be able to have travelled here. You were never supposed to be able to leave Earth. I can't risk missing something again. I have looked into your soul, you're a good person, I know it. You would never endanger lives on purpose, but it's the accidental I'm worried about. This is the end of your journey, my son. I respect your tenacity, but it's time to die. You will feel no pain."

He raised His giant arm and pointed a giant finger at me. "Any last words?"

A mobile phone ringtone rang out. Terry went in his pocket.

"Sorry about this chaps." He held up his hand in apology.

He answered the phone and seemed to be listening intently. "It's for you," he said to me handing me the phone. God watched with an amused grin as I took the call.

"Hello?" I said as I put it to my ear, but no one replied. Instead I felt a familiarly horrific sensation – like being hit with a hammer whilst being stuffed into a suitcase, which was being thrown off a cliff.

Chapter 34
From Bad to Worse

"You've just saved the world from a notorious terrorist. How do you feel?" said the reporter.

"I feel fantastic. Justice served, lives saved and evil vanquished," said Satan winking at Jeff when he did so. The young female reporter holding the microphone was getting the scoop of her life, but little did she know it was about to get significantly bigger.

"So, what's your name?"

"My name?" He hesitated.

"Stick to the cue cards," hissed Jeff from a few feet away.

"Yes, my name is Andrew Harris, I am a plumber from Basingstoke."

"Andrew Harris? A plumber from Basingstoke? Wonderful and how long have you been doing that?"

"A few years now and…"

"Yes?"

There was a pause. Satan felt something dark stirring within him.

"I'm a plumber," he said distractedly.

"So you've said, yes. And any wife or children in the crowd tonight?"

He felt an old feeling that he'd pushed to the back of his mind resurface. He tried to suppress it, but it was far too strong. It was giving him urges he couldn't control.

"Anything to say at all?" the reporter prompted nervously, worried about dead air.

He stared at her and his eyes went black. The old Satan was rising up within him, as if on some automatic setting. The temptation to try and take over the Universe was too much. It was in-built.

"You know what? Fuck it. I'm Satan."

"What?"

"The devil, Beelzebub, Lucifer, Old Nick, the Prince of Darkness – you know? Satan."

"You believe that you are the actual Devil?"

"I am the devil sweetheart." And with that, he burst out of

his mortal shell, rose up to twelve feet tall and bright red, and released his dragonish tail which he whipped round and swiped the microphone from her hand.

“I am Satan and I have saved you from certain death. Now bow down idiots.”

“Absolutely none of that was on the cue cards,” said Jeff worriedly. “I knew I shouldn’t have let him watch Iron Man.”

****

God jumped back in shock, as the human went into the phone, and looked at Terry.

“Where’s the human gone Terry?”

“Yes, sorry – I gave him a way back to Earth. I like him and I don’t want you to kill him. I’m sorry.”

“You’re sorry? You’re sorry!!!! I just explicitly detailed that if that man reaches Earth, he can end all lives. He can destroy all universes; he can finish existence as we know it across every atom of all worlds and you…you let him go. If you knew all that, why would you possibly let him go?”

“Oh, right sorry, it’s just I wasn’t really listening properly earlier,” he showed his phone with the game of snake in progress.

“Jeez-o,” said God, turning away with His hands on His head.

Terry had got up and started backing away from God awkwardly. “If I had known that I might have reconsidered the old escaperoo, you know?”

Terry’s phone rang again. “Oh look, the phone’s ringing,” he said, unconvincingly. He picked it up and before God could say anything, he too had disappeared down the line.

****

In Paris, Satan had claimed to be the saviour of Earth on every news channel in every language. He had gone off the deep end and was loving not having to conceal himself now. Unfortunately, the world’s religious extremist communities did not deal with the emergence of Satan too well and launched everything that they had at the stadium. The resulting fireball killed 33,000 people and France retaliated against four different countries with cruise missiles of their own. By the time eight hours had passed 1 million people had died in the various bombings. This was why he wasn't allowed to do press – ever.

Satan, the demons and Jeff, were able to fly to safety and were unharmed by the blasts.

The bombings had pushed some worldwide alliances into action and conflict broke out all over Earth on a massive scale. By the end of the night in almost every country the picture was the same – armies were mobilising, missiles were filling the skies and panic had gripped the streets.

Satan made things even worse later by sending all world leaders an invitation to 'Bend the knee to the almighty Satan'. It may or may not have intimated that he would burn their country if they did not comply.

Fate and Satan's immortal bodies were also causing havoc with the Universe's construction. They were putting undue pressure on the fabric of time and space. Earthquakes, rips and reality glitches were springing up all over the planet. A family of four going in their kitchen door had emerged out of the Sultan of Brunei's nose which caused a stain down the front of his robes and killed him instantly.

As Satan stood watching the carnage unfold from the top of a block of flats God teleported in looking worryingly flustered. He took one look at the inferno that was Paris and turned to Satan.

"What the actual fuck has happened here?"

"Um," Satan said, the desire to be in charge suddenly draining from him to be replaced with shame.

"Did you fight Fate, here?" God persisted.

"Maybe."

"And?"

"He's gone."

"And how did you achieve that?"

"Not important."

"Probably not, but if you used your God Killing knife then that would have probably worked." God winked.

"You knew I had that?"

"I'm God."

"That is not an explanation for everything by the way."

"I didn't really think you'd use it."

"Well I kept it because he was a truly evil looney."
"I always thought he'd eventually toe the line."
"No. He booted the universe in the baws instead. He took a lot of people with him when he went."
A gas main exploded down on the street sending up a huge fireball in front of them.
"Holy hell though – this place is a mess. How did you explain that carnage away?"
"Um…"
"Tell me. Tell me. Please tell me, that you did not go on tv."
"I did a bit yeah."
"How'd that go?" God gestured to the city in ruins beneath them.
"He tried to take over the world," said Jeff.
"Ah. Yes. I may have got a bit tempted in your absence," said Satan.
"And that always works out great for you."
"I might have started a world war."
"Hold on, are you in your fucking immortal body?"
"Maybe," mumbled Satan, looking awkwardly at the floor.
"You've fucked it."
"I might have, yeah."
God stared at the devil. Sweat ran down Satan's face as he anticipated God was about to destroy him.
"Well – so have I. Completely and utterly shagged it," God said. He gave Satan a bleak grin.
"Where's the human?" asked Jeff.
"No idea."
"Well let's find him, we can still save this!" said Satan.
"No, we can't. Look at it – this is not going to be saved. This is the end. Lines have been crossed that cannot be uncrossed. There's an empty bag on the ground and the proverbial cat is roaming about the neighbourhood."
"So that's it then. You're chucking it? Throwing in the towel?"
"Yeah I reckon so. I have a strong sense of impending doom."
The two of them stared out over the wreckage of Earth – God put His hand round His friend's shoulder.
"Kind of beautiful in a weird way isn't it," said God.

"Yeah – very beautiful actually. If you hang around long enough for the Middle East to get involved here, we might even get a nuclear sunset. I've heard they're lovely."

"Sounds good. Would you like a beer?"

"Yeah – I'll just have a few thousand though. I've got work in the morning."

God laughed and produced a huge cooler. They all started to tuck in.

"Actually, I think you're just about to get a few days off."

Satan smiled. "Well in that case…"

He grabbed eight bottles of beer, ripped the lids off them and downed them all in one expertly swirled swig.

They drank their delicious beer and watched the world burn.

****

I had teleported into a small circular metal pod; it was dark and cold. The teleport system had its customary effect and I vomited all over the place. I flopped down onto the only chair. In front of me was a small porthole window, outside of which were the stars.

As I was cleaning myself up with some of the rags I was wearing, the power came on with a jolt. Interior lights illuminated the stark pod. There was one chair, with a harness; a life jacket and an axe were fixed to the wall. There was a button marked 'Exit' on the wall. I tried it, but nothing happened. There was no obvious door.

The low hiss of a PA system being turned on was apparent. I had a sense something awful was to occur, so I moved across to the seat and strapped myself into the harness. Friendly music began to fill the pod.

"Hello Traveller!" On the wall a familiar projection had appeared. "I am Peter the Pod Pal."

"You look a lot like Graham the gravity goose."

He looked exactly like Graham the gravity goose. In fact the Moon's systems had only one animation: this was because although all the computer systems were unique, there was only one animator with any coherent talent and he died of old age after completing just one goose character.

"Thank you traveller! I will take that as the compliment it undoubtedly is," Pete said cheerily.

"Am I on the Moon?"

"You are traveller! But not for long! In just thirty-two seconds we will blast off from the MOON and travel through space to the planet Earth! How exciting!"

"I can't go to Earth."

"Of course you can – it's easy! All you have to do is to remain seated!"

"No, I mean it's dangerous for me to go. Everyone will die as a result."

"The launch sequence is not reversible!" he said – his voice straining to remain jolly in tone. His eyes had a worried quality, but his programming instructed him to remain positive at all times.

"You need to find a way Pete, to stop this vessel or you won't exist quite soon."

"Haha, such fun, calculating now!" His voice was extremely stressed now.

There was silence aside from the ticking countdown clock.

"How are you getting on there, Pete – time's ticking."

"Wonderful thank you! I am working hard on our little snafu."

A deep electrical current noise began to fill the air.

"What's that noise Pete?"

"I am working to deal with that – in the meantime here is some light jazz for your aural pleasure!"

The noise became much more urgent sounding. It was now mixed with Kenny G.

"Is that the launch powering up?" I asked.

"No that's Kenny G powering up his saxophone to delight your ears."

"I mean the launchy rumbling sound Pete."

"Unfortunately, it appears that we may have a non-optimal result."

"What does that mean?"

We were fired out of the Moon's orbit like a bullet from a gun. I was thrown back into the chair and was extremely thankful to have strapped myself into the harness.

"Is there a self-destruct sequence Pete?"

"There most certainly is not! This is an escape pod and is therefore specifically designed not to blow up, destroying its occupants, yay!"

"Is there a way to open the door?"

"No! Once we're in flight there is no door, the pod is a sealed unit. This prevents mechanical failures in space – safety is a top concern!"

"Is there a way to break the window?"

"Why would you want to do that? It would result in your immediate death!"

"So it can be done?"

"Oh yes!"

"Then how do I do it?"

"Oh, you can't do it sir! I said it CAN be done, but you'd need a gun or a laser or something more powerful to break it open."

"What the hell is that axe doing on the wall then, if it's not for escaping?"

"This is an interesting story. We did a study and people feel 25% more calm in a confined space if they think there is an emergency exit which only requires brute force to operate."

"So, an axe is useless?"

"Not at all!"

"So what should I do with it?"

"Well you could chop wood, break down a door or throw it at a target!"

"How will any of that help here?"

"Oh, it won't! There is actually a slight negative value to having it here as it takes up space that could be occupied with oxygen vital for your survival. You asked if an axe was useless though. Axes have many uses and are one of civilisation's oldest tools and weapons."

"That's great."

"When we get to Earth you are free to keep it!"

"I don't WANT TO GET TO EARTH!!!! You need to help me die or help us miss the Earth."

"We won't miss the Earth, we're on a locked trajectory and I can't change that – because of our wonderful security measures!"

"Ok then I'm going to kill myself with that axe then."

"I would rather you didn't do that sir."

"Why, are you squeamish? I didn't realise digital geese got squeamish."

"We don't – I happen to like you sir."

"Well that's nice Pete, but me being alive is something of a Universe-level problem at the moment."

I unclicked my harness and floated over to the axe on the wall. I pulled it off its holder and was immediately struck by its plastic construction and flimsy nature. As I tested it against my arm it bent.

"This axe doesn't look like it would cut anything?"

"Oh no – it definitely won't cut anything. We can't have a real axe in here, imagine if it got detached from the wall somehow and started floating around being a danger to escapees? It's a decorative axe which has been painstakingly constructed to look like a real, practical axe."

"You really are the biggest lot of twats out there. This is so much effort for a slight calming effect."

"We aim to please. If we have not met your expectations in any way, I would be happy to fill out a customer feedback form on your behalf."

I floated back to the chair and looked out of the window at the ever-growing image of the Earth.

"What do you think would happen if I didn't get out of the pod when we arrive and just get someone to shoot me before I touch the ground."

"The pod will actually dissolve as soon as it comes to a stop."

"So, I can't stop myself from touching the ground."

"Can you fly?"

"No Pete."

"Digital geese can fly."

"Good for you." I said glumly.

****

Satan and Jeff were nodding. They hadn't got a word in edgeways. God was on a rant.

"I tried really hard to be a nice guy, you know? I tried. They are so violent and scary though." God was drunk.

"Hey, this wasn't your fault," said Satan, taking a sip.

"Yes, it was."

"Ok it was, but you couldn't have predicted some of these outcomes. You did your best. Nobody's perfect."

"They think I am. They complain about it all the time. It's

a lot to live up to. I'm just a good guy trying his best."

"They don't know what they're doing. They're only humans, they're just mortals, babies – I mean look at this place. They totally blew up a city because they disagreed with my press conference."

"To be fair to them – you were being a dick."

"Well at least I stayed true to myself."

They clinked bottles.

Satan drifted off to sleep then woke up with a start. "Oh!"

"What?" said God

"After we all disappear, you get to nominate a successor, don't you?"

"Yes."

"Are you going to pick me?"

"No offence, but no."

"None taken, I was going to tell you it was stupid idea anyway. Just didn't want you messing up a whole other set of universes just because you got sentimental at the last minute."

"Don't worry, I'm in full command of my emotions." Although the country of Taiwan strongly disagreed.

"Who are you going to pick then?"

"None of us are fit for it. Has to be one of them," God gestured towards the humans below.

Satan laughed. "Well that should go just fine. Are you going to tell them that before or after they've nuked the world to fuck?"

"It actually should be over already, the world I mean."

"Because?"

"The human. He understands. Terry transported him here. I was expecting it to be instant."

"Maybe it takes a while to deconstruct seven universes?"

"Yeah probably. It took me a while to build them," said God.

"Maybe he died in the transfer though? How do you know it's over?"

"I just do. I have an intense feeling of peace about it. A wave of certainty which told me 'it's over don't worry about it'."

"A feeling?"

"A God feeling. I think I know somehow, but I don't know

how I know. And I don't know why I don't know how I know."

"I don't know what you're talking about."

"Well just sit back, enjoy your last beer and trust me. This is the last reel. Take it in and be thankful."

"Yes boss." Satan threw back another twelve beers.

****

We were almost at the atmosphere.

"Pete, do you ever have creatures in the pods who are not human?"

"Yes."

"Can you suffocate me with their alien air supply?"

"No sir I cannot!"

"Why not?"

"Because all of the planets use a similar mix of gases in their air. You would comfortably breathe on any of the other worlds."

"Can you raise the temperature and get me that way?"

"No temperature controls on-board I'm afraid."

"Could we activate the landing sequence early? Have it disintegrate in space?"

"I'll check."

There was a second's pause.

"No can do. It's locked in, no overrides."

"Any ideas whatsoever about how to kill me?"

"I have analysed the vessel and the available materials and I think your best option would be to attempt to choke yourself on the axe handle."

I looked at the rubber floppy axe handle. It was pretty wide and pretty thick. I tried to get it in my mouth, but it was not a snug fit and I could breathe perfectly well either side of it.

"This is rubbish." I tried to beat myself with it, but the floppiness and the zero-gravity made it impossible to wage a proper attack on my skull.

"What about your clothes sir?"

"What about them?"

"You could stuff them down your throat and choke to death?"

"Oooooh. Nice idea." I started stripping off my sack clothes.

I was thrown to the floor a few seconds later. The craft was rumbling and roaring as we had hit earth's atmosphere. The temperature rose significantly as we began re-entry. The whole pod was vibrating and I was seeing double, triple, a thousand of everything. I could barely keep my hands steady enough to grip the clothes, never mind get them down my throat.

****

On the rooftop God, Satan, the demons and Jeff were drinking and watching the city in flames.

"So, you're choosing the human?"

"I think so."

"Because he's been around?"

"He's got more perspective on the mistakes of these worlds than anyone. He's had plenty of chances to be horrible and he's passed all of them. He's like me I think, a nice guy, just trying his best."

"Ok. I think that's fair."

"He seems sharp enough and I know he has a good heart."

"Well, that's a start."

They all turned as a sonic boom made them look to the sky. The escape pod was hurtling towards the city. It launched a set of chutes, but didn't slow down appreciably and still hit the ground at a ferocious pace. It threw up a hail of sparks as it rattled along the cobbles and it continued scraping along the street for another few hundred yards until it came to a stop just in front of the building God, Satan and Jeff were sitting on. They all leaned over the edge to take a look. The craft's walls burst into blue neon dust and revealed a human sitting on the floor of it – he was naked, he was eating his own clothes and was holding what appeared to be a wooden dildo.

"This guy?" said Satan pointing.

"Well... Yeah actually," said God and they both started laughing hysterically.

****

I could hear loud booming laughter above me. The pavement

was delightfully warm against my naked arse and I was momentarily thankful for that at least.

I traced the source of the laughter and saw God on top of a nearby rooftop. He raised His bottle of beer in a 'cheers' and I nodded back, shrugged my shoulders as if to say 'I tried'.

"It's ok. Not your fault. This one's on me I'm afraid," He said loud enough for me to hear.

"Well I'm still sorry. I tried really hard to kill myself, but it just didn't work," I said, it was drowned out by the commotion but somehow, he heard it like I was standing next to him.

"We've all got different things we're good at. Don't worry about it."

"Is this really the end?" I asked, looking around at the mayhem.

"Seems like it – I actually thought it would have started by now. Oh, here it goes," He said, pointing at me.

I looked down and spreading slowly out from my feet was a wave of blue light, it coloured everything blue as it touched it and it was touching everything in every direction. I began to laugh in a scared and hysterical way. Watching the blue light colour my legs and spread up towards my body. There was much commotion around, people unsure whether to run or hide or fight. Above me I thought I heard God's voice say "WU-TANG!"

As the sound of His voice echoed across the street everyone dropped to the ground apparently unconscious.

The blue light was now covering everything and had started to turn a darker more intense shade. It felt tingly. I realised I was about to die. I was intensely sad that I not be remembered by anyone, as all my friends were dead too. I was pleased that I'd had an adventure though. My life had meant something to others, even if what it meant was that they were all going to be destroyed in an apocalypse. I had enjoyed my adventure. I had lived, truly lived. I had discovered the point of life. It's just a game, but not one you can win like Hungry Hungry Hippos; more like one you play to pass the time enjoyably, like Swingball or something.

If I could have gone back in time to my younger self I'd have said – "This is it, this is all you get. No credit is built up for afterwards. Heaven is just a waiting room, this life is the thing, this is it, we should make the most of it. Fall in love, go skydiving, just fucking finally try an avocado, whatever; say yes more."

I had missed out on things by playing it safe in my youth, but in the last few weeks I had seen the universe from an angle no-one else ever had before. I truly got it now, albeit a little bit too late to be of any use. *Ah well*, I thought, *no sense worrying about it now – it's just about death o'clock.*

****

As God watched the blue light spread across the world, He tilted His head back and took a final swig of beer. As the cool, delicious beer swirled around His mouth He looked at His magnificent sky one more time. The stars and the heavens above.

So beautiful was the Earth sky; the humans called it 'the heavens', but it was not truly the heavens, technically. The phrase echoed around His mind – *not truly the heavens.*

It was then a rather radical idea occurred to Him. He needed a word of power: "WU-TANG!" He shouted as He carried out His final play.

Everything began to shake and at one point it looked like fifteen Earths all next to each other. The blue light turned to red and the shaking reached its peak. A rushing sound began which would have deafened a dead God. It built and built until you could feel it across all worlds in all universes; it intensified a degree further until the whole fabric of reality was at breaking point.

When it cranked up another notch every atom in every universe exploded into sparks.

Chapter 35

Everything that has an end, has a beginning

IN the end there was nothing. God said let there be light and there was light.

After the light appeared, God stood in the void alone, unnerved by the quietness and bowed His head in silent reflection. He would now carry out His final act and leave the message in the stars for His successor. He crafted it exactly how He remembered it from His youth. At that moment He realised, for literally the very first time, that He must have been just a person once. Before He was God, He must have been a person who lived a life somewhere and they'd made Him forget everything. Perhaps the act of dying makes you forget everything.

It was sort of amazing that as God, there was still so much He didn't know, still so much mystery left in life.

He mused on what He must have done to convince a previous God that He was worthy of becoming the successor, He marvelled at the honour that He Himself was about to bestow.

It started to make Him wonder about the message He was leaving. Does history have to repeat itself? Does the message need to say what it said before? Does the successor have to forget what he knew or can he learn from the mistakes of the past?

Should the next universe be forced to live by the rules of long dead Gods?

He made a decision to change things – He left a different message, a more detailed message and He named aloud His successor. He would allow this man to remember, He would allow this man the benefit of his past mistakes – the benefit of God's past mistakes. He looked at the message in the stars – it glowed warmly and pleasantly, felt good upon His skin. God is great – people would shout that at the sky sometimes. He didn't know about great, but He was definitely a good God who had tried His best. That was who should be running things – a good person, trying their best.

He also created a door. His final gift to creation.

The supreme being paused, reflecting. Despite His flaws, He felt pride. He had created every beautiful thing, ever seen, anywhere. Every moment of joy, every laugh and all the love that ever existed was all possible because of Him. His final creation was a gold sticker. It said 'Great Job!' and He popped it on His robe. A smirk crossed His big face.

"Good luck" He said aloud to the ether. He took a deep bow to an imaginary crowd. When He straightened his back, He was ready. Everything that has a beginning has an end.

He added the final full stop at the end of the last sentence and slowly faded from view for the last time ever.

****

I awoke, bathed in the light of a billion stars.

My eyes took a minute to adjust to the brightness. I went to rub them and realised I didn't have any arms or in fact, a body to which arms could be attached. I then remembered being blown up and ending the Universe. This freaked me out somewhat and I briefly had an imaginary anxiety attack with my non-existent heart. I wished I had a body again and at that moment I immediately did. This freaked me out again and I reasoned that I must have been imagining the part where I didn't have a body and decided to continue as if that were the case. I used my new hands to rub my new eyes and the stars became clearer in front of me.

The message was pretty long and very detailed. It was from God and it was written in beautiful cursive despite being crafted from stars.

There was a paragraph about the consistency of sand. There was a think-piece about the morality of ducks. He had obviously been at this for a while. I got through the long analysis of what objects you could appear as to your subjects without causing alarm and the reasons why.

There were some more important pieces of information though.

My eye was drawn to the opening paragraph:

"Good evening. As you may have guessed, the Seven Universes as you know them have been completely destroyed. A new era will begin when you have finished reading this message, please pay close attention to it. The main news you need to be aware of is that you are now God."

This took me about six days to process.

"I am God," I would say. Then stare, in shock for hours. "I am actually God." More hours would pass. "WTF".

When I got it together and started reading again, the message started to become much more direct. He warned me against arrogance, against complacency, against the thought that I was all powerful. He instructed me in significant detail about how to make life. He was very specific about how green, 'green' should be.

One of God's most ardent assertions was that having a council of some sort was immensely helpful and He regretted that He hadn't thought of it until late in His tenure. Companionship, friendship, competition and different perspectives were vital to creating sustainable worlds.

The most important paragraphs though were concerning the free-standing button backed door which was situated to my left. It had a big H on it and if you held your hand near it you could feel warmth.

However, when I got to the section about the door it was not Hell as I had originally thought; God, in His final moments on Earth had realised that He'd created heaven in a space which was not in any of the seven universes. In fact, it wasn't really strictly anywhere. It was the same place I was now. The staging area. The bubble from which to observe and to create all things.

So, with His final utterance (wu-tang) He'd killed everyone on every planet and granted them all admittance to Heaven. Through the door was every soul on every planet, ever – fully intact, enjoying heaven's modest pleasures (it wasn't the perfect paradise people imagined – there was a recreation room with a good selection of games, but you would regularly have to queue for the pool table).

The possibilities were myriad. I could rebuild everything just as it was or I could innovate. I could bring people back; I could leave people exactly where they were; I could do anything.

I committed the message to memory as it began to fade. I spent a long time considering the implications of the message and the possibilities open to me. After seven days I walked across and opened the door. There was work to be done.

A few days of creative activity later I was sitting behind a nice desk, on a nice cloud in my staging area. Around the table my council were taking their seats. Today was planning meeting #1 for a new Universe. "Welcome everyone!" I said.

"Morning God."

I smiled at them; excited about the day ahead.

"Let's take a quick attendance." I said, "Handrew?"

"Here."

"Nohaz?"

"Here."

"Terry?"

"Here."

"Jim?"

"Baaaaa!"

"Sonia?"

"Here."

"Nigel?"

"HERE"

"Ok. Let's get started."

The Beginning

Acknowledgements

To Jen. Once again, it is important to thank her. Not only the person who believed I could write, who encouraged / consoled as necessary, but also a wife who had to listen to 17 iterations of 900 different jokes about talking sheep and sentient phlegm. An actual deity.

To Peter Buck, who said yes to a silly book, when others saw risk. A gentleman to deal with and a man who patiently educates as he works. Because of the pandemic we've still never actually met, so although I think of him fondly, I could not confirm beyond all doubt that he is real. For the sake of my own sanity, I have chosen to believe that he is.

To Sofia, who is deserving of accolades for the sheer amount of editing work she did during the difficult circumstances of the pandemic, not solely on this book. Her detailed notes on my manuscript were like a free writing lesson for me. She was precise, insightful and the author of my favourite ever note I've received on anything in my entire life – "Is The Devil Scottish?".

To all at Elsewhen Press, not just for their faith in the book, but also for their hard work in terrible times, which ensured not only this book's release but many others. In a perfect world, Sofia and Peter would ideally edit this sentence to suggest something better than 'thank you'.‡

To Gordon and Fiona Miller – For his excellent artwork and a beard that could stop a bullet. For her regular encouragement and for being an unpaid advice service.

To my parents, for never once discouraging me from pursuing creative endeavours (even when I wasn't any good at them) and for making sure I read plenty of books. Mum, your copy will have all the f[redacted]ks and c[redacted]ts redacted, like a CIA file.

To Tess Milligan and Kyle Wilson – For the assistance, for reading, for the feedback and for being thoroughly nice. We will get together and watch a terrible film when such things are once again permitted.

To (Mr) Kenny Pieper, the teacher who cared when certain

‡ We would never dare to edit an author's acknowledgements! – Peter

others did not. Thanks for the very specific cultural education, it stuck and this is (for better or worse) the result.

To Graham Jardine for teaching me to never judge a whale by its cover. You'll be pleased to know that I never have.

Elsewhen Press

delivering outstanding new talents in speculative fiction

Visit the Elsewhen Press website at elsewhen.press for the latest information on all of our titles, authors and events; to read our blog; find out where to buy our books and ebooks; or to place an order.

Sign up for the Elsewhen Press InFlight Newsletter at elsewhen.press/newsletter

Other Elsewhen Press titles you might like

THE EYE COLLECTORS

A STORY OF

HER MAJESTY'S OFFICE OF THE WITCHFINDER GENERAL

PROTECTING THE PUBLIC FROM THE UNNATURAL SINCE 1645

SIMON KEWIN

When Danesh Shahzan gets called to a crime scene, it's usually because the police suspect not just foul play but unnatural forces at play.

Danesh is an Acolyte in Her Majesty's Office of the Witchfinder General, a shadowy arm of the British government fighting supernatural threats to the realm. This time, he's been called in by Detective Inspector Nikola Zubrasky to investigate a murder in Cardiff. The victim had been placed inside a runic circle and their eyes carefully removed from their head. Danesh soon confirms that magical forces are at work. Concerned that there may be more victims to come, he and DI Zubrasky establish a wary collaboration as they each pursue the investigation within the constraints of their respective organisations. Soon Danesh learns that there may be much wider implications to what is taking place and that somehow he has an unexpected connection. He also realises something about himself that he can never admit to the people with whom he works…

"Think *Dirk Gently* meets *Good Omens*!"

ISBN: 9781911409748 (epub, kindle) / ISBN: 9781911409649 (288pp paperback)

Visit bit.ly/TheEyeCollectors

Other Elsewhen Press titles you might like

HOWUL

A LIFE'S JOURNEY

DAVID SHANNON

"Un-put-down-able! A classic hero's journey, deftly handled. I was surprised by every twist and turn, the plotting was superb, and the engagement of all the senses – I could smell those flowers and herbs. A tour de force"

– LINDSAY NICHOLSON MBE

Books are dangerous

People in Blanow think that books are dangerous: they fill your head with drivel, make poor firewood and cannot be eaten (even in an emergency).

This book is about Howul. He sees things differently: fires are dangerous; people are dangerous; books are just books.

Howul secretly writes down what goes on around him in Blanow. How its people treat foreigners, treat his daughter, treat him. None of it is pretty. Worse still, everything here keeps trying to kill him: rats, snakes, diseases, roof slates, the weather, the sea. That he survives must mean something. He wants to find out what. By trying to do this, he gets himself thrown out of Blanow… and so his journey begins.

Like all gripping stories, *HOWUL* is about the bad things people do to each other and what to do if they happen to you. Some people use sticks to stay safe. Some use guns. Words are the weapons that Howul uses most. He makes them sharp. He makes them hurt.

Of course books are dangerous.

ISBN: 9781911409908 (epub, kindle) / ISBN: 9781911409809 (200pp paperback)

Visit bit.ly/HOWUL

Other Elsewhen Press titles you might like

Working Weekend

Penelope Hill

Sometimes authenticity sucks!

Marcus Holland, European Folklore expert and award-winning writer of Horror and Fantasy fiction, is guest of honour at the CoffinCon convention being held in an old gothic mansion-turned-hotel. He's looking forward to the weekend, as he's hoping for a break from the pressures of work, the enthusiasm of his agent and the demands of his ex-wife. There's to be a midnight masque, a Real Ale bar, and the convention committee have even arranged to have a 'real' vampire wandering the halls, to help add to the atmosphere.

From the moment Marcus arrives he starts to feel uneasy, but can't quite put his finger on the reason why. Although he soon comes to realise what is wrong, he knows he can't broadcast his concerns without being thought insane. Far from being a relaxing break he will be working harder than ever in order to safeguard his friends and fans.

ISBN: 9781911409717 (epub, kindle) / ISBN: 9781911409618 (240pp paperback)

Visit bit.ly/WorkingWeekend

Other Elsewhen Press titles you might like

A series of novels attempting to document the trials and tribulations of the **Transdimensional Authority**

Ira Nayman

If there were Alternate Realities, and in each there was a version of Earth (very similar, but perhaps significantly different in one particular regard, or divergent since one particular point in history) then imagine the problems that could be caused if someone, somewhere, managed to work out how to travel between them. Those problems would be ideal fodder for a News Service that could also span all the realities. Now you understand the reasoning behind the Alternate Reality News Service (ARNS). But you aren't the first. In fact, Canadian satirist and author Ira Nayman got there before you and has been the conduit for ARNS into our Reality for some years now, thanks to his website *Les Pages aux Folles*.

But also consider that if there were problems being caused by unregulated travel between realities, it's not just news but a perfect ~~excuse~~ reason to establish an Authority to oversee such travel and make sure that it is regulated. You probably thought jurisdictional issues are bad enough between competing national agencies of dubious acronym and even more dubious motivation, let alone between agencies from different nations. So imagine how each of them would cope with an Authority that has jurisdiction across the realities in different dimensions. Now, you understand the challenges for the investigators who work for the Transdimensional Authority (TA). But, perhaps more importantly, you can see the potential for humour. Again, Ira beat you to it.

Welcome to the Multiverse*

*** Sorry for the inconvenience**

Being the first

ISBN: 9781908168191 (epub, kindle) / 9781908168092 (336pp paperback)

You Can't Kill the Multiverse*

*** But You Can Mess With its Head**

Being the second

ISBN: 9781908168399 (epub, kindle) / 9781908168290 (320pp paperback)

Random Dingoes

Being the third

ISBN: 9781908168795 (epub, kindle) / 9781908168696 (288pp paperback)

It's Just the Chronosphere Unfolding as it Should

A Radames Trafshanian Time Agency novel

Being the fourth

ISBN: 9781911419113 (epub, kindle) / 9781911409014 (288pp paperback)

The Multiverse is a Nice Place to Visit, But I Wouldn't Want to Live There

Being the fifth

ISBN: 9781911419199 (epub, kindle) / 9781911409090 (320pp paperback)

Visit bit.ly/TransdimensionalAuthority

About Craig Meighan

Craig Meighan was born in Lanarkshire, in central Scotland. Both a keen drummer and a fan of science fiction, he grew up wanting to be either Animal from The Muppets or Douglas Adams. This has led to an unfortunate habit of smashing up his computer at the end of each writing session.

With the ambition of becoming a screenwriter, he attended film college in Glasgow. He spent a short time making corporate videos and then after attending one chance meeting, he accidentally joined the civil service. Intending to stay for one summer, he ended up staying for 12 years (so think carefully before inviting him round for tea).

He is too polite to say which of the killer robots, demons and other assorted antagonists that appear in his book, are based on his interactions with actual government ministers.

His first novel, *Far Far Beyond Berlin,* was written in the evenings, after work, every day for a year, at the end of which time his wife Jen convinced him it was time to finally leave the safety of the office job and pursue writing full-time. She cunningly incentivised him by promising that if he managed to get his book published, he could get a big dog.

Craig lives with Jen, just outside Glasgow, where they like to play softball, enter pub quizzes and do escape rooms. He is delighted to announce that they are expecting a greyhound.